THE SHADOW OF CAIN

THE SHADOW OF CAIN

The Renaissance Trilogy - Book II

HENRY VYNER-BROOKS

Henry Vyner-Brooks

Contents

Dramatis Personae

Fictional Characters marked with *

Rhodes:
*Fra Hugh de Erpingham
Grandmaster Emery d'Ambroise
Guy de Blanchefort, Prior of Auvergne
*Fra Marcantonio Vendramin (the knight who has disappeared)
Guy Borel Valdiviessa e Maldonato (Knight of the Langue of Castille)
*Wilfred Carter (manservant to Hugh de Erpingham)

ROME
Cardinals and Papal Curia:
Pope Julius II – Giuliano della Rovere, the Warrior Pope
Giuliano Leno – Former Papal Chamberlain & nuncio to England
Angelo Colocci – Papal Secretary
Sigismondo de Conti – Private Papal Secretary
Johannes Burchard & Paris di Grassis – Papal Masters of Ceremony
Donato Bramante – Military Engineer and Papal Architect for the new St. Peters
Agostino Chigi – Banker, Treasurer and Notary of the Apostolic Camera
Cardinal Ippolito d'Este – archbishop of Milan and brother to the Duke of Ferrara
Cardinal Riario – Pope Julius's cousin
Cardinal Giovanni de Medici – exiled Florentine, future Pope Leo X

Others in Rome:
Pietro Bembo – Poet, literary scholar
Raphael di Santi – Painter from Urbino
Edigio da Viterbo – vicar general of the Augustinians
Jacopo Galli – aged banker and collector of art
Desiderius Erasmus of Rotterdam – Augustinian author
Alexander Stuart – illigitimate son of James IV of Scotland
Fr Giovanni Rafenelli – Dominican Inquisitor, Master of the Sacred Palace

Fedro Ingirami – Deacon, scholar and (in 1510) Prefect of the Palatine Library

Florentines in Rome:
*Giovanni Battista – Prior of Rome for the knights of Rhodes
Giuliano de Sangallo – Sculptor, Architect, friend of Pope and Michelangelo
Michelangelo di Buonarotti – Sculptor, reluctant painter

Island of Ischia
Duchess Constanza D'Avalos – Duchess of Francavilla, *la Gioconda*
Vittoria Colonna – Poetess & Grandaughter of Duke Frederico de Montefeltro

Bracciano
Madonna Felice Orsini - (ne. De Cupis) business woman & daughter of the Pope
Duke Gian Giordano Orsini – Felice's husband, warlord allied to the French
Lady Emilia Pia – lady-in-waiting and sister-in-law to the Duchess of Urbino

Assisi
*Fra Francesco i Bisognoso – runs the leper colony
*Fra Paolo Todesco – Fra Francesco's assistant

Urbino
Duchess Elizabetta Montefeltro (ne. Gonzaga)
Emilia Pia – Lady-in-waiting, sister-in-law and cousin to the duchess
Baldassare Castiglione – ambassador, and author of *The Courtier*
Gian Cristoforo Romano – sculptor from Ferrara
Count Ludovico Canossa – Italian nobleman
Gaspare Pallavicino – Marchese di Cortemaggiore
Giuliano de Medici – exiled Lord of Florence, son of Lorenzo *Il Magnifico.*
Marco Vigerio della Rovere – Bishop of Senegallia, relative of Pope Julius
*Sister Clemente – *La Bafana*, Vittoria Colona's governess

Ferrara
Ludovico Ariosto – Poet
Duke Alfonso d'Este – Duke of Ferrara
Duchess Lucretia d'Este –ne. Borgia, daughter of Pope Alexander VI
Girolamo Donato – Venetian ambassador, composer, musician, sage.
Cardinal Ippolito d'Este – duke's brother, archbishop of Milan.
*General Manozzi – Commander in Ferrarese army

Mantua
Francesco Gonzaga – Marchese of Mantua
Isabella Gonzaga – Marchessa of Mantua, ne. d'Este of Ferrara

Niccolo da Corregio - diplomat

Venice

Niccolò di Pitigliano – Commander of Venetians troops, of Orsini blood
Doge Leonardo Loredan – Doge of Venice from 1503-1522
Angelo Trevisan – Naval commander at the battle of the Polesine
Titziano Vecello (Titian) – artist, "the sun among many small stars"
Girolamo Donato – Venetian ambassador to the papal court
*Prior Enrico da Mosta – Grand Priory of the Knights of Rhodes, Venice.
Giovanni de Medici – exiled son of Lorenzo *Il Magnifico*, future Pope Leo X
Alvise Contarini – noble merchant
Gasparo Contarini – son of Alvise Contarini

Asolo

Catherina Cornaro – Last Queen of Cyprus, Armenia and Jerusalem
Ferdinand Francesco d'Avalos – Marchese of Pesaro, Vittoria Colonna's fiancé

The Deceased:

Rodrigo Borgia – Pope Alexander VI
Cesare Borgia – Duke Valentino of Romagna, son of Pope Alexander VI
Francesco Todeschini Piccolomini – Pope Pius III, murdered
Magister Pierre d'Aubusson – late Grand Master of the Knights of Rhodes
Guidobaldo Montefeltro – Duke of Urbino, husband of Elizabetta Gonzaga
Lorenzo de Medici – Florentine statesman known as "*Il Magnifico*"
Ficino – Platonist scholar, reluctant tutor to the House of Medici.
Francesco Petrarca – (Petrarch) Priest, poet, early humanist
Dante Alighieri – Poet of the *Vita Nuova* and the *Divina Comedia*
Michelotto – friend of Cesare Borgia
Savonarola Dominican – friar, prophet and reformer
Bertoldo di Giovanni – 15th c Florentine sculptor, pupil of Donatello
*Pico – Orphan, Wilfred's helper

The Soule

When once the soule has lost her way
O then how restlesse do's she stray!
And having not her God for light,
How do's she erre in endlesse night.

Robert Herrick (1591-1674)

Map of Hugh's Journey 1509-1510

PROLOGUE

LETTER TO RHODES – MAY 25ST 1509

Most Illustrious Magister,

I write you on this feast of Saint Anselm with news from all quarters:

Firstly, and to the point, I finally came to grips with Vendramin in the tunnels under Siena. Through fire and water and great travail it was; I fell into his hand, yet he delivered me. Yes, you read aright. Vendramin saved me from drowning before escaping me. My part in the affair was not wholly satisfactory, but I did come to understand that he is motivated partly by private emnity against Pandolfo Petrucci – who was responsible for Pope Pius' death. Beyond that he has taken upon himself to sunder his vows, indeed to set himself up as some sort of magistrate above the wisdom of the Holy Church, to wit: he will not release to anyone the gold or that weapon I have written of because, as he sees it, they will be directed toward bloodshed in Christian lands. What exactly he has done with them, or will do, is uncertain. It is indeed a strange era of change in which we live, Magister, is it not? When a man can make himself 'the measure of all things'. (I believe Protagoras first wrote it, and verily these *Umanista* bandy the phrase about readily enough.)

Vendramin, like a lawless knave, now places his own opinions above those to whom he is foresworn. Howsoever deluded he may be in our eyes, I do not believe he has either treated yet with any of our competitors, or disposed of either item for which we seek. So we may at least be optimistic on that count, though at present I have no means of pursuing him. My only remaining course, is to see whether this deluded knave is hiding in his native land of Venice for he said that I would 'find him among his own people'. This will be an arduous journey – and doubtless a slow one too – for Venice is blockaded. I plead your patience and beg you remember what Euclid said to Ptolemy Soter when asked if there was any shortcut to understanding his *Elements*: 'My lord, there is no royal road to geometry.' So too in the present case to Vendramin, I fear it might even be that this troth-breaker will seek me out and so me harm. He warned me of the consequences of further pursuit, and though he is now old he is also exceeding cunning and well connected by some secret associations which I have not yet fathomed. If he learns that I still seek him, and he thereby come upon me, then all shall be put to the test. Necessity drives me on. Concerning the war in the north, it seems at the present that Venice may soon be humbled sufficiently and Christendom finally able to give attention to the Turks. Unsure as to whether others have written to you already, I will give a brief account.

On 14th May at Agnadello, Venice capitualated before the French, who fought for total mastery, unlike the manner of these hired, Italian *condotierri*. Pitigliano has been forced to *volte face* to Treviso with a remnant of the Venetian army, and it would seem therefore that the Venetian capitulation is more or less complete. The French, with your own illustrious brother's leadership, occupied cities as far east as Brescia without encountering new resistance. Not to be outdone, and swift on the undefended prey, the emperor's army also descended on Padua, Verona and Vicenza, which are all in his hands now.

His Holiness, aided by Alfonso d'Este, Duke of Ferrara – whom he appointed gonfalonier on his joining the League – have invaded the Romagna. The pope now has Ravenna, and the duke has seized the entire Polesine for himself. In less than a month it seems, if the reports are true, we have witnessed the reversal of a century of Venetian conquests.

Have our brothers from the priory of Venice written to you similarly? Perhaps we should comfort ourselves that the war was swift, and hope that the various parties can secure their new domains against any Venetian reprisals. Julius is currently in Bologna with the army, and if he does not return to Rome this summer I will journey there to discuss again the crusade. King Henry of England died on 21st April. His son Henry, though young, is known to be a man of honour and chivalric sentiment, and will be no wit less a supporter of our cause than his father was. I will write again when I receive the next riders from the north.

Until then, *adieu.* Your servant, et cetera.

THE GRAND PRIORY, ROME - MAY 26TH 1509

'You seem—' Grand Prior Battista fishes for a prudent verb. 'Agitated.'

Hugh observes the prior's wizened upper cheeks as they smart into a smile. His private correspondence to the magister lies open on the prior's desk, unsent. His superior's last sentence seems to linger overlong in the rafters of the priory's great hall. At Hugh's back and to his side, the breathing and bristle of armed men. And beyond their shuffling, beyond the smell of their acrid sweat; come the sounds of birds fussing over their offspring in the orange grove; and distant choral music from the church of Santa Sabina. The prior sits forward and opens his hands magnanimously. 'Is something troubling you perhaps?'

Hugh re-crosses his legs and straightens his back. 'You order me here *unarmed* as if I were some bishop's catamite, and have six armed men stand over me. And then you tell me I look agitated? Some men I know would take offence. Some men would feel their honour impugned. Some might even ask for satisfaction, nay, might insist on it. But not me, your servant who has come lamblike, so perhaps you would cut to the chase and tell me what the hell is going on.'

'My dear man, you should take no offence. After all I am only taking the precautions you yourself would in my position.'

'Precautions? What are you talking about?'

'Come now. You know that often the hawk flies beyond the call of the handler. You turn up back here in Rome having, by your own admission, had two meetings with Vendramin and tell us blithely that you are no nearer obtaining either item that we know he possesses. Indeed—' the prior fills his cheeks with air and shakes his grey curls, but then continues. 'Indeed, you tell me that it is now most likely you will never find them. All you have – ' The prior flutters his fingers. 'Is a handful of flies, uh?'

'Yes, all that, and that he threatened to find me if I did not give up the chase.'

'And our gold?'

'What of it? Think you not that I know my own business?' Hugh says, layering an acid sarcasm over the rage growing deep in him. 'Why in God's name are we even having this conversation, seeing you take it upon yourself to read my correspondence? It's all in the letter, as you know.'

'Yes, I know what you wrote, and there is no need to raise your voice. I have my orders as have you, and I am instructed by those above me to ensure that Vendramin has in no way tricked you into his confidence – for, as I am sure you have been told many times, he is the subtlest of tacticians.' Prior Battista's eyes feign a smile and his lean fingers bounce against each other forming the shape of a cathedral spire. 'You will forgive me but we must be sure.'

'I see.' Hugh glances left and right to assess the positions and order of the other men, then leans forward carefully rolling his forearms over at his knees so that the prior can see his wrists scars and the flesh crackled like bacon from the Greek fire. A bead of sweat is appearing on the prior's temple. Hugh speaks slowly with a measured monotone, first using his tongue to dislodge some breakfast in his teeth. 'You want to be sure because my word is not enough. Do you see these hands, Prior? These wrists? A year and a half under the Turkish lash, and those godless bastards didn't break me. Nor did Michelotto and his *strapado*, nor Petrucci with all his wiles, not even when the bastard tried to have me thrown from the balcony. I've earned my spurs, Prior, God knows it. So, you had better be damn sure of what you are asking me. Because if it is thumb-screw time, I'd suggest you send for some more men.' Hugh snorts a great lung-full of air and places both hands resolutely on his knees. 'Or did you think a man like me even went for a piss without at least taking a set of boot-knives?'

'I did hope you would follow orders.' The prior says calmly, yet glaring at the captain.

'Hope!' Hugh says, 'Isn't much of a strategy, Prior.' He pumps blood into his fists, and shakes his head with tight lips and maniacal eyes. 'No, they didn't frisk me. And *yes*, if it comes to a scuffle I will make sure you get it in the neck and then also the four to my right. The other two will have to take their chances.'

Boot knives. How much speed for this; how much force for that?

Table, prior, prior's sword, two weaker guards, the guard by the window, possibly escape through it?

He can see his limbs doing the moves, can feel the motion.

Neck, ribs, parry, thrust, gore, inwards, tripe, blood, screaming. The shadow of Cain, all over again, and again.

He breathes in deeply, and lets his ready fingers flutter on his knees as a desire more primordial than obedience possesses him. The red mist is beginning to descend. His focus shrinks to the necessary. Hip and thigh, hip and thigh. One move from anyone of them, and he'll start and not stop. Red mist thickens. No bastard will chain me ever again.

'The confidence of youth.' The prior's fingers are motionless in their cathedral spire, his eyes unblinking, searching for bluff, for weakness.

'Do not you push me, Prior.' Hugh's steadies his breathing. He fixes his gaze somewhere between the prior and the window, from which point he can detect the movements of the men either side of him. 'This face has been the last many people have seen, these hands the last things many have felt before they were ripped untimely from this world. Many who never expected it. You want to summon the piper, then we will dance, but be assured that I have kept troth with the order. I am no traitor. The magister will know it.' Hugh nods towards the letter. 'Everything I have discovered is in that letter.'

The prior opens his hands slightly, his face all affability. 'And that is *all* I wanted to be assured of. All this talk of thumb screws and traitors, really! What imagination you English have. We are brothers and fellow servants. As I said, I just wanted to be sure, and now I am.'

'What.' Hugh blinks rapidly. 'And I am free to go?'

'Of course. You always were. You are our honoured guest here.'

Hugh blinks again. Then sniffs. He can feel his eyes become more lucid, watery. His knotted stomach loosens, then tightens again. 'Then I thank you, Prior Battista. I am glad not to be needing these.' Hugh reaches deliberately and slowly into his riding boots to draw out two twelve-inch Basilard daggers. He's not going to turn his back on the prior and walk through those men without something in his hands. *It's as well we all know where we stand.*

Bembo said Petrucci had someone inside the priory. Now he knows who it is. The prior said he had his orders. Maybe he does, but they aren't from the magister; it is too soon for anything from that quarter. It takes two months to get correspondence from Rhodes. And it couldn't be from Petrucci or Michelotto. *I've dealt with those bastards.* Who then? Venice, the pope, the emperor? *Perhaps even this White Cardinal that everyone tells me that I should shit my hose about, the one who pays well for information about me, yet never reveals his hand.* He's been busy has Prior Battista. Hugh rises slowly and nods to him. 'Please don't rise, I'll see myself out.'

Hugh eyes each man as he passes. They bristle as he nears. Their eyes show how close a call it had just been. Hugh glances back from the door to see the prior gazing intently at him from behind his fingers. He knows that look; staying in Rome is no longer an option, unless he wants to wake up with a cold knife in the belly.

PART I - PROCOPIUS' FOLLY

THE VILLA BELVEDERE, VATICAN, ROME

They are waiting in line to be announced. A long line. Hugh can see Prior Battista's spies milling with other guests further back: two tall fellows in vermillion doublets and only lightly armed.

Hugh and Bembo are on Bramante's giant spiral stone ramp which connects the courtyard of the palazzo directly to the street. Around him Hugh observes the simple Doric columns in granite and the herringbone pavement illumined by a shaft of dying light through the oculus above. Warm currents waft upwards, miasmic vapours of streets just after rain laced with the smell of ladies' pomanders stuffed with every herb, but also the dung of pack animals as this is usually a service entrance and somewhere Julius can enter the upper levels of his own palace by horse and carriage. *Why make everyone walk up here? Probably so they can all admire how exceedingly clever their host is.* Everywhere the titter of excitement; the pope is away and the great architect is entertaining at home in Pope Innocent's palazzo – the one adjoining the Vatican.

Bembo whispers to Hugh while both of them eye the other guests shuffling in line. 'He was so inordinately pleased with himself over this spiral ramp that he decided to rent the entire palazzo while his star was rising in Rome. I suppose that and it being so near the works at Saint Peters.' Hugh does not respond to the sniping comments. 'Ah,' Bembo exhales. 'There is nothing that makes for a jolly party like the absence of Julius in Rome. Oh look, there is Sangallo with Michelangelo. I did hear that Sangallo was so confident of the Saint Peter's commission that he moved his whole family here from Florence, poor sod.'

Hugh nods, but is all the while catching fragments of others' conversation. He decides to forget the spies altogether. What are they going to do here anyway? He can hear Sangallo chuntering. Everyone can, and he obviously doesn't care if they do. He is telling Michelangelo that Bramante copied the spiral ramp design from his nephew's ramp in Orvieto. Michelangelo looks like he's heard the story before. He also looks like he's slept in his clothes again; a crumpled brocade and beard as unkempt as an Athenian stoic. The venerable and ancient banker Jacopo Galli is also with them but has just turned to the side to lecture some younger bankers whom Hugh recognizes as Chigi's employees.

'Eh what? You must speak up my boys. What I said was, there was a time when we bankers loved our cities and prized virtue more than lining our own pockets as it is these days. In those days we would brag not about how many palazzos we had, but how many young men we had launched on prosperous careers, how many convents and orphanages we had endowed, how many artists we had employed to the honour of theirs and our cities. Back then we did not hoard our capital but risked it to create wealth among the next generation. What? Pardon signor, you must speak up. These ears of mine. We sent men across the world back then, had branches in Constantinople. That was where I learnt my double accounting you know, not Florence or Venice. Yes, I did.'

Galli has been in Constantinople. Hugh's mind is sent in whirl, spinning with memory and emotion. That place, that other possible future for the west, a future that will probably never be. He has seen it through cracks in gunwales of a Turkish goke. *Dio mio*, it was only a year ago, yet it feels like another age, almost like another man. *I was a stretched-skin-on-bone savage that had forgotten what it was to be a man. They had made me forget it. They had made me worse than the devils. Irredeemable, unpardonable. They, the infidel Turks, drove me to it, made me more an abomination to God than ever Balaam made the Israelites. Now I wander as Odysseus wandered, warmed only by self-pity and all the while certain that there is no home in this cosmos for me.*

Hugh's thoughts are overtaken by Bembo's chatter. He has been talking about money, particularly his lack thereof. 'Look at Chigi's co-conspirators around old Galli. How happy they are.' Bembo points further up the ramp to the confident youths bedecked in gauche silks and standing contrapposto. 'They are the real alchemists, Hugh, for surely as the old kind are dying out, these new ones have found a way to make gold appear from nowhere.'

'Have they?' He finds it hard to share Bembo's admiration. *Wasn't it Thales, or some other Greek, who made his fortune trading on a failed olive crop just to show what an unworthy thing it was to make oneself rich?*

'I think we would find that they have merely found subtler ways to tax other men's toil.' Hugh has learnt by now the expression on his companion's face when he is not listening because of some new tidbit to deliver. It would be a fault inexcusable in a less interesting man.

'It is said of Abbot Prokrop, or Procopius, a Benedictine from Bohemia, that God gave him power to harness the very devil, yes, the devil! He would get Lucifer himself to plough the monastery fields. It was many years ago, but I am told Prokrop became a very great saint in that country, indeed, even confessor to their ruler Oldřich. I am told that at his monastery Břevnov there is a fine carving of him with the devil in chains under his feet. Exhausted most likely.'

'Do you believe that, I mean, that it is possible?'

'To plough with the devil?'

'Yes. Do you think it is possible? I mean, to use a crooked stick to draw a straight line and so forth?' Hugh is thinking of himself, of the knights, of the church even. But then he thinks the crooked stick is a bad analogy.

'You mean at a philosophical level?' Bembo always squints skyward when he turns his mind to metaphysical matters. 'Could we use the darker forces and passions of our fallen nature to create good somehow? Put sin in the service of good? It is a difficult question.'

'Yes, and perhaps one we must not answer, *caro*, for I think I know what you will say. You will say 'yes, within reason'. But consider how such a thought might itself begin to change us, our view of ourselves, our natures, our dealings with each other. It might change *reason* itself. Perhaps Prokrop did harness the devil. But perhaps Lucifer let him. He is no fool is the devil. He couldn't tempt Christ to turn stones to bread so he just waited to find others who were less sceptical and—' He glances at the young mercantile *arrivistas*. 'Better dressed, like those pricks.'

THE DUKE & DUCHESS OF MANTUA

They are interrupted by a clatter of hoofs below and the shouts of heralds. Hugh, like everyone else, moves to the iron balustrade to see what the commotion is. Bembo recognizes the livery and exclaims with a jocular but amiable voice, 'I see the Marchese and Marchesa of

Mantua did not fancy the ascent on foot.' Each is mounted on a black and white steed, whose trappings are red velvet fringed with gold and silver. He is clad in simple black damask and attended by six grooms dressed in doublets and jerkins of black and yellow satin. His face and nose are spread broad like a frog, his long moustache trailing over his chin like some Mongol chieftain from the lands north of Cathay, or somewhere. Yet for all that, his bearing is military and confident – one hand boldly on his thigh in a fist, the other giving magnanimous gestures to fawning Romans as he passes. Hugh has heard of him often, one of the most famed knights in Christendom, onetime gonfalonier of the Venetian forces, leading armies before he had even grown a full beard.

'He looks pleased with himself,' Hugh mutters.

'Probably just glad he didn't side against Julius in this war.'

Behind the grooms the marchesa ascends gracefully on her mount. Plump but not too matronly, quick eyes but hard. She does not look up the great spiral but rides as one who knows all eyes are on her, as they should be. She wears a petticoat of bold geometrical patterned brocade, with dark red velvet sleeves and large sprays of beaten gold in floral designs. Walking swiftly in the rear are six ladies in waiting attired in simple red damask without further ornamentation, for they are not to outshine their mistress. They all—each horse, every fabric, every ornament—are to compliment the duchy's coat of arms, a moving stage piece to show the Romans that Mantua is still a leader in the thing that matters - style. The Romans and other guests keep to the railings as they pass, doffing caps, bowing, curtseying as necessary. The marchese acknowledges Bembo by name with a small tilt of the head. A moment later the marchesa passes with a similar nod, then the perspiring ladies. The rustle of fabrics, the wheeze of overtaxed lungs, the smell of saddle leather, of horseflesh, of sweat. Hugh comments on the rather unnatural yellow colour of the marchesa's hair. Bembo confides quietly behind hand. 'She dyes it. Always has. People say it is because of her husband's passionate affair with Lucretia Borgia – a famous blonde, you know.'

'When she was Duchess of Ferrara?'

'Oh yes.'

'Before, during or after her affair with y –

'Not so loud, it was at the same time, though I did not know it then. What are you smiling about?'

'The great poet blushing is a most becoming sight! Forgive me, *caro*. I believe you were declaiming on that most important topic: your former patron's hair colour.'

'Ah well, Lucretia, as I said, is justly famed for her golden hair, but I happen to know that the marchesa dyed hers long before her knowledge of the affair, in fact, since her wedding day.'

'Most interesting.'

'Not really, but there it is, and there is no need to be sarcastic.'

'Were they a good match?'

'Mantua and Ferrara are two lambs among lions up north, an alliance was obvious.'

'No, not that. I mean them.'

'Why?'

'No reason.' Actually, he is thinking of Vittoria, how she might be in fifteen, twenty years, what the duties of womanhood will exact from her. He broods and strokes some skin on his temple that has nearly recovered from the burns. It always seemed to him that it was an unfair burden women carried, but he knew he could never really weigh the matter, for he could never know the corresponding joys that they alone knew.

Bembo cuts across his thoughts. 'As far as the world knows they were the perfect couple: he the not-so-handsome but illustrious knight, she his beautiful and accomplished lady with a dowry of many thousand ducats.'

'And you? What does the all-seeing eye of Pietro Bembo see? You were there.'

'Ah!' Bembo's eyes come alive. 'I think they, like many couples, had at least one big thing in common while courting. She was in love with him, and so was he. It was only a pity he couldn't have married the true love of his life, himself.'

'Himself? Really Pietro, that is what Lady Emilia Pia said to you. We have been together too long if I am to bear such humour twice.'

'Did she? What a memory you have, Hugh. Don't miss a thing.' Bembo brushes some fluff from his doublet and casts it with flickering fingers over the railings and into the void. 'But back to our subject, I would say there was no meeting of minds. That is what I would say privately, to friends you understand. She was always precocious – raised by the best minds and proved herself their equal in letters, rhetoric and taste. He, on the other hand.' Bembo shakes his head. 'Well, let us just say that he is not the most luminous body in the heavens, and leave it at that. I think it is possible for a woman of merit to love a man like that if his deficiencies are compensated by other qualities. And I don't believe the marchese is diverse in that department, indeed I am sure he hasn't had many thoughts from above his belt in years. She gave him eight children, and organized his court, while he got himself the French disease from his endless whoring and now she will not share his bed, and so you see'– Bembo's voice trails away.

'Pietro, *caro*, there are many slow ways to kill a woman.' Hugh is thinking of his own mother. He is suddenly glad that his vows will spare him at least the sin of killing a thing he had once loved.

'Indeed, all that brilliance of mind turned brittle. They say that the marchesa doesn't need a steak knife at dinner; she just uses her tongue. Still, no use our dwelling on the fact that others have not found happiness. Let us rather compliment ourselves that we have been spared the trials of marriage.'

Before Hugh can answer, he hears their names. It is the architect Sangallo, who has seen them and is calling them to come up higher. Michelangelo is remarking to Signor Galli, somewhat loudly because of the latter's hearing, that the Gonzagas were more *his sort of patron*. Apparently, they employed Andrea Mantegna for forty-six years to be their court painter. 'Not by individual commissions but for fifteen ducats a month, with a house, grain and wood allowance for his family of six, grants of land even.'

'Really, really?' says the octogenarian with surprise. For though this former banker is one of the more generous of art patrons, his hearing always seems to spring to life at the mention of ducats. 'I seem to remember that Fra. Angelico was paid sixteen ducats a month, but I suppose a Dominican Friar did not need a house and wood allowance. And, now I think of it, poor old Gozzoli only got seven ducats a month. There is no justice for some artists. Paolo Uccello, whom I knew, spent long weeks puzzling over the difficulties of perspective until he fell into poverty, poor man. Donatello remonstrated with him and at last he agreed to work for the abbot of San Miniato. But the monks fed him only cheese until he cried, "I shall become cheese and be used as putty." Poor man that he was. And then of course there was Cennini, who wrote nine whole chapters on the laying of gold from where? I'll tell you: from the debtor's prison. The world has truly gone mad when a maestro like Cennini, who could write so eloquently on how to imitate velvet, how to use iridescent colours and ultramarine and paints fishes and so forth – how could any sane city chain a man like that? What madness? What waste? Though if he had not been imprisoned, we would not have his *Libro dell'Arte*. I suppose you read that as an apprentice, Michelangelo, *caro*?'

'Yes,' Michelangelo says absently, seeing Hugh and Bembo approaching, and nodding as only an artist can before a wealthy *collectore*.

'Hmm, well there you are,' Galli muses, adding immediately, 'But I like what you said about the Gonzaga and their treatment of Mantegna. Fifteen ducats a month with a house, grain and wood. I approve. An artist needs stability like anyone else. Patrons should be more responsible.'

'Though, perhaps not like Borso d'Este then,' Bembo says, laying a hand on Galli's shoulder and cutting across their conversation as is his usual, amiable manner. He and Hugh bow, and then Bembo continues. 'I believe he paid some fellow, ten Bolognese lire per foot, to fresco his palazzi. Now that is my kind of prince: give me twenty-one and a half square feet of fresco and no more. Can't say fairer than that. You know where you are with a man like that.'

General mirth and re-introductions follow. Signor Galli wants to know what has happened to Hugh's hands and face.

'I was making friends in Siena, signor, but I think I am over the worst of it now.'

'Which,' Bembo adds, 'is more than I can say for the Petrucci.'

'Ah yes,' Galli says. 'Word is that Pater Pandolfo has rather extended himself and has withdrawn from public life altogether.' Galli's eye is alight with a malevolent delight which suddenly turns melancholic. 'I hope he enjoys retirement, though I am afraid old age is a part hard to play in this present day – especially for men who have consolidated our fortunes by usury. The church has ruled that a usurer should restore in his lifetime, or at the time of his death, all that he gained unrighteously. It is ambiguous. Restore to whom? To the church or state? To the poor? Or mayhap, give it in commissions of art and buildings that would benefit the public. And how does even the best bookkeeper calculate the true amount? Tell me that. Does one deduct previous taxes and donations, expenses etc.? It is a very delicate thing when one is preparing to meet his Maker I can tell you.'

EN ROUTE TO THE POPE'S NEW APARTMENTS

'What? "Two faced?" Said I. "Surely not. If she'd had two, she'd hardly have been wearing that one!" No, my friends, as I always said about her, butter wouldn't melt in her mouth or anywhere else for that matter.' Bramante is a great wit, a great *rex convivii*, if a little coarse when away from the ladies. He beckons his countryman toward the knot of hangers-on that wait on his words. 'Come on Raphael, if you haven't got anything nice to say about anyone, come and sit by me.'

Raphael sniggers. He laughs at all Bramante's jokes. It is a sort of reciprocal arrangement for these men from Urbino—helps them get on in the world. Sangallo isn't amused, but Papal Secretary Angelo Colocci laughs too, sounding like a drowning goose. While anyone's star is rising in the Vatican, he is Colocci's kind of person. And Bramante is nothing if not that. Others laugh and faun. He is very much, as Bembo remarks, a stupid person's idea of a worthy intellectual.

Bramante is inviting them to see Raphael's finished fresco 'The School of Athens' in the pope's new apartment across the courtyard. 'Because I am sure nothing has ever yet been achieved as good in Rome. I tell you all the very truth: a new day is dawning for artists. Gone are the days when all patrons cared about was how much gold was used, or the quantity and grade of ultramarine. *Now* the preciousness is not in the things of this earth but in the divine skill placed in the hands of artists like my young countryman here, Signor Santi.'

Raphael effects a small bow, and adds that he has only tried his best to honour His Holiness. He says this for fear of another figure who also hovers near them uninvited, and not the sort of man you can easily send away.

Hugh follows Raphael's nervous side glance, to a prelate with a face as long as Sunday, and whose long, inky shadow seems to follow him like an admiring pupil in the last of the dying sunlight. The prior's spies are there too, but Hugh takes no thought for them. For the moment his eyes are glued to the wraith-like creature spreading his darkness about poor old Galli.

Hugh feels a hand on his elbow and hears Bembo whisper, 'Giovanni Rafenelli is a Dominican of Dominicans, *Domini Canes* – hates his neighbour as himself. It's why they make such good inquisitors and tax collectors.' The man's black cloak and scapular hide the white undergarments as he walks crow-like alongside Jacopo Galli, perhaps the only person old enough not to fear him. 'He is the *Haereticae Privatiatis Inquisator*, Master of the Sacred Palace and the pope's private theologian. They say his hero was his fellow Dominican Tomas de Torquemada who burned over two thousand heretics twenty-five years ago. So tread very carefully, my friend. If he hears something he doesn't like, then he has the power to stop you talking. Permanently. Try saying *odium theologicum* without a tongue.'

Hugh observes Rafenelli from the side as they enter the shadow of the north wing of the papal palace. He walks like a man wrapped in thorns, pained and grudging. His face is creased with disdain. *God save us*, Hugh thinks. You know your god is man-made when he hates all the same people you do. All Italy knows that Cardinal Caraffa is reviving the inquisition. Perhaps there will be openings for a man like Rafenelli, promotions even. For the moment, he seems content to stick his long nose into the intents and meanings of Raphael's frescoes.

Bembo whispers again, 'Raphael should beware, too. Rafenelli has only been in post a year and so has had no input in the fresco's content, but that's not to say he can't grill an artist in retrospect.'

'What?' Hugh hoots back. 'Even a divine genius?'

The jest is severed by the inquisitor, speaking above the general murmurs of wonder and approbation. Rafenelli's voice is thin, nasal. 'I believe that you, Signor Bramante, influenced His Holiness in the content.'

'Me? Well, His Holiness does speak to me about many of his ideas.' Bramante looks back, and Hugh can see his nervous glance at the inquisitor, then a lame gulping of his Adam's apple. 'But you know him, Fra. Giovanni; the Holy Father knows his own mind. But Michelangelo on the other hand has been given a free rein on the vault, for he would not paint the holy apostles as His Holiness asked. Have you had a chance to see what *he* is painting yet?'

'I have asked. He has not showed me so much as a cartoon.'

'Really?' Bramante finds it hard to sound sincere at the best of times. 'That is a shame, almost a scandal. Still I believe it is a sign of the times. There was a time when no patron would dream of letting an artist paint what he liked, but I can well imagine a day when they will, and make the patron pay all the same.'

More titters of praise. Bramante is pleased with the way he deflected that one, and even got a laugh to boot. They walk in a loose group from the Palazzo Belvedere, which he designed, across the *Cortile del Belvedere* which he designed, to the new papal apartments, which he also designed. The air is still warm, fragrant with apple and almond blossom. He leads them with the occasional gesture here to a capital, there to an arch or here to a window reveal or pilaster.

Sangallo has been invited, too, probably so Bramante can rub his nose in it. There's not much call for Corinthian capitals and fluted columns when you've been demoted to military engineer. Also invited was Michelangelo, but he declined, murmuring that he'll not have people saying he ever copied this upstart from the Marches, when the truth is precisely the reverse.

Hugh draws alongside the aged patrician in order to save him from Rafenelli's questions about Plato and theology. The inquisitor has learnt 'the whole truth' about the matter from Augustine's earlier writings – a truth which he has fashioned into a sharp point upon which he can impale any who disagree. Galli is showing all the recalcitrance of an octogenarian and looks liable to get himself and any others with broader views into trouble. Hugh gives a little cough and speaks congenially, 'Signor Galli, please forgive my intrusion but I heard you saying earlier to some young men that you were at one time in Constantinople before it fell.'

'Indeed I was. Have you seen her?'

'Once, but I was not trading as much as being traded.'

'Signor?' Rafenelli's head turns. The others have already entered the Apostolic Palace. It's just the three of them left by the entrance door helping signor Galli on the stairs.

'I was a galley slave on a Turkish man of war. My hosts were not keen on shore leave though I would have dearly loved it. They say you could hear near seventy tongues there, probably an exaggeration. Please take my hand, the stairs are steep.'

'Thank you, dear boy. No, it was not an exaggeration. Not at all. Every nation under heaven was there. Coptic monks chattering a language older than the pharaohs, side by side with Aramaic speaking Syrians, Latin speaking North Africans haggling in the bazaars. Jewish glass blowers, Persian silk traders, the swarthy descendants of Gepid, mercenaries who had crossed the frozen Danube a millennium before. Herule slave traders speaking some debased version of old German – no one ever understood them. I remember it all like it was yesterday, yes, all of it. The Armenians, hah, the Armenians: goldsmiths, silversmiths, jewelers, experts at inlaid enamel and mosaics, sculptors, weavers of brocade. There we all were—vying, haggling, spending, in the world's most diverse and well situated market. And don't think it was all in dusty agoras. No, we met in leafy cloisters or on manicured lawns, sitting in the shade of great magnolia trees, drinking their morning wine or Persian sherbets while the great cream blooms hung around us like angels. I have fond memories, I do.'

'So it seems, though for myself—' Rafenelli chooses his words as a surgeon chooses his instruments. 'I do not think I could be happy among people of – let me be charitable – such heterodox religion.'

Galli either does not hear or chooses not to, but rather, carries on up the smooth marble steps on Hugh's arm. 'I don't think this generation realizes what we lost when Constantinople fell to Mehmed. She was a jewel of a city. Eight huge public bath houses and one hundred and fifty three private ones, imperial and princely palaces, over three hundred monasteries, not to mention the churches built with stones from Libya, Lebanon, from the Atlantic coast of the Franks, even Mons Porphyrites from the distant deserts of southern Egypt, and green marble from old Sparta.'

Rafanelli follows behind, but he's not helping the aged patrician. 'I am told that the Venetians continued trading with Mehmed and the infidels before even the canon smoke was cleared. His Holiness will make them pay dearly for their pride and treacheries. And afterwards he has promised to crusade against the infidel in person, and God willing regain Constantinople and Jerusalem.'

'There, Signor Galli,' Hugh says, reaching a landing where the window looks eastward past the Castel Sant Angelo just as a flame of dying evening light ignites the Travertine of the Medici Villa on the Trinita dei Monti in a blaze of pomegranate red. 'Then maybe you will once again walk the streets and cloisters of Constantinople.'

'It is a pleasant thought, Fra Hugh,' Galli says between wheezing breaths. 'But I am old enough to know when a dream has died.'

BEFORE RAPHAEL'S *SCUOLA DI ATENE*

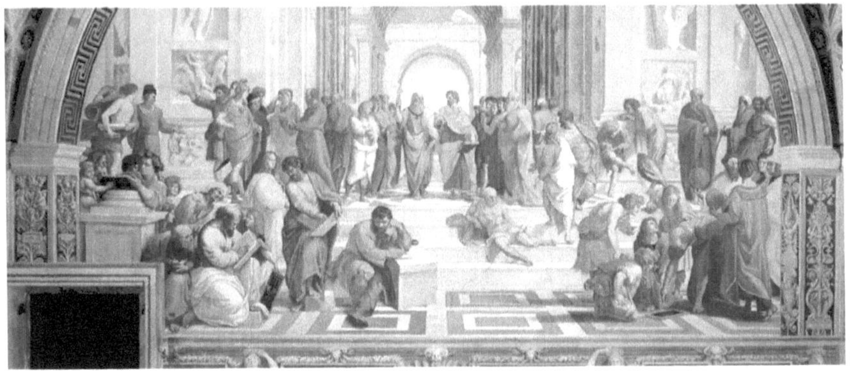

By the time Hugh arrives he can see that they are not alone. The sight of red cardinals' caps sends a shiver through him. What if one of these is the White Cardinal? He could be anyone. Hugh fights the fear as it grips him, forcing his hand away from his dagger. *They don't see me*, he reassures himself. *They don't know me here. Whoever this white devil is I will deal with him when the time comes. Until then I will not yield to this terror.*

With consciously controlled breathing Hugh surveys the faces, trying to remember who is who. Cardinal Riario, Julius' wealthy cousin is there with Egidio da Viterbo, vicar general of the Augustinians, and two other scholarly clerics, black caps with dense beards. One he recognizes as the brilliant Fedro Ingirami, but the other he does not. Hugh pauses and looks closer and sees that they are, by their nods and gestures, deferring to another slighter scholar who is standing in their centre with a well shod youth. The youth has a tinge of ginger in his curly locks – most unusual for Rome. But the scholar's alabaster-white face is more intriguing still. It is sharp, almost shrew-like but not unkind. He wears the black wool beret of a scholar and long woolen cloak with fur trim. Hugh sees Bembo looking intently too and draws near him by the window. There is a general noise as Bramante and the cardinal talk over each other about Raphael's new fresco, so Hugh and Bembo are not overheard.

'I see you observe the foreign scholar, Bembo. You seem to know everyone else's business. Who is he?'

'Desiderius Erasmus of Rotterdam – though in truth he's like Plotinus: nobody knows where he is from. His young pupil is the bastard son of James IV of Scotland, Alexander Stuart. They are guests of the cardinal.'

'Here to teach the boy the Classics?'

'That and get a dispensation from the pope so he can obtain an ecclesiastical position in England.' Bembo smiles to see Hugh's quizzical expression. 'The young lad is not the only bastard. Apparently Erasmus' father was a priest who had not kept to his own bed or his vows. Erasmus wishes the pope to make it otherwise.'

'Ah, thank you for explaining it to me. You are a mine of information, my friend,' Hugh says somewhat absentmindedly, for he is now examining the semicircular fresco at door height on the wall opposite. 'It is magnificent.' It is all he can say.

The cardinal congratulates Raphael on the architecture, but Bramante speaks yet again, this time to say that the architecture was his own modest contribution – that and the content.

'And your bald head!' Sangallo says pointing at the figure of Euclid in the right hand corner of the fresco, surrounded by some young admirers. The group gasps, then laughs. 'So it is,' some say, then clap their hands. Bramante bows good-naturedly with his cap removed so they can see the likeness. 'I have always prized geometry. It is our elevation of math and geometry in education that has led to all these marvels – made this renaissance.' When he sees that they will not stop laughing and that his cheeks only get redder, the architect bows one more time. 'Yes, yes. It is a fair likeness, is it not?'

Hugh then sees other faces in the fresco that he recognizes: Raphael himself in the right hand corner looking outward. Leonardo da Vinci as Plato perhaps. And then right there on his own, like he had just stepped off the scaffold, not even in ancient dress; the booted and grumpy Michelangelo.

When the noise dies back Cardinal Riario speaks to Raphael. 'There is no gold leaf and precious little ultramarine. Did my good cousin run short of funds?'

While Raphael is still thinking of a politic answer, Erasmus says in perfect Toscana, 'I suppose it is the preciousness and not the art that pleases you?'

Those near him gasp, but the cardinal pretends he has not heard. The pointed nose of the scholar broadens into a winning smile. 'I did not intend offence, Eminence, but merely quoting the voice of Reason from your own poet Petrarch. I believe your poet perceived rightly that the just index of consumption should be "the genius of man" wherever we find it. So I stand here amazed in your presence yet again, Eminence. You take me to catacombs that inflame my piety, such as it is, and then to libraries – where I would happily pass the rest of my days. And now to see frescoes such as this! You have verily ruined the rest of Europe for me.' He removes his scholar's black beret to reveal the thinning grey hairs and receding hairline of a man in his forties. When he has finished shaking his head, he says, 'My guidebook by Canon Albertini says that I must yet see this great fresco under construction by the *maestro depinctor Michaelis Archangeli* in the vault of Sixtus' chapel, but really signors, can anything be finer than what we are now seeing?'

'Indeed, you shall see for yourself, signor,' says Sangallo stepping forward keen to defend the prowess of the Florentine republic. 'For half the vault is now complete and scaffold ready to be taken down. Rome just awaits the triumphal return of His Holiness for the unveiling – though it may be possible to prevail upon Michelangelo to let you see sooner if your business will take you away before then.'

'That is most kind, Signor Sangallo, most generous of you.' Erasmus bows again. 'But let us not steal the thunder from our young friend here. Signor Santi, these good men have tried to explain your methods to me, but I am afraid that you must remind me; is it true that these pigments here – the azurite, terra verde, vermillion, malachite – are all added *a secco?*'

'Indeed signor, all but the azurite. I am flattered that you approve so. My only hope is that His Holiness will commend me thus himself when he returns in health – and victory.'

A voice from near the cardinal sounds loud and truculent. 'And indeed he shall, I have said so all along.'

It is the Augustinian Egidio da Viterbo. 'It is as I said from the pulpit of Saint Peter's Basilica: our noble pontiff is the very fulfillment of the Cumaean prophecy, "justice returns to earth, the Golden Age returns, and its first born comes down from heaven above."' He steps in front of the fresco, so that he might be better heard. 'Venice is all but humbled; the Papal States secured; God has exalted our most holy pontiff in the camp as in the forum. Surely now the golden age spoken of by the Sybil will come to pass.' He turns to the cardinal. 'Your Eminence, we should take Signor Erasmus and young Stuart to the cave at Lake Avernus where these things were foretold.'

Hugh observes the inquisitor's eyes narrow, the cardinal's roll, and Erasmus look as if the Vicar General of the Augustinian order had just lost his mind.

'What on earth is he talking about?' Hugh whispers to Bembo. 'Did he really proclaim *that* in Saint Peters?'

'Apparently. Can't help admiring the fellow's cheek. It's from Virgil's eclogues. The prophecy, I mean. "Now is the Virgin made herself known, and the reign of Saturn on earth," something, something, "rejoice at the birth of this boy who will put an end to this wretched age, from whom golden people shall spring." Something, something, I can't remember, and then, "now does your Apollo reign". It is an extraordinary prophecy, the bits I remember. How can we explain it? Virgil had never read Isaiah. How then? Surely there is a deep desire at work in all men for *ille dem vitam accipiet*, the gift of divine life. The Romans claimed it for Augustus, Augustine claimed it for Christ, but Egidio evidently knew better. The brown nose.'

'He's not the only one. I've seen at least another three of Raphael's frescoes where Julius is painted as some hero or other. I am surprised the pope's humility will stand it.'

Hugh's sniping whispers are interrupted by a commotion at the fresco. He looks up to see the inquisitor addressing Bramante and Raphael in front of the illustrious assemblage. It appears that people were beginning to relax and enjoy themselves too much. And so it was time for the inquisitor to ask why this composition had no reference to ecclesiastical authority in it. 'Particularly at a time when enemies without and within seek to usurp the power of the church – schismatics, heretics, sectaries. There are some who would dearly love to just have Aristotle and Plato and do away with the church. Yes, shake your heads and tut all you want. It is my business to know that it is true.' Hands on hips, the Dominican glowers about the room as if each person present might be plotting to overthrow the papacy that very night. 'Natural philosophers, who will build a new world with reason's large conscience—that is why I say, as I will say to his holiness, that some of these bearded stoics should be repainted as doctors of the church. Reason indeed.'

'But surely Aquinas tells us that reason is God's representative to man?' Erasmus talks quietly, but everyone hushes for the foreigner, even the cardinal. 'Therefore I cannot think but that the saint intended us to believe that our reason was not affected by original sin.'

'I doubt a man like Aquinas was as easily beguiled as some of his interpreters. "The heart of man is corrupt and wicked above all things," as says the prophet Jeremias. Reason has been made as much the devil's whore as all our other noble faculties.'

To everyone's surprise the northern scholar bows in acquiescence. 'It is well said, Your Grace. Perhaps stronger than I would put it, but well said. And I have lived long enough and studied long enough to see how sins of ambition, pride and avarice have tainted even the pursuits of knowledge. It is fairly spoken, God have mercy on us all.'

'Let us hope so,' Bembo whispers to Hugh. 'For the inquisition will not.'

Hugh, as if not hearing him, speaks his own thoughts. 'I hate to agree with a man like that, the Dominican I mean, but I think he is right, Pietro. I think we might follow Aristotle in many fields of enquiry but with caution, for our hearts always desire to separate some small parcel of the cosmos and call it our own. Torture facts long enough, and they will confess anything. I see a danger, *caro*, do you not?'

'Of course, little minds with small philosophy, arguments from undesign *ad ifinitum*. Hugh, you know the sort of thing. *Nequaquam nobis divinitus esseparatum, naturam rerum, tanta stat praedita culpa:* had God designed the world it would not be a world so frail and faulty as we see. But really, Hugh, are you so pessimistic when the scriptures and the church are able to answer such truepenny sophistry as easily and clearly as they do?'

'Perhaps, perhaps. But times change, and often before we even know it. Do you think there was a Roman alive who could have told you the day when the Roman Empire had passed that slow curve from rise to decline? Did Horace, Livy, or Seneca? I don't think they did. Maybe they all woke up one day and wondered, "How can Jove the Thunderer be the same as Jove the Adulterer?" Maybe they all decided then and there that they had never really believed at all—that it was all one grand charade to hide themselves in. Maybe we'll wake up one morning and think the same thing. Maybe in the future people will pity us, as we pity Cicero and Pompey now, for the fig leaf of religion that we professed but that we never really believed.'

'Hugh, are you all right, my friend? Where has all this come from?' Bembo leads Hugh into the window seat for even though the general conversation is now loud enough to mask their voices, Hugh's face is stricken with emotion.

Hugh folds his arms and looks toward the Tiber and the soft orange roofs. 'I don't think I am quite all right and have not been so since the tunnels of Siena. I have many things to think about, but I cannot do so here in Rome.'

'Well, let us go to Urbino. *Dio mio*, Castiglione sends to me weekly saying that he needs my help on his new book *The Courtier*. I know you would be most welcome too. The surrounding courts will be eager to hear your news from the East. You haven't yet visited Bologna, Ferrara, or Mantua either. It will all serve, Hugh. You might as well be seen to be fulfilling your outward mission while you are about it.'

'Yes, I agree, it would serve. But I think I should like to call into Assisi on my way first. Unfinished business.'

Bembo draws back, the whites of alarm in his eyes. 'Really?'

That business with the olive press still haunting him at weak moments? 'Not with you, Pietro, you dolt. This time it is something I must confess.'

Relief floods Bembo's face as every muscle relaxes. 'You have a confessor there?'

'Yes, if you can call him that. My prior on Rhodes said I should get one, yet I think in truth he found me. I cannot explain it to myself much less you, but either way I should like to go there again. Do you mind?'

'No, it is on the way after all.' Bembo gazes at his friend with a sympathetic stare, and says softly once more, 'Are you all right?'

'I might be better than I have ever been since childhood, but I cannot be certain. And there is another matter that weighs heavily on me. In the tunnels Vendramin told me things, things which almost all Christendom repudiates.'

'I should think that to believe something that four-fifths of Christendom repudiates is one of the prerequisites of sanity.'

'It is not a laughing matter, my friend. I mean, would you turn traitor to all you hold dear if you found it unjust, wrong, contrary to the truth? To the church even?'

'Well...' The whites of his eyes grow then subside as a smile masks the evident shock. 'I am like every honest man Hugh, always willing to consider any additional evidence that confirms my existing opinion.'

STABLE YARD, GRAND PRIORY, ROME. MAY 28TH

'Why we meeting here?' Wilf is scowling and scratching his small clothes.

'Because it's quiet and the only ears here are the horses.' Hugh glances back from the stable doorway into the priory yard to make sure that it is true.

'Trouble, master?'

'We leave tonight for the Marches, but I don't want the prior knowing about it.'

'Why the hell not?'

'Not so loud.' Another glance. 'He suspects me of disloyalty with regards to Vendramin, and I begin to suspect his motives are not entirely fueled by zeal for our order.'

'Eh? Speak English like.'

'Do you remember that night at the olive press in Assisi? Bembo said that his masters had someone on the inside of the Grand Priory, but he didn't know who, someone who left the cellar door open.'

'You think it's the prior?'

'Perhaps. I had a little chat yesterday with him and his men.'

'And how was that?'

'The wrong side of exciting.'

'I see. Serious.' Wilf stops grinning. 'Well, what's his game?'

'With Petrucci and Michelotto gone? I don't know, and I'm not staying in Rome to find out either. He'd be within his rights, as my superior, to have me in his dungeon, and flogged if he wanted. No one will question his jurisdiction in Rome. So we're best out of here, but quietly. You take our stuff a bit at a time today to the Hay Market. Don't arouse suspicion. I'll let the prior's men follow me today and give them the slip after vespers, and meet you there.'

'I'll be ready.' Wilf is rubbing the scar where his ear used to be. Hugh has noticed that he always does this when he hears Michelotto's name. 'And then what?'

'We have an invitation to visit the court of Urbino, a few week's ride. We'll stop at Assisi on the way.'

'Why?'

'Someone I want to see.'

'That monk.' Wilf's eyes light with interest.

'He's a friar, you halfwit.'

'Whatever. Do you think he can help you?'

'Not sure. What d'you think, Wilf? Is there any hope for me?' Hugh feels his toes involuntarily curl in his boots.

'Yeah, I think you're getting better, master.'

'Really?'

'Well, you ain't tried to hang yourself for a while. That's a start, like. And I'm not having to clean your sheets as much neither. Yeah, there's hope, master.'

'You're a good man, Wilf. An idiot for sticking with me. But a good man.'

'Hah, I serve the most famous knight in Europe. The ladies love that. What's not to like?'

Hugh is about to answer but turns inward again. *You serve a monster, Wilf. It is only because you do not know what I truly became, that you are still here. I keep you by deceit. I am unworthy of any such fealty. And that's the truth.*

Wilf tries to find Hugh's eyes again. 'So we travel north. Then what?'

'We visit the courts where we are invited, talk about the crusade – just like we've been instructed. And we keep our eyes and ears open. The usual.'

'Oh yeah, and find Vendramin?'

Hugh pauses. 'Of course.'

'Don't sound convinced. What about this gold?'

'Yes, that too. Of course the gold.'

'And the Greek fire?'

'What? Yes, yes, and that. But you understand that means we must go to Venice.'

'What? Them lot what are at war with everyone else?'

'It's our best chance of catching Vendrammin. They are his people.'

'Aye Hugh, and they'll bloody kill us if we cross the front line and all. Or else our lot will.'

'There is a risk, of course, but we have immunity, and we have no enemies among Christian nations.'

'No enemies, bollocks, you can't go to the Jacques for a piss without making enemies for God's sake. Holy Mother!'

'That's enough, man,' Hugh snapped. 'Just have the baggage and victuals ready.'

Wilf shrugs and prepares to go. Hugh breaks free from his own inner wrestlings. 'Wilf. One more thing you should know, should be watching for.'

'Oh yeah?'

'When you're among the servants and so forth.' Hugh stumbles over even speaking the name. He is amazed at himself for a moment. *Why is my heart beating so? Why this outbreak of sweat?*

'Yeah?'

Hugh swallows hard. 'There is someone else who is after us. Not new; he's been there all the time. Petrucci and Vendramin warned me about him. He's called the White Cardinal, and no one knows who he is, but he is after me, or at least information about my progress. So I mention it now. If you hear someone mention *il cardinale bianco*, then tell me straight away.'

'Is he dangerous?'

'Aren't they all?'

'What's he after?'

'Who knows? But he's a clever bugger so be on your guard.'

'Fine,' Wilf says, puffing out his cheeks and surveying what lies ahead. 'So we wander about like sitting ducks, travelling with that sweet-talking dago what might murder us in our beds, chasing a man who is as good as a phantom and being chased ourselves by another. We've got the magister with a pike up our arses, his holiness holding us by the short and curlies and now, on top of it all, we're wandering up north into someone else's war in the hopes of speaking with the enemy. That's nice, that is. Life ain't dull, but shit master, don't fancy our chances, like.'

'It's all we have, Wilf, so just be ready. Oh, and bring that carrack sword of de Blanchfort. I'd best be wearing it today.'

'Aye, bloody right you should. And what time are we meeting?'

'Just after the bell for prime. I'm going with Bembo to see Michelangelo and a few others, to say goodbye. We'll not be long.'

'Bembo! I still say you're a fool to take him again, master. That shifty dago, with all his fine talk! I wouldn't show him your eggs again, master, not after what he did to us.'

'Peace Wilf. I have my reasons.'

'Yeah, that's what I'm afraid of.'

ON THE SCAFFOLD IN THE SISTINE CHAPEL, ROME - MAY 28TH 1509

'Yes, England was well when I left her. It is the feast of Saint Augustine of Canterbury today. Did you know that?' Erasmus' slender hand grips the ladder with white knuckles as they ascend to the vault. The scholar glances down again to the floor now thirty feet below them and gulps. 'King Henry is to marry his brother's widow in a week or so. You say you are familiar with Cambridge?'

It is strange for Hugh to hear someone speaking to him in such good English. He has been introduced to Erasmus at the bottom of the Sistine scaffold. It is a strange meeting, like having air. They reach the final platform. Sangallo is standing by Michelangelo's grinder and general *manino*. Hugh has forgotten his name. Sangallo is rubbing his hands, deferential. So is Bembo, who for once is hushed in the presence of – as he put it himself – one greater than Solomon. Europe's first free floating brain. The first man to actually live from his pen. Printing is changing everything. For Bembo it's an apparition and epiphany in one. Think of it, he had said to Hugh the night before: no more hanging on a duke or duchess' coat tails, total freedom to write what you would. In the School of Athens fresco, Raphael seemed to foresee the same possibilities, the arts equal to or perhaps even supplanting the sciences. Artists and writers, the new high priests of culture, covert legislators of mankind.

Michelangelo is rubbing his hands together, though merely to get the *intonacco* from them. He'd do anything for Sangallo, but he looks world-weary, hunched and resentful. Time is always against him. He never has done one half of what he wishes. He is muttering as much to Sangallo, words turbid, tone terse. Hugh knows the feeling. He and Michelangelo exchange nods. The chapel is almost half complete. He has had help, Hugh thinks as he glances about. Good. The incense from morning mass still wafts under the vault, illumined by shafts of bespeckled light rising from between the planks. Hugh breathes in deeply now he is finally up the ladders and on the scaffold. Along with the smell of wet plaster, odours of frankincense, saffron, pepper and sage fill his nostrils. Erasmus, two shaky footsteps in front of him, turns to get the answer to his question.

'I studied there, and my family's estates lie between there and Norwich.' Their conversation going up the ladder has overrun the proper time for introductions. Erasmus says that it is a pleasant part of the country; that he doesn't care for the inhabitants of Yarmouth, but at least has always obtained a reasonable passage from his homeland there. He stands uneasily on the boards, his hand always reaching out for something to grab every time one moves slightly. 'I'd be a poor sailor!'

He laughs nervously and then bows unevenly when introduced to Michelangelo. Erasmus points out the Cumaean Sybil on the far side of the vault, monolithic, monumental. Erasmus is near speechless for half a minute, forgetting himself and uttering small comments in his native tongue. Hugh knows how it feels. Compared to the finesse of Raphael's work, the sheer scale and brute, masculine force of these frescoes takes the wind out of the proudest sail. It is like facing the immortal gods. Nor is the shrew-like scholar any more calm when he is invited to turn his head up to behold the temptation of Adam. Hugh joins him, turning about and craning his neck back to take it all in. Adam is reaching boldly for the fruit from a feminine serpent. Eve reclines, voluptuous, her head sensuously close to Adam's parts. Hugh feels a tingle. Well, it's different, Hugh thinks.

'It is good, no?' Sangallo tries to break the awkward silence by angling for an encouraging comment.

'Indeed, and most intriguing.' Erasmus takes three steps backward and almost knocks the brushes over. 'Tell me, signor, it has been the standard interpretation that Eve sinned first in giving the fruit to Adam. That is, if you will pardon me, how your countryman Raphael has painted the scene.'

'Did he? I'm sure I've not seen it.' If an injured bear could speak, it could not sound as gruff as Michelangelo does. 'And what would he know anyway, with a conscience that stops at his belt? He's so young I doubt he could even claim to know himself. Does he? Him and his many ladies. Probably thinks it's all their fault that he can't keep his dick inside his hose. Dante has it right to have the lustful perpetually blown about in hell.'

Sangallo is beginning to smooth the remarks over, but Erasmus won't have it. 'No, your countryman touches on very big issues that affect many areas of life and theology. All have sinned in Adam, not Eve. We wrong women by blaming them for the violation of a command that the man was given. Have you heard of Cornelius Von Nettesheim's new book, *On the Nobility and Superiority of the Female Sex*? No? There is no reason you should have. He is German and speaks of these very things. And as for your colleague's unchastity, yes well...' Erasmus pauses to examine his own hands, finishing the sentence into his boots. 'Even licentious Ovid said he didn't need Muses to tell him about the *Ars Amatoria*, the art of love. We all have passions enough in our own breasts to school us, and ample opportunities to indulge or refuse those appetites.'

Michelangelo, chin raised slightly in pride. 'You speak with experience then, signor.'

Erasmus, cheeks already flushed from the ascent, removes his scholar's beret. 'Indeed. As a younger monk I felt the power of strong affections. Almost too strong for me, I confess. But even so, by some miracle of divine grace, no doubt, I was kept from a great fall.'

'No doubt. You did the right thing.' Michelangelo, hands on hips, speaks with almost Julian authority. 'Because to indulge the body in such things saps the spirit, enfeebles the brain, causes heart problems and bad digestion.'

'Oh Michelangelo, *caro*, enough of that Platonism of Ficino's.' The happily married, and grandfatherly Sangallo, shakes his old wizened head so that his turkey neck flaps back and forth. 'You must pardon my young friend, signor. He speaks after the philosophy of the Greeks.'

Michelangelo insists, 'You may disagree, all you like Giuliano, but let me have an answer from your guest.'

Erasmus is moved by the boldness of Michelangelo, the same elemental passion that has created all they see around them. For a moment he purses his lips and looks about him, nodding gently then says, 'I left because in my case – and according to the scripture – it was illicit, a sinful liaison. My prior was understanding, and by his permission I was able to leave the occasion of my temptation. It was my choice. It has not been an easy path, but it has been a true one. If a wise man may overrule the stars, then how much more his passions. I know your Boccaccio believed otherwise—that all us, prelates are scoundrels and hypocrites —but I cannot see how anyone could take as normative, every passion he might suddenly be given to at any moment, and then try to live that way without ruining his life and everyone else's around him. I was able to walk away, and I thank God I was able to. But I judge no man.'

Erasmus speaks with an easy grace and precision that are such unlikely companions that the group continues to observe the ceiling in silence. Hugh looks hard at Adam and Eve expelled, thinks of his own orphan journey in the world. 'Do you mind to be thus?' Hugh says.

'You and I both wander far from our homelands, signor, but perhaps in this world we are all wanderers cast from Eden. I think, since that time men have tried to be at home here, tried to imagine a possible civil society that could be perfect. Plato, his Republic. Augustine his City of God. Even a friend of mine is writing a book called *Utopia* to explore these issues. But perhaps you will know him for he is a member of parliament from Yarmouth which is in your Norfolk is it not. Thomas More?'

Hugh shakes his head. 'I have been from the country some years, signor.'

'Yes, of course. Well, I believe my friend's book is much in the high style of *The Republic*, minus the ban on poetry and music! And I think, if my memory serves me, that in his society children are even allowed to have parents! But I am digressing from the matter at hand. You ask if I mind my wandering, and I say that I yearn for a heavenly country, the way to which is through the path of gospel salvation and not higher political action. It is internal, not external, and if I am to be any use in this world then I must be a redeemed man. I am, Signor Bembo, more with Petrarch than Dante on this matter. In his *De Monarchia,* Dante believes the right worldly system will produce the right men. But I believe, and I rely on you to correct me if I have misunderstood the matter, that the emphasis should be the other way round.'

'But surely, Signor Erasmus,' interrupts Michelangelo, on hearing a Florentine criticized. 'You would agree with Dante that a world where the pope did not meddle with the temporal powers would be a better world? I mean, at least we wouldn't have what we have now: this war, this bloodshed.'

'Michelangelo.' Sangallo lays a hand on the artist's arm. 'You must not speak ill-advisedly on matters concerning the church.'

'Why not? That inquisitor prick isn't here. We're men of sense, aren't we? Signor?'

'It is all right, Signor Sangallo. I speak as a guest, Signor Buonarotti.' Erasmus' quick eyes dart about the assembled men to see he has their discretion. 'Dante was a most perceptive man. He spoke truth and was persecuted for it. I will not say or write more until I am back in England, but I perceive at every turn in Europe, momentous times are upon us. Some man once said, "May you never live in interesting times." I cannot remember who, but you know what I mean.'

'Please, by your courtesy, continue signor.' Hugh rubs his neck, stiff from looking up too long.

'I have been, because of the success of my work, somewhat like your Francesco Petrarcha, an independent observer of the European. And everywhere and in many different ways I see a legitimation crisis – a crisis of authority – causing great tensions. Why, not even our maps can be trusted since this fellow Columbus has found this New World!' Erasmus licks his lips and swallows to moisten a throat dried by lime dust. With each point he makes fluttering gestures with his delicate white fingers as if he were spinning a web of ideas. 'I don't know where I should even begin. I have spent much of the night in thought about it. We simply cannot agree who is the final arbiter of truth. God through the church? God through the state? Dante thought it should be both severally. Or, as we saw in the school of Athens fresco, God through Plato and Augustine's idealism or God through Aristotle's and Aquinas' natural philosophy? A veritable abyss of limitless, and as yet undetermined, possibilities is their new science.'

'Well, I'm with Dante,' Michelangelo interjects, sniffing loudly then muttering under his breath. 'Don't care what anyone else thinks, least of all Raphael.'

Erasmus nods affably. 'Yes, well and good signor, well and good. But how precisely does the church bring truth to the sacred spheres, by what measure shall she measure? It has been divided east and west since the great schism. The failure at the Council of Florence to reunite the church seventy years ago only underlines the point. The fall of the Eastern Church to the Turks, while we stood by, only highlights our joint shame. And what of the spiritual example of the church and of the papacy? I will say nothing of the present pontiff while I am a guest in his private chapel, but was it not the pope's uncle who excommunicated your Lorenzo do Medici? And what did your bishops do but excommunicate him right back? Authority is like soap: it diminishes with use. Pope Callistus III excommunicated a comet! And let us not forget the Borgias, an example of wickedness unparalleled even amongst the most barbarous civilizations. So, you say, perhaps we devolve power to the Conciliar Council? Is that better? I cannot think it. Jan Huss questioned their authority, and they burned him for it. I think the final authority God intended must therefore rest outside the earthly structures. Concretely in this world but not of it.'

Michelangelo picked up and blew the dust off his copy of Savonarola's sermons. 'He is a brave man who would challenge the corrupt powers in this world. If all that Savonarola did and taught could bring no change, what could anyone do?'

'Ah,' Erasmus says, 'Fra Savonarola too was beguiled into using the power of this world. His authority rested in the public belief in his infallibility. That claim betrayed him. You can kill a man, but you cannot kill an idea. You cannot kill truth.'

'So, you have a better way, have you?' Michelangelo was getting bullish again. 'Better than Fra Savonarola?'

'I do.'

'Well?'

'It seems to have escaped everyone's notice that since the Turkish conquest of Constantinople, even before its fall, many monks, priests and scholars have come west bearing manuscripts previously unknown to us. Many of these were Greek copies of the New Testament gospels and epistles. Now, what if someone were to collate the best of them and make a full Greek New Testament with a parallel translation, say in Latin or even national languages, mass produced by these new printing presses?' Erasmus lingers on the last S and his dark eyes burn under his cap as the others take it all in.

'But who can speak Greek?' Michelangelo says, winding his neck back shamefacedly.

'I can.' Erasmus says quietly and turns his sparkling mouse-like eyes uncertainly toward Bembo. 'You asked me on the way in, what an independent writer might do if he had no need of patrons. Well, this, signor, is it. Would it not be something to reform the church bottom up rather than top down? Of course, to re-form one must either know, or have means to discover, the original form to be aimed at, the form before the Fathers even, *ad fontes*. It is a project, Fra Hugh, that has been much on my heart since my years at Cambridge and my friendship with your most excellent compatriot John Colet. If any good were to come out of those frustrating years, then let this be it. These texts are, after all, the title deeds of our religion, the patrimony of all mankind. That is why I think the project has merit.'

'Well,' Bembo chuckles nervously, and shifts his feet as he tries to visualise the result of Bibles in German, Spanish, Toscana, Veneziano, English even. 'That would be something different, I suppose. Savonarola would cheer you from his grave, I think. He chided *Il Magnifico* and the others for the pagan bent of their scholarship and caused many to apply the new learning to biblical exegesis. Yes, Savonarola would love this, but he found himself on the wrong end of the *strapado* and then the pyre. So, if I were you, I wouldn't undertake such a task in Italy – or Spain.'

'Indeed no, but perhaps England, or Switzerland.' Erasmus smiles meekly. 'Jerome's translation is held as high as the very high shelves on which it mostly gathers dust – especially by those who never read it. Jerome worked with what was at hand during the collapse of the empire. He did good work in difficult times. And besides all that, today's versions are far removed from his original work, and even further away from his original Greek sources. And now, at our end of history, if there is a silver lining to the infidel menace it must be this: these manuscripts, coming now to us as they have. In the present crisis it is up to each man to wage war for truth with the weapons God has given him. I believe we will conquer through Christ if we fight according to Christ's example only. My sword is the pen, and with it I only look to reveal truth as it was first revealed to mankind through Christ and the apostles. Think brothers! If people could read the scriptures as received – or as close as the best scholarship can get them. Might we not begin to rid ourselves of religion by rote, by simonism, by superstition and amulets. We might at last see a new devotion, a genuine piety among the masses.' Erasmus concludes in a tone that belies his best convictions, 'It could be a source of unanimity, of concourse even.'

Hugh raises an eyebrow at Bembo. *Apres moi le deluge*, more like.

LETTER TO LADY VITTORIA COLONA AT ISCHIA

From Page Two

With regards to those other matters, my lady, Bembo says that the woman's name was actually Alessandria Bardi. Some of what you heard was true. Bembo says that she was so tall she never wore patterns. He also says she was never seen idling in the doors or windows and always wore a veil when she went to mass – which she did with her mother, though she was the ornament of every fete and reception. Bembo is sceptical – I think you know him by now – of some other details. Though the architect Sangallo, who knows the city's history, says most of the stories are *se non vero e ben trovato*, if not true then well founded. At least they serve as an example to young women of your station. For she did not scorn to go around with a linen napkin over her shoulder offering trays of confectionary and cups of wine. Further she deprived herself of comforts; wearing rough undergarments and sleeping on a straw mattress of the floor.

These I say, are what is said, the rest I am assured is attested by an historian whose name I have forgotten already. You heard correctly that her father and husband were exiled, and she was left alone with her children. Her husband was forced to become tutor to the Lord of Gubbio and was eventually murdered by him. Alessandria was left in Florence where she dressed in a narrow widow's skirt, with an unpleated hood and headband above her eyes, and a cloak that almost completely concealed her face. Still beautiful, she resisted an avalanche of temptations and brought up her children respectably, she died after a fever in her fifty fourth year. I hope that suffices. Tell the duchess that if she would know more, then Bembo says a letter to Francesco Giucciardini might yield greater detail, or at least more certain confirmations.

From Page Three

Thank you again for the verse and your prayers. I know not whether you write to me these days for your instruction or my edification. I fear that I have not been the tutor that you deserve. This past winter has been hard for me. I feel the presence of enemies within and without. Of the latter I am not at liberty to write further, but of the former, this villainous and accusing conscience, I may pen something for it hath much bearing on this pious verse that you last sent. Indeed, it comes with fresh hope, and I will write out in full those cantos which have been a solace to me on the road north from Rome.

When on my many sins, I gaze intent,
From God the father, then my face I hide
In shame, and unto thee, who for us died
On cross of Calvary, my heart is bent.
Thy love and wounds to me a shield heaven lent
To turn all past and present wrath aside.
Thou art to me a sure and precious guide,
Who our deep woes has turned to glad content.

In line one you talk of many sins and hiding from God. Surely this is exaggeration on your part, you who are so young and have been kept in such innocence from this world. I know of what you write, but you should not strain for effect, if indeed this is the case. If not, then forgive the impertinence. We must write only of what we know. And I would know this, lady. You say in lines five and six that the love and wounds of Christ do offer a shield against the past and present wrath. How does this surety happen upon you? And what of the sinner whose future duty demands he sin again cruelly? I cannot explain myself in ink and likely would not in person, only believe me that I find myself in Italy about a business for which I have no stomach, but which leads me on. Sometime I dream that I will be dragged bodily to Hades, not for what I have done but for the things I must do hereafter.

From Page Four

Another canto follows, which, too, fills me with questions.

For us, Thou didst entreat in death's dread hour,
Saying, 'I would, O Father, that above
Be those who trust in me.' Whence my soul free
From earthly fears acknowledges the power
Of that pure zeal, which led Thee in Thy love
To crucify my sins upon Thy tree.

I know the verse which speaks of the plea of Christ for us. It is well known. I give assent in my mind – feverishly so in darkest times – but what is this trust you speak of which banishes earthly fear? You speak of Christ's love as if it may be experienced in this earth. I do not know whether to believe you in earnest, or whether these are the noble and pious sentiments of a virtuous woman. Write more anon, but please do not give me a theologian's answer, or some lines from a catechism. It need not be in rhyming couplets or *tersa rima* either! But please write of it in plain language how all this happens upon you.

But what do I ask, fool that I am? Is not verse without affectation the plainest speech? So write as you will. All our earthly lives we are named by others, our fathers, our masters. Surely God alone can truly give a man his name? These verses of yours make me dream that a man might be more than his past. No, that is not it, not at all.

What I meant to express is above that. In very truth, they make me believe in the impossible, that a man might escape his name, escape himself, his nature, escape from what he has been called – been called to do even.

I fear, having read the above, that I am less than clear in my writing. The Trebiano frustrates my purpose, so from now on, hock and water. The news that you shall be visiting your late grandfather's palace in Urbino this summer is news indeed, as Bembo and I are headed there after many delays, and so we have hopes that our visits will coincide.

Keep me in your prayers, lady, for I have need. Adieu.

I am, *pro gloria Rege*, et cetera.

ABBAZIA DI SAN SALVATORE, 31ST MAY 1509

The Abbey of San Salvatore on Mount Amiata is a day's ride north of Lake Bolsena. It's a ridiculous haul up the Tuscan mountain, but not too much out of their way. They met the abbot, earlier that week when staying with Gian Giordano Orsini in Bracciano. The Duchess Felice was at her other estate on the coast, but this abbot made up for it. Indeed he insisted they enjoy the hospitality of the monks in this hillside village. They are fed bear, a first for Hugh, and after dinner the abbot – a diminutive Benedictine with a deeply veined, red face and slapping sandals – leads Hugh with a feverish sort of excitement into the crypt of the abbey. Two other novices attend with lamps. It is cold but only slightly damp. *Why the fuss? What does he want to show me?* Hugh is not anxious. *They're all good sorts here. No harm in them.* Only it is a strange business. It all started at dinner when the abbot asked Hugh whether he knew of Coelfrid of the English? He didn't.

The warm flickering glow illumines squat Romanesque arches, smoothed by the ages and redolent with incense and mold, prayers and tradition. The abbot and first novice leave the central colonnade in the crypt and enter a small side chapel. Hugh follows. As the lamps are set in alcoves, Hugh discerns an ossuary in the center of the altar. At the abbot's invitation Hugh goes forward and lets his fingers run over the stone sarcophagus in miniature. Strange patterns run under his fingers, and strange dragons or lion creatures meet his thumbs, round head, round jaws. It is the work of Northmen, Danes, or their descendants.

'It is very old,' is all Hugh can say, then afterwards feels stupid for saying it.

'It is from the time of Gregory the second, eight hundred years ago. They are the bones of Coelfrid of England, of Yarrow in your north country. I am surprised you had not heard of him at all. He is venerated here.' *Jarrow. He means Jarrow where Bede lived out his days.* No sooner has Hugh thought this then the abbot says, 'He was abbot to the Venerable Bede and made his last pilgrimage to Rome to make a gift to the pope but died en route.'

'It must have been some gift, abbot.' Hugh says, withdrawing his hands and taking a step back.

'A great Bible. The work is very fine, and all the more so because – pardon my saying – it has come from the fringes of civilisation.'

'I should like to see it.'

IN THE SCRIPTORIUM

The next morning, Hugh and Bembo are shown this gift from the English that never quite made it to Rome. Bembo is intrigued; it is a book after all. Over two feet by three, and surely over a foot thick, the behemoth sits daintily as a millstone on the scribe's table. How many hundred calf skins to make this? A thousand? The leather bindings are worn and the oak boards show splinters on the edges and corners. Mildew dots the spine and lower pages. Brother librarian insists that it did not get damp on his watch. But who's listening? Certainly not Hugh and Bembo, who are now lost in the text, in the illustration. They are not just touching vellum. They know without saying that they are touching another world almost incomprehensible to them. Smell that musty peppery odour, feel that crisp edge of the page. If anything the librarian has kept it too dry. Holy men, who carved out a place for the true God amidst a barbarian nation, wrought this with their lives. The ink is their blood almost. *We should be kneeling, not before the book, but kneeling in dedication, that we might walk as they did. Have I sold my life too cheaply? What have I left behind but blood?*

While Hugh is fixed with pious thoughts, Bembo is piecing the story together with a childish fervor. He is never really more himself then when his mind is gambling off by itself and he is taking no thought for an audience. He keeps saying "by the immortal gods" over and over. The librarian leaves them to it, and returns to a back room where he is doing something that requires him to shuffle papers and curse at regular intervals.

Bembo chatters like a child while he turns the huge pages, sometimes by whole quires. 'Coelfrid died in Burgundy, so how did the Bible come here? No one here seems to know. Probably best that they don't. Did the brothers travelling with Coelfrid seek to fulfil their abbot's last wish, traveling on afterwards with his bones and the Bible? Perhaps they were waylaid as you and I have been by the offer of hospitality. It's a nice spot up here, not too hot in the summer for someone from your neck of the woods, Hugh. Suppose they were offered a permanent place? Would they turn down a slice of the *dolce vita* for another twenty English winters? Not lightly. They were a tough lot, hard cases bred on gruel and the green martyrdom. But even so?'

Bembo leaves the book for Hugh to handle. He steps back a little, folding his arms, but then raises a forearm and finger toward the vault. 'And then there is the matter of textual precedence and authority and so forth. This is probably the oldest complete translation of Jerome's Vulgate. I know that Cassiodorus' Vivarium yielded one, but I don't think it is complete. I have not seen it, have you? Of course you haven't. Sorry, Hugh, for a moment I thought you were Castiglione. He gets about, you know. But you see what I am getting at?' Hugh doesn't. 'We talked with our learned friend Erasmus this week about his Greek New Testament project – and every success to him, of course, of course every success – but this is what he'll be up against if the inquisition get hold of him. They'll say that their Vulgates are older, attested by western history and tradition. But how can he prove his eastern manuscripts are older still. I wager he can't. Provenance is a tricky business, and the inquisition do not just argue with words. They call them weapons of virtue. God deliver him, for a Dominican like Giovanni Rafenelli won't.'

THE LAZAR COLONY, ASSISI. 2ND JUNE 1509 - FEAST OF SAINTS MARCELLINUS & PETER

At the dung gate, things are different.

Shanties beyond the city walls are no longer dry-rot and wood-worm-ridden beams draped with moth eaten rags, but stone built cells with new pantile roofs. *Four of them, no five.* Hugh releases the scarf he placed over his mouth. It doesn't even smell miasmic any more. In fact, it smells better than Rome here. Warm winds bring the scents of almond blossoms and saffron from the olive terraces below. *What change is this in only eight months?* The piles of household waste with lepers picking through them are all gone. So are the fires and the putrid, fly-ridden pools of stagnant water. He sees a stone fish pond, the cement joints new and without mold. Labourers are laying slabs of limestone near it. To his left Hugh hears the clinking of the *scapellinos* preparing coin stones with their rhythmic hammers for yet another barn.

It is early morning. Hugh has left Bembo and the servants at their lodgings. He is eager to find the Franciscan. The cock crows, and bees hum as the morning light illumines the thousand sparkling cobwebs on grass and trees. It is a new day. *I will see the friar. He will help me.*

There is a scuffing of boots behind and the murmur of chatter. Hugh turns to see some friars coming down through the gate, among them the squat form of Fra Paulo Todesco.

Hugh approaches with a hand raised in welcome. 'Good morrow, friars.' He notices how two of them draw back slightly when they see him. Or is it the colhonna swinging on his belt?

Fra Paulo's pudgy features break into a nervous grin. 'Fra Hugh, you are here. Brothers, this is Hugh Erpingham of Rhodes. Remember I was telling you about him.' A significant look. The brothers bow slightly then move to their duties, leaving Hugh and Paulo alone. 'So you have come again.'

'I have.'

'And you are well?'

'Tolerably.'

'Any special reason for the visit? You are alone, I think.' Paulo glances about furtively.

'I have friends at the convent, sleeping probably.'

'You're not with the pope's people this time?' He smiles unevenly.

'No.' Hugh lets something of an enquiry rest on the word. *He asked me that last time I came here.*

'Well you are welcome all the same, and you will see we have made wondrous improvements since you were last here.'

'Wondrous indeed, brother. A new benefactor?'

'God is good.'

'Indeed, and a generous one, too.'

Paulo smiles, and raises his hands to heaven slightly. 'The cattle on a thousand hills.'

After a pause Hugh looks at his boots. 'And Fra Francesco is well?'

'He has kept to his pallet this last week. Fluid on his chest, an ague. The travelling does not agree with him.'

'He travels?'

Paulo's eyes and mouth open slightly, as if he has been caught out. 'Occasionally, to visit the destitute. With his condition, travel is not easy.'

'Condition?'

'Oh. Perhaps you did not know.'

Five minutes later Paulo is leading Hugh into an upper dorter at the friary, inside the gate. Sixteen pallets with straw mattresses and grey blankets. Shafts of dusty light fall from two upper windows. The smell of thatched rafters and human sweat are faintly detectable. The furthest pallet is occupied by a hunched bundle of coarse blanket and a tuft of grey hair.

'This is our infirmary while the new one is under construction. Francesco will be happy to speak with you, I am sure.' Paulo gestures toward the pallet and then speaks up. 'Fra Hugh of Rhodes to see you, Francesco.'

While the grey bundle shifts with a groan, Paulo says that he must leave them for he has chores. Hugh nods and approaches the bed. The old man, facing the farther wall, starts to cough great, lungsful of fluid. But when finishes, he is able to turn and sit up.

'You.' He grunts, in a way more accusatory than anything else. 'What are you doing here? Thought you were busy making war on the Turks.'

'It is my day off. May I take a seat?'

'Suit yourself.' Francesco elbows himself up against the stucco-plastered wall.

Hugh sees the dried skin and small pustules around the forehead and neck. 'Paulo told me you have had the disease for a year. I confess I didn't notice when we last met.'

'Really? Well, I would suppose a famous man like you doesn't notice a lot of things.' A small rumble of phlegm rises in his lungs as he barks defensively from the pallet. 'You came here to discuss my leprosy or yours? I told you last time, didn't I? I'm just a leper binding the wounds of other lepers. Now what do you want? I'm busy today.' He hunches away in a full fit of coughing.

'You don't look busy.' *It was a mistake to come here. And this old fart is certainly no saint, that's for sure. What was I thinking?*

Hugh is turning to go when he hears the friar start up again.

'That's right, run along. Best not contaminate yourself. Or don't you know, brave knight, that diseases like this come on men who are guilty of great sins. Pope Gregory said we lepers must be heretics, and the Third Lateran Council said we should be banished from city limits. So go on. Run along to your fine palaces and gentle ladies.'

'You said you were busy.'

Cough. And no answer. Hugh looks to his eyes—fierce blue, but afraid. Francesco sniffs sullenly and rubs the two brown moles near his left nostril with his thumb. He is tensely hunched like one in pain, as a soldier sits defensively when wounded. Hugh picks up a three-legged stool and places it deliberately near the pallet. *I'm not afraid of you, you old bastard. Some confessor!*

Hugh decides on being vulnerable. It'll make it easier on the old man's pride. 'You know why I have come.' He speaks quietly and non-rhetorically.

'Yes.' The old man draws his knees up under the covers and looks away slightly. 'You wear your hunger like a livery.'

'Like you Franciscans wear a taste for martyrdom.' *Two can play this game, mate.*

'What!'

'Well, coming down here, exposing yourself to these diseases. What disregard, what self-loathing is that?'

'You know nothing. You speak of what you know not, churl.' The older man snaps back. 'I see that you loathe yourself. That is plain. I see it in your eyes, your shoulders, the way you look at others. I suppose you even try to convince yourself sometimes that it is the gospel virtue of self-denial, yet in truth it will make diabolic in you what common selfishness would have left merely animal. Look at you! And you think we are here because we hate our own lives like you hate yours.'

'You—' But this is all Hugh can say. He is broadsided by the fierce words of the friar and feels too morally winded to reply further.

'Let me tell you something, and this will help you, but only if you listen. This is what I, Francesco, have learnt on my brief sojourn.' He coughs and swallows more phlegm and fixes both eyes on Hugh. 'I have found two voices inside me, and I must decide which to love and which to hate – to hate with an endless hatred and to kill at every opportunity. First I hear the voice that claims that I am God's creature, which is a good thing, and though I am fallen, yet I am to be cherished, healed and rescued. And I am to love others – in this way – as I love myself. This I have learned.' He uses his right fist to pound his own heart as he speaks, but then raises a squat finger. 'But then I hear that second voice that claims the self which is called me, Francesco, should be preferred beyond all other selves, even God himself. This voice claims that all should be behind me, my needs, and my desires. That all should be beneath me. You know that voice don't you.' He pauses for a significant raising of the eyebrows. 'But if I carry on like that, then I will soon discover that the object of all my affections and partiality is so disappointing that I begin to loathe it and then others. I am sure you have seen more of this than you care to admit, Hugh.'

For a moment Hugh just breathes steadily, regarding the old man with a numbness of mind and emotion. The old friar's grunt brings him to himself, and Hugh says with a dry throat. 'And so you are free from this plague of selfishness that destroys everyone else?'

'No. But by making war on it by the way I think and live I have come to know our adversary perhaps more acutely than others. Perhaps you have found this with your enemies too, eh? Maybe not, but that is how I see it anyway. We do as Christ himself did, and would do.' Francesco's ruffled hair shakes as he speaks. 'We do what we see our Father doing—binding up wounds. While others do what they see their father the devil doing.'

Touchez. 'Christ may have touched lepers but he never caught the disease.'

'How do you know? It doesn't say he didn't have leprosy.'

Hugh is about to say that it is obvious by omission but then thinks better of it. *If I say that, he'll probably twist it round somehow and say that I am wrong to bear a sword in Christ's name. Can't reason with old men.* They sit for a few silent moments before Hugh concedes with a sigh. 'So you know why I came then.'

'Yes.' The friar's shoulders relax slightly. 'Yes, I do. And I suppose you've been blundering around Italy these last months not believing a word I told you last time. Do you remember? I told you hell's half acre has already been harrowed, but you looked as dumb then as you do now. And I said to myself, Francesco, I said, you can't wake a person who is pretending to be asleep. If a man won't hear good news like that, then he'll never hear it.'

'I'm not pretending anything.'

'Then confess what it is you have done and move on. *Dio mio,* you're young enough to!'

'It is something I have not told anyone.' Hugh's hands clamp shut as he gazes at his boots.

Francesco's words soften. 'Look, what does Isaias say? Some men's sins are scarlet, obvious. But others are crimson, deep, hidden. You think this scarlet sin is the thing that will keep you from God because you are a fool. It is not the scarlet, but the many deeply rooted crimson ones that do the most damage to a man's soul – those continuous sins of pride and independence that a man thinks are part of him, perhaps even what he thinks is his righteousness but all of which stinks to high heaven – it is they that will keep him from God in the end.'

Words form on Hugh's suddenly parched tongue. He is about to say it, wants to. The words are there, but then he draws back. He laughs defensively and takes a deep breath. 'They say that Aquinas' deathbed sins were only those of a five-year-old child.'

'The man was a saint. What do you expect? Besides, God makes saints out of fools and sinners because there is nothing else for him to use. Anyway, the rest of us must come as we may.'

'Even you?' Deflection tactic.

Francesco lowers his grey head, snorts a chuckle then looks up again. 'There are no saints here Hugh, if that's what you think.'

'Even you?' Delay tactic.

'Especially me.' Francesco coughs again.

'What were you then, a village brawler? A horse thief?'

'Hah! If only.'

He's looking at his hands. Curious.

'We all have our stories, even an old man like me. But we're not here to talk about me, are we?'

Hugh shuffles, delaying again. 'No.'

'Well, then confess and have done.'

Still he pauses. Again his boots shuffle. His stomach squirms and contracts. Hugh looks up from the floor to see Francesco puckering his dry lips in contemplation. *He's changing tack perhaps. He'll come at me from the side maybe.*

Francesco sighs. 'Still hunting lions then.' When Hugh looks askance at him with knitted brow, Francesco says, 'Aesop's fable. Remember?'

Hugh nods and lets out a pent up breath. 'Suppose I am. Sometimes I feel I could face that lion, Theseus before the Minotaur.' He gives a half-hearted, self-deprecating grunt. 'But more often I am only too aware of being myself that monster, pursued by Christ down the labyrinth of my own evasion, a darkness of my own creation, my comfortable hiding place. I am evading Him now. Even by my cursed learning and literary allusions, I run from him. Yes, you may look at me as piteously as you want, Fra Francesco, but that is the sober truth of it all. I want to be clean, yet not so much that it interferes with what I have to do. And I am bound by many ties to do some terrible acts.'

'Last time you were here you said you were looking for someone, wouldn't say who or why. But I got the impression – forgive me if I am wrong – that he was an enemy and that you intended him harm.'

Hugh quickly casts his mind back to his first abortive confession with Francesco, and then further to what he had told Paulo on the Island of Procida. *He knows it is Vendramin that I sought; Paulo must have mentioned it. Does it matter now? Probably not.* Hugh releases his right hand and raises it dismissively as one might shoo a fly. 'You are right, Fra Francesco. I did pursue this man across Italy. A Venetian, a knight of my own order. A man they call Vendramin.'

'Vendramin! Pah.' The old man cocks his head back and tuts. 'I have heard he is a phantom; that he is everywhere and nowhere. A fable to frighten children.'

'He is no phantom.'

'No? You surprise me.'

'I found him, or at least he found me. I intended him harm, I don't deny it. But when we finally met, I fell into his hand, yet he spared me. Nay, he not only saved my life, but thought to lecture me on metaphysics as if *I* were the villain.'

'I see.' Francesco seems pleased, almost smiles. 'And are you a villain?'

Hugh feels a shudder move through him. Is he being tricked into something here? He'll not have it; outwitted by a holier-than-thou self-righteous friar. 'No, I serve my order. I serve the church.'

'Really? With a clean conscience?'

'Well, I...' Hugh pauses, the words escape him like spilt water. He exhales in resignation. 'I struggle, am struggling. At night I cannot – ' Hugh breaks away and scrunches up his eyes as the demons of memory break in upon him. One thousand accusers and tormentors.

'I see, I see,' Francesco sits more upright with some coughing. 'Have you ever read *The Spiritual Meadow* by John Moscus?'

'I've heard of it, but no.'

'He was a monk a thousand years ago, and he writes of a muleteer from Rome whose donkeys trample and kill a small child at an inn. The muleteer was overcome with remorse and so takes ship to the Holy Land to seek forgiveness. But what do you thing happens?'

'I don't know?' *Is there a point to this?*

'Well, he does not seem to find forgiveness, even after much searching in that holy place. So what does he do?'

'I don't know.' *Please get to the point and let me know this is not another wasted journey.*

'Of course, he considers suicide as the only alternative. That is right; he will take his own life. Because, as you can imagine, Hugh, a world where God will not forgive is a very dark place.'

Francesco pauses and Hugh watches the slate grey-blue of his eyes stare deep into his. He feels a lump in his throat as he remembers the feel of those sheets choking the life from him. The look on Wilf's face as he rushed in. It is not many men who have felt the weight of their own boots and lived to tell the tale. He breaks with the old man's eyes and says with dry mouth. 'And what happened?'

'Ah well, that's just it, you see; before he can accomplish this great and final sin the muleteer is set upon by a lion. It brings him down but does not kill him. Eventually it even releases him, and he, marveling at his escape, begins to consider that perhaps the forgiveness of God may yet be possible even for a man such as him. I mean, could God be any less merciful than a desert lion? Sin itself makes us believe strange things about God and ourselves.'

'Ourselves?' While the old man continues to stare, Hugh is at once concocting his next shield and hating himself for doing so. His voice is thin, almost jocular. 'The Mohammedans do not believe they are made in the image of their god.' No response. 'It seems easier to believe sometimes.' No response. 'Sometimes I think we're made in the devil's image.' Still no response. A tear is forming in Hugh's left eye. The shaking is returning.

'Are you going to confess or prattle on like an old spinster?' The voice is familiar, paternal. 'Was it when you had killed that Almain knight?' Hugh is nodding, and screwing up his facial features in order to control his emotions.

'What did you do?'

'We were hungry.'

'What did you do?

'We were dying.' Hugh is holding out his palms a little. *Don't make me say it.*

'And what? What did you do?'

'I wasn't the first. I mean, I did not start it. They tore him apart with stones and gorged themselves. Black fingers turned red, like harpies. Wouldn't wait until he putrefied and waste all that flesh.'

'And you?'

'I,' Hugh feels his bile rise and his mouth fills with saliva. 'I was jealous.'

'Is that all?'

Hugh shakes his head in short spasms of denial. It is not all. He bellows. 'We were starving. You cannot judge me. I sank my teeth into his flesh and cursed God as I did so for letting me do it. There, I've said it. Are you satisfied now?'

'Are you?'

Hugh shouts again. 'Don't speak to me with riddles and questions, damn you. Now you know what I am. Now you know why God will not hear me. It wasn't my donkey that got loose and killed a boy. It was me, Hugh Erpingham, sworn knight of Rhodes, defender of the faith, *pro fides,* who did this thing. That is worse than anything Dante can imagine among the denizens of any circle of hell. His Count Ugulino of Pisa, imprisoned with his sons, most likely only ate their flesh after they had died. Hunger for him overcame grief. But I killed a baptized Christian and ate him.'

'And cursed God.' Francesco says unmoved. 'And are you contrite for these sins? You repent of them?'

'Of course.'

'Then receive, *you receive*, the forgiveness of Christ and be free.'

'What? You still say it is that easy after what I have just told you?'

'Yes, I do. I may not be a priested confessor, my friend, but when it comes to absolution I know what I am talking about. So you ate a man's flesh, and you're a sinner. Do you think the rich haven't always eaten the living flesh of the poor, torn it from their backs to make the great fabric of commerce, the grist of progress? Yes, God cares what you've done. You stink; you're a leper. What do you think he sent his Son for? To tell pretty stories and lead a moral life where we could not? You idiot, he came to give his life a ransom for many; "he who knew no sin became sin for us, that we might become the righteousness of God through him." Your past is irrelevant. "Christ died for us while we were yet sinners." Forget this pride that offers vain sufferings as recompense. Reach up and take his pardon. Then tell me what you will do with your future, and I'll listen to you some more. Reach up, I say.'

'Don't you think I can read? I know what the scriptures say. Only nothing has happened – '

'Oh, so you don't feel forgiven. That is rich. God's own words on the matter are not sufficient for you. What do you want, almond blossoms to fall from the sky and angels to appear to you? You have the wrong religion, my friend, the wrong religion. You need to accept forgiveness and then live it. So tell me what you intend to do, and we'll talk some more.'

'What?' Hugh's mind is astir like hornets disturbed in straw. 'I don't know. I cannot think.'

'Very well, I will tell you something you can do while you're making up your mind. You can stay here and help us. Just for a short time, a few weeks maybe.'

'Stay here?'

'Yes. Do something useful while I recover. Just while our physician balances my humors.'

'But I have people with me. We are expected at the Court of Urbino.'

'So send them on ahead of you with apologies. Do you think the world can't live without you for a few weeks?'

THREE WEEKS LATER

Hugh stays; and it is during a torrential downpour on the Feast of the Nativity of John the Baptist, that the leper Giacomo comes once more. Rain, like you only see in the Marches in midsummer, as if someone has decided to pour all of Lake Trasimeno on Umbria. Thick and warm like a bath on dusty feet it falls, life-giving, liquid diamonds, each drop bursting with sunlight, dancing off the pantiles, cleansing the cobbles. Hugh is watching from the infirmary door, about to cast out the mop water. Bembo is long gone to Urbino, and Wilf, still here, thinks Hugh's mind is far gone for staying in Asissi – here with the off-scouring of the world.

Today Hugh begins to think Wilf is right. Three weeks, and nothing. He has thrown himself into every task, taken upon himself the worst of them: the latrines, the burials, the arse-wiping, vomit-washing, puss-canker-shite-cleansing. Tireless, joyless, driven, desperate as a man with the devil after him. Three weeks and he will do more if it can make him right again—succour every leper and beggar this side of the Apennines. *What will a man give in exchange for his soul? I will show my contrition. I will be worthy of his sacrifice.*

A ragged figure shuffles through the gate and heads along the dancing cobbles towards him. *Sodden foot-bindings and soggy rags of yet another leper come in from the country for fresh bandages, free food, free bed and any number of gullible friars to hear his sob stories, give him money for supposed relatives that probably don't exist. It probably all goes on the drink and whores if they can get them. "Thank you," they say. "Obliged to you," they say. But do any of them ever lift a finger? Do they ever offer to clean up after a meal? Do they ever heed the advice given them about their condition? Freeloaders all, and mostly happy to be so. And everyone else, the healthy townsfolk, says how much they admire your work, doff their caps, give you two scudi and then move on as quickly as possible, glad there is someone else around to appease their consciences.*

Hugh's grim recollections are cut short by Fra Francesco's voice shouting from a window somewhere above him. 'Giacomo, you old rascal, you return to us!' The beggar raises his stick. Hugh sees the facemask and remembers the name. It is the leper that Fra Francesco was ministering to on that first visit to Assisi. 'The poor are always with us,' Hugh mutters coldly, then pours the mop water into the running gulley. In the mood he's in today Hugh wonders whether Jesus said it with the same sneer he's been wearing all day. *No, of course not. Just me in my black dog moods.*

Francesco shouts again. 'Is that you done down there with the mop water, Hugh? Then welcome our old friend back with some dry clothes.' *Of course, get me to do it; saint in training.*

Ten minutes later, he is irrigating Giacomo's foot sores with wine, while Fra Francesco stands over him. The rain hammers the pantiles of the infirmary like French artillery, and the fire which slowly warms the leper also brings out the pungent aroma of his cankered wounds. They are alone. Giacomo is naked apart from his small clothes such as they are, soiled and ragged. Even his head-cloth is gone to reveal what was once a face now ravaged by decay. His dialect is from the deep, impoverished south, and Hugh still cannot divine what the man is saying, though he seems to understand Hugh well enough. The friar, on the other hand, is all *bon mot and bonhomie* and the rest. They chunter and chuckle like two old starlings on a vine, an incessant prattling broken only by Giacomo's ungrateful groans at Hugh's energetic hands.

'Hold still, will you,' Hugh says, scraping away the last of the puss from a cankered fissure running deep from the ball of his left foot toward the calluses where three toes should have been. 'This wound has been left too long. It will need salt rubbing into it, you know.'

'But not the salt of the earth, I fancy.' Francesco crouches down and looks at Hugh. 'A little more kindness, perhaps brother?'

'Well he has left it too long. Look!'

'And so did you. So did I. But God forgave us, restored us and bound our wounded souls.'

'I don't feel restored.' The words are spat out with a sourness that even surprises Hugh. Remembering his new saintly self he counters like a penitent. 'Forgive me, friar. I thought that working here would help, but as you can see it has done little for me.' The martyr avoids Francesco's gaze and reaches for the salt.

'It is not for you that you are here, but for them. Why must you always think everything is about you? You are here to serve others because you have received the free gift of God's pardon. But no, you can't do that, can you? You have to be like Naaman, who went to see the prophet Elisha. Yes, you remember him, don't you? He was a great knight like you, and a leper like you too. But he wouldn't simply wash seven times in the Jordan as he was told, no. Do you know why? Because great men like you always have to do great things to appease their pride.' Francesco takes a pinch of salt from Hugh and sprinkles it onto the open wound. 'But it's easy for old Giacomo here. Isn't it, you old flea dog?' The old leper chunts and chuckles through a twisted and lipless mouth. 'Yes, that's right. Giacomo has nothing to be proud about so he comes here and takes help freely, like a child would. You pity him, I dare say, but you are the one to be more pitied.'

'I thank you for your sympathy, good friar.' Hugh is still kneeling, bearing the insults in a manly and pious way. After all, it is to be expected that country friars living among the unlettered classes will reduce complex theological verities to the base simplicity of their usual audience. 'Each man must make his own way, make peace with his maker as best he can. I may not have reached your level of child-like faith, but I am trying, believe me.'

Francesco reaches out a hand to take up some bandages and shakes his head wearily. 'I do believe you. I do. You are like those written of long ago by the misguided Bishop Theodoret. Read him?' Hugh shakes his head. 'You should have. His subjects could teach you a thing or two about this self-mortification that you embrace.'

'Really.' *I think I prefered it when you were prattling on with Giacomo.*

'Yes, really. For example Baradatus of Syria. You should listen to this, Giacomo. You will like this. Baradatus lived in a coffin which he made himself. Fancy that, eh? When ordered to cease, he decided that he would stand up for the rest of his life – stand on his own two feet as it were. But this in itself was not harsh enough. So now guess what Baradatus did, guess what?' Giacomo chunters incomprehensibly again, with something that ends with a chuckle. 'I will tell you. He wrapped himself in a tunic of skins so that he would bake himself alive in the Syrian sun. Fancy that now, Hugh, a baked saint! And then there was Thalelaeus, who lived in a cage suspended above the earth. He had been like that, in his self-imposed limbo, for ten years when Theodoret asked. 'Why are you living like this?" *Dio mio*, the poor man had been bent double with his chin on his knees! He said that he knew of the purgation that awaited in the afterlife, and he wished to atone for what sins he could in this one.'

'And there is me thinking a man like you would admire the desert fathers.' Hugh says, ignoring the friar's caustic stare and starting to tidy away Giacomo's wet clothing. 'All that self-denial and purgation.'

'You think we are the same?'

'Aren't you?'

'I dare say we look the same to a blind man,' the friar's familiar and weary tone rankles Hugh almost to violence. He can feel his chest tighten. *Don't think I ever came across anyone who outstepped me more than this provincial friar. It's as pointless as trying to go up against your own father. Already think they know everything.*

Hugh makes his excuses and gets up to go. He skirts along the street under the shelter of the overhanging roof. Beyond the roofline the rain still comes down in unending torrents.

JULY 3RD, LETTER TO THE GRAND PRIORY, ROME

My dear Monsignor,

May God give you health, nay, may he also give you faith in our cause on this day, which after all is the Feast of Thomas – who almost fell through doubt. Your letter regarding the disappearance of Fra Erpingham betrayed a certain disquiet, as if providence itself were yet counted among the excellencies of man. I trust that in good time the divine hand will so arrange our affairs that even Erpingham will be where he is needed at the right moment.

His movements are not hidden from me even though you write that your men have made a diligent search. He is, right now, sojourning among the lowly friars in Assisi. I do not think that he hides – not from us at any rate – but he is there of a certainty.

In truth, I am not sure what to make of him. My heart is stirred within me, moved as with the swelling of Jordan. I am as Alexander before Diogenes. I confess that he reflects back on me a challenge I have not yet adequately met. Everything, my dear signor, as you know, is a matter of heart. Character is the need of the hour. When I think of our young friend I hear those words of Socrates, "he is richest who is content with the least, for contentment is the wealth of nature." What does his time with these Franciscans mean? He lives and works as one of them, I am told. I am perplexed.

There is some national characteristic of independence among the

English that I noted well during my time in that dank place. The natural propensity of an island race, perhaps? An obdurate nonchalance borne of the foul weather they endure? As I say, I am vexed, but not in despair. Indeed it is not unpleasant to contemplate something new. He does not yet know his worth to us. I entrust him to your capable hands. Keep the faith, and Saint Thomas bless you.

Your liege lord,
The White Cardinal

1ST JULY, ASSISI. FEAST OF THE MOST PRECIOUS BLOOD OF OUR LORD JESUS CHRIST

During high mass at the lower basilica Hugh has been standing under Giotto's fresco of Francis being married to Lady Poverty. She looks gaunt, and he feels it by now. The friars only eat meat on Fridays—if you can call fish meat. Hugh feels faint. He had been near the censer belching out incense so caustic that during the early chants he felt he would pass out entirely. But he did not, and now the smoke, like the townsfolk, is departing with the bishop and his dolorous benediction. He would dearly love to depart for his own meagre lunch too if only Fra Francesco would come away. But the old man, leaning on Hugh's arm seems rapt in thought, his eyes gazing into the distance, possibly at the image of Francis and the pale woman.

Hugh shuffles slightly then says, 'Shall we go, brother?'

For a moment Francesco does not answer, but eventually he speaks in a faint, almost breathless voice. 'I shall not come here many more times. They will not permit it much longer now I have the disease.'

'You are tired brother, perhaps I can –'

'I have been thinking of what you said to me, about poverty. I should like to talk to you about it.'

'I see.' Hugh's stomach groans within him. *Could we do this after lunch?*

'We are not, even in our best moments at least, like those desert fathers, Hugh. Look at Francis. It is not mere external poverty he sought, but the total denial of self. It is not poverty per se, Hugh, or denial per se. A martyr is not the same as a suicide, is he? A martyr loves something more than life, but the suicide does not even love life. For Francis it is, I think, self-forgetfulness – do you have this word in your language?'

'Not really brother.'

Francesco nods, for even the word in Toscana is almost an archaism. 'It is to be conscious that you are a "self" but then to have the freedom to give that up to the will of another instead. Lovers know this, so easily at first, but even they often forget with time. It is a terrible thing.'

Hugh feels the old man's hand suddenly tighten on his shoulder as he begins to shudder. Hugh looks and sees eyes closed and brimming with tears. 'Brother?'

'We are.' His voice breaks. 'We are more deeply broken creatures than any of us know. That is something only old men know, Hugh, and we keep it from you young.' He recovers with a sniff of a man unused to showing emotion. His eyes open, and he gazes up again at Giotto's fresco. 'What do you see?'

'Of Lady Poverty? She is tall, bigger than he is. Pale, too, austere even in her visage, clothes are patched yet clean, but she is beset with thorns.'

'Yes, and so you know what Christ offers his followers, even the rich young ruler, even me and you. For Francis, for him it was not just to do Christ's work; it was to do Christ's work in Christ's way. That is the difference, Hugh. Do you see that? Do you see how much ill we do *pro fides*? To do it any other way is not to do it at all; it is to work for the other side. There, I have said it, and you are probably not listening anyway.'

'I am listening, brother.' *And I am also hungry.*

'No, you are not. You think of your belly. You think of food and glory, the gods of this world. You think maybe it is permissible for some to follow Francis as he followed Christ, but for others, like you English and the men of Aragon, to follow Saint George, or what you think Saint George meant.'

'I did not say that.'

'You didn't have to. Your sighing speaks; your foot shuffling speaks; your life speaks.' Fra Francesco bats the air with his right hand. 'Never mind, I don't want to argue with you. I am hungry too, but let us go to the house via the garden so I might see whether my grafted pear is taking. It won't take us long and while we go we can talk.' The old man begins to shuffle, slowly then faster, all the while using Hugh's right shoulder as a support.

Why does he do it? Hugh has seen him walking on his own quite well, even this morning. *Does he want sympathy for the affliction*? But Hugh thinks not. He allows his right arm to support the friar under his left as they ascend into the upper basilica and toward the light. He glances up to see the fresco of Francis casting the demons out of Arezzo. His mind drifts between Francis and Saint George but in another moment his attention is called back because the old man is talking again between heavy breaths, something about the saint.

'He was not popular everywhere, you know. A saint is a medicine because he is an antidote. He or she restores the world to sanity by bringing to the fore whatever it has neglected. Indeed, he may often be mistaken for a poison and thus often martyred. But in general each generation seeks its saints by instinct like goats going higher up the mountains to find the right herbs to restore their health.'

'You believe that?'

'I do. You may think me a pessimist, Hugh, but I am not. I believe that at some point, each generation is converted by the saint that contradicts it most. Why do you look like that?

'I only wonder, where are the saints of our own day then?'

'Why? So you can gawp at them, congratulate them? It is the wrong question, Hugh, the wrong question. The question is why am I not a saint when he has called me at this moment in history? We ask, "Where is the God of Elijah?" And he asks, "Where are the Elijahs of God? Where are the ones who make known to Jacob his sin?' The old man stops to scratch the moles on his nose with his thumb while eyeing Hugh carefully and with intent. 'That is the question for you, Hugh. It is why you are here, now.' They start to walk again. 'And that is why I say again, each generation is converted by the saint that contradicts it the most.'

'So you've said' Hugh surpresses the heaving in his stomach, not hunger this time but a yearning so deep in his own bowels that something akin to dread mixed with joy grips him. But he hardly trusts the frigidity of his senses as he has been so long without the commonest feelings, even less his interpretation of them.

'Yes, of course. That is why here, in Asissi, when the world grew saturated in worldliness and *laissez faire* commerce, Christianity came as a holy vagabond, overturning the world as Christ overturned the moneychangers' tables.'

'Of course, I agree that Francis was a great man, brother, but...' Hugh reaches for the right words even as he reaches for the large iron handle of the basilica door. 'We cannot all live by begging.' He tugs at it, and light floods in with odours of horses, saddle leather and cooked chestnuts from a nearby brazier. The day has turned out fine now the rains have passed and great white clouds like ships billow high above the verdant Umbrian plains.

'Yes, I agree that we cannot all beg, nor should we all. Francis responded to the deadness that he saw. His instinct was right, and so was that of his followers. But times change; I know that. A generation later, perhaps when the world had grown a great deal too wild, Christianity returned as a teacher of logic.'

'You refer to Aquinas?'

'Of course I do.' The wheezing friar leans even more heavily on Hugh as they descend the steps. 'Those two men that stood like one colossus over their age—the vagabond and the student, the merchant and the aristocrat, the nature lover and the booklover, the wildest of all missionaries and the mildest of all philosophers. You know, what they started was really a bolder and a freer thing than we call our renaissance. For *we* labour to resurrect old things drawn forth from a dead thing. *Nova veritas, onva veritas,* our truth, new truth, we bleat. What bollocks. Was ever such a confession of poverty so glibly spun? Can you imagine the great artists and builders of Francis' or Aquinas' time talking such utter bollocks? Eh, eh? Did they model their cathedrals and monasteries on the obsolete tombs of antiquity? Of course not. They shot spires, vaults and buttresses skyward in an explosion of new life. Did they call upon the dead gods from Hades? Of course not. They erupted everywhere in new songs and music fit for angels.' At this point Francesco has released Hugh's shoulder and is using both his hands to gesture skyward. He now brings his hands back down and takes hold of Hugh once more. 'But whatever they were, they were about the same great work—one in the study, the other in the street.'

'The work, brother?' Hugh can see the house now further down the street, perhaps he can persuade the old man to forget his trip to the orchard.

'Why, bringing God back to earth of course. Look; there is Paulo. He will tell you about Aquinas for he studied in Paris where the saint taught. He knows much of this matter and almost became a Dominican, though thank God, he did not. Paulo, Paulo!'

The diminutive friar looks up from the ragged woman to whom he has been speaking and salutes them. Hugh does not like him for he is always cheerful, a sure sign of a hypocrite. Besides, he can never escape the feeling that when these two men are together, they are in a conspiracy against him; that everything they do seems somehow choreographed in some sly way. Paulo joins them after bidding the woman goodbye and at once busies himself by taking Francesco's other arm and asking how they enjoyed the sermon.

'Never mind that, old friend, never mind that. I am telling young Hugh here about how Francis and Saint Thomas fought the spirit of their age, and how he should become a saint too, but he seems reluctant for he would rather be known for his valour in other fields.'

Hugh does not respond or even contemplate the jest. *You cannot talk to old men who know everything, even when they are not in earnest. Or is he? Perhaps he is. And oh God, look at Paulo. He's almost slavering with excitement about Aquinas, licking his damn lips ten to the dozen to get the words out.*

Paulo is talking about the saints metaphorically as the Ox and the Ass attending Christ at his nativity in Bethlehem. Apparently Thomas' university nickname was 'the Dumb Ox', and Francis affectionately referred to his own body as 'Brother Ass'. Hugh all the while is fighting off the awful thought, that dread possibility, that ultimate challenge: why should he not be a saint? But between the two of them, these men will give him no space to think. They are always at him when they are together. *Look at their eyes, always on me. What do they want of me, the scoundrels? They are like dogs.*

Fra Francesco cuts across Paulo. 'Yes, yes, that is what I told him, Paulo, that they brought God back to earth, in the courts, the university and the streets.'

'It is well said, brother, well said.' Paulo is always deferential and agreeing with the older man. Hugh has noticed that, too. These old men love to be agreed with. Paulo continues, 'But how did they do it? That is your question, Fra Hugh. That is your question, is it not? Their tools, nay their weapons, were nature in Francis' case, and the philosopher of nature in Aquinas' case, for he called forth the newly recovered manuscripts of Aristotle in the fight for Christ. Of course, their detractors, who were many, accused them of resurrecting a pagan goddess and a pagan sage, but in truth they were defending the very incarnation.'

'I see,' Hugh says, avoiding their eyes and pretending to be more observant of possible obstacles on the street for the older man to avoid.

'There is no need, Paulo, to speak down to Hugh for he studied at Cambridge and has no doubt read some, if not most, of the extant works of Aristotle.'

'Just some.' Hugh nods. *How did he know I was at Cambridge? Did I tell him? Did I tell anyone here? Why does he look at me like that?*

'There, you see, Paulo, he knows a thing or two already. Good for him. And he wants to know how saints do what they do. He is not satisfied with mere fame, but he does not fancy the poverty of Francis, I think. So perhaps he can be a saint in the study instead. Is that what he was really put on earth for perhaps? I don't know.'

Hugh demurs and lets Paulo warm to his subject with more lip licking. 'Aquinas rejected the life of a prince to become a friar, you know. His family kidnapped him, but he would not yield to them. Under Albert the Great and afterwards he worked to reconcile faith with reason and even expanded it towards experimental natural philosophy. He insisted that there were two great agencies at work; reality and the recognition of reality, that senses were the windows of the soul and that when God said through Isaiah, "Come let us reason together," he really was affirming that our rational faculties are indeed valid, that reason has a right to feed on facts, that external facts can fertilise the internal intelligence as a bee does a flower.'

Hugh begins to be interested. He remembers Milan and his conversation with Maestro da Vinci and all the thoughts that have plagued him since. If only he could have space to think, to arrange his thoughts. His eyes dart across the Umbrian fields toward the north, visible as they descend the slope from the basilica toward the town. The fields are golden yellow directly below but on the horizon, all the way back to Perugia, they are greens and blues. He recalls Leonardo's landscape behind the picture of La Giroconda and tries once more to grasp the threads about the limits, if there are any, of enquiry in natural philosophy. Hugh clears his throat. 'I suppose it was a humbler, homelier thing to walk in Aristotle's footsteps when the fashion was Plato and Augustine.'

'Yes,' Francesco adds, leaning harder than ever on Hugh's shoulder.

'Yes, indeed, but no humbler than God when he made tables and chairs in Joseph's workshop at Nazareth.'

Paulo, agreeing as ever, says, 'Indeed brother. Aquinas wanted the body with all its senses because he believed it to be a holy thing, a Christian thing. He said reason could be trusted, if only it could be rational enough, and rational *long* enough.'

'Aye, and there's the rub, Paulo. *If only*.' Hugh thinks he has the centre. 'The study *sine ira et studio*, without passion or partisanship, has been a maxim more preached than practiced.'

'I admit the point, Hugh. I do. Aquinas was optimistic about human beings I grant you, but remember that when he was confessed on his deathbed, his friend Reginald said his sins were only those of a five-year-old child. But of course he was no fool. This is a man who, without hubris, could claim that he had understood every word he had ever read. Imagine that, would you? And he was no *braggadocio*. In fact, he did insist on the special importance of revelation—that we could only receive the highest moral truths in a miraculous manner. And of course, there were many of his day who saw the dangers, too. William de St Amour wrote *The Perils of the Latter Times*. The freedom of the friars was dangerous enough, but this awful apparition of Aristotle rising out of the east, like some sort of resurrected Greek god was too much. He challenged the French king and the pope to hold an enquiry. These writings, these thoughts should be stopped. Thomas attended and spoke out. So did Stephen Tempier, Bishop of Paris, though he spoke against the new learning too. The bishop thought those who studied Aristotle today might worship Apollo tomorrow. But he was a fair man was the bishop, unlike some of Aquinas' Augustinian adversaries who were happy to class Thomas and his students along with the raft of equivocal Muslim metaphysicians.'

'Did he win?' Hugh says. 'I suppose he did if he was a saint.'

'Yes, he won. Yes, he beat the controversialists, and even later beat Sigar of Brabant, who at first you might think would be his ally, for he was as ardent a student of Aristotle as ever was. But Sigar had learned Aristotelianism from the Arabs. Here was the greatest danger, and it came as a blow to Aquinas, who for the first time saw that there were people like Sigar, who really did wish Christ to go down before Aristotle in a way like Philo, in all his exegesis of Genesis, had wanted Moses to go down before Plato. But that was never Aquinas' stance. He was of Peter Abelard's spirit, who said, "I would not want to be a philosopher if it meant conflicting with Paul, nor be an Aristotelian if it cuts me off from Christ" or something like that.'

'But few men are of that stripe, Paulo.' Francesco says, then sighs. 'These are days of infidelity.'

'Not totally, Fra Francesco. Not totally,' Paulo retorts gently. 'But I will own that in Sigar's sophistry Aquinas glimpsed the awful possibility of another age of even weaker reason, where deceivers and deceived would together let Christ go down before Aristotle, the end of all religion, even the idea of truth itself as a solid and knowable thing. Sigar would have Christ as merely the first among men, a man who could do no more than weep alongside us because we were indeed alone, all of us, without a father in this universe. What would we be? I do not know. Hardly men at all. Just creatures who favour endless change with no reference point outside it, one long curve of progression."

'Hah,' Francesco half says, half coughs. 'But progression to what?'

'I suppose, they would not be able to say exactly. A deceived man can only deceive, and perhaps the most dangerous and credible deceiver is the one who does not know he, himself is deceived. He is a deception in himself. Either way, I am sure they will assume it is change for the good.'

'But what would good be?' Francesco interjects again, as the three stop at the orchard entrance.

'I suppose they would not be able to say either. They might say that change itself will decide. It is enough for them, perhaps, that there is a beyond.'

'But suppose that this beyond is beyond bearing?'

'Then they will adjust, and re-adjust their souls to cope. I suppose.'

Hugh imagines further if there had been no champion, no saint, no

Aquinas to resist the spirit of the age. *What if Sigar of Brabant had not been defeated? Is it possible that men would not even weep about this, as the more realistic poets of antiquity wept? Was not Heraclitus, who insisted everything was in flux, called the weeping philosopher? It was the pagan's greatest fear—his terror even—to have no fixed identity, to be like the rest of reality, essentially fluid, inessential. What if matter and force were primary in the universe with life derivative of it? What if God did not create a cosmos and us in it but counter wise—the cosmos created us and God? Surely that is why the ancients contrived to escape the torments of life on the Great Wheel with the peace of a good Roman exit – a hot bath and razor.*

But is it really credible?

Could men revert to a dehumanizing mental servitude to elemental nature and not weep for the tragedy of mere mutability? Is it possible that they would, in some beggarly way, even be cheered that movement of any sort would at least afford relief from the sheer agony of boredom? Imagine it! And they call Hope an uncertain goddess!

While Paulo opens the gate into the orchard and the scents of the field and humming of insects fill his senses, Hugh has another startling thought. *What did Farranata and Boccaccio think of Sigar? Surely those atheistos would have approved. But even sceptics can never believe themselves enough to work sceptically. No fatalist can ever actually live fatalistically. That arrogant little prick Boccaccio wrote that truth was subjective, but he certainly did not hesitate to treat it as objective. Lucretius may have believed his mind to be made of mud, but he had no trouble making it up, and writing voluminously about it. His poetry rhymed, had design and symmetry even if his universe did not. Forget Lucretius; forget Epicurus for that matter. They were answered ably enough by Cicero in his Somnium Scipionis. Their wings are broken. No one will believe that madness again.*

Hugh follows behind the older friar as they pass through the narrow gate. He closes it behind him, letting his fingers caress the grain of the chestnut wood and aware, as a man sometimes is when experiencing the early stages of inebriation, that he is analysing his thoughts even as he thinks them. *A man might be a fundamental skeptic, but he cannot be anything else, certainly not a defender of fundamental scepticism. For if the movements of the heavens, indeed his own mind, are meaningless then it does not leave anything worthy of discussion. Life is a trick, a joke, a prison.*

Francesco hobbles unaided to his pear trees. Paulo looks round to see if Hugh is following. 'Fra Hugh, you look troubled.'

'I was thinking about what you said, brother.' Hugh watches where he is now stepping on the wet grass, as he cannot abide wet slugs in his sandals. 'I was wondering whether you thought it possible that we might ever let Christ go down before Aristotle. In another time, I mean.'

Paulo tucks two thumbs under his hemp belt and looks to the side with his lips puckered as he always does when he is thinking. Eventually he looks up, his eyes betraying the beginnings of a smile. 'Perhaps, but not if there are saints on the earth.' He glances away from Hugh to Fra Francesco. 'Has the graft taken?'

Francesco is bending at the bandaged limb of a large pear tree tied to the wall that borders the orchard. He mumbles something, but as he is facing the other way, they cannot hear. Hugh approaches, holding the skirts of his habit high as the grass is long. *They should tether two goats here, or let the sheep in.* When he is within a few feet he asks, 'Has it taken?'

The old man's nose wrinkles as he squints under the rags at the cutting. 'I don't know. I just don't know. I think it needs a little more time.'

14TH JULY, 2 WEEKS LATER ON THE FEAST OF SAINT BONAVENTURE. ASSISI.

Hugh first notices the disturbance by the uncanny silence. No one is at their work in the yard, at the well, on the new walls. He and Paulo are walking up the steep hill through the olive groves after taking offal to the swine. Dried olive leaves crunch under his feet. The vinegar smell of squashed olives fills his nostrils. Above the hum of bees and insects there remains a penetrating absence of the usual bustle. Hugh's knuckles clench white about the hemp ropes of the buckets he is carrying.

'Where is everyone?' he whispers, by instinct letting his feet fall quieter.

'I don't know. Surely I don't.' Paulo sets his buckets down and wipes his brow. But as he finishes speaking, Hugh discerns a lone raised voice somewhere up toward the gate.

'Stay here. I will go to see.' With eyes fixed on the gate, Hugh pads swiftly and silently over the gravel toward the city. He passes the well. A board with lime cement has been left with the trowel in it. He glances across toward the lazar house. Three lepers are peering out of the window toward him, but the door is tight shut. Again the sound of a raised voice inside the gate. He keeps moving; each step raises his heart until a steady sweat spreads under his Franciscan habit. Through the gate and round to the right at the friary refectory, he hears words, the scuffing of thick boots, riding boots, and the dull clank of weapons. From around the corner up the end of the street comes the whinnying of horses straining on the halter. Visitors. He approaches the doorway and listens. Blood—still red—stains the doorstep.

'I will repeat, gentle friars. There is no need for further trouble.' The voice is deep, gruff. He does not recognize it. 'No one else needs to get hurt. Just tell us where we can find the foreigner, the knight of Rhodes.'

Hugh steps in, fists tight round the hemp ropes of the oak buckets. The refectory is not large, perhaps forty feet by twenty. A space is cleared in the middle, and the twelve friars are on benches around the side. In the middle stand five well booted men in black doublets with no heraldry. Mercenaries? Spaniards? They don't look or sound like them. Two of them have Fra Francesco on his knees in the middle. One eye swollen closed, teeth missing and blood flowing freely from a blow to the head. They have a knife to his throat. Hugh returns his attention to the threat. Pity can wait. Four of them are thick set, erect, military sorts. The fifth is tall, wiry with wily grey eyes that see him first, hovering on the step.

'Another peaceable friar come to help.' He levels a blade with a Spanish swept hilt at Hugh's eyes and gestures with it for him to join them. Hugh raises his chin slightly. The brothers cower rabbit-like on the benches. 'Where's Erpingham, Friar?'

Hugh ignores him, then says, 'I see you have softened up the old man. I bet he didn't tell you anything. Old men are stubborn.'

The wiry knight cranes his neck out and levels the blade again, this time even closer. 'He got where he is for giving lip, and not doing as he was told. So I say for the last time, meek friar; sit down and tell me what I want to know.'

Hugh smiles in the direction of Francesco. 'D'you hear that, brother? Meek. Never been called meek before. Perhaps I will inherit the earth after all.'

'Oh yeah?' Wiry man is stepping forward using his left hand to retrieve a knife. 'And shall we send you to your reward then, blessed friar?'

'Friar Hugh, though I am not very blessed, I'm afraid.' He bends down, twisting to the right as he speaks. It appears he is setting the buckets down, but not releasing his grip. The wiry man pauses for the briefest moment as his mind processes the word 'Hugh' as he matches it with the image of the man he's been tracking. It doesn't matter anyway; he may as well kill himself as Hugh won't stop now. The hornets of his mind are stirred, and the demons take control. The man's face is still only registering when Hugh straightens up, uncoiling like a spring, buckets flying and more deadly than a mace.

Hugh the monster, Hugh the fury, with insatiate bloodlust and stone dead eyes. The left hand bucket sends the blade up. The right hand bucket – iron bound – shatters the man's jawbone. He spins back like a ragdoll, pivoting midair, skull hitting the flagged floor with a hollow thud. Hugh continues his pivot, increasing momentum and laying into the next two unprepared soldiers. They should not have sheathed those fancy Spanish blades. *Knuckles may be all well and good against timid friars, but you've come looking for Hugh Erpingham, my friends. You wanted trouble? Well, here it is—by the bucketful.*

The first soldier raises his hand in defense only to have the iron rim shatter his knuckles like celery. The second slams his temple. The red mist descends over Hugh's mind as malice and rage course through his torso like hellfire. One, two, three, four. Thud, slash, dash, mash, screaming. He rains blows on his enemies. Soldier two is thrashing on the floor like a landed fish. Hugh's arms flail like a wrecking ball sending bone splinters, gore, brain white as tripe across the tables, floor and walls. *Thought you'd catch old Hugh Erpingham with his arse in a bucket? I will kill you all. Bastards. Horse gelders. Whoremongers. You want some of this do you, ponce? Buck-kets-ful.* Soldier three gets one in the gut that folds him forward, then a second bucket which bites deep into the skull. Blood sprays upward in a bright crimson fountain.

The friars shriek hysterically. Hugh is roaring like a demon, baying for blood. 'Come on. Come on.' *Come on the rest of you, in your fancy black doublets. Leave off old friars and pick on someone your own size. Bastards. Come taste the bucket, boys. Come taste the wrath of God.*

The last two let Francesco drop to the floor as they unsheathe their swords. Necks thick as capstans, they curse him as they observe the writhing remains of their comrades. Hugh flings his right bucket at them by way of distraction and retrieves the sword with the swept hilt from the floor. He'd have loved his carrack sword, but Wilf has all his stuff at the inn. He doesn't need it. He has plenty of tricks up his sleeve.

'We'll take him together,' one growls, but his fellow can't resist Hugh as he bends for the blade. Hugh sees it coming, but parries the lunge with a swipe of the bucket followed through with the sword he's just got. It is a sloppy thrust, but even so it pierces the man's shoulder. As he dances back, the other fellow lunges. Hugh, still rising, gives a sloping parry and uses his upspring to shoulder the man backward against the tables. Hugh spins about to meet the next blow from the injured man. He catches the cut high, bringing the assailant's blade down hard and sandwiching both blades against the side of the table. Rearranging the fellow's face with two swift head-butts, Hugh levers himself away from the tables, slashing wildly through the blood in his eyes.

The man's comrade is coming, too. He is fast, but Hugh sidesteps rather than parry. The blade passes, and Hugh uses a flashing up-thrust to clip his opponent's wings. The man doesn't even scream as his own blade drops from his hand, and the tendons give that familiar twang. Nor when Hugh brains him with the bucket a moment later. He just collapses ingloriously as a sack of oats on the floor that now more resembles a charnel house than a friar's refectory. Blood. So much blood. The last soldier, already injured in the shoulder and face, is skirting for the door. Hugh counter steps him, a crazed and feral gloat in his eye. Hugh the murderer. The Master butcher. Bloodlust. Hatred. The shadow of Cain.

'Hugh.' The raspy voice of Fra Francesco is behind Hugh's back. 'Let him go.'

But you can't talk to Hugh when he is like this; he cannot reason for he cannot hear you. His whole being is bent on ignoring all but the pleas of destruction. Hugh makes to thrust for the man's chest. He goes to parry, but Hugh drops his blade, rolls it under the other's blade, then brings it back up at the original angle. *Oldest one in the book.* It slides in like butter, and the startled man withers against the wall in a series of spasms and groans. Should have thought twice about coming after Hugh Erpingham.

Hugh is breathing like a horse, face contorted in hatred. But suddenly he hears an inner voice: a man like me, a brother unknown. He stands over the vanquished slain, knees trembling as the red mist is replaced by exhaustion, exaltation with numbness, focus with disorientation. His knees are shaking violently, eyes blinking rapidly.

He feels someone at his side. It is Francesco relieving him of the bucket. The blade falls from his hand, and Hugh grips the friar's sleeve in horror. The other friars beat a hasty retreat to the exit, not daring to meet Hugh's eye. He feels it now if he never felt it before. *God, what have I done?* His eye strays past Francesco's shoulder to the twitching corpse of the wiry soldier. The place looks like hell's antechamber. *This was me – is me. I did this.* He breathes in, grimaces and looks up at the old friar. Despite his own wounds, his own scrape with destiny, Francesco displays none of the terror of the other friars, no particular sense of excitement or weakness. He is serene almost. 'Are you all right?' He exhales and surveys the mess. 'Here let me help you. Come, sit down.' He leads Hugh sideways to a bench.

'No, no. I am all right,' Hugh says, yet complies.

'Your hand is bleeding.'

'So it is.' Hugh stares at it incredulously. Hemp blisters from the ropes and a deep slit across the knuckles from soldier four's blade. Never felt it. Hugh glances up at the friar, who is still standing, 'So is your head.'

'It will mend, and so might two of these fellows if we help them.' Francesco shuffles toward the mangled bodies. 'It is hard to tell with head wounds. Do you know who sent them? Was it Vendramin?'

'No, I think he'd come himself. Besides, if he wanted me dead he could have done so himself in Siena.'

'He must be a remarkable man, this Vendramin. They say he is Venetian, the son of a doge.'

'They say he is the devil.'

'And you believe what people say, don't you?'

'I used to.'

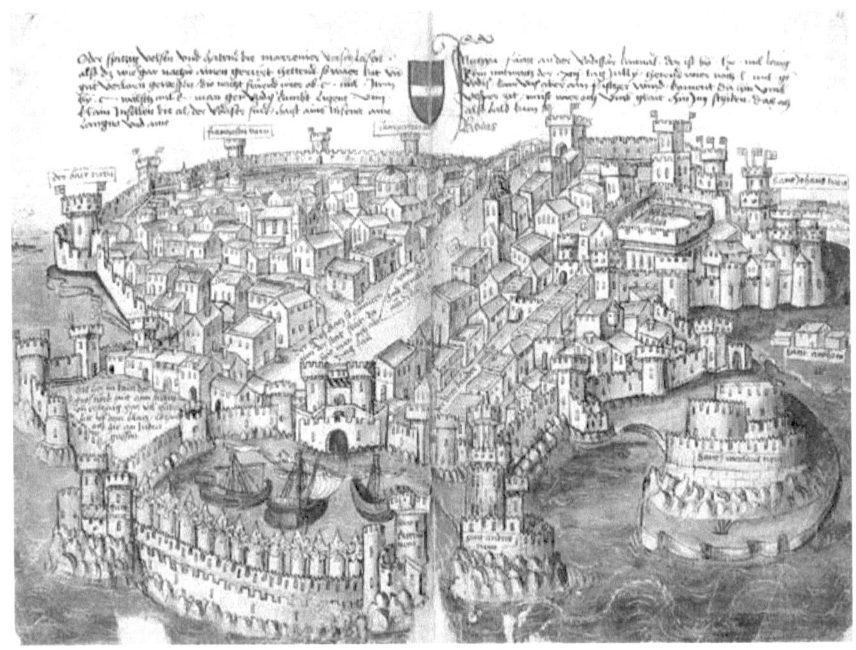

LETTER TO RHODES FROM ASSISI, JULY 19TH

Most Illustrious Magister,

I write to you on this feast of Saint Vincent de Paul with the gravest of news, not knowing what you have already heard but fearing that I have been maligned by unjust slander. I have evidence, written evidence, that the Grand Prior of Rome is complicit in some way against the interests of the knights. I suspected as much in Rome this spring, but now, as I say, I have written evidence from his own hand, which I forward to you. He sent men after me, who found me unarmed in Assisi. I had been the guest of some Franciscans and had entered into various spiritual disciplines myself as a physic for malignancies that torment me still. One elder friar in particular has been a help to me. You may tell Prior de Blanchfort that I have been watchful to observe his advice to obtain a good confessor. In this way I had been serving at the lazar colony with the good brothers, thinking to stay for a few weeks and then to rejoin my party in Urbino as a guest of the duchess, and so resume my duties.

The mercenaries sent by Prior Battista are regrettably all dead, but this missive I recovered from their saddlebags. It is the prior's hand. I do not know who else's hand is behind this. Possibly it is His Holiness, possibly one of the cardinals. I am afraid my mind is wearied by these continual intrigues. And how you shall deal with this Judas I leave best to your own wisdom, only do not believe him if he has tried to cover his betrayal by maligning me.

As for Vendramin I have no new news. And as to the state of my own soul I have no news either. You may be sure that I have less melancholy than I did, but this sojourn in Assisi has done little but confuse and perplex me.

As for news of the war, Venetian envoys have finally arrived in Rome at the beginning of this month led by the scholarly Girolamo Donato. I am told the pope knows him and knew his father too, which of course is good. But apparently the unfortunate envoy has not received adequate powers to negotiate. And besides all this, the pope already suspects that the Venetians have been writing privily to each of the pope's allies and perhaps even Signor Turco for assistance. I do not envy Donato his embassage, a lion in a den of Daniels. Even the lifting of the interdict is a complex matter under canon law. How much more that His Holiness has demanded, at their first audience, that Venice give up Trevisio? If I am right, Venice will now be weighing her seven thousand against the emperor's twenty-two thousand, with rumours that the king of Hungary may yet join the league, and so begin a campaign despoiling Venetian possessions in Dalmatia. I would say that His Holiness holds all the best cards.

Please give orders regarding the Grand Prior with all speed. I intend to be in Urbino until the breaking of winter.

I am, as ever, your obedient son in the faith, etc

Addendum:

Fresh news from the north. A rider brings news that only this last week, the League has seen an unexpected reversal in the papal alliance. Padua was retaken by Venice two days ago. The Imperial governors made themselves so odious to the inhabitants that they, aided by detachments of Venetian cavalry under the command of Andrea Gritti, successfully overran the Landsknechts garrisoning the city. It appears now to me that the allies have been too slow to seize their advantage. Under-garrisoned cities like Padua and Verona still not taken even though they are the gate of the Veneto? They have been ill-advised and ill prepared.

I need not tell you that this bodes ill for us, Magister. Any lengthening of hostilities here will only dissipate the strength of Christendom for the fight with her real enemy. The crusade was discussed at Consistory about ten days ago along with letters from King Ferdinand and King Henry of England. They pledge a somewhat ambiguous support for the crusade, but what will be left of Venetian, French, papal and imperial power by the time this war among Christians is resolved, I cannot say. Adieu.

JULY 20TH 1509. THE FEAST OF SAINT GIROLAMO EMILIANI, ASSISI. 6 AM.

The horses whinny at their halters. They are eager for the road, and so is Wilf who holds them. Cocks are still crowing, and it is a fair day for travel; clouds like pillows jostle in an otherwise open heaven. Hugh puts his gloves on carefully while bidding farewell to Fra Francesco. The two are alone outside the gate, and Wilf is not near enough to hear. Once more, spider's webs and dew cover the grass, an intricate network that is always there unseen but only revealed by the dazzling light of morning. Hugh places a hand over his heart.

'I must thank you for your hospitality, brother.'

'And I you for saving my neck.' Fra Francesco shuffles awkwardly. They have not talked since the attack. 'I hope we send you away a better sort of man.'

Hugh looks to the sky, then to the gate, then to the ground. *Shall I tell him why I have been avoiding him these last weeks? No, he's a good man, stupid like all good men, but innocent of people like me. I will let him keep his innocence and his easy forgiveness.* 'When the wax is hard it does not make a good impression. I know you did your best, friar.'

'My best? What is that supposed to mean?' The old man's face for a moment borders on a scowl. 'I thought we had been talking about the grace of God here, not *my best*. You should clean your ears if that is what you think.'

Hugh drops his hand and clenches his fist tightly within the glove. Francesco sees it and looks now at Hugh as if to goad him on, to unleash the demon. Hugh straightens and sets his jaw. 'I will tell you something, good friar, not in anger, but in sober truth. I have wandered about this place these last weeks struggling within myself. God knows I have. I told you what I had not dared tell anyone else. I told you and you accepted me, still accepted me even though you knew. You said that forgiveness was there for the taking, that God forgives all. You accepted me and I hated you for it. I let you know me, see what was in me. I gave you that power over me, and no sooner had I done so than I regretted it, and so hated you the more. Yes, hated you, that's right. I loathed with a passion I have never known before. Can you understand that? No, of course you can't. But it is God's truth. It is not that I thought you would tell anyone either. It was just that I had made you my judge. And while you lived, while you knew, I could not be at peace. I thought that by confessing my great sin I would exorcise the demon – that I would have peace. I really thought it would be that easy. You tricked me, but now I find seven stronger demons in its place. I began to say to myself, he is the only one who knows. Blot him out and all memory of the deed will be forgotten. And that night I brought you the herbal infusion for your breathing – '

'It was very kind of you – '

'No, it wasn't. It wasn't!' Hugh glowers at him, his face contorted like a claw-mad lion, and eyes so intense that it would have sent a lesser a man running for his life. 'You were never nearer death that night, I tell you. We were alone, and I knew we would be with the others at Vespers.

I planned it that way you see. You can't imagine such diabolical cunning can you – a good man such as you are? But there it is. I intended to let you drink it as a last rite and then suffocate you with your own pillow. Those were the thoughts in my head, you know. God is silent in me, but these thoughts go on and on. Such thoughts, such thoughts, friar, that not so much drive me mad as make me question whether I was ever sane in the first place – whether any of us are.'

'But you spared me, Hugh.' If he is surprised, Francesco does not show it. His words are even, his eyes still. 'To be tempted is no sin.'

'They were just thoughts, a legion of thoughts that pricked me on, my black dog thoughts, but when I saw you, so frail, so like my own father – yes –' Hugh sighs and for a moment drops his eyes, his bottom lip quivering. 'I did; I spared you. But do not think any better of me. For the next day, when those men came and put that knife at your throat? The first thought that came to me was, ah good, someone to do the deed for me. And so I goaded them with the bucket. I knocked them about a bit thinking that I could have them kill you as David killed Uriah with the sword of the children of Ammon. But it was no good, nothing ever is. So I killed them all in my anger, and you still live.' Hugh pauses to draw breath, exhales, sniffs and looks to his horse. 'So you see why I must go away from this place. It is not that I killed those assassins. It is so I do not commit a greater sin. I think you can see that now, friar, and believe it.'

'I believe you are a tormented soul.' The friar moves a step closer, as if to take Hugh's hands. 'And if you would just stay a little and let us help – '

Hugh withdraws his hand with a sharp breath that sounds more like a hiss. 'We both know that would be a mistake. Suffer it to be so for now and permit me to write to you if anything changes. If a problem has no solution, it may not be a problem after all but a fact.'

'You take very dark council, my son.' The friar shakes his head slightly and continues. 'But I will pray for you. You know, I suppose, that Aquinas never wrote another word after he had a certain experience of

God at mass. He said that it made all his writings seem like straw. But an experience like that is not given to people who seek experiences. Be careful. I know you would like more than just the oath of God on the matter, but there it is. We are plain men.'

'Still trying to make me a saint, even after what I just told you.'

The old man looks as if he would say something, but he bows his head instead. Hugh observes his eyes for a moment longer. Tears. *He weeps for me. And I like a scoundrel will hide in a scoundrel's last hope: that I will be different in a different place. Do I still believe that? No, if I ever did, I do not believe it now.* He mounts the horse from which height he can see over the wall to the orchard. He shouldn't leave it like this. He glances toward the treetops as he gathers the reins. 'Has it taken?'

'What?'

'The grafted pear.'

'Yes, with patience, it has.' Francesco is smiling.

LETTER DATED 25TH JULY, TO THE GRAND PRIORY OF ROME

My dear Prior,

This letter will be brief and, by your courtesy, I hope I shall not write the like again for your sake. Verily you have disappointed me in this matter of Erpingham. Think you to frighten the quarry while the hawk is still with the handler? What is this I have learnt about mercenaries and blood at the friary? Force has no place where there is need of skill. You have acted foolishly.

But, and here I am affirmed in my trust in the divine providence,

Fortuna hath spared the Englishman, and thus I am content to let it be so for now. Let the hare run out his strength. Time is the wisest counselor.

Yes, let life and health for him continue in Urbino whither he has now gone. Leave him to me now he has come north. Let us hear how he quits himself there. Let us probe him, to see whether he is indeed worthy. Seneca wrote that one of the most beautiful qualities of true friendship is to understand and to be understood. I have few, Prior, if any, who have truly understood me, yet this man might. Providence shall bring us together, it is fated. We cannot escape destiny. He and I are competitors – in the correct meaning of the word – co-seekers. We seek the same objects, with the same passion, perhaps even the same ends. Our whole wills and cunning are bent toward the same goal. God will see it aright, of that I am sure. Plato says that "courage is knowing what not to fear". He does not fear me yet for he does not know yet that I exist. But he will hereafter.

And you, my friend, must not fail again in strategy, sense or execution.

Yours etc.

The White Cardinal.

JULY 24TH, 1509 URBINO, FINALLY

'You all right, are you?' Wilf shouts with exasperation from the wagon as they descend the last pine-clad hill before the road finally rises to enter Urbino.

Hugh, thirty yards in front, does not answer straight away. His mind is still laden with all that he has done and said at Assisi. It was churlish to say things he had only half felt, half meant. Sometimes it is like a demon is driving him, an irresistible force seeking to eschew helpers and to cast them off like last year's rushes.

It is late afternoon, and he is saddle weary, thought weary, world weary. The smell of warm pine so familiar to his nostrils from Rhodes and Norfolk are no comfort today, not after all that has happened. He cannot be saved, but perhaps he can be diverted here at Urbino. He will play the part for them, talk high thoughts out with them, and all the while fret over his own lost soul – that and Vendramin. It is irrational, he knows, like having an itch just out of reach, a thread that he must keep pulling even if it undoes the garment. He does not even know why he should go after Vendramin now. Is it for them, his masters? For the order? For Christendom? For righteousness? Certainly not the latter.

'I said, are you all right? You haven't said two words since Fermignano.'

'I'm tired, Wilf; that's all. Just tired.'

'I see. Well, we're here now. Presume that's it, is it?'

'It is.' Hugh glances through the trees at a vista of yet more steep rolling hills. But this time the tops are crowned with a walled town. Its stones gleam under the late afternoon sun. They are biscuit brown with marble reveals, and the pantiles a warm brown like those of Assisi rather than the russet red of Florence. Most noticeable are the twin cylindrical Torricini towers which face them as they approach from the south. They rise skyward in a stately shaft of early renaissance confidence. The ambassador Castiglione often boasted of them when they were riding on Hugh's first circuit of Ischia and Naples. They were designed, he said, by a Dalmation called Luciano Lurana. Good for him. It is like riding into a fairytale. Hugh feels his stomach unknot slightly. He will enjoy seeing Castiglione again. He feels diverted already. Fickleness is such a blessed failing.

1 HOUR LATER, PALAZZO DUCALE

He has left Wilf with their gear in the bowels of the palazzo which is almost like an underground city in its own right. He is being led up an eighty-foot, rutted brick ramp into an exquisitely proportioned courtyard, where a clean colonnade on all four sides and an inscription above the frieze assures him that the Montefeltros were under no illusion about their own worth, taste and honour.

White marble interiors are cool as a spring lake – heaven compared to the heat of the road. Shallow stairs seem to raise even the weariest traveler – which Hugh is this afternoon. Carvings of milk-white flowers, urns, lion's feet rise gracefully to greet him from the wall panels. The cool marble bannister brushes his left palm like kisses. In a niche he spots a sculpture of Frederico da Montefeltro, the man who brought the place into the sixteenth century fifty years ago.

Strange, he muses, *when they say a man is ahead of his age, they usually just mean that he agrees with theirs.*

'This way please.' The page leads on. His golden bowl-shaped hair bobs at the nape. The lad is nervous. He almost fainted with shock when Hugh gave his name.

When they arrive at a landing, light floods the stair, and Hugh's weary mind also. He has longed to be here. He comes to Urbino at the setting of the sun. Its golden orb dips beyond the grey Apennines towards Florence. Duke Frederico is dead; so now is his son Guidobaldo. The Duchess Elizabetta remains in this afterglow, but the dukedom is now seeded to the pope's family – so it is a noble, yet wistful twilight. This moment is a pause between breaths, while Pallas Athena, goddess of the arts, graciously bows out. Something great has happened here.

Yes, Hugh thinks, Castiglione and Bembo have talked about this Salon of Ideas, this town of knights and courtiers. Certainly they have, but now he sees it himself, and feels it. Though for all that, it is almost certainly a pause between breaths, he thinks again. And in that pause Castiglione and Bembo squirrel away at their books. *That's the thing about magic: no one knows when it will end.* He and the page ascend another flight and arrive in an ambulatory that runs on all four sides of the courtyard below.

'The *Sala dei Jole* is this way please, signor.' The page points toward a tall doorway whose architrave is magnificently carved with shields, drums, harps, swords, griffins, bows and winged helmets. His eyes move slowly and peacefully over them. Horns, urns, swags of foliage, birds and other heraldic emblems. All marble, all creamy white like heaven, like a mother's milk. None of the dark oak of his grandfather's generation. And none of the gaudy colours of the new. No heavy leather embossed wall coverings, no frescoes even, just this creamy lime-white marble and lime plaster, which leaves his eye free to delight in the serene proportions and noble detailing about the window reveals.

Hugh walks through the doorway into a rectangular reception room, where a central fireplace is supported by Iole and Hercules, the latter looking none too sure. Above the over mantel they support, sits a double frieze with putti and festoons, which to Hugh looks like the triumph of Bacchus and Ariadne. And on the mantle-hood two cherubs hold up the duke's shield, a lone eagle. It is well done, as are the leafy architraves about the window recesses to his left. He could get used to this room. At the nearest recess, a grey cat is crouching on the delicate window seat, with dabbles of green and golden light on its fur from the bottle-end window glass above.

'There are no people.' He says quietly, and letting his riding gloves, which he clutches in his right hand, flap against his leg.

The boy has shrunk back in the doorway as if he had been caught stealing. 'I...I...I apologise, signor. I forgot. The household and guests have been hunting, and now will be dressing for dinner.'

'Do not fret over such a little thing, lad. I will not tell anyone.' *It is not so long ago that I was a stripling, falling over my words and wondering when my beard would grow. Not long ago at all, and yet so long ago.*

'I thank you, and I shall fetch someone for you.'

'There is no need for the duchess to see me in my riding boots, smelling like I've slept in a hayrick.'

'Oh, of course not.' The lad's mouth gapes for a moment. 'Of course not, signor.'

The page casts his eyes about like a landed fish. He cannot remember what he should say next, and when Hugh sees it, he laughs. 'And perhaps I should like to go to my room and have my man prepare me for dinner too?'

'Oh yes, that's it, that's it exactly, your room. Sorry, sorry. Yes of course, by your courtesy signor, I will take you to you room. It is very close.'

He leads Hugh back out and round the upper gallery. A gentleman and his small retinue are dismounting from their horses in the courtyard below. *More people sent by the prior after me?* Unlikely by the look of their tailoring and baggage. The gentleman is too high born to throw his lot in with Hugh's enemies, and his retainers don't look too handy either. *Still, I'd best not be about this place unarmed or even alone if I can help it.*

The lad rounds a bend and turns midway down the next side of the upper gallery. Hugh sees two women on the lower gallery. One is the lady Vittoria Colonna. *She is here, praise God. And what a vision in flowing blue silks, and what a laugh – it's like a celestial chorus. She is an angel come among mortals.* For a moment Hugh believes all the trite verses of the troubadours. He wants to cry out to her but refrains for decency's sake. He will see her in the evening. Before then he will have time to separate his desire for innocence from merely possessing it in another.

The page coughs politely from the doorway. 'In here, signor, is your room. It is a fine one. We would have given you the suite near the duke's, God rest him. We had got it ready, but then Giuliano de Medici has come and so, you see. And the household enjoyed Cardinal Bibbiena's

Comedia *Calandria* in his honour. But this is a fine set of rooms, and they get the morning sun. *l'ultimo.*'

'I thank you. They are fine indeed.' Hug pauses in the entrance. 'I did not get your name?'

'Guido, my lord, I mean, signor. I am the son of the chief steward.'

'Well, Guido,' Hugh says passing him into the spacious apartment. 'I am sure you will bring honour to your parents.'

'Yes, signor. Thank you, signor.'

Hugh turns back to see the lad fingering his velvet cap and lingering at the door. 'Yes?' *What does he want? To be like me? I would trade places with him in a trice, poor child.*

Guido arranges his feet, looks down at them and says, 'Signor, I was just wondering. I mean the other pages won't believe that I have actually met you. And I was wondering if it is true, you know, that when you captured the corsair galleys that you made Barbarossa appear before you without a sword or dagger? That even the Sultan is afraid of you and won't have your name mentioned in his court or harem.'

His harem! That is a new one. Hugh casts his eyes about the room; the tapestry showing some faded scene of martial glory and the chipped crests 'F' and 'B' of Duke Frederigo and his wife, Battista Sforza, carved on the chimney breast. *What do I reply to this boy? Do I encourage him? Embellish the story with details that he will repeat for the rest of his life, no doubt keeping my name alive long after I am dust, or worse. No, it is base; I will not do it.* 'Do you heed the Sunday gospels when they are read to you?'

'Yes, signor, always.'

'Then you remember that Christ says it is possible to gain the whole world and yet forfeit your soul?'

Guido's words and facial expression grow uncertain. 'Yes, signor.'

'Then you admit that a man's soul can be lost eternally, even though all the world admires and envies him.'

'I suppose so.'

'Is your father a good steward Guido of Urbino?'

'Yes indeed, signor.'

'And does he enjoy his position, his honour and his family?'

'Yes, signor.'

'And does he sleep well and rise refreshed each day for his work?'

'He does, signor.'

'Then I will tell you something, Guido. Your father is to be envied and emulated more than a thousand knights of my acquaintance. Do you think dukes and cardinals sleep well? Does Giuliano de Medici?'

'He has our finest feather bolster.'

'He'll need it.' *Now that Florence has rejected him. What can a prince do sans terre, without a province to rule?* Hugh broods with pathos over the fates of the Medici, and particularly this son of Lorenzo who has just arrived, this man to whom Machiavelli would address his book. *Just when you think you have history on your side, Fortuna shits on you. There may yet be discovered a theology of history, but there will never be a philosophy of it.*

'My lord?' the lad rouses Hugh from his introspection.

'Do not you envy me, the Medici or any *magnati*. Envy rather your father, Guido, that is what I say.' Hugh does not bother to observe the lad's face but turns and walks toward his balcony. *He's probably not listening anyway. Why should he when I sound like an old fart?* He would never have listened at the boy's age. A low stone parapet with a smooth, sculpted bench runs on all side of his spacious terrace. To his right is a door, more buildings with ramshackle roofs, and below a garden with fruit trees and the rising smell of lemon verbena. 'You may leave me and have my man sent with the baggage when the horses are settled.'

'Yes, signor.'

'Good, and think well on what I have told you.'

'That I will my lord, I mean, signor. Goodbye'

10 MINUTES LATER, PALAZZO DUCALE

Wilf, red faced with blunt admiration, says, 'Well, I seen it all, I have now, master. This place is a cut above, I can tell you. This lad called Guillaume showed us round the kitchen and ice house. A *neverea*, they call it, or something like that. And what do you think? It's the size of our entire stable block back in Norfolk and bleeding stuffed full of snow even now half way through the summer, and stables the size of – "

'I've seen the stables, Wilf.' Hugh looks up from where he sits, legs crossed, on the balcony, resting his haunches from the ride.

'Ah, but you didn't see the saddle room, and some of the leather work those lads have got would make some of our nobles back in Norfolk green with envy.'

'What I want,' Hugh says with a weary sigh, 'is water to wash. Water. Are they bringing some up?'

'Water? They've got hydraulic engineering down there, and the lad Guillaume says you can use the old duke's cold room. It's got heated floors and hot water, though why they call a hot bath a cold room I dunno.'

'*Caldarium* you idiot. It's Latin for – oh, never mind what its Latin for – just get the trunks unpacked and let's get on with it. I'm starving.'

Minutes later Hugh follows Guido and Guillaume in a roundabout route to the duke's *caldarium*. They return first to the central stairs and ascend to the second floor. It is to avoid going through the duke's apartments where other guests might be studying, Guido says. Guillaume keeps gawping and sniggering back to his fellow. Hugh wishes he'd sent for water to wash in private. To meet someone here would be humbling. *No man is a hero in his bathrobe holding his fresh linen.* He laughs inwardly, mocking his own 'great honour'. They pass around two sides of the upper loggia and pass through some plainer apartments and eventually down the spiral stairs in one of the Torricini towers. One floor down Guido remarks, 'This floor was the duke's apartments. The duchess allows the poets and scholars to study there now.' Another floor down he says, 'And this door leads to the duke's private Chapel of Forgiveness.'

'Forgiveness,' Hugh says almost involuntarily, lingering for a moment at the doorway. 'Let me see it.'

The boys come back up the few steps they have gone down and lead Hugh through a small vestibule set out as a private study and towards the doorway opposite. Hugh feels the cool of the marble even before he enters. Guido moves aside to let him pass for they are in a small corridor-like anteroom. 'It is in here signor, but there is not room for us all.'

Hugh waves them aside and enters without a word. He instinctively lets both hands reach out to touch the walls after he has crossed himself. His fingers run from the marble partitions into the dark-veined granite inlays, while his eyes remained fixed straight ahead toward the altar and perfectly formed little apse. There is a faint smell of incense, wax and mop water. His eye catches the faces of a hundred angels with golden wings amid the geometric plaster designs on the barrel vaulted ceiling. They look on now as they have done in the dark before the door was opened. *What do they see?* The altar is bare, the tabernacle left open, and there are no candles in the brass candlesticks. *What have they seen?*

No sooner has the thought formed in his mind than the word "tears" is there. Tears. A man has wept here, has wept an ocean of tears. He senses this with an irrational swarm of emotion that begins to choke him up. *Was the duke who died last year so young, so ill? Or was it the great Federigo his illustrious father? What is this place?* 'Who calls his private chapel a Chapel of Forgiveness? Why would someone do that?'

'My father says.'

'Huh,' Hugh does not realise that he has spoken his thoughts in whispers, and so when Guido answers, he comes about with a start. 'What?'

'My father says that Duke Federigo named the chapel thus when his half-brother was killed.'

'Killed?'

'Well, yes, signor.' Guido shoots Hugh a reverential look. 'Oddantonio hated the duke even though they had grown up together. He mounted a rebellion against him, but the duke's men killed him. And some say that it was on the duke's orders, so – '

'So,' Hugh says with a finality that lets Guido off having to say any more. He turns back to face the altar imagining that bold knight prostrate on the cold marble, his bitter tears mingled with pleas that his brother's blood not be required at his hand. And the angels looked on. And heaven looked on. Even when the candles were snuffed and the door shut, and there was no more light, they all looked on. And the tears were mingled with the mop water when the serving girl came with her bucket. And maybe some of the tears are still there in the cracks and joints of the marble. Maybe they are washed away. And the shadow of Cain? Can that be washed away? Can anything wash a shadow but light? Is there any hope for anyone in this world? *Madre Dio, it is not just the vile things that we have done, but the tainted good, we thought I had done, nay, even the truer good we should have done. That is what has made this whole place an antechamber of hell. It is not just that we are sinners, but that we are not saints. The old friar is right in that much, at least. But how is a man to have hope in such a world? How is he to live? How is he to sleep? That is what I want to know, and who is there to answer that?*

They descend the last few spirals into what Hugh guesses must be the level of the cellars, stables and kitchens. The smells of wood smoke and tallow become obvious, and he can hear the distant bustle and shouting of the servants as they near a large oak door at the bottom of the stairs and then another noise—someone singing. A chestnut-haired boy comes out of the bathing room, remarking to Guido as he passes, 'He has sent me for a lute, as if I can play. Says he can't sing without it.' The lad sniggers, but then bows when he sees Hugh come round the corner.

'Who cannot sing without a lute?' Hugh says, doubtful from the din that a lute will help in any case.

'Why, it is Signor Pietro Bembo, the great poet.' The lad bows again, trying to keep as straight a face as he can.

'Is it indeed?' Hugh says. He shouts as he enters the steaming room. 'Bembo, in God's name stop that infernal racket and make room for a weary traveler.'

'Hugh, is that you? My dear fellow, so you have finally come when we had given up all hope of ever seeing you again. Did you have trouble?' Hugh approaches the sunken bath where a red-faced Bembo is sitting forward and blinking the sweat from his eyes.

'Trouble? Why do you say that?' Hugh says, scrutinising whether Bembo's wide eyes betray a sort of guilty surprise or a genuine delight. He has been trying to shake thoughts of yet further betrayal from his mind. Those assassins knew where he would be. Bembo alone knew his location. Well, him and anyone he innocently told. And then of course word may have reached the prior via informants in Assisi itself. He doesn't want to contemplate Bembo as a betrayer again, but he cannot take chances.

'Because you were so long. I told everyone you would be a week, maybe two. And now here you are a month later. The ladies have grown restless my friend. It was all I could do to keep them entertained by our recent exploits. As you know, a true friend, such as I am, loves you even despite your achievements. Many here still remember Michelotto, and so to hear of him tossed from the Duomo has brought succor to more than one pious soul.'

'Ah yes, of course. I forgot he had been here with Cesare Borgia.'

Hugh steps down into the recessed pool, his bare feet feeling their way from the hot mosaic tiles toward the even hotter water.

'I am surprised the boys have not come in to actually watch you. You know that they are taught here that the English do not bath at all, and they have forgotten how to even make lye soap.' When Hugh doesn't rise to the bait, Bembo adds. 'Suit yourself. Bloody water here so thick with lime that you'd think they had boiled macaroni in it first.'

'I was shown the duke's private chapel just now.' Hugh eases himself into one of the stone seats and lets the water wash under his arms. It feels good. He looks at the flushed cheeks of the poet and the red tan under his neck, just below the beard. *Heat like this makes any man look guilty*. He suddenly remembers the expression of Bembo's face that day. That dreadful day in Florence when all his own betrayals and infamy were manifest. *Bembo had hope because I forgave him, or at least I said I would. Is it the same thing? He does not suppose that I have forgotten his betrayal does he? Perhaps he thinks that even though I can recall, yet I should never count it against him in our future dealings. He has my word on it. No affidavit, just my word. I don't know whether he deserved it necessarily, or whether he really believed me totally at the time. But he seems resigned to it now all the same.* 'This water is too hot.'

'You get used to it the longer you are in. Almost feels lukewarm to me now. The duke's chapel you say. Did they show you the Temple to the Muses next door? You should see it.'

'Why would a man build a temple to the Muses, *caro*?'

'Bit of fun, I suppose. A place to go for inspiration.'

'Inspiration for what? He didn't write. Couldn't even read, some say.'

'Well, for the young courtiers then, and the poets. It's a bit of fun anyway. Why always be so serious about everything.'

'I just think it tells forth the age. I mean, right next door to a chapel. What are we saying? What are we really bloody saying with all this?'

'Come now, Hugh. You know what they say: hopes can be disappointed but nostalgia is irrefutable. Besides many of the ancients were, as the fathers said, *homines naturaliter Christianus,* naturally Christian men. Their words not mine.'

'Oh, so that is it. Having acknowledged some we must take all. Having tasted the saner wine that accords with reason and truth, we must therefore re-drain the dregs of antiquity to avoid stagnation?'

'Hugh, Hugh!'

'I mean, *madre dio* Bembo, the Muses! Come now. The daughters of Zeus of the Aegis were not even claiming to be moral guides. When Hesiod saw them dancing on Mount Helicon – no let me finish, damn it – they said, "We know how to tell many false things as if they are true, and the truth when we want." They didn't care whether what they said was true or false so long as it was diverting for the audience. It doesn't exactly bode well for your poetry, scholarship and natural philosophy, does it? I mean to say, if we rebuild their abandoned temples knowing all this, then more fool us.'

'I hope you don't intend to be a miser in front of our friends when Castiglione and I have told them what a decent fellow you are. It's hard enough here for the duchess as she prepares to give over to the pope's nephew without you droning on about her father-in-law's decorative tastes.'

'Yes, very well. God I am so tired.' He knows he only mulls over things like this to distract him from his own downfall. Hugh tries unsuccessfully to smile and then says, 'I shall be an angel, but answer the point. Do you not think there is something monstrous, unnatural – dangerous even – to court such folly?'

'Well,' Bembo says slowly, at the same timing moving aside as fresh hot water splutters out from a pipe near his head. 'First I would say we must know what the ancients meant by their attachment to the Muses. They were older than the Olympian gods, you know. Their mother, whom they believed to be Memory, had mated nine times with Zeus. Surely this all speaks of something metaphorical—mans' innate humility perhaps, you know, that he acknowledged that real genius, real inspiration, real answers come from the outside. I don't think you need to be on your high horse about it. I don't think they worshipped them as we worship Christ.'

'How can you say that?' Hugh says, craning his head back in mockery. 'Horace calls on any number of muses like you Italians call on your Umbrian saints. The Spartans sacrificed to them – said it was the Muses who taught Apollo how to sing. Even Pinder, who should have belonged to the later sceptics, prayed to them. The point isn't what *they* thought – it is obvious to me they were serious in the main – the point is what are *we* about? Do these *Umanista* care about truth absolute or are they happy to go on projecting their own wayward opinions and call it inspiration or the new learning? They say, "Man has come of age; he is the measure of all things; he will remake our world to reflect the new learning. He will perfect the arts, the sciences; even nature herself will yield, even man himself. We will establish objective branches of knowledge *sine ira et studio,* without passion and partisanship. My arse, it's all bollocks. Can't you see that? They are willingly beguiled by their own hubris. What is progress? What is perfectibility? What is this processive future they see if not a barely hidden assumption? And, I suppose, each new development must be sensational. Yes, yes, of course it must be sensational, because the Muses know how to hold the public attention, whatever else they do while they are screwing you."

'Stop, stop it!' Bembo splashes water at Hugh with the back of his hand. 'Of course we are earnest in seeking the truth. Really, I wish you wouldn't go on as if you were the first person to have questions about the times we live in, Hugh.' Bembo splashes him. 'You are a visitor here. Anyway, I am not going to talk to you seriously about anything when I see your humors are quite out. Have you eaten? I suppose it's because you have been holed up in that friary. I dare say they fed you nothing but boiled parsnips all week and fish on Fridays. You have too much black bile; that's your real problem.' Bembo looks up momentarily as he hears light footsteps descending the stairs. 'Aha, hear is Giulaume with the lute.'

'Oh, no.' Hugh sinks further into the water. 'He says he can't play.'

'Nonsense, boys are born with lutes in Urbno, they are—fully formed from their mother's wombs. And as you know, the muse Erato's specialty was poetry sung to the lyre so perhaps you would not mind imploring the nymph to attend us and aid my endeavors.'

'Very funny. But I think I would rather get changed and have something to eat.' Hugh splashes water back in Bembo's direction. 'Or failing that, send for a razor and drown here and now, before you start wailing again like a feral cat.'

AN HOUR LATER. APERITIFS ON THE ROOF GARDEN, URBINO.

'Do you remember the last time we drank Greek wine Malmsey together?' Hugh asks Ambassador Baldasarre Castiglione. He leans on the balcony of the hanging garden, loosely clutching his fine Venetian glass and admiring the panorama of blue hills. On the cultivated terraces, workers can still be discerned bringing in the hay. Because of the precipitous slopes they do here as they do in the Alps: tie it in vast bundles and carry it down on their backs to waiting carts. They look like walking trees in the half-light.

Hugh glances at the ambassador. The man is in fine form this evening, sporting the very latest vermillion velvet doublet with slashed sleeves to reveal his rich cream, silk chemise. His cuffs are gathered with a lace cord and secured with a pearl fastener. His nails are immaculate as ever, hands so milk white that you would never guess he'd been outside or indeed written anything that week, which he has.

'Malmsey? Yes, of course I can. It was on the terrace at Castello D'Avalos on Ischia. It was a memorable night. I miss those times.'

'So do I. It is good to see you again, *caro*.' Hugh raises a glass, which Castiglione meets. During the clink, the light of the flaming torches that line the terrace refract in the wine and illumine the ambassador's calf-like features with a golden glow.

'It is good to see you, too. And here in Urbino, as well. Is it not everything I told you? On this side of the garden are the duke's apartments, and on that side are the duchess's. When they wanted to spend a night together, one or other of them – I suppose it was him really – would have to descend his private stairs and cross the garden to her door, up her private staircase, so to speak. Sorry, that sounds crude, I didn't intend it to be. I'm rabbiting on because I am so glad you are here and hope so much that you approve of the place.' Castiglione gestures over the terraced garden, perhaps a hundred feet square, and up the towers and parapets.

'I don't know why you would need my approval, but for what it is worth, yes, it is a fine palace and garden.'

'Splendid. And would you believe that their harness room is under this very garden?'

'I would.' *And I can tell you three ways to get there and out via the stable should it come to it.* Hugh had Guido guide him about the place before coming to the garden. He doesn't seriously think the prior's people will try anything here, but it doesn't hurt to be cautious. 'Tell me,' Hugh says while surveying the gentlemen and ladies that enter the garden. 'Who are these people? They look very important. I hope you will introduce me. I promised Bembo that I would not let him down here.'

'I should think we had more need to worry about him. You know that he is apt to exhibit when he has been drinking. But as to the guests let me see. There is Signor Ludovico Canossa with the Gonzaga's sculptor Gian Cristoforo Romano. Yes, him with the unfortunate collar talking to the young man.'

Hugh casts a quiet glance towards the group of *grandees* and *magnati*, and particularly to a young man wearing a pink cape, edged with a broad band of velvet, white velvet hose variegated with silver lacework, a white satin jacket, and velvet cap set off with a feather. His companions all sport velvet shoes, delicate, calf-skin gloves, gold medals, daggers, swords and gold chains worth fifty crowns or more. One fellow, directly under the lantern, has so many rings that his fingers are almost invisible. Next to him is a man who turns away in their direction to cough.

'That young man is Gaspare Pallavicino,' Castiglione says. 'He has very poor health but an excellent wit. He's want to be impetuous, though of course, that is not a crime in the young. The others, over there, are family members, country cousins, hangers on. And of course, on this side is Giuliano de Medici with his affinity. I see the musicians play to honour him. Do you know this piece? It is called "Corinto," but it is set to one of his father's poems.' Castiglione turns his head to hear, nodding in approval at the pitch and cadence affected by the young soprano whose face reminds Hugh suddenly of poor Pico.

Quant'e bella giovainezza, Che si fugge tuttavia!
Chi vuol esser lieto, sia, Di Doman no c'e certezza.

How beautiful is youth that slips our grasp and flies away!
So go on, be merry and gay,
for uncertainty is tomorrow's only truth.

'How true, *caro*, how true.' Castiglione says, 'Lorenzo was a good man. His son Giuliano is, too, in his own way. Have you been introduced yet? No? Then I shall do so presently. And look, here is the duchess with her cousin, and lady-in-waiting, Lady Emilia Pia. Oh, and Bembo, who already looks like he's had a skinful. I think you have been introduced to the lady? Oh, but here she comes, let us bow for they are close.'

Castiglione, fastidious to the point of exhaustion, bends his knee and removes his beret, letting his hands sweep in a studied arc so that the feather brushes the grass. Hugh sees him readjust his feet a moment later and curse quietly under his breath, blaming the wine for his poor execution. Hugh places his wine on the stone rail and follows suit with a slower and more gracious motion. The ladies curtsey and fall into conversation with the Medici party, leaving the two of them alone to finish their wine.

'It was well done, your bow. I don't know what was going on with me. The wine is stronger than I thought.'

Hugh tries not to sound too patronizing. 'My dear friend, you would do well to think less of your technique. Truly your scrupulousness does you great service, but well, you know, perhaps a little less effort?' Hugh phrases it like a question so as not to offend an otherwise warm hearted man in his area of peculiar weakness. 'Remember: Protogenes is said to have been censured by Apelles because he did not know when to take his hand from the tablet.'

'Ah, *touchez.*' Castiglione smiles somewhat abashed. 'Less effort, of course. You are absolutely right. It is only the Germans that prize sweat above all else.' He glances into his glass and sees that it is empty. His fingers fidget around the stem. 'Do you remember that I said all those months back, that I was working on something.'

'Your book, *The Courtier*. Of course I remember. Is it coming on?'

'In fits and starts yes. I have gathered many pages of notes of all that I wanted to say. I think I should now start to set it down in earnest.'

'Good, I am glad. I hope it goes well.'

The ambassador shrugs with a studied modesty and speaks into his beard. 'The Lady Vittoria has been writing and asking for the first draft, and now she has arrived here in Urbino, I am ashamed not to have done more.'

'Is she in the garden yet?' Hugh says, suppressing the urge to seek her out.

'I think not. She knows I am writing it mainly for her sake – that she might know once and for all that her betrothed is truly the full worth of any knight in Europe. Or at least that is what I suppose it is. Maybe she is just humouring me. Either way, I believe the project is a noble one. And though I may not be first in the camp and the forum, yet I flatter myself that, having travelled to so many illustrious courts, I may sketch many useful lessons.'

'I have no doubt in that regard. When Bembo calls you *maitre l'ambassador*, he does not jest, though perhaps you think he does. He respects you in his own way. Have you decided on the form the work should take?'

'Oh yes, platonic dialogues, set here on a night like this, in fact, just like this. Why not? Though in my mind I wanted perhaps to set the evening a few years back when Duke Guidobaldo was still with us. He does not need to be present, but a duke should be in his palace, the direct heir of Federigo, the last in his line. It seems right to me anyway. It adds poignancy.' Castiglione sighs. 'My days are probably numbered here. It is good to remember things as they were. I do not know whether the pope's nephew will have need of me as an ambassador when he takes up his residence. This book might be something of a swan song, but at least it will go out with some strength.' Castiglione straightens his shoulders and gazes boldly across the valley. 'Yes, I will set it on a night like this, with these guests and you, yes, why not? Why not when Il Magnifico's son is present? Why not when the most famed holy knight is in our midst in Urbino? It is fitting.'

'I would reconsider that point, *caro*.' Hugh speaks slowly, to temper the excitement and volume of his friend.

'But why not you?'

'Because people who appear in books are sure to be remembered for generations, who then might make further enquiry. And I would not that people enquired over much into my life. If they did, it might diminish your noble work.'

'Hugh? I saw this sadness in you at our first meeting at the Castel Sant'Angelo. Does it follow you still? What is there in your life that is not worthy of emulation? Who would you protect by this humility?'

'My mother, my father, my brother and sisters.' *Would you like a full list?* Hugh breathes heavily through his nostrils, and looks away. 'I am happy to assist, you know that, but please let my name, my part be assigned to another more worthy of memory.' Hugh forces a smile. 'Give it to the fellow with the pink satin doublet and silk slippers.'

At this point by the rustling of silks and taffeta behind them both men are made aware of approaching ladies. They turn and bow. It is the duchess, Elizabetta Montefeltro, escorted by Giuliano de Medici, son of *Il Magnifico*. She wears the apparel of mourning – a black bologna silk *gamurra* trimmed with dark furs. Small white emblems that Hugh cannot make out in the dying light are appliquéd on the lower sleeves. She honours her husband's memory but shows hope for the future perhaps. It is a fine brocade. Hugh lets his gaze rest only momentarily on her. He glimpses her face when no one else is looking. It is full of a quiet solemnity, December remembering May. But a gracious, heartfelt smile breaks through the retrospection when her eyes meet each guest.

Hugh also observes *Il Magnifico's* son. He has the famous nose, not quite Roman, more like a knobby Brescia sausage. His features are dark, saturnine but not unhandsome. *We are of an age*, Hugh thinks. Though affable in appearance, he projects a layer of aggravated haughtiness, no doubt designed to mask the ignominy of being Lord of Florence *in absentia*. It must be hard to fill such big boots, particularly when some republicans have run off with them. He has been a guest of the Venetians but also has been careful to keep within the papal curia for he knows it is they who are his best chance of regaining Florence.

The duchess tilts her head in a second bow. 'You do us honour in your coming, Fra Erpingham.'

'On the contrary, Duchess, the honour is all mine.'

'May I introduce my friend Giuliano of the illustrious house of Medici?'

'I am honoured yet further to make so noble an acquaintance.' More homage.

'And I you, signor.' Giuliano arranges his black velvet beret which is the harder to reset after bowing because he is sporting a Moorish silk turban under it. It is, at least as Hughes sees it, an eastern affectation prevalent among the Venetians and spreading like the pox. Giuliano continues. 'I have heard much of your exploits from our bank on Rhodes. They say that by your vengeance on the infidel you provoke open war, and jeopardize the bank's interests. In fact, they advise us to invest in the manufacture of arms, for a war is eminent. Can this be true, do you think?'

'We are already at war. Whether we choose to fight, to ignore, or profit from it is another matter.' Hugh speaks quickly and ill-advisedly. *How dare he speak to me as if I were one of his junior bank clerks. Look at his stupid turban and lily-white fingers. Prick.* 'The Turks amass a monstrous fleet to level Rhodes. This I have seen with my own eyes. If Rhodes falls, God forbid, then they will overrun Europe – which is too busy butchering itself to mount a proper defense. So yes, war is coming, and we must have money for the defense of Rhodes if you do not wish to see the crescent moon above the Vatican palace, or have Saint Peter's another grand mosque like Hagia Sophia.'

For a moment Giuliano's mouth is agape, but it soon closes to make a firm jaw.

'Such *un homme serieux*.' The duchess unexpectedly steps between them to take Hugh's arm. 'Let us not talk tonight of wars that may never come. You have suffered, signor, at their hands, as has my friend here at the hands of his countrymen. There are many wrongs in this world. We have all been part of this world's wrongs to a greater and lesser extent, and we might yet be part of this world's good, too. We do not know. Though we do know that the wrongs will not last forever, and one day all of this will seem so very small. I am reminded of those lapidary Horatian verses of your dear father's, Giuliano.

"Quanto sia vana speranza nostra,
Quanto falace ciaschedun disegno,
Quanto sia il mondo d'ignoranza pregno,
La maestro del tutto, Morte, il mostra."

How vain is every hope, each breath,
How false is every single plan;
How full of ignorance is man
Against the monstrous mistress death.

The duchess takes Giuliano by the other arm and leads them along the terrace, with deliberate steps and deliberate words. Every few paces she glances from one man to the other and then out to the harvest moon, which casts an ephemeral pewter light onto the fields, towers and crenulations. 'There is time to talk of war in the day, but now it is night and we rest from the day's work. I know you have both suffered loss, but let us rest tonight even from tomorrow. We are God's creatures first, are we not?' She gently tugs a nod from Giuliano before continuing. 'So we rest. We will not fret about the future; it does not belong to us. We are his creatures first, yes?' And she gently shakes a nod from Hugh, too.

When they reach the end of the terrace, she turns to bring them close to the stone balustrade. Silver mists have formed in the valleys two hundred feet below them, and it seems that they are floating above the clouds. 'We may yet suffer further loss, gentlemen,' the duchess says, 'but tonight let us rest and remember. Moonlight is the great restorer of vanished kingdoms.'

VITTORIA COLONNA

As he is about to exit the garden for dinner, Hugh comes face to face with Vittoria coming in the opposite direction. 'Fra Hugh!' she says, forgetting to curtsey, but then doing so as Hugh bares his head.

'Signorina,' Hugh returns, rising and replacing his beret.

'You are in health?' Vittoria asks.

'Yes, and you?' *Stupid question.*

'Yes, and you?' Vittoria asks again, then stammers, 'Sorry, I have already said that, haven't I? Forgive me. You have caught me by surprise. Am I late for the party? Oh dear, everyone is coming in already for dinner.'

Hugh proffers his arm. 'Let me escort you.'

'No, I cannot. Sister Clemence is quite ill from the journey, and I should stay with her.'

'*La Bafana?*' Hugh says.

'Oh dear, did I call her that to you? What a dreadful girl I was. She is not such a dragon as I now understand. I was a petulant student, but she bore with Olympian patience my failings, and now it is right that I should bear with her ill health. There is always merit in sacrifice, as she would say, and I would so have loved to be at dinner tonight with you all. But I am needed upstairs and I will not be much missed, I dare say.'

'You will be, lady, and you know it.'

'It is very kind of you, Fra Hugh, but you mustn't flatter me. You have borne with my ill verse. That is enough for me.'

'Your ill verse!' Hugh says, moving to the side to let the pink silk gentleman pass, and then waiting until no one else is in earshot. When he speaks it is in a hushed and urgent whisper. 'You know very well that your verse has brought consolation to a drowning man. I am in your debt, lady. Surely you know that.' Hugh raises his eyes from the ground to look into hers. 'Never say that it is ill verse when it has brought one soul hope.'

Vittoria suddenly opens up like a flood. 'I had to come down just now, for I so wanted to see you. Duchess Constanza and I have prayed so much for you.'

'I think the duchess has the measure of me,' Hugh mumbles into his collar. 'And I do not blame her.'

'You are wrong, Hugh. She feels something immeasurably strong with regards to your destiny. She has such a prophetic soul, you know. When you wrote that you were going to Assisi, she even began to fast and pray for you that you would find what you were searching for. She said to me, made me promise in fact, that when I met you here, I would write without delay. You cannot know how she has prayed for you. We both have. And now I am here and still see a sadness in your eyes, and I am afraid of what you might tell me.'

Hugh's shoulders suddenly melt, and the breath leaves him. For a moment he is numb and insensible in his mind. She is saying something else to him, asking if he is all right. She touches his arm and he looks up at her again. 'You may tell her, thank you. I am undeserving of any favours. I know that. You may reassure her that I have confessed all my sins.'

As Hugh pauses, mouth still open, jaw cocked slightly, still searching for some nice conclusion, Vittoria jumps in.

'But that is good, Hugh. Surely that is good.'

'Is remorse true repentance? Is regret?'

'But Hugh,' Vittoria takes hold of his sleeves with both hands. 'The things you wrote about made me so afraid. You said there was some dreadful thing you must do. But now you say that you have confessed. Well, surely this is good news? Hugh?'

Hugh gazes into her eyes again. *What can I tell her? How can she understand? Will I destroy her innocence with my guilt? Will I undermine her faith in divine redemption by my unbelief? That God should redeem repentant sinners is worthy in concept and manifest in execution – I cannot deny the cross. Who can deny history? But how repentant am I, bent on this course of assassination as I still am. I will not add hypocrisy to my sins. Let me spare myself that indignity. If I am bound for eternal torment, let me at least have my pride as a companion.* Bembo and Castiglione's voices loom up behind him. He crosses his right hand to lay it on hers. 'You may tell her that I have confessed. And do not forget me in your prayers and in your correspondence. You cannot know what they mean to me.'

As the other two arrive and renew acquaintances with Vittoria, Hugh stands back and wonders if he truly knows what those letters have meant – these two women, these two latter day Mary-and-Marthas tending their sickly Lazarus, hoping that the Saviour won't be too late to cure him, or else raise him from the dead.

LATER THAT EVENING, SALA VEGIE.

The Sala Vegie is a well-appointed room for a small dining party, perhaps forty feet long with windows facing north and south. These are not courtyard views either, but great vistas of the dukedom's prosperous streets and rolling hills under cultivation, if not for crops then for swine, goats, figs and chestnuts.

The room has two entrances that Hugh cannot help diverting his eyes to every time someone enters. The one to his right goes to the double length *Sala dei Onore*, which is the chief reception room. The one to his left goes to the duchess' apartments. It is this door through which the servants come and go. Just beyond it, as Hugh well knows is a spiral staircase leading to the kitchens, stable and freedom if the need should arise.

But, he thinks, casting his eyes upward, *Tonight I may be set upon with words, but not with knives.* He examines the high ceiling, broken up by a series of fan vaults, simply covered in lime plaster. The fire, ablaze with dense olive-wood logs, casts dancing orange shapes over the walls and in and out of the vaults. The mood has been good; no one has mentioned the war and people have eaten well: veal, other meats of castrated animals, capons. There remains the anticipation of a final sweet course. He looks about the table. The ladies seem outnumbered three to one, which is probably an occupational hazard when running an artistic court of bachelor poets and painters. He sits to the right of the duchess, which he knows to be an honoured place.

Emilia Pia smiles at Hugh from across the table as the plates are being cleared. She is wearing a white damask under-gown, with embroidered *sarcanet* sleeves, taffeta cuffs fringed with white musk fur. She has been talking to the bishop of Senegallia and enquiring whether he thinks the price of grain will rise above ten ducats a *rubbio* because of the war. The bishop pinches his nose, which he seems to do constantly, and says he hopes not, adding that he can remember it at two *scudi* a *rubbio* when he was young. He looks forlornly at the remaining white bread rolls when they are removed. Perhaps he would have had just one more.

Hugh's attention is diverted back to the duchess who is talking to Giuliano de Medici about a certain tomb belonging to the Lord of Lucca. 'He married Ilaria of Carreto, acknowledged by all to be one of the most beautiful and accomplished ladies of her day. They were very happy, but she died bearing their third child. I have seen the tomb; it is very fine. Fra Hugh, you should visit Lucca.' She looks between the two men, then smiles. 'A man might have everything and yet death, that Last Enemy, may take it in an instant. We must be thankful for all the happiness that may be ours in this life, gentlemen. Christ will make all things right in the end, and in the meantime let faith, hope and love abide.'

Giuliano nods. There is something so solemn and deep about this woman, as if she is aware of verities behind the curtain of youth that the middle-aged politely keep to themselves.

A servant refills Hugh's goblet, and he places his hand to stop him overfilling. He brings it to his nose. It is more aromatic Greek wine called *Retsina,* which is flavored with the resins of maritime pines. He can smell the pine resin, and it takes him back. Many a Turkish goke is made from the great pines that grow on the Bosporan peninsula and round to Bodrum. He can hear the creak of timbers, ropes, rowlocks, of chain and lash; smell the timbers, the sweat, the excrement, the puss from a thousand untreated wounds; hear the cries of unnumbered and unnamed tormented souls. Abandon hope all ye who enter. He lost hope sooner than he thought possible. Love and faith faired no better. Man is like the grass.

'Fra Hugh, Fra Hugh, are you quite well?' The duchess touches his arm.

'Pardon me, I was lost for a moment,' he says, adding quietly. 'In thought.'

'I can see that we must have diversion now that we have eaten a little.' She raises her hand and eyebrows in Castiglione's direction. 'My dear Baldasarre, you may tell the guests what you have been about.'

The ambassador places his goblet on the table and then stands deliberately. He clears his throat, straightens his sleeves and begins to tell the assembled group about his plans for the book. After no more than a minute of summary, he coughs modestly into his hand and finishes with. 'So you can see what I have set myself to do, for the honour of this court, my noble patroness and her illustrious husband's family name and memory. I would welcome your thoughts, my honoured guests, that perhaps you would add to my limited knowledge on what is needful for the aspiring courtiers and knights of Europe. In such a time of change we must, I believe, give form to a standard for which all men can aspire.'

'Permit me to say, with all humility that you take upon yourself too great a task, my friend.' Ludovico Canossa pushes his plate forward and shakes his head. 'Such perfections in a courtier cannot be taught. It cannot be broken down to a set of rules or precepts. I would not do it.'

Castiglione is amicable but clearly ruffled. 'But surely to perfect oneself fulfils a public and private moral duty to elevate ourselves and act as a model for others. But it cannot be if we do not define it, even broadly.'

For a moment no one answers. Hugh can see that the young man Gaspare Pallavicino has something to say but is holding back out of deference to the older and more illustrious guests. The bishop has no such scruples, for he has reached that age in life and that station where he feels every opinion in his head is a universal axiom. 'First I should say, he must be of noble birth.'

He is about to elaborate when Castiglione gently interrupts. 'Do others agree?'

'No indeed.' It is young Pallavicino. 'Many outstanding and virtuous men have been of humble origins. History attests it.'

Others agree with nods and names. Castiglione smiles, bows at each comment with the sort of vacant look of a man taking mental notes. After a few minutes Castiglione concludes with a literary benediction worthy of Bembo himself and evidently something he has already been working on. 'Dante expresses this in Convivio IV in the canzone "*Le dolci rime d'amor Ch'io solia* – the sweet song of my own love." In another place he breaks the word *gentle* from its original meaning *gens*, that is, from noble stock. But rather "Here, neither birth nor riches but a gentle heart." And Guinizelli almost makes this sentiment his manifesto: *A cor gentil ripara sempre amore* – a gentle heart always loves remedy. It may, my dear bishop, be easier in practice to achieve these perfections if one is nobly born, but we must concede that many have risen above and sunk below their stations. A wise man may overrule the stars and so forth. What we are discussing in the ideal courtier is surely a work of art, not nature: a man from the courts of Charlemagne or Camelot, learned, meek and yet also fierce in battle.'

Hugh can hear Bembo muttering. 'Doesn't need to be a soldier. War is a fearful inconvenience when one is busy.'

Giuliano places his wrists on the table. 'The French, despite all that their forefather Charlemagne might teach them, now assert that education leads to effeminacy on the field of battle. And are we Italians to teach them otherwise after their extraordinary conquests of recent years?'

'Certainly we shall.' Castiglione assumes a mock aggressive position. 'The French may well enjoy their new military prowess. They may conquer half the earth, but what will they make of their half of the earth? Make them all Spartan warriors? To what end? No, I say, and I can see you agree, my lord, that a courtier should be deeply versed in Greek and Latin and moreover should know enough to be able to discriminate between good and bad writing. These rude and uncultivated French who despise letters, who disdain one who can read with the name clerk, are to be pitied rather. Let them light a candle to a knight like Fra Erpingham here. Let them produce a man to compare to him in arms and in learning. Here is proof that they are wrong surely.'

Hugh raises his hand. '*Caro*, I wish you would not – ' *Why does he insist on this folly? To even talk of maintaining virtue in this way seems to make it a sunset debate. Odysseus's Ithaca was, by the time Homer wrote it, a lost ideal, a fallen utopia of aristocratic virtue.*

'I know, I know. I understand, you speak little and boast little, which is right. Better than another who is forever sounding his own praises, which is naught but affectation, and wishing to appear bold. But you,'

Castiglione opens his hands in Hugh's direction as if he were releasing a dove. 'You have nobility enough for the bishop and learning enough to chase even Bembo away, and as for arms we need not speak. You do not overdress, as the French, or underdress like the Germans. You do not ride bolt upright in the saddle as the Venetians, but with an easy grace as is befitting. And your speech? Who will not agree that it is with grave simplicity that belies your years? But beyond all this you possess *sprezzatura*, that easy grace, or as Quintilian says: "the art that conceals art". For this essential quality is not simply a kind of superficial dissimulation, as it may also be the result of such assiduous practice, so that what one does becomes second nature and seems inborn. Indeed – '

Emilia Pia, who has been fidgeting with her pearl necklace, interjects over the top of Castiglione's next sentence. 'But surely such studied grace will always be found out as affectation.'

'Oh, no. No indeed, my lady. Verily, a courtier does well if he can avoid all forms of affectation into which fault many fall. Why, even some of us Lombards, if we have been a year away from home, on our return at once begin to speak with accents Roman, sometimes Spanish or even French, and God alone knows why. But I think all this comes from over zeal to appear widely informed. In such fashion do men devote care to acquire a very odious fault. And truly it would be no light task for me, if I were to try in these discussions of ours to use those antique Tuscan words that are quite rejected even by the usage of the Tuscans of today. I think everyone would laugh at me anyway.'

'Laugh at you, my friend?' Bembo says with a comic roar. 'Never.'

Amidst the ensuing mirth the young sculptor Gian Cristoforo Romano speaks. 'I should like to ask you, signor, aware that I among such an august party, whether you would consider that this courtier paint or sculpt even?'

'I do not think these arts of man are in the least beneath him.' Castiglione raises his palms again in Hugh's direction. 'See for yourself, Fra Erpingham himself is – so I am told – a fine painter.'

'Please, signor.' Hugh shakes his head with shame remembering his coarse efforts, which were given him to aid his recovery and stop him fighting. 'I am indeed glad that Rhodes is so far from here and that you will not have cause to compare my humble technique with that of Signor Buonarotti or your own Raphael.'

'He paints,' Castiglione says, partly ignoring Hugh's remonstrations and gesturing between him and the pink cheeked Romano who seems pleased. 'He paints. Perhaps he sculpts too, but I do know that he writes verse.'

'Not that we have seen any, he keeps it close!' Bembo with jealous eyes speaks with a wry humour from inside his glass.

'And—' Castiglione speaks over him. 'He can sing in tune unlike some others we could mention.'

Into the general mirth and table patting that follows the ambassador's jibe, Lady Emilia Pia speaks. 'And grace in the company of ladies?' She gives a pert smile and glances with raised eyebrows toward the other women. 'Is he devoted to a lady? Is he constant in his devotion? Surely this will be on your list, Baldasarre. With whom does Fra Erpingham correspond, for example? What secrets may we know of so discreet a guest?'

'Shots fired, shots fired.' Bembo smirks and places his goblet on the table. 'Answer that, Hugh, won't you?'

Hugh feels his humours rise. The heat in his cheeks is evident to Lady Pia as he catches a fleeting glimpse of her spiteful smile. *Does she know about the correspondence with Vittoria? Does she wish to damage the marchese's reputation in some way?* He glances at Castiglione for rescue. But it is Bembo again, prompted by a cautionary glance from the duchess who steps in to deflect the comments.

'You know, my dear Emilia, there is the love of a man for a woman which is sensual, and it should not be gainsaid, for without it none of us would be here. But since reading Ficino's commentaries on Socrates's speech on the nature of love in Plato's *Symposium*, and since writing my *Gli Asolini,* I begin also to see another species of love at work between people of the same and opposite sexes. Don't stare so, I say, these friendships are valid and beneficial to our health. You agree, I am sure. The divine nature and origin of love must be among us most highly prized.

It is the father of true pleasures, of all blessings, of peace, of gentleness, and of good will; the enemy of rough savagery and vileness of which we have already spoken tonight.' He glances about the table and brightens considerably as he sees their undivided attentions are placed on his words. He nods, then continues. 'Ultimately each manifestation of love in our experience lifts the lover and beloved to the contemplation of the spiritual realm, leading to Love himself – to God.' Bembo raises his hand in a theatrical gesture, seeing again that the guests appear happy to defer to him in matters like this. He smiles tightly and then says, 'I understand that Plato supposes pederasty at some point – what the Florentines call their *bottom game* – but I think here he is was speaking only out of the illness of his own times. My friend Fra Erpingham has taken vows of chastity. He is wed to his Order and by his commitment has dashed the hopes of a thousand potential selves, and perhaps even the hearts of not a few English maidens. Be that as it may, my lady, we must not impugn his character or any of his *familiaritas* merely to satisfy a waspish love of gossip.'

Hugh watches Lady Emilia and Bembo fix each other's stare long after the conversation moves on. *She's not finished with this.*

'What about music then? You have said nothing of music,' Canossa says, raising his palms in appeal to the older guests. 'Surely you will insist on this in your book, signor?'

'Please, no,' says Pallavicino. 'In a man of situation this would surely tend to effeminacy.'

Canossa replies 'No, my friend, no! There is no better way to soothe the soul and raise the spirits than through music. Think of the great generals and heroes of antiquity who were keen musicians. Why, even Socrates himself began to learn the cithern when an old man. I say parents should have their children taught from infancy for it promotes habits of harmony and virtue.'

'He's right, Pallavicino.' Giuliano de Medici nods seriously, raising his glass toward the similarly red faced youngster. 'The pup is right, concede the point. Music is not mere ornament, but a necessity. Even the wisest philosophers taught that the heavens are composed of music, that there is a harmony of the spheres. Phaedo says that Socrates was writing verse just before death and that all his life he'd had a recurrent dream where Apollo encouraged him to keep on with his music. He had always taken this to mean he should carry on with philosophy. But now, with the hemlock before him, he was not so sure. So, as I say, let Castiglione's courtier learn music, to read and play it, in moderation, of course. He should not give the impression that music is his main occupation in life. I think it was Epictetus that said to spend too much time in exercise, eating, drinking, even evacuating the bowels or copulating is a mark of lack of refinement.'

Giuliano begins to extol the polyphonic excellences of the northern composers Guillame Dufay and Joskin Van de Velde. 'And what of the Venetian ambassador Girolamo Donato, poor man? They say he is more tuneful than Orpheus on his lyre, that he listens to birds and can sing with them, that he writes poetry and even composes music for performances, though privily as he fears it would not be fitting for a patrician. But I say, why not indeed? Why not?'

The bishop guffaws. 'Well, he should sing a pretty song indeed if he wishes to appease His Holiness. That, at least, I do not envy him.'

Hugh's attention drifts. He is distracted by Lady Emilia who has been teasing the bread\crumbs into a tidy cluster with her unbanded ring-finger. Her eyes often dart to Bembo, he thinks. *Bembo ought to get a wedding band on that finger. They could torment each other quite mercilessly to their hearts' content.* As soon as Giuliano finishes, Emilia looks from Bembo to Gian Cristoforo. 'What think you of this opinion? Do you admit that painting is susceptible of greater skill than sculpture?'

Gian Cristoforo, conscious of a trap and that his words might well be recorded by the eager-eyed Castiglione, gulps, and nervously fiddles with the midmost silk button on his doublet. 'I, my lady, think that sculpture needs more pains, more skill, and therefore may be said to be of greater dignity than painting.' He casts a wary eye about for approval.

Giuliano de Medici folds his arms and then places a careful knuckle under his chin. He begins to caress his beard and then shakes his head slightly. 'Let me answer that. As you know, my noble father's sculpture garden in Florence gave rise to such formidable genius as Michelangelo. Many times growing up I watched old Bertoldo, who knew Donatello and others, teaching the young men, and I have thought about these matters. It is true that statues are more enduring, so perhaps we might say they are of greater dignity. After all, if they are being made as memorials, they fulfil better than painting the purpose for which they are made. But besides serving as memorials, both painting and sculpture serve also to beautify, and in this respect painting is much superior, for if less diuturnal, so to speak, than sculpture, yet it is of very long life, and is far more charming so long as it endures.'

But almost before he has finished Gian Cristoforo exclaims, 'I think that you are speaking against your convictions, my lord, in that you speak in preferment of your friend Raphael. Perhaps the excellence you find in his painting seems to you so consummate that sculpture cannot rival it, but consider that this is praise of an artist and not of his art.'

The outburst of an impassioned sculptor in front of a superior is perhaps not so shocking to the party as the argument *ad hominem* about Raphael. Hugh sees Emilia smiling with pleasure at the raised eyebrows. She is still moving her little pile of crumbs left then right.

The young sculptor, perhaps emboldened that no one has seen fit to contradict, least of all Giuliano, continues with words almost tumbling out in the wrong order. 'It is, of course it is, you know, very fine. I do not deny it. How could I here, where he grew up and trained? Of course not. But it seems clear to me that both sculpture and painting are artificial imitations of nature. I do not see how you can say that truth, such as nature makes it, is not better imitated in a marble or bronze statue, wherein the members are round, formed, and measured, as nature makes them, than in a painting, where we see nothing but the surface and those colours that cheat the eyes. Nor will you tell me, surely, that *being* is not nearer truth than *seeming*. More, more, moreover I think sculpture is more difficult because if a slip is made, it cannot be corrected. You cannot patch marble as you can repaint a wooden panel or a fresco which you may change a thousand times, and add and take away, improving always. Always. I think.' The voice of the young sculptor, aware there are no nods, no murmurs of approval, is beginning to waver in confidence and trail off.

The duchess moves her left hand along the edge of the table toward Giuliano. He sees it from the corner of his eye, catches her smile and takes the hint. He looks toward young Romano and bursts into a laugh that makes even Emilia start. 'I am not speaking for Raphael's sake, signor. Nor ought you to repute me as so ignorant as not to know the excellence of Michelangelo in sculpture. He is a Florentine after all, and he came to us when he was sixteen. No, I am speaking of the art, and not of the artists. Anyone who does not esteem the art of painting seems to me to be quite wrong-headed. Why, doth not this whole world bespeak itself in beauty and diversity and immensity of the Creator's mighty artistry? In my opinion, whoever can imitate it deserves the highest praise. And in this I believe we have achieved in Italy a perfection in these last fifty years from which the next five hundred will scarce equal and surely never surpass. My own family's small part as patrons is, as I am sure it is for our hostess's noble family, a source of the greatest satisfaction.'

A small crease of a frown appears on Lady Emilia's forehead. 'And our artist knight? Does he have an opinion? Surely he does when he excels in all things. Come, signor, let us defer to you as our friend the ambassador would have us. Speak truth and we will submit.'

'My lady,' Hugh says quietly so that those at the other end of the table bend over with greater attention. He sees it and loathes the thought that perhaps they think he spoke quietly out of affectation. Bembo is muttering, 'Shots fired again', which irritates him further. *I've faced death in a hundred skirmishes and waded in the gore of my enemies, I'll not be unmanned or bated by this donna non amata with her pert smile, feral tongue and borrowed pearls.* He clears his throat so as to speak a little louder. 'At this moment and in this company, I am only aware of my own ignorance, and I would certainly not have anyone own my opinions on the matter.' Emilia opens her mouth with, no doubt, a well-rehearsed retort, but seeing it, Hugh speaks on. 'Accept this: on this subject as on all others, none of us speaks from, as it were, the outside, but from within our own native traditions and national tastes. It is good for us, in doubtful matters, to speak with circumspection. After all, we might later find ourselves guilty of the folly of the haberdasher's children who argue which blade of their father's scissors is sharper or more useful. Or of those who want to argue over which of the sexes were the greatest.'

Gaspare Pallavicino raises an eyebrow and then his goblet to be filled again, remarking to Canossa in an insolent manner, and at an unintended volume because of his inebriation, that as far as he is concerned, 'Women are only good for bearing children, keeping the keys, telling their beads, mending linen and cleaning the silver.'

The duchess, and the lady Emilia, neither of whom have been delivered of a living child, immediately remonstrate with the young man, and call upon Giuliano to defend them. This he does with verve, citing some of the women who excelled in philosophy and others who waged war and governed cities—Hypathia, Xenobia, Cleopatra etc. He admits that, as with men, some specimens are better examples than others. He references those coarse creatures who live only to scold their husbands and children, and who always shout like country wenches who bellow to their neighbours from hilltop to hilltop. 'Some are well known as the devourers of patrimonies and possess the morals of children, but of course that may be as much our fault as men, as theirs.'

'And if you could educate us all, noble lord, how would you have us pray?' Emilia's eyes are wide with something more than impish wit. They burn with a barely suppressed rage at the injustice she has seen. Before Giuliano can speak she cuts across him. 'Come, come. Verily I have read the books on how we should behave. That we should not display any more than six teeth, and that our lips should always have a dimple and not be too thin. We should greet no one in the street, never call out from the upper windows, and always wear topaz. That the softness of our skin should be pallid enough for a monk, yet comely enough for our youthful admirers; our sweetness charming enough for dinner parties and our spirit tempting enough for any duke or count. Above all this, and after bearing our sire's ten or more fine children – all sons – we should still possess the lightness of limb and thigh of Venus just born. You see my point, I hope? When you think of us, you think only of decoration and appendages to your illustrious personages. How many powders to clean the teeth? How many boxes and phials of ointments to cleanse the hands? You men will go quickly to your slumbers tonight – or is it near morning? – while we women must stay up further to give treatments that our hands may be smooth as alabaster for your delectation. Long after your noble snoaring fills these corridors, our maids will be heating lemon with water and white sugar, adding mustard, apple and bitter almonds, that we may rub it on our hands and then put on our chamois-leather gloves which we must always sleep in. You may well snigger, Signor Pallavicino, but we do all this for you men each night. And then rise each morn to wash them dutifully with water and benzoin oil. Sometimes maybe even sweet almond oil and white wax and camphor! And with all these and many more remedies we must travel too. One could fit out a ship from stem to stern in less time. All this and more we must do in our fight against nature and our competition for your approbation.'

More comments follow about the efficacious nature of comfry and other remedies, but Hugh is hardly listening now. Rather his eye is captured by Elisabetta's dolorous, chestnut eyes as they flicker carefully about the table guests. They remind him of Felice's the night she talked of the death of her child. They suffer, women do, from the belly outwards. Perhaps to be a woman is in the end to know that the world will break your heart, whether you bare children or not. Most are widowed by fifty, if they survive childbearing. It is a mystery how they bear it all. They are a mystery.

Pallavicino is trying to laugh it off. Someone has attributed his misogyny to his failed attempts to woo a certain lady. He deflects by saying Giuliano is of the same opinion and that he only flatters the ladies present. It goes on and on, in a weary tit for tat. Eventually, Pallavicino begs pardon. 'It was the wine, I swear it. How could I mean it in the presence of such ladies? Does not the Apostle Paul himself say we are equal? The first mention in ancient literature. Isn't that so

Signor Bembo? I am sure it is. Look, he's nodding. So let that be an end of it; the scriptures and Bembo have spoken.'

Emilia turns to Elisabetta. 'Perhaps he is sincere, my lady. Maybe he does hold Fra Erpingham's position after all, that men and women are complementary like his scissors. But I doubt the English knight really believes it despite his protestations.'

Elisabetta shakes her head. 'Emilia, you do our guest a great disservice, and you know it. Forgive her, signor. She has an over-exercised wit and does not mean it.'

'Oh, but I do mean it,' Emilia says. 'Or don't you know he is the oldest son of his family's line and yet, so I am informed, he refused an advantageous match, and all so he could join the knights, that he might chase Turks about with his little sword. Let him deny it if it is not true. Surely if he were to stand by the sentiments he expressed he would have honoured the marriage his parents arranged for him, rather than be a lone scissor cutting up Saracens right under the sultan's nose. Come now, Fra Hugh, why do you look so? Do you wish to frighten me because I tease an irreproachable knight of Rhodes? It will not work, I tell you. I have faced the wrath of Bembo and survived his heat. And besides, surely a mere woman is beneath your contempt.'

Hugh clenches his fists under the table. How did she know that? Who told her of the betrothal? He places his hands together back on the table, fingers joined, thumbs rubbing each other. *I will not be provoked. I will not be – damn her. In front of all these people, too. Damn her. Who is she anyway?*

Through the fog of his own anger and the coiling black serpent of his own injured pride, Hugh feels the salvic touch of the duchess's feather-like fingers on his wrist. 'Tell me, Fra Hugh, if you agree with me.' Above the tuts and whispers she speaks as all become immediately silent. Her voice is the equipoise: gentleness and authority. 'I always thought, that despairing Dido is the most haunting and enduring image of that lost world of our ancestors. How our sympathies are torn—' She looks up, at the other guests, gazing steadily for a moment in each of their eyes. 'We, the descendants and heirs of those first Romans. We know, as does Aeneas that he must sail away from Carthage to found the city of Rome. Does he know that his destiny, his ambition will be the death of her? I do not know. But he sails into the sunrise of a new and glorious future while she is left with her curses, a cold sword and funerary pyre. I think men often kill the thing they love without knowing it, just by following the course of honour. I don't say it as a condemnation. I do not think it is my place to be the judge – or any of us. To be a public man in our age, perhaps any age, is very difficult. Consider: Aeneas broke Dido's heart and *his* mother was Venus. So you see, it is difficult, is it not? What we women want from men seems incompatible sometimes. Perhaps a man is wiser and freer to pursue his public duty without the encumbrance and distraction of the hearth. Perhaps that man is kinder, Emilia, and not to be teased.'

And then it happens, the transformation in Lady Emilia's face. The words of the duchess work like a magic salve, and all the tension and bitterness temporarily ease around Emilia's eyes and mouth. 'Oh,' she exclaims, 'would to God that I had been born a man. What a thing it is to be a woman. Surely we bear the burden of Eve's transgression more than a man does Adam's. We live as secluded virgins or secluded matrons. We have no prime as you men do, only a season of ripe virginity followed by a season of overripe maturity, divided only by a wedding night. It is not just, I say, when you men may have such freedom. Why may I not lead armies and take cities for my honour?'

Bembo is chuckling for he knows her too well. 'Because as you well know and as Galen attests, you did not receive enough heat in your mother's womb. We may doubt it in your case, but nevertheless your monthlies are proof that even you have not enough heat to burn up the excess fluids. We men on the other hand are furnaces under pressure – '

'We have heard enough wisdom from you, signor,' Emilia retorts. 'What we want to hear, what the ambassador wants to hear and no doubt squirrel away for his book, is whether an elite man like Fra Erpingham – yes, I use the word elite, from the Greek *eligo*, released – does a released man, a man whose life is filled with honour and purpose, still notice us weaker vessels as they sail to glory in the path of honour? We often wonder it of saints too. Does Venus still work upon them and you as upon other mortals?' At a guffaw from Bembo, she looks straight at Hugh and adds, 'Do not heed him, my lord. I ask as an honest maiden, as one who would be your friend.'

'*Timeo Danaos et dona ferentis,* beware of Greeks, even bearing gifts, Hugh. *Timeo*!' Bembo says.

Hugh gathers his wits. He blinks and tilts his goblet, rolling it on its base slightly as he speaks demurely but gets louder as he continues. 'Yes, of course, I notice. *Homo sum: humani nil a me alienum puto,* I am a human being and nothing human is strange to me. We, that is, I, have forgone the comforts of the hearth so that I may dedicate myself to a certain end, but of course...' Hugh searches for the prudent way of expressing it. He tilts his head and looks at the glass, and then it comes to him for the stem looks like the swaying mast of a skif. 'The crew of Odysseus had their ears stopped with wax, but he himself was lashed to the mast with his ears open. I cannot speak for others, and certainly not for saints, my lady, but perhaps I am like Odysseus; I have made my sacred vows and with those I am lashed to the mast of my choice.'

'As a young man you made them.'

'Yes, as a young man and perhaps as I gain years, I glimpse more fully those comforts, those loves which I have forgone – a wife, children, a country here on earth to call my own. But I trust God, my lady, that he sees it and will recompense.'

'Still, it is a great oath to take as a young man.' Emilia's voice has softened for perhaps her own imagination is now at work. Perhaps she has fought the chains of her gender for so long that it comes almost as a new thought: what would I actually do with a man's freedom? Certainly not give it away as this man has done surely. She speaks now with a broken voice. 'When did you consider such a pledge?'

'To myself? The first time I read Homer.' Hugh smiles and looks straight at her, and past her into the far distant memories of his own. A twelve-year-old boy sitting under a laden pear tree, having escaped a beating from his tutor. Sweet fruit and epic poetry. Bliss. 'War was glorious to a boy seeing it only between velum pages.'

'And as a man?'

Hugh cannot answer. *They know,* he thinks, *they all know. Let them see my face and they will know. Everyone wants to be Hugh Erpingham except me. Every schoolboy from Cadiz to Paris wants to be me, or someone like me, to have songs and stories multiplied about them like the corpses they dream of piling up to honour God.* He does remember moments of sublime glory and comradeship, but even they now seem like the memories of another. The worm of Vendramin's accusations have fastened onto his mind. *I will find him. You do not just opt out of an oath. You do not just choose to be free of obligations because you have decided to be a law of conscience unto yourself. I will find him. I will find my accuser, the one who seeks to break apart all I've worked for, given my life for, my damned conscience.* 'I will find him.'

'Signor? Fra Erpingham? Find who?'

'My lady?' Hugh comes to with a start. *Did I speak?*

'Leave off now, Emilia,' the duchess says, 'As Italy descends yet again into conflict we shall be reminded soon enough anyway.' The duchess' voice trails off as there appear, at least to Hugh, those familiar ghosts in her eyes.

Emilia however has not seen but seizes the gap to speak again. 'I am sure we shall, and well I remember the night when Cesare Borgia came here and we took flight from him. How our gentle lord, your husband was forced to flee over the mountains. It is all monstrous, and it is usually we women who are left to bear the burden of famine, siege, the bereavement of sons, husbands and fathers.' Emilia glances up to see her mistress' face. 'Oh my lady, and here I am talking in the abstract while your poor brother Francesco and of course our most beloved sister Isabella...' She rolls the r's and labours the s's while saying *soror amantissima*, reaching out her hand in comfort to Elisabetta. 'While they are up there in Mantua, pressed between the great powers. How you must feel for them. War, this war. It is all monstrous, I say, and yet...' She turns her eye back on Hugh and speaks without any further sisterly affectation. 'My original point was, rather, how can a boy who knows little of the world be asked to make commitments so young?'

Elisabetta says, 'I do not think that is necessarily true, my dear. I was always struck by the words of Abbess Hildegard who, you know, took vows to be an anchorite at seven. She says that parents may lead a child toward such a vocation – she likens their role as a bridle about a horse's neck. But she says the child must have taken the bit between his or her teeth for the lifetime's commitment to be successful. Many children are apprenticed at those ages anyway; it is little different.'

'Aye, and many noble women are married or betrothed, too.'

'My dear lady,' says Bembo. 'I can see there is nothing for it but you make vows. Yes, take vows, attach yourself to a nunnery, be a virgin of Christ. Virginity is an honourable estate. The very word Parthenon meant virginity, and did not the light of our Roman civilisation go forth from the flame of Vesta? Take vows lady, and you shall be unharmed by the passion of the lion and the horn of the unicorn. You will drive all before you like the pikes of the Swiss, like Alexander's phalanxes. Get thee to a nunnery, and you can then be free of us men, as Hildegard was. And as a bride of Christ you will find a husband of infinite patience – which you will need, of course.'

Before Emilia can give her retort, the bishop, who up until now has been cracking walnuts noisily and eating them almost constantly, is roused with a scowl of either indignation or indigestion. 'What? Saint Bernard was too easily won over by that woman. Did you know that her nuns dressed like princesses, on feast days. That's right, princesses in white silk gowns and gold crowns, hair unshorn, worn long, with many rings and bracelets on their arms that clinked and clanked as they processed into church, like it were some Babylonish pageant.'

'Oh, but I fear it is worse than that, my good bishop.' Emilia looks at him with the sort of mock seriousness that only someone like him could mistake. 'I read somewhere, or perhaps heard from one of the serving girls, I cannot now recall, that Hildegard called on Christ to be to her as a mighty lion-lover whom she enjoined to rend the skies and come down to her in *aulum virginis*, virgin's vestibule, to make the word flesh in her.'

'Pah, it is as I say.' The bishop raises and waggles a well fleshed finger upon which sits a sizeable emerald ring. 'The Alamani are a vulgar and barbaric race, without taste. Rude of speech and thought.'

Elisabetta looks not at him but at her glass. 'But really, my lord, you are too harsh when even the writer of the Song of Songs in the Bible writes in similar terms.'

'Yes, well, the Song of Solomon is a difficult book to interpret, and perhaps – '

'"I am my beloved's and he is mine. Grazing among the lilies." Has such a ring to it,' Bembo says with an impish tone in his voice. Perhaps, Hugh thinks, he is rescuing the bishop from inconveniencing the party by saying something rash. 'I do not think such mutuality, such equality had ever been expressed before in ancient literature. As far as I know there is nothing quite like it in Greece and Rome. No, I am sure there isn't. It is like a clarion call, shocking to us in our current state but obviously not for the hearers of their day. Lady Emilia may take hope that there is yet felicity to be found in the conjugal state.'

Emilia says, 'I will take hope, signor, on the day you take vows, become a monk, a knight, anything. Only spare the weaker sex, I pray you, your unwanted attentions.'

'Nonsense,' says Castiglione. 'The pair of you should be wed one to another, for we all know there would be scant pleasure in this life if it were not for women, Bembo. And besides, by marriage you would spare the misery you might otherwise inflict on two monastic houses.'

'Why Castiglione, that is a very fine idea. For has she not the mind and soul of a man?' Bembo says.

'Hah,' Emilia snaps back. 'No doubt the highest compliment you could pay a woman, sir. But I say better your insincere compliments than your sincere criticism.'

'Come, come. Let us not quibble, darling. What say you, *midons*? Would you submit to me as lord and do my laundry? For as you know a poet's life is a harsh one.'

'It is hard on your small clothes at least, my lord,' Emilia says. 'For verily, you spend your life sitting on them and, indeed, you are so full of wind that it is a wonder that there should be anything left for me to wash.'

'All true, I must own it,' Bembo says, beaming from ear to ear. 'But surely one less obstruction between our final *rencontre*. So marry me. Submit to trial by ordeal. Give in to Eros, give in I say. Why battle a god?'

She tosses her head. 'I wonder whether he refers to himself or Eros? A poet's head is so full of fancies.'

'And his heart, my lady; that may be full, too?'

'Pah, full all right. It is the wine speaking. It is wine that pricks you on. You are all talk, but you will sleep anon.'

'Why talk you of pricks when I talk courtship?' Bembo pretends to be aghast. 'You must learn to take matters forward more slowly, my love.'

'I am not your love, nor could I submit to a man who does not truly hold me as his equal.'

'Oh my love, I, your slave, would not have you trade at less a rate. But surely surrender is also necessary for a woman's happiness, and dare I say, pleasure.'

'You would not know or ever know, my lord. Be content to look and tease, for your words pierce no hearts here. We know you, Signor Bembo. We know you of old.'

'Alas, friends, you see I am undone. I am as the tragic lover Diego of Teruel. He loved the fairest and most submissive of maidens that ever graced the courts of Aragon. But he was of a poor family and lightly esteemed.'

'Perhaps his father was a poet,' Emilia says.

'Aha, very good but hear anon. "Five years," says Don Seguras the maiden's father. "You have five years to make your fortune before you can marry my daughter." So he goes his way and five years pass. Isabella waits in her window – as no doubt Lady Emilia waits for me when I, by cruel circumstance, am torn from Urbino – but there is no sign of Diego's return. "Alas," she says, "for I am undone and must marry my father's other choice, even though he is an old knight." And so Don Seguras prepares the wedding feast for that very evening for Isabella and the elderly knight. But after the ceremony and during the great feast, who should appear laden with gold? Yes, it is Diego who had counted the five years from the day he had left, not the night before when he had received the charge. And so here he is, arrived too late. And what does he do? What can he do? What would you do, or I do? I will tell you. That night he creeps into her bridal chamber and begs for just one kiss. "*Besame, que me muero*. Kiss me for I am dying." But she, remembering her vows, turns away. How could a pure maiden break a vow made before the altar? At this second rejection, poor Diego falls dead at her feet.' Bembo places a theatrical backhand upon his brow. 'Alas, the cruelty of fate and the fidelity of women. And thus the wedding is followed by a funeral. But that is not all my lady, for Isabella, seeing the bier passing, halts it before all – her father and husband. In front of them all she bends and kisses Diego tenderly on the lips. And then drops dead herself. Thus those *amantes* of Teruel – so cruelly separated in life, as Lady Emilia and I are – were united in death. And thus seems my own fate. What tragedy.'

Emila laughs. 'Your tragedy, signor, is that you were not born a *jocateur, jongleur* or a fool.'

Bembo replies, 'And yours, my lady, that you were not born a queen, or better a king even, for I would gladly then have been your fool.'

'You have been fool enough for us and the kings of France. Away with you.'

'And you have a tongue equal to the queens of France. Truly we should marry and live happily ever after.'

'So you say, my lord. But we have read your *Asolani* and all your lofty hymns to Cupid. From your own pen, via Signor Perottino, you say that *amore,* love, will turn *amare,* bitter, in the end, if not in you then certainly in the poor object of your affection.'

'Too harsh, too harsh,' Bembo replies. 'In book two, Gismondo finds true and lasting love as shall we.'

'And in book three, Lavinello refutes them both with Platonic idealism, and so if our marriage should follow the pattern of your book, then we shall end up spending all our time contemplating the eternal beauty in each other's love, and who then will be left to launder your small clothes?'

The guests, who have up until now been laughing and cajoling the two paramours, now erupt with roars of unrestrained mirth. Giuliano de Medici roars through his tears. 'Give in Bembo, give in, or we shall all die of asphyxiation.'

Emilia is staring between Bembo and the others, but always back at him. Her eyes are aflame with the approbation, and her lips curl into a tight smile. Bembo keeps looking like he wishes to speak above the noise and have the last word, but the others drown him out on purpose. He stands to give an oration, but Canossa and Romano pull him back into his chair. He begins to smile and then bursts into fits. Even the bishop is laughing, and also the duchess who shakes her head at her friend. The only other that seems to be laughing out of politeness, Hugh thinks, is Castiglione. The beleaguered ambassador sits at his end of the table looking on in a dissatisfied, matronly manner, like a teacher whose pupils will not cooperate. *He won't be recording this for his book. More's the pity.*

Into the order restored by Castiglione, the duchess nods to one of the retainers who in turn opens the door to others who file in with trays, plates and platters laden with sweet meats: pastes, cakes, biscotti, tarts, leaches, candy, marmalets, milk gnocchi, almond stuffed peaches and royal marchpanes. The conversation drifts for the following hours between various literary projects, the current political situation and the nature of true love. *Do they do this every night here?* Hugh takes less of a part, but even so is surprised when night fades into the cool blue light of dawn. By now the guests are not all at the same table but rather in the window seats holding private conversations or else leaning against the mantelpiece.

Hugh looks round to see Castiglione scratching words with a reed in a notebook at a small desk that he has pulled up to a window seat. He gets up to stretch his legs and walks alongside the ambassador, glancing over his shoulder. 'One minute, *caro*,' Castiglione does not look but re-dips his reed. 'I have just had some thoughts about my book's end and didn't want to miss the moment.'

He doesn't seem to mind Hugh leaning over him, so Hugh reads for himself as the words take shape in the notebook in a very uneven hand.

THE MORNING AS REMEMBERED BY CASTIGLIONE

So when the windows on the side of the palace that faces the lofty peak of Mount Catria had been opened, they saw that the dawn had already come to the east, with the beauty and colour of a rose, and all the stars had been scattered, save only the lovely mistress of heaven, Venus, who guards the confines of night and day. From there, there seemed to come a delicate breeze, filling the air with biting cold, and among the murmuring woods on neighbouring hills wakening the birds into joyous song. Then all, having taken leave of the duchess, went to their rooms, without torches, for the light of day was sufficient.

Baldasarre Castiglione, *Il Cortegiano*

AUGUST 21ST 1509 THE DUKE'S *STUDIOLO*, URBINO

The duchess perches on a low stool in the corner of her late husband's private study. Hugh has been here many times over the past month, to read, to write, to think. It is his favourite room in the palace. *The books this place has! I could live a thousand lives here. Is it wrong to be like that? Is this only for the man who would escape this world? No. Surely not.* Hugh knows what that feels like right enough, but the desire to study is surely an acknowledgment that this world in all its dimensions is rich almost beyond words and worthy of exploration. These libraries, these great palaces and noble courts do honour the Creator as much as Francis. Hugh feels caught between Francis, Aquinas, and Augustine – pulled between the polarities of this triangle. Perhaps all Christendom is.

He closes the door carefully, and as he turns to her, lets his eye survey the wondrous marquetry designed to make solid panels look like opened lattice doors, and cupboards filled with musical or scientific instruments, or an alcove with a statue of the Virgin, or even a cage of birds. It never ceases to fill him with wonder each time he enters, though today his eye is quickly drawn to the slumped shoulders and shrunken demeanour of the duchess.

'Fra Erpingham, how good of you to come.' She is holding an opened letter in hand and casting a baleful eye about the cabinets and bookshelves and then above them to the paintings of various prelates, dukes and kings as if imploring them for succour. She releases a pent up breath and lets her eyes settle once more on her lap, and the letter. As he approaches, he discerns the redness of former tears about her eyes and also the *scorpione* insignia on the wax seal. He knows by some ineffable twist of the cursed fates that this letter will somehow involve him, and the premonition, such as it is, sends a shudder throughout an already heavy-laden soul.

'My lady?' He bows gently.

'Please.' She motions to a walnut chair next to the writing desk. 'I come here sometimes when I know no one else will be here, when you are all out hawking and whatever else. It is right for these apartments to be what use they can, and I am happy that you men find them so agreeable. My husband would have wanted it, I am sure. But still I do come myself sometimes as I used to in the former days of our happiness. This was his retreat, you know.' She lets her white fingers caress the wooden panel to her right, but pulls them back to her lap when they touch an area where the sun has blistered and curled the marquetry. 'Here the pressures of the world did not impinge, not much anyway. He was always calmer here. I know people say that he was irritable and often fractious, but that was because of the pain that vexed him. They did not know him truly, not as a wife knows. Here, in this little room, he was his true self. He never raised his voice here. I always fancied that if I came alone to see him here, he would always grant me my request. I seem to remember him telling me as much once, but now I am not sure; perhaps I imagined the memory. As time passes it gets harder to hold the threads together. Even the portraits seem not to be him but some other man.'

'I am sorry for your loss.'

'Thank you.' She gives a weak smile. 'We had hoped to grow old together; his father achieved a good age. But there it is. My burden is light compared to others. But...' She sighs and reaches out her hand toward the window and angles it back and forth gently. 'I fear I grow shallow, walled up here in my widowhood – like a plant cultivated indoors with brackish roots and always shifting its foliage to capture any glimpse of sunlight from outside. I remember a relative telling me that being a young widow is like death by drowning – delightful enough if you cease struggling. And I am trying to be pious in resignation, but it does not come naturally.' She glances at the desk suddenly as if catching herself in a day dream. She moves a stray hair from her eye, smiling as she does so. A sweet smile of remembrance. 'Once I even spilled his ink over a letter he had almost written, a long letter, but even then he was not angry here. Even then he responded to my request. He was sitting right where you are now at that desk.'

'I am glad for your happy memories,' Hugh says, shifting uncertainly in his seat. 'I heard that the duke was greatly respected.' It is not quite true, but he is hardly going to repeat what he has heard of the deceased in his own house in front of his widow.

She smiles thinly as if she knows all his thoughts. 'He was less the warrior than his father, but even so I wish he were here now in this time of distress.'

'My lady?' Hugh leans forward. 'Is it this letter?'

She nods pursing her lips so as to hold back more tears. 'My sister-in-law has written from Mantua.'

'The Marchesa Isabella Gonzaga?'

Elisabetta nods again without looking at him but rather at the letter which she unfolds. 'At first she writes with news from England. Can you believe it—England? Your new king is to marry his dead brother's wife which will make our friends in Aragon happy, she says. They should be crowned together later this month, and one of our Tuscan sculptors, Torrigiano, will carve the old king's tomb in their great abbey in London. All this she writes before she tells me of my brother's fate at the hands of the Venetians.'

'Your brother, my lady?' Hugh starts, remembering the night of Bramante's party when the marquis, victor of the Battle of Fornovo, one of Christendom's most noble and honoured knights, and the only one to answer the insolence of Frankish might, sending them packing over the alps – Yes, he, the Marchese of Mantua, rode up the spiral ramp with the marchesa. A sudden shifting of the clouds to the south allow a shaft of sharp morning light to pierce the room and make everything suddenly strange, intended even.

'He was captured while riding with his men, not more than a hundred. They were surrounded, and he is now held in that vile dungeon next to the doge's palazzo. He has written to her to say they have given him a cell on the ground floor and that when they have an *aqua alta*, which they will have many times as winter draws on, then the water will be two feet high in his cell and he will surely die of the cold and miasmic vapours.' She flings the letter on the ground and kicks it away with her foot. 'He is a marchese. He has generaled their armies before now, and they treat him thus. Oh, my poor wretched brother.'

'Take comfort, my lady, for I am sure his captors merely wish to create an effect so as to obtain the ransom money quicker.'

'But she will not pay it in any case.' She looks at him frantically, her eyes wild with a childish terror. 'She only writes now to tell me how it is so I can prepare for the worst. Oh, she is such a woman, but I do not blame her, not really. She has borne so much from him, so many infidelities, ones never specified in the pre-nuptial contract. Poor Isabella, but who could have predicted that Borgia woman? My brother was ill equipped to resist her siren charm. And now what? Should Isabella bankrupt Mantua for a man who has treated her thus when she has sons of her own and such a head for politics as he has not, nor I? She has eclipsed him, and for all his bravery, and for all his former glory, the world will soon forget him. Mantua is better off, they will say. He has the French disease, and his mind has become unreliable. That is the way people speak. The pope will not give a *scudi* for his release. That is the way it is. You are indispensable until you are not. Poor Isabella! I blame her not; we are like sisters, but oh, my poor Francesco. Though the world forget you, can your sister forget—she whom you cradled in your arms? I cannot stand by and let his life end thus – like a drowning rat. He is my brother, kind and brave, and I am resolved to help him if I can.'

Hugh feels tingles all over his spine and down to his fingers. 'Help him, my lady?'

'Yes, I am determined to exert all my powers in his defence. But I know that a woman's power, such as it is, is quite insufficient in such a case as this. Even if I were to throw myself at Doge Loredan's feet, offer myself in exchange and all I have, it would not be sufficient. Who can even approach *La Serrenissima* now they are at war? We are for the moment their implacable enemies. Any embassage from the Papal States would be met with extreme prejudice. I suddenly find myself in a position where nothing I have or do can help. Have you ever been in such a position? So, I said, my person and my wealth are all but dust in this case, worse than dust, and yet I still have connections. For, thought I, there is one who stands outside this conflict, who may yet act on my behalf, whom I may yet petition, whom I may not be so proud as to beseech with all my heart.' She clasps her praying hands to her bosom which heaves with emotion as she speaks. 'Yes, this I may yet do.'

Hugh looks toward the statue of the Madonna and nods piously. 'Yes, my lady, God is merciful.'

'I know he is, signor, but are you? Did you think it was of God I spoke just now? I spoke of you. Why the very timing of your coming here.'

'Me?'

'The knights are neutral, foresworn not to fight other Christians. You have your reputation, a fine priory in Venice to visit on the *Rio della Pieta*. I remember the place from happier times. Why not visit Venice while on your grand tour? What could be more natural? I seem to remember you saying that you wished to visit when the war is concluded, but why not now?'

'But my lady, I am hardly – ' The words die on his lips even as she pursues her assault.

'Who better than you, signor? Who else is there anyway? The doge will no doubt be pleased to receive you as an ambassador from a neutral sovereign state, you will be immune from suspicion – you are Hugh Erpingham. You could request access to my brother, devise a plan. Forgive me, signor. I know I am speaking as if I were beside myself. Perhaps I am, but with my husband gone, well that is to say, I am only a woman, a sister – Do you have sisters? Yes, you do, you spoke of them. Can you imagine how they worry about you, how they suffer?' The duchess drops to her knees before him, all her elegance and leonine dignity melting away in a flood of tears and entreaties. She clasps his hands in hers. She looks up through her tears. 'You will help me, say you will. I know you to be a man of endeavour. You will think of something I am sure. Only do not deny me my last hope. Not while you sit in that chair, in this place. I beg you.'

'Please, don't.' Hugh casts his eye about the room, flailing about inside his soul like a landed fish. He instinctively turns his hands over to take hers in his. He does not think of who might suddenly come in or who might be listening. Convention, mores, the whole world disappear when one human being is reaching out in the darkness to another. *You can say what you like, Bembo, about platonic love, aye, wax lyrical about it and denigrate what you call the lower loves of earth, but if the touch of a woman's hand can make a man feel like this, call forth such virtue as this, then the half has not been told of the joys of marriage.* Her hands are warm, delicate, yielding, and yet they clench his fingers tight as if they were a rope and she were drowning, which she definitely is. Her soul has weathered the bereavement of the children stillborn and unborn, and now a husband buried. These she has born, but the unknown and accumulated sorrows of the future, looming and ominous, may yet sink her. There is no greater sadness than to remember happiness. *Who said that? Dante probably.* He squeezes her hand resolutely. The connection has been made. What else can he do?

Queen takes knight. Check mate.

PART II - THE DEVIL'S WHORE

BOLOGNA, PALAZZO LEGATO, SEPTEMBER 15TH

After Urbino, the stone ramp they ascend towards the cardinal legate's palace seems more than a bit – as Bembo put it – *rusticci*. Mind you, after Urbino, everything does. Below them, beyond the inner courtyard, garrisons of soldiery litter the *Piazza Maggiore* in never ending clusters of discontent. They had all expected to be rich by now; feasting in the *Palazzo Ducale* and lounging about in the *Piazza San Marco* – not here waiting like beggars for the onset of winter.

Hugh and Bembo turn a corner of the ascent, and somewhere below them Hugh hears men shouting. He glances down in case it means trouble. The noise comes from between the Swiss guards' quarters and those of the light infantry, who are similarly billeted on the lower loggia of the vast, red sandstone palace. Bembo trips on a raised stone, and curses. 'We'd have been better bringing the horses and mules up here with us. Bloody safer. I nearly went headlong just then.'

They pass the great studded doors into a hall, seventy feet long, roofed with painted oak beams and plasterwork stained by leaks. Fifty or so people, ambassadors and the like, well-heeled but weary looking, are dotted about the place in clusters, whispering and occasionally casting furtive glances. Beyond the next doors, some seventy feet off, are the papal legate's apartments, temporary court of Julius. The bear pit.

'Cheery as a wake,' Bembo says, hands on hips. Hugh follows the poet's eyes toward the windows on the right where the shutters are peeling. Hugh then notices a man on a low scaffold talking down to the only gentleman. 'Ah, the Venetian ambassador, Girolamo Donato. What happy providence; I know him. Do you remember how Giuliano de Medici praised him that evening in Urbino? Yes, you remember. His music and poetry. I'm sure the half has not been told. Come on; come, Hugh. If anyone can ease your access to Venice it is he, but let me do the talking. And remember whatever your initial impressions, everything with him is calculated for effect.'

'What, even the black and gold surcoat,' Hugh says with a smirk. 'Looks like an exotic beetle.'

Hugh and Bembo approach the slightly hunched man in his fifties, wearing a black velvet surcoat. The garment is gathered at the waist with a belt and embroidered with sections of gold brocade so that from a distance it looks like a map of golden islands on a black sea. In contrast, he wears a simple linen chemise, pleated and gathered at the neck with draw chords ending with two large pearls. When nearer Hugh sees that the older man's fingers rest on the scaffold, tapping out a rhythm. He and the fresco artist are conversing in French, and the latter is explaining that the fresco is to commemorate the earthquake that shook the city a few years back. Hugh observes the likeness, and it is well wrought. Not perhaps the two hundred patrician towers and fifteen gates that the city is famed for but certainly a few towers piercing the rooftops and fair indication of the most important or at least the oldest university in the world. It is not an easy thing to attempt such detail in fresco. Hugh should not like to attempt it himself, at least not with others looking on. But this artist seems happy to pass pleasantries and let others observe.

As Hugh and Bembo approach, the artist doffs his cap, causing the ambassador to turn and see who is coming. A knowing smile creases the already creased face, making the points of his *moustachio* tilt upwards and his long nose flare at the nostrils.

Bembo bows. 'Pietro Bembo. Grace and peace to you, Ambassador.'

'Signor Bembo.' Donato steps forward without bowing and takes him heartily by the arm so that Hugh can hear he is wearing a plate harness under his coat. *He fears more than just harsh words.* He talks quickly. 'My dear fellow, of course. How long has it been? Eight, ten years? How are you? You look well, yes, very well. I cannot tell you how much my wife and I enjoyed your *Gli Asolani*. To our shame we only read it last winter after our return from Crete – the life of a governor gives one little time for recreation I can tell you. It was given to us by dear Caterina Cornaro when we stayed with her at Asoli. Can you believe it? So we actually started reading it during our stay, you know, in the very place where you set your story. Can you believe it? Signora Donato was most diverted by it, I can tell you, and not a few of the signorinas too. She says we talk too little of love. She often says that, but with nine children, signors, nine children, our conversation more naturally runs to education and positions for them all, marriages and so forth. Oh, the cares of this world. Contemplating those higher platonic plains you write of so well, signor, can seem a long way away sometimes. But listen to me going on like this when you have not introduced your companion. Forgive me, please, but these days my job is to say little and be shouted at much from all sides.'

'Not at all, Ambassador, not at all. This is my dear friend Fra Hugh Erpingham of Rhodes.'

Hugh bows and so does the ambassador, removing his brown velvet beret. His face showing a wide-eyed surprise which he does not try to conceal.

'So it is to you, signor, that I must give my thanks. The scourge of the sultan and the corsair. My children shall want to know that I have met you. Indeed they shall. We who have lived in the jaws of the Turk, as we did as your neighbours on Crete, understand in a special way the need to repress these rapacious heathen. Why, it is not ten years since their fleet was blocking even the lagoon of Venice. They only grow in insolence and rub their hands to see Christian nations weakening each other in war. It is an *annus terribilis*, signori, *annus horibilis*, when the lords of Christendom join together to achieve our destruction. But enough of that, I know already of your mission, Fra Erpingham.'

For a moment Hugh reads from the man's grey-eyed stare that the ambassador really does know all. There is something in the movement and insinuation of his eyebrows that suggests he knows more than he says. Remembering Bembo's warning, Hugh bows slightly. 'Then you will know, signor, that we are of a mind you and I. That this current war should be speedily concluded and the real enemy countered by land and sea. I myself have seen – '

'Yes, I know, the sultan's new fleet being assembled and expanded in the arsenals of Gallipoli. I have heard these things, and I should say you would like to take this news before the council in Venice, before Doge Loredan, too, perhaps. Yes, it can be arranged.'

Bembo raises an eyebrow. 'I see you have read our every thought and intention, signor.'

'Well, they didn't send me here to talk about my children and Signor Bembo's literary endeavours, however much I would prefer to do so.' He sighs theatrically. 'And seeing I have little leisure for speaking, I have all the more to listen.'

'And to whom have you been listening, do tell?' Hugh says, trying not to sound irritated, or sarcastic – which for him is a feat in itself. He throws his riding cloak over his other arm, using the opportunity to see if anyone else in the room is listening to them. 'Come, we are all ears.'

'Oh, this one and that one. Really, I don't want you to be offended. I am not your enemy. *Dio Mio*, don't you think I have enough trouble of my own? No, but take my advice as a somewhat independent observer: be on your guard, you have as many enemies in there as I do, my friend. And not just there either.' He motions to the far doors.

Hugh puts his free hand on his hips and spreads his legs slightly. 'Care to be more specific?'

'No, indeed. That is all I am prepared to say. But if you wish for safe passage to Venice, I can arrange it for you. My personal guarantee of safe passage, for what it is worth in such perilous times.'

Hugh is about to press the point, but Bembo speaks over him. 'That is very kind of you, Ambassador, very kind of you indeed.'

'Not at all.' He bows with elegance, concluding in a lower voice, 'Frankly it is refreshing to be busy at anything rather than await my next mauling from His Holiness. The way across the frontier is not an easy one these days, but I can give you a letter with my seal. You, as a citizen of our republic, Signor Bembo, and you, signor, with your diplomatic immunity, should be as safe as any. Of course, both sides will think you are a spy even if you give them your word as a knight and a gentlemen, but what can we do, *O tempora! O mores!* Oh, the times, the morals!' Donato breaks off speaking as new steps approach.

Hugh turns to see the equine visage and pigeon chest of Angelo Colocci, the papal secretary, approaching at speed. After the faintest homage, and other sinister expressions of goodwill, he says, 'Where have you been? His Holiness was expecting you before mass. Come at once please.'

'And it is a pleasure to find you in health, Angelo.' Bembo remarks. 'Does not this northern air agree with you? For my part I find it bracing, if a little damp, though certainly less miasmic than Rome.'

'I said, where have you been?'

'Why, admiring this fresco, of course.'

Colocci ignores Bembo's jest and beckons with hurried arms. 'Come away at once, will you? Forgive us, Ambassador, but His Holiness is very busy today.'

Donato bows. 'Then let me not be the cause of further vexation.'

Slap, slap, slap. Colocci's slippers flap and snap on the boards as the crowd divides before him. Slap, slap, slap. Hugh and Bembo follow with set faces and tightening stomachs. Hugh had not wanted this, but you can't pass through the Romagna during wartime without everyone knowing your business. The governor of every town from San Marino to Bologna knew that the pope was looking for Hugh. Letters had been sent. Now he's here, waiting for a mauling of his own. Slap, slap, slap. Hugh hears the whispers left and right: it is the knight from Rhodes. He hears, or thinks he even hears the name Vendramin uttered. He shoots a glance in the direction of the voice but sees only ambassadors and smiles. Ambassadors and smiles—that is Bologna. The war has seen such unlikely reversals in the last months that he bets some of them are wondering whether they ought not rather be down near the fresco scaffold making overtures to the Venetian ambassador, themselves. Slap, slap, slap. Colocci waves aside the halberds at the door and turns the iron handle which gives an unlikely squeak, then clank. The smell of oak, wax, lock oil and then the wafts of wood smoke and yesterday's mop water rise in Hugh's nostrils as they pass through.

The chamber is large enough to garrison a number of tables and desks at which or around which sit and stand the pope's advisors. Rays of light from the large gothic windows pierce the smoke that sporadically escapes the marble fireplaces when the wind outside gusts. The glass and lead-work and window tracery seem to almost want to implode at one such gust, and all eyes temporarily are off Hugh and Bembo. Winter is coming, they know it. The *tramontana* wind will bring rain, snow, mud, disease, inertia, death, if they can't resolve this war soon. Worse, the pope will have to winter an army who can't earn their way by conquest and despoliation. The wind abates temporarily, and they return their gaze to the intruders.

They are all there, like a line-up of who's who in the Papal Curia: Giuliano Leno, Papal Chamberlain; Sigismondo de Conti, the other private papal secretary; Johannes Burchard and Paris di Grassis, the Papal Masters of Ceremony, all hunched in a window seat and looking gloomily over a thick folio of papers. A side table near them still shows the remains of breakfast mostly uneaten: plates of beef, goat's meat, poultry and salted pork with cabbage, roast pigeon, milk, butter, white cane sugar, spices, onions, spinach, nuts and other vegetables and fresh fruit.

To Hugh's immediate left is Donato Bramante, stroking his bald head at the table nearest the fire and pouring over a plan with Agostino Chigi, the banker and chief notary of the Apostolic Camera. It's a thankless task being the chief military engineer. Bramante looks like death warmed up. Every *scudi* on ramparts and bulwarks is one stone less for his new Saint Peters. Where will he get the money now if they don't get to plunder Venice? Sell more indulgences perhaps. And now Francesco Gonzaga is locked up under the Doge's palace. Morale is slipping. Hugh remembers them the week they were leaving Rome, so pleased with themselves, so sure that war was mere finance, just our credit, our mercenaries, our banks against yours. The Chigis and the Fuggers against Venice and the Jewish bankers. They didn't reckon on anything so mundane as Padua not actually wanting to garrison idiot governors and German Landsknechts. That sort of thing doesn't appear even on a double accounted balance sheet. And now winter comes to break further fantasies with hard reality.

Others are spread about the place whom Hugh does not recognise, trying to look busy at desks. There is a cluster of crimson cardinals in one corner speaking in whispers, most with their backs to the room. Hugh recognises Ippolito d'Este, whom he last saw in Konstanz. Lean faced, angular cheekbones and sunken eyes; there is some uncanny look of death about the man, as if he had been a corpse disinterred for the occasion and dressed in finest crimson. *Odious little turd, I was well rid of his company*. Their eyes meet briefly, and he sees the other smile and caress the area of skin just under his lip.

Bramante hails Bembo, and Hugh is led away to yet another door on the far right. The master at arms relieves Hugh of his colhonna and boot knives, all four of them. Hugh does not flinch, he expected as much. He follows Colocci down a corridor but all the time examines the window fastenings and the position of doors. Numerous rooms open off the left. They pass three of them and enter the third. It is dark, a bedroom with the shutters half closed. Hugh knows this meeting with the pope could likely turn out ill, very ill indeed. If Julius needed money before, how much more now? With Julius' infamous bad temper, that *terribilta* that petrifies half of Italy, Hugh is already preparing an exit strategy – just in case. A large bed with a half-tester in scarlet Bruges silks. Candlesticks on the mantelpiece—possible weapons. A gilt stool, better. A four-foot-high wrought iron candelabra near an ebony writing desk, even better. *Who needs knives?* And then he sees the hunched form of Julius on the far side of the fireplace, slumped on an unsubstantial wooden chair, gilt and finished with lion's claw hand-rests and acorn-topped backrests – della Rovere, 'the oak'. But the pope's face is drawn, his cheeks almost collapsed inward for want of teeth, and eyes that stare from sunken sockets beyond the letter he holds, toward the grate. The milk white beard twitches, and Hugh looks about for the source of the tapping sound he hears. Is it the window catches? No, it is the three rings on the pope's right hand, tapping the chair arm as his hand shakes almost imperceptibly.

Colocci steps closer like a cat. 'Holiness. Um, Holiness, I have brought the knight.'

'Hmm, what?' The life suddenly returns to the face and limbs, making a tremor on his pleated linen chasuble and filling the shoulders under the red velvet surplice. 'The knight? Why didn't you say so? Show him in. Where has he been?'

'Huh, admiring your Holiness' new fresco by Francesco Franci.'

'Oh, has he.'

Colocci picks up a dish of doves on a table near the pope's chair. 'You have not touched your food, and it is your favourite. Are you well?'

'Of course I am. Don't be impertinent.' He brushes the secretary away. 'Healthy as a fish.'

Hugh steps beyond the doorframe and bows. He leans to kiss the ring and can feel the sweat spreading down his back. The pope doesn't raise the hand from the chair arm, so it is just his bejewelled fingers and the lion's paw underneath that Hugh sees as he leans closer and closer. Julius's nails are unkempt and inked black from signing his voluminous correspondence. Hugh's bottom lip inadvertently touches the skin as he kisses the emerald ring. They are both alike stone cold. Hugh espies the emperor's eagles on the letter's wax seal. *News?*

'You may sit, and you, Colocci, may go.' He sprinkles his fingers, adding, 'To the outer chamber with the others, and mind we are not disturbed.'

Colocci scowls at Hugh, then bows. 'Of course, Holiness.'

When the door is closed and the footsteps fade, the pope leans forward and fixes Hugh with a cold eye. Hugh does not avoid it or lower his. *I've got nothing to hide from you, you old bastard. Let's just get this over with.*

'So you like it?'

'Holiness?'

'My new fresco. Francia is no Michelangelo, but it's good to remember past sorrows and deliverances. Talking of Buonarotti, did you see his iron cast of me on your way in? Impressive isn't it?'

'Indeed, Your Holiness.' Hugh mouths the words, but in his mind the words of Cato ring louder. *After I'm dead I'd rather have people ask why I have no monument than why I have one.*

'It is. They said we couldn't cast that large, but Michelangelo did it, and I rewarded him handsomely for it. I remember giving him his reward standing where you are right now, a thousand *scudi* one time, and five hundred ducats another. He is very lucky to have my patronage, he is. Do you know he wanted to model me with a book in my hand. "What know I of books?" said I. "Put a sword in it." And he did. Just as long as they remember and are grateful for all I have done for them. Not just him. I mean, Bologna, all of them.' He shifts uneasily on his cushion and grinds his few remaining teeth for a moment before concluding. 'I'm organising a terracotta statue of Hercules killing the Hydra of Lerna to go in that room too, the one with the fresco. It is fitting that the people of this city remember that it was me who liberated them from the many headed viper of the Bentivogli.'

A silence falls between them, even as the pope's eyes narrow, perhaps remembering a lifetime of battles. 'People are rarely grateful,' he concludes bitterly.

The duomo bell sounds across the piazza. The pope brings a finger before his lips and points it gently at Hugh with a sigh. 'Today is the Feast of the Madonna of Sorrows, and you know, I suppose, that she bore the betrayals and pains of her son even as I do those of my people —this war, these recalcitrant children. As I have said before, I am of your stripe, Erpingham. We must have done here in the north as soon as God wills it and be at our real enemy before the heathen overtake us. But dealing with Venice has proved a harder task than my commanders and those dolts of the emperor's army foresaw. The emperor writes to me to say that he has finally arrived from Trento and will start the siege to retake Padua. It's taken him a month to get there. Says it was a lack of horses. God alone knows how many more troops Pitigliano has stuffed in there in the meantime. A month! Took him a month! Anyway, I cannot worry about him as well. I have enough here to deal with. We cannot run a campaign on fresh air and promises. Sixty thousand ducats a month they cost, that lot,' he motions to the window and the piazza. 'That's right, sixty thousand: thirty for infantry, five for commanders, twenty five for men at arms, light horse and others. Padua yielded less than we expected, and now here I am looking at you and wondering what news you have for me.'

'Me, my lord?'

'Yes, you, of course.' Julius' lips close tight for a moment while he inhales sharply. 'Where is Vendramin? Where is my gold? We had a deal.'

'But Holiness, I have not found Vendramin, nor am I any closer to this treasure than when I first started.'

'Liar. You were with him in the tunnels under Siena. You tell that much in your own correspondence with your blessed magister. So don't play with me, or I'll have the guard take you below. You are in Italy at my leave. Do you hear me? *My* leave.' Julius slams his palm again and again on the chair arm, his face ashen. He snorts like a stallion and looks for his bell which is with the dish of doves and some unopened brevies on the side table. His forefinger and thumb rub each other feverishly. Perhaps that is what he intended all along if I didn't turn up laden with ingots.

'I said that I did not find Vendramin which is only the truth. He found me, or at least I found him, he then escaped but rescued me.'

'Really, you sound confused.' *His fingers. The bell.*

'Not confused, Holiness. I still have hopes of tracking him down to his own territory: Venice.' *The bell.* 'I, er, I have made arrangements even now with the Venetian ambassador for safe passage to the Veneto.'

'You did, did you? Very enterprising. You will go in among our enemies and ask about, will you?' His fingers move away from the bell.

'The knights have no enemies in Christendom, my lord.'

Julius' eyes suddenly ignite with fury, and he bellows. 'And how in God's name do I know you are not on your way to sell your secrets to those whores? How do I know that, eh?' A huge vein bulges on Julius temple. Hugh does not answer or even breathe. He just stares wide mouthed, expecting to be dragged away at any moment. Julius hovers uncertainly for what seems like an age but then slumps back in the chair, placing again the finger on his lips. Hugh dares not so much as blink. *The bell.* His stomach tightens and he swallows hard. All thoughts of weapons and escape seem like nonsense. What was he going to do? Kill the pope or the papal guard to avoid capture and then escape? Escape where? Where would a man like that escape? The mark of Cain already follows his every waking hour, how much more the man who has slain God's vicar on earth?

Eventually Julius exhales abruptly and says less sharply. 'Vendramin has caused much vexation. He has been a worse enemy to Christendom than any infidel Turk. He has stood against everything that we have laboured to build. He stands against civilisation. He is an enemy of all mankind. If you find him in Venice, you will make him pay for his sins against us. You make him pay, you hear.' Julius observes Hugh as a man might look at his favourite hunting dog. 'Yes, I think you will.'

Hugh blinks rapidly. 'Then I am free to go?'

'Yes, yes. If you think he might be there. And God be with you, my son. God go with you and bring me word before winter; straight to me, mind, not these others. They are not all about God's work as you and I are. Remember that. So no more silences, you hear? No more silences, or I shall start to believe what others are saying about you.'

A LETTER TO THE GRAND PRIORY IN ROME, SEPTEMBER 16TH

My dear Prior,

You write of your plans as if by compensation for your incompetence with regard to the Englishman, but I write again now as I wrote before, that you should have faith in the divine providence. Even with your double blunders, the omnipotent hand has been at work on our behalf and even now Erpingham is coming north to me. As the apostle says, 'Where sin abounds, grace doth much more abound.'

Naturally, in his own mind Erpingham is still setting himself against the villain Vendramin. But he does not know of what spirit he is. Age and experience will always triumph over youth and idealism. We made that mistake with Vendramin once, but will not do so again. That Vendrammin has not killed Erpingham already is the mystery. It is the riddle for which I hope Venice will provide the answer. The strange dance that these two perform for us is our best chance of catching both. One for the brazier and one for the pot.

I saw long ago, before Michelotto, before Petrucci, that one should arise, anointed to wrest back from Vendramin that which he kept from those verminous Borgia—a new Jason to recover the golden fleece, a new Odysseus to bend his mighty bow against the enemies of virtue. I perceive the knight to be such a man, and this is why I let him live. Each man has his part to play, Prior, remember that. Vendramin has kept safe what providence meant for our cause. Erpingham is the Perseus who will bring me Medusa's head, so that I can be the Theseus who slays the Minotaur of our age.

It was Thucydides, I think, who said that the bravest are surely those who have the clearest vision of what is before them, glory and danger alike, and yet notwithstanding, go out to meet it. The Englishman is dauntless, that is to our favour, for we will need such as him. And if Erpingham does draw out that viper, then we'll be there to sever its head and discover its eggs. Do not you worry, for he shall be well attended in Venice, and if he endure and come south again, I shall tell you what you shalt do thereafter.

Yours, etc.

The White Cardinal

LA VIA FERRARA, MORNING, SEPTEMBER 17TH

'So glad you took up my little offer. The weather up here can be unseasonably coarse at this time of year for open travel.' Cardinal d'Este's pale face rocks back and forth as the four-poster Hungarian carriage heads north from Bologna. He is inordinately proud of it, and says so. It is lighter and faster than anything else in Italy. He is even prouder that he, on his return from those lands, was the one to introduce what, he assumes, will become high fashion in the rest of Europe.

As he talks, Hugh observes him with barely disguised distain. The cardinal has a narrow, beaklike nose and deep blue eyes circumvented by unfeasibly long eyebrows that dip down to the bridge of his nose in one seamless arc. His beard is sparse on the chin and shows tinges of ginger in the dark brown. He ruffles his thick black cloak and reseats himself, thumbing the scarlet braid on the hem of the cloak and crossing his right leg over his left while he reclines on the crimson velvet of his seat as if he were anticipating a second breakfast.

Hugh grunts, nodding in deference, trying to make out whether the eyebrows are in fact painted on. Cocks crow over the dung heaps outside the city gate as the pale light of dawn appears in the east. It has rained steadily since before matins. They are the first through the north gate. The cardinal's new crest on the carriage doors works wonders at getting you anything you want—that and the hundred light horse that ride fore and aft. The farmers and other traders have to wait while they pass through the gate. Wilf comes behind with the horses and baggage but knows he'll soon lose them. The cardinal's carriage is pulled by six fine boned black mares. They hope to make the thirty-seven mile trip by late afternoon. The whip is not spared as the road north opens before them. Bembo is a *persona non grata* in Ferrara because of his indiscretions with the duchess, so he will come along privily and stay with the poet Ariosto.

Seeing the bowing peasants and traders sprinkled with mud as the carriage wheels gather pace, Hugh says, 'I congratulate you on your elevation.'

'This?' The cardinal pats his red berretta as if not sure of which elevation Hugh might be speaking. 'Julius and I have not always been on such good terms, but I helped him deal with the Bentivogli, and he was grateful.'

That and an offering to the war coffers, Hugh thinks. It is well known that Ippolito has had lucrative benefices and abbacies from Italy to Hungary since before he could speak. Julius may well have been grateful for Ippolito's betrayal of the Bentivogli, but it's hard cash he needs right now, and if that means getting in bed with the devil, he'll do it. Ippolito must seem like small fry compared to doing the deal he's done with the French. *Dio Mio, the bloody French! It was only this time last year that the pope couldn't mention them without flying into a purple rage and reigning a maelstrom of curses and anathemas on anyone north of the Pyrenees and west of Savona.*

Hugh's thoughts are curtailed by the cardinal's fingers which stroke a small fringe of hair that protrudes onto his forehead from under the berretta. He seems to think they look better caressed toward the right. A prelate of his exalted stature does not need charm, Hugh supposes, which is good because he has none. He probably knows it and makes up for it with the meticulous and relentless manicure of what he can control, like his blessed fringe. What did his brother's lover say to his advances? Hugh casts his mind back, ah yes, "Giulio's eyes are worth more than your whole person." So, he had his eyes put out. His own brother. He is the sort of man who thinks happiness is having a large, close-knit family – in a dungeon, or in mortal fear of their lives. *His own brother!* Hugh recoils at the very thought. *The Mark of Cain, wherever I go. We are all monsters.*

'You left Lake Konstanz so suddenly last spring.' Ippolito leaves the sentence unfinished, looking hawk-like for a reaction from Hugh. Hugh nods and waits. The cardinal tries to mask his irritation. 'Well, I have not seen you this six, seven months and wondered how your mission was proceeding.'

'It proceeds well, thank you. The need for a crusade is –'

'Your real mission, I meant.' His eyes narrow suddenly as he cranes his neck forward.

Hugh can smell the herring Ippolito has just eaten for breakfast, mixed with the acrid tinge of last night's wines. 'Your Grace?'

'Come, Fra Hugh. You need have no artifice with me. Do you think every minor ambassador from the Levant gets sought out by Julius with such desperation and then ushered into his bedroom, his *sanctus santorum,* just to talk about the crusade? You have something he wants, and maybe I, as a man with connections and means, can help you get it for him. What are we, after all, if we cannot oblige the successor of Saint Peter? Is this not what we live for, to serve the Holy See? I have pleased him once in respect to the Bentivogli; perhaps I can be of service again.' Ippolito lays alabaster smooth hands open for a moment and then lets them fall together on his lap.

Hugh nods slowly. After a very brief smile, he says, 'Such loyalty is indeed rare, Your Grace. I shall be sure to mention your zeal to the Holy Father in my correspondence. But as to any understanding between me and His Holiness, *that* you may hear from his lips only.'

The cardinal fixes a tight rimmed smile and sits back on his perch. He uncrosses his legs and spreads his knees wide, putting both hands on them, like some avian predator bulking out its plumage to subdue an opponent. 'I think you mistook the gentleness of my approach, signor. I was not asking. I was hoping that as gentlemen we could discuss the matter with some delicacy but perhaps that is not possible. I know what you are here for, know all about it. Is that plain enough for you? And I will tell you something else: you are entering d'Este country, and we make very good friends. But also – ' He raises his ridiculous eyebrows and nods in a knowing way, as if not wanting to have to complete the contrary inference. 'This dukedom has strong alliances from France to Hungary. I am my brother's political advisor. I can speak to him, and together we could help you in your search perhaps.' Again, the drooping lily hands held out in supplication.

'Your Grace, permit me to say that you have greatly over estimated my progress or ability to grant His Holiness that satisfaction he desires in this matter. If you know all about it, as you claim – '

Ippolito with a seething whisper: 'I know that you seek that dog, Vendramin.'

Hugh speaks over him. '– then by all means use your utmost powers. For myself, with scant hope of success, I go to Venice to seek him among his kinsmen.'

'Pah, Venice!' Ippolito sneers and points an accusing finger toward Hugh. 'You go to those whoremongers, our enemies at such a time? Perhaps you will treat with them. After all, your interests and theirs both rest in the stability of the east. I would not have allowed it if I were the pope.'

'But you are not pope.'

'No, I am not.' Ippolito snaps, and Hugh observes the words *yet* appear on the man's lips before being withdrawn. 'And you, signor, are not innocent in this matter. It is written in your face – this high-handed approach with me now, this insolence, your disappearance in Germany, these reports I hear from Florence and Siena. We're not in the , oh what are they calling them now, ah yes, the Dark Ages. You are a guest among our people. Do you think because there are songs about you that you have friends here? The crowd sing songs because they like singing. It is the way with the mob. But they change their tunes with their hose. You should remember that. You have no real friends, signor, not where it matters anyway. You are not even beyond my reach in Venice, remember that. Whatever you do, your sins will find you out.

I will make sure of that. And—' He smirks and reclines, re-crossing his legs. 'If you are an honest man, as you claim, make sure you report back to me on your return to Bologna. Then I will know, and you can walk freely without fear of, well, shall we say, incident.'

Hugh feels a twitching in his neck, spreading to his left eye. *Threatening me in a confined space? People have died for less. This man has balls of brass or else he has the postilion with a scopietti pointed at my back.* He twists his neck partly to relieve the twitching and partly to check if there is some secret hatch behind him. He straightens up, sucking his cheeks in and nodding gently. 'Your Grace.' Hugh falters and shakes his head mildly. *What the hell should I tell him?* He is alone with a man world famous for his reckless actions. *No one will hear him suffocating beneath one of the velvet cushions over the sound of carriage wheels. Over garnished prelates die everyday in their carriages from various agues and distempers of the bowels. What does he want? The gold. Maybe the Greek fire. Why? He wants power. He wants to be the pope. Let him flatter himself that he has me, the prick. Let him tell his friends and his petite femmes that even Hugh Erpingham is at his beck and call. I am beyond caring anymore. I will choose my own battles. Carpe Deum, qualm minimum credula postero. Seize the day; trust little in tomorrow. If I snuffed his wick now, ten more pricks would appear in his place, just as ridiculous. If he's so stupid to bait me when I have the advantage, he is no adversary worthy of rage. Any fool can double-cross his friends and send assassins after his enemies, but it takes a special sort of deluded cockscombe to think he can make this knight soil his breaches. Besides, he cannot desire my death more than I do myself on most days.* 'Your Grace, you can rely on me as a devoted son of the church, ready to comply with all her worthy ministers.'

'Good, then I will wait on your correspondence.'

Hugh nods, rests his head on the deep cushion and then closes his eyes. *Wait all you want.*

FERRARA, THIRTY-SEVEN MILES LATER

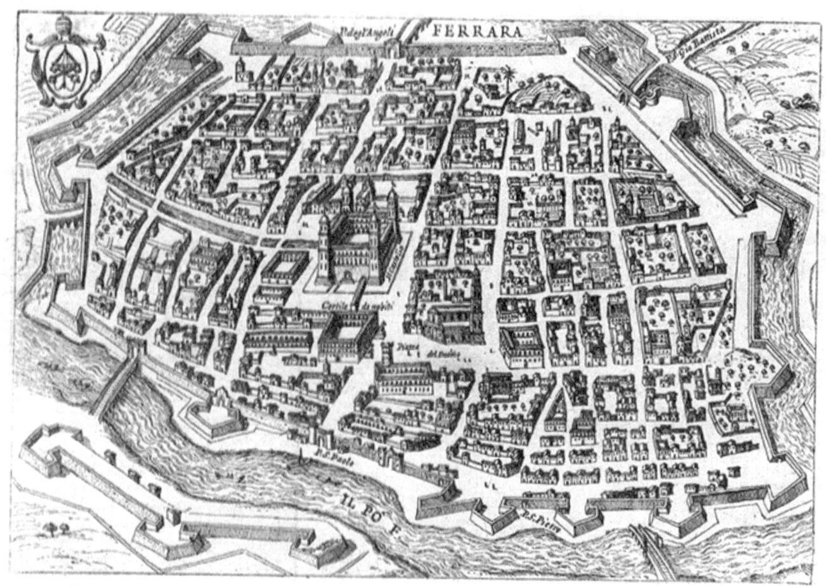

As their carriage approaches the Porta Paulo Hugh's eyes rest to the left on the fortress at the southerly most corner of the city. *Shows where they most expect trouble from*, he thinks, – *the Papal States*. The angled walls, scarp-back ramparts and redoubts are the finest he's yet seen in Italy. *Could use some decent bastions though*. State of the art, French. Duke Alfonso d'Este, Cardinal Ippolito's brother, is thick with them, another reason why the pope hates him and wants the dukedom back with its salt monopolies. The duke is also a man who knows his ordinance. Hugh squints in the afternoon light to see the tell-tale glint of iron on the walls. They say he has amassed near three hundred pieces of artillery, that he supervises the casting of his own, and that his largest piece, called the Lord's Devil, will force its way anywhere.

The hooves of a hundred horses clatter on the wooden bridge as they cross the Volano, a tributary of the mighty Po River which inches its way east to Venice just two miles to the north of the city. Beyond the river, the largest in Italy, Ippolito had said an hour or so before, lies the Polesine da Rovigo, ancestral lands of the d'Este family, annexed by Venice over twenty years ago. 'This war is a gift from God. My brother and I will get them back from that "whore that trades on many waters". You cannot know the ignominy of having a usurper occupying your lands.'

Actually, he could. The confiscation of the Erpingham estates after the Battle of Bosworth had broken Hugh's father as much as any public execution could. It was a lifelong traitor's quartering, a mortification of every affection, a tainting and poisoning of every pleasure, until all that remained was the *rigor mortis* of daily routine. Despite his affection for his mother and siblings, Hugh couldn't escape Norfolk fast enough. A man dies without purpose, as a woman dies without love. That is what he had learnt at home, what he had learnt from his father. A man dies or becomes a brute. The Boleyn marriage his parents proposed offered land and some regained status, but not purpose. The knights offered purpose, and he has gambled all on it – every inch of his soul. If that narrative fails, if Rhodes falls, if Vendramin is right in his judgement on Christendom, then Hugh Erpingham will sink irrevocably. And that, he muses finally, is why I am here in Italy: fighting for my life - the whole story of it. *And that is why Vendramin must die.*

Later afternoon sun glints off the green-grey waters of the Volano, which runs right up to the city wall and along the wharf, where men hurriedly unload the last of the day's cargo before the marshal closes the city gates. They don't have to worry about water erosion here as the river flows so slowly. Water surrounds the whole city wall, in fact. It's like Norfolk: you dig down and there it is, handy but miasmic in summer. The Ferrarese are great diggers and have made canals everywhere. They could probably even teach the Flemish engineers a trick or two.

The river view is quickly eclipsed by the red and brown brick walls of the city and classical pediments atop the Porta Paolo. Once inside the walls and the shaded streets, Hugh can hear the rhythmic compline bell from San Paolo's campanile echo from around the Byzantine quarter to his right.

'Welcome to Ferrara,' the cardinal says with a look of satisfaction. 'The centre of our web, so to speak. I have had long absences for various reasons, but to come home each time, well, what is a man without a city? I hope you will find your time here useful. Do you plan to stay long?'

'Few weeks perhaps. Give me a chance to build bridges with your brother.'

'Oh, he will love you, I'm sure. Any talk of artillery and bulwarks, and he comes alive. But remember, at the end of the day, the Estense look after their own. Don't get him carried away with notions of crusade and enemies far away when we have an abundance on our own hunting grounds. Ample chance for him to earn undying glory fighting here for his own people without bankrupting them across the seas. He is prone to chivalric sentiment, fed on a veritable diet of Provencal love lyrics since he was a boy. Right now he – that is we – have Ariosto furthering the tales of Boiardo with a large work on the madness of Roland. And even had your Mallory's *Morte d'Arthur* translated into Veneziano so everyone can learn, what they call, true courtesy.' The cardinal sniggers and then takes hold of the door frame as the carriage makes a sharp left and begins to rattle less smoothly on the cobbles. 'What I mean to say is, and I ask this now that we have an understanding, is that you do not use your fame and standing to feed an already inflated appetite for that sort of thing – picturesque though it is. Please me in this little thing, and I will make sure that Ferrara will be more than generous when the time comes for the *Cruciatae* tax. You have my word on it.'

'Of course, I will oblige Your Grace, wherever it is right for me to do so.'

His Grace looks noncommittedly at Hugh but eventually smiles. 'I am staying up here—' The cardinal directs Hugh's eyes to the window.

'In a little place I am making comfortable for my visits. It became vacant after Ludivico *Il Moro* Sforza lost Milan so suddenly. It is spacious, but his décor is as barbaric as a Magyar's. Still it cost us nothing.' As he is speaking the carriage swings right and through a red bricked Romanesque arch and up a shallow ramp into a moderate courtyard. Around two sides stand white columns, with Corinthian capitals and a second tier of round arches on the upper storey. The cardinal is helped out, stretches his back and then holds a hand up to Hugh. 'No, no, you are not to get out here. My men will take you to one of our *delizia*.'

'*Delizia*, Your Grace?' Perhaps his euphemism for a torture chamber.

'Oh, it is our name for *petit palazzos* that we have built for amusement. This one is within the city walls and only a few minutes from the ducal palace.'

'I hope I won't be inconveniencing the family if it is one of their retreats.'

'I very much doubt anyone but the servants will be there. You will like it I am sure. Spacious gardens. We will be expected at the palace for dinner after vespers, but I think you will have sufficient time to prepare. If you need anything, you can send a servant round here. It is not far.' The cardinal clicks his fingers in the direction of the coachman. 'Deliver our guest to the Palazzo Schifanoia, and then have this delivered to the ducal palace, put it in my brothers hands only.' Hugh observes the sealed parchment. Written before the journey? Almost certainly. About him? Perhaps.

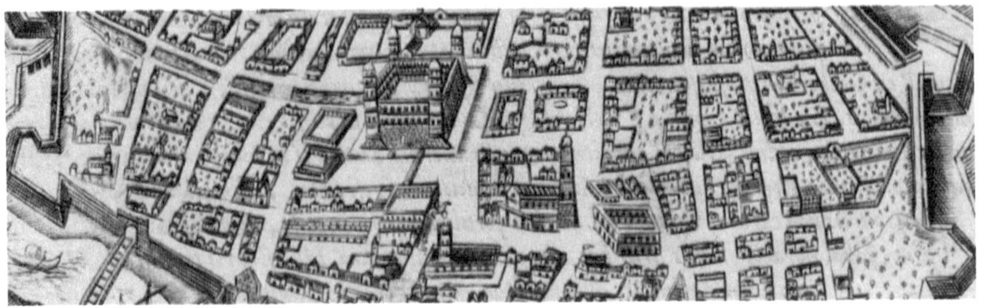

PALAZZO SCHIFANOIA, FERRARA

Hugh is ushered through the hall of the Palazzo Schifanoia which stands on the street like all the palazzi of this pocket dukedom. It could have been a warehouse, if not for the marble pediment over the door surmounted by a further relief sculpture of the duke's shield. The outer plaster and fescoes, of geometric designs and poorly executed marble effects are now pitted, peeling with some sections crumbled right back to the brick. *Schivar la noia;* literally to "escape from boredom". A strange luxury peculiar to the indolent rich, he thinks with an air of self-righteous indignation, glancing from the white marble floor and up the modest stairwell to his left, as a harassed retainer in light blue and white polychrome banded tights leads him straight out the back of the house into the gardens so he can be introduced formally to the family. *The family are resident?* Hugh straightens his sleeves, much creased as they are from the journey. He says he would rather change before being introduced, but the man is too busy talking to hear him. It is not the whole family apparently, Hugh picks up, but just the duchess and children. The duke is busy at the court. There is a war on, or didn't he know? Hugh said he was aware of it. The duchess is in seclusion, recovering from the safe delivery of a child. A male child, God be praised.

'Oh, I see,' Hugh glances furtively about the shrubs and orange trees.

He can hear children laughing somewhere further on. 'Then perhaps I should not intrude.'

The servant, past fifty and slightly hunched, turns quickly as if grieved. 'Ah, but we can't have that if his Grace the duke's brother has sent you here. His Grace must be obeyed. If he heard I turned you away to sleep in some inn or station, he would have me skinned.' He turns back and rattles on down the gravel path lined with orange and lemon trees. 'No, signor, the cardinal is a precise man, and he expects his servants to obey, which of course, we are pleased to do.'

The parkland stretches beyond Hugh's vision. It is a few acres at least. The cypress trees, which are evenly spaced along high walls are still wet from the rain. The ripe fruits of apple and pear trees, which are trained on the wall, also glisten. Hugh is led to a leafy arbour where vines and wisteria drape precariously over wooden trellises. Inside the arbor is a circular stone table, surrounded by a shallow curved stone bench, draped in fabrics and cushions. On it two nurses hold infants, one a newborn wrapped against the cool of the late afternoon, the other a ruddy-faced and drooling one-year-old, sucking on a wooden horse. A sallow faced youth of about ten years is near the table, switch in hand, teasing the bees off the remaining bougainvillea flowers. They all glance at the newcomers. Hugh bows. *Where is she?* He wonders. The arch temptress, femme fatale, of whom he has heard so much on his journeys round Italy. Hugh is suddenly hyper-conscious of himself, his appearance, his awkwardness among beautiful women. He arranges his feet and puffs out his chest, as if she might suddenly appear on the table for him – ready to test him, his resolve, his vows. The servant enquires after the duchess. The children stare at Hugh with the unbroken gazes of innocent disdain. Strangers always mean disturbance and the loss of parental attention. The older boy's eyes seem fixed on the hilt of the carrack sword. He's probably never seen one. A lizard scuttles unseen by all but Hugh, between the nurses' feet. Somewhere far off to the north Hugh can hear the low murmur of ordinance. Bells are tolling somewhere else in the city, and the air is redolent with the scent of honeysuckle and rose. Hugh senses a movement on the grass behind him and immediately the children's faces come alive. She is approaching behind him. He waits a moment longer, steels himself, breathes deeply, then turns.

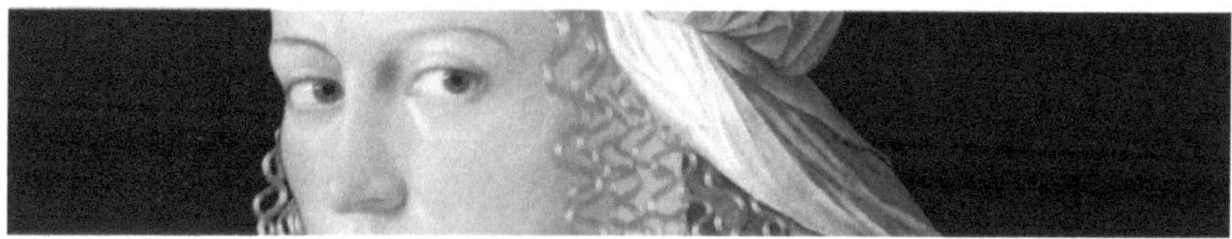

She approaches soft and catlike. The folds of her white linen dress fall easily and noiselessly over her hips. The dress is gathered at her slender waist, just under a compact bosom, with a light blue silk sash – her husband's family colours. She smiles graciously and falls into an easy curtsey as Hugh doffs his beret and bows. On coming up he sees that she is still approaching untamed. Waist-length golden hair, thick as sheaves and gathered at the sides, is tied around the back with white and blue ribbon. She glances, almost guiltily, behind her as if dismissing her past. And gives Hugh the view of the rest of her golden tresses cascading like a golden waterfall down her back and resting on her buttocks. The servant announces him, and at his name her full lips part to reveal the dimples in her pale cheeks and milk white teeth. She has come unashamedly close, so that he can now look full into her chestnut eyes, which do not seem ever to blink.

'We have heard much of you, signor.' She glances at the older boy. 'Giovanni, Cavaliere Erpingham of Rhodes!' Her sapphire eyes are alive and searching, perhaps hungry. Yet |Hugh also detects an unstudied reserve in her glance. It is not coyness but a self-knowledge, perhaps piety even. The lad approaches and glances at the hilt.

'Is this the sword you fought the Turks with?'

'No.'

'Are you here to fight them now?'

'No, there are no Turks here. Yet.'

'Then why do you carry a sword? It is a strange one. May I hold it?'

'Giovanni! Forgive him, signor. My little brother forgets his manners sometimes.'

'It is all right.' Hugh unsheathes the sword and with a flick of the wrist, turns the pommel so the boy can take the hilt. Brother? This must be the infamous *Infans Romanus*, he thinks, which people believed to have been Lucretia's child by her brother or worse, but was later declared to be – by two separate papal bulls – the illegitimate son of Cesare, or his father, the pope. The boy has her eyes, but what is that? These idle courtiers dispel their boredom with such vile gossip. Nothing was considered true under the Borgias until it was officially denied. Hugh watches as Lucretia fingers a ringlet near her chest. They say that one of her rings has a secret poisoner's compartment full of canterella. People say all sorts of things. He holds the hilt out and smiles at the lad. 'It is Portuguese, called a colhonna, and very sharp.'

'Why does it have these?' He points at the rings on the hilt before taking it heavily with both his slender hands.

'So I may catch the blades of my enemies.'

'Like Barbarossa and the sultan. They say he is very fat and that he has to be carried on a litter. Do you have enemies here?'

Hugh pauses, smiles, then shakes his head.

The lad begins to swing and jab the blade as he has been taught. 'They say you are brave as Hector, strong as Ajax, and fast as Achilles.'

Hugh smiles and folds his arms. 'The same people say that I am eight feet tall, but as you can see, I have shrunk a great deal since I arrived in Rome.'

The boy stops swinging the blade and gives a wide toothy grin.

Lucretia laughs and gestures with a bejewelled right hand. 'What a child you are, brother. Now give the knight back his sword. We must prepare for dinner tonight. The evenings are cooler now, but I like to have the children outside as much as possible for when the winter rains and fogs come...' She pauses, shakes her head slightly and flutters both fingers. 'Listen to me, quite the matron. All I was going to say was, it is a long time for little ones before the spring, and they do so love it outside. I see that now.'

She gestures to the nurse holding the babe who has been restless and giving out little whimpers. The nurse passes the tiny bundle, and the duchess cradles it. 'Now then, now then. What is this fuss, little one?' She sways, pivoting her hips and looking at Hugh. 'This is Ippolito. His older brother there is Ercole, named after his grandfather. Such treasures and such good children, yes. Yes, you are.' As the nurses smile unconvincingly, Lucretia kisses the protruding hand and then the forehead. 'Marianna, take the others inside, and I will show Signor Erpingham about the place.' Marianna curtseys and takes the babe from Lucretia who leads Hugh toward the house. Hugh follows alongside, and Giovanni falls in step behind Hugh. *Pere et Fils.* Sons looking for fathers.

Hugh is lost in thought for a brief moment as the strangeness of the occurrence settles on him. He is looking at her hands, now drawn under her chest and fidgeting girlishly as she walks down the path. Her slippers fall not on the gravel but just off to one side on the grass, noiseless. But how strange this is. Until this moment the Borgias were names, spectres, a different era, a different papacy, a different epoch almost. But now here are two Borgias, the last fruit of those diabolic insatiates for whom all Italy was too small. *Did more heinous men ever walk this earth, except perhaps me?* It is easy to hate the Borgias from a distance. But here, now?

After ten or so paces she turns. 'It is strange, signor, but you remind me so much of my own brother, Cesare, the way you walk along looking so purposeful and yet saying so little. I hope you don't mind my saying it. I am sure it is not an ill comparison, for you are both famed for your martial vigour. Why, he even dressed as a knight of Rhodes once when he stole away from Urbino with only three men so that he could meet King Louis in Forli.' She sighs, looking toward the high garden wall with eyes reaching for fading memories. 'But I do miss him around his birthday. You know he would have been thirty-four this month if he had lived. Are you about that year of age?'

'I have not yet reached my thirtieth year, duchess.'

'Nor have I. Yet, you look older.'

'Thank you.'

She stops to look at him, and when he sees her impish smile, they both laugh. As she begins walking again her cindery eyes crackle with mirth, but immediately her expression dissolves with the strong emotion of remembrance and bitterest grief. 'He once took a hundred mile detour to visit me here. Whole armies waited on him, and yet he waited on me, his sister. We were very attached. It was the last time I saw him. The day I heard of his death I almost cursed God. He was so dear to me was Cesare, my own flesh and blood. I couldn't bear the thought of him dead in another land so far away, stripped of honour. The more I cried out to God, the further He withdrew from me. That was then.'

As she mounts the steps into the covered portico, Hugh says, 'And now?'

'Now? Now I have received some instruction and consolation from the sisters here, who are very good people, you know.' She motions with one hand toward a protruding bell tower beyond the garden walls. 'I was raised with all finery and indulgence, but I think I could have been equally happy if I had taken the veil.' She turns on the steps and catches his eye. 'Aha, now you do looked surprised. Well, it is the truth.'

She leads him through the lower vestibule, up the stairs *d'honneur* and into an upper salon at which point Giovanni slinks off. 'He is a fine young man,' Hugh remarks.

'Yes,' she says without turning. 'He is dear to me as a reminder of all that we lose in life but that the divine mercy gives us back in other ways. I have a son Giovanni's age by my first husband, the Duke of Bisceglie. The duke departed this life – still young.' *Ah yes,* Hugh thinks, *through a window, twice, at the hands of Michelotto.* She continues. 'I have not seen my son Rodrigo in all these years, but I hope to soon. The grief of my husband's death combined with losing my infant made me unwell for a long time. I tried to surfeit that loss in many ways, which I now regret. It is hard to understand, let alone explain. The sisters have been very kind to me. And having borne more children – ' She turns on the landing at the entrance of a grand salon. 'I begin again to feel rightly and trust in those sentiments. I am a mother now, a mother in truth, and that has changed me, I know it. Grief changes us, yes, but so does joy and love.' She catches his eyes and chides herself. 'Oh, listen to me talking like this! But there it is, I see grief in your eyes, sir knight, and I offer help where I can. The sisters taught me thus. We are all beggars, they say, sharing where we may alike find bread. There, I shall make a good nun myself one day, shall I not? But pray do not answer, for I would not have you lie.' She turns to the doors of the salon and half whispers, half talks. 'But come and I shall show you the Conquest of Venus!'

Hugh obviously does an unmanly job of hiding his alarm, for she laughs. He glances about the corridor and vestibule below. There are various maids and liveried retainers in pale blue and yellow hose and doublets on duty in the house, and so Hugh does not feel altogether like Joseph about to be unclothed by Potiphar's wife. He smiles at himself for his feigned piety. *I am no Joseph either in virtue or visage. I remind her of her syphilitic brother. Let us keep it thus and by God, let not the duke have cause to sunder me with horses along with Bembo.*

Even as he entertains these thoughts, he is struck by how different he finds her than he had imagined. There is, as they say in that part of the world a *pieta*, a mercy in her every gesture that unnerves him. She is as one freed and arouses both a hunger in him and disdain. He follows her as she pushes the door. She turns one last time before entering, as if she had just remembered something. 'They tell me that Don Michelle, my brother's lieutenant, fell to his death from the duomo in Florence recently.'

'It is true.'

'I did not like him.' Her nostrils flare with indignation and then the dimples appear in her cheeks again. 'I hear that you were in Florence at the time.' She does not wait for his reply but leads him through.

The salon is capacious and reverberant, though not as large as he remembers the grand salon at Urbino. It is spanned by monumental beams, hewn square and painted in vibrant designs, as at Bracciano, but the walls here are frescoed from top to bottom and all around, without a tapestry in sight. She turns him to the right, pleased to see the stunned expression on his face and hear his gasp as he first glimpses the south wall.

'You are pleased. Good. I thought you would be. They were commissioned by my husband's uncle Borso forty years ago, but they still have the power to impress. It is magnificent, no? There are over six hundred and fifty square feet of frescoes here, so I am told. Hugh remembered what Bembo had said, that Borso d'Este paid by the square foot. He views twelve scenes divided by twelve frescoed columns. With her help, he begins to understand the cycle. Each section represents one month, with each month divided into three horizontal levels. The upper level shows the Triumph of the Pagan gods, the mid-section, the signs of the European zodiac with other motifs from oriental astrology. And the lower section shows many scenes from the court life of the last generation: horses, ladies, courtiers, festoons. She leads him under one panel where he follows her hand up to Venus enthroned on an ornamental barge, pulled by swans with Mars kneeling before her. On the banks either side are young men and women, dressed as they did in Hugh's grandfather's day in romantic groups. Some kiss, some talk, some flirt in amorous poses, some with instruments. Three naked Graces are on the top right. A lad in the lower right has his arm around a maiden and his hand between her thighs.

Seeing him staring toward the lower right, Lucretia says, 'Think you that the maiden is pushing his hand away from her or down deeper? The white rabbits everywhere are for fertility, you know.'

Hugh smiles noncommittally and lowers his gaze further to the panel where Taurus the bull is jumping across the sky. His mind is immediately taken back to the Parrot Room in the Vatican apartments all those months ago where Lucretia's father used the bull motif everywhere as the family symbol. Julius has had them removed, exorcized. One rumour is that Vannozza dei Cattanei, the *cortegiane onesti* who is Lucretia's mother, was Julius's lover when he was a cardinal. More rumours. He looks at Lucretia again. It is from her mother she got that golden hair. Perugino painted her in the fresco. He recalls the image. She was thinner, smaller of face, he thinks, but it was still the same beauty. He looks again at Venus enthroned and thinks that she is very like the duchess.

'Mars is chained,' she says, with something almost breaking in her voice, 'and he kneels before her. It is an enigma or a prophecy perhaps: one day all war will be quelled by love. I have lived around courts all my life and I have seen what Venus can do.'

'And what she cannot perhaps?'

A knowing smile. She has the white thread of an old scar on her lower lip. It is tiny. He sees it as she moistens them before speaking. 'July is one month in twelve.' She turns those same cindery eyes in his direction once more, but this time he fancies it is not to search him but herself, for her gaze is distant, mute somehow. 'Lilies fester worse than weeds, they say. I think the old troubadour poetry deceived us into making too much of Venus.'

'I think you are right.' He stares at the fresco then down to his feet, adding bashfully. 'Though I am but a very distant observer.'

'Yes.' Long pause. She buttons her lip and gazes at the adjoining panels. He hears the breaths through her nostrils, almost hears the cogs turning. This woman has lived through tumultuous events. Eventually she points up and down on the panel in front of them. 'It progresses from the human to the divine world, that we might understand the will of God. The divine mind!' She laughs with a hint of scorn. 'There was such optimism and naivety in our father's generation, so sure they could give us an answer for everything. I think some of them believe it even now. I don't think the artists knew any more than we do, and besides, they are long since dead so we cannot ask them. My husband remembers them—Signor Cossa and Cosmè Tura—but only as a boy. For myself I think we are fools to make the heavens so small. God has already told us what we should do yet we will not do it. That is plain. So what do we do? We seek instead to make ourselves masters of providence itself by way of compensation to him. We failed to improve ourselves, so we say we will not believe in a God that we ourselves cannot improve. There, I've said it. Spoken like a good nun too.'

'Yes, the sister would be proud, your grace.'

The sisters would be proud of me. They are right about many things. But listen to me talking anon, you have had a long journey, and you will want to rest before this evening. I will have the servants attend you.'

20TH SEPTEMBER, THE HOUSE OF ARIOSTO

Hugh enters a modest house in a modest street just off the Via Arianuova, Ferrara.

'It is a great honour for me to have you visit my home like this. Please excuse the books and majolica ornaments everywhere; we are barely moved in.' The poet Ariosto, of whom Bembo has said so much, dismisses the serving girl and leads Hugh out of the cramped hallway and along the red brick garden wall at the back of his house toward a leafy bower. The wall radiates the heat of the afternoon sun. Hugh can smell curing *intonacco*, wet cement, and hear the chimes of the bells at San Benedetto, whose campanile he saw on his way. The bell must be cracked, or else made of some very inferior metal as it clanks more like a goat bell than anything else, dolorous, brief, hollow. The garden, mostly vegetable beds and fruit trees, stretches for a hundred feet in front of him. It is bounded by six-foot walls, newly built, with a pig sty and hay ricks at the far end, chickens everywhere, pecking, squabbling.

Ariosto leads Hugh down the garden, glancing back every step and chatting affably. 'I read somewhere of a man of Alexandria called Cosmas the lawyer who had more books than anyone else in that fair city, but nothing else save a chair and table. Can you imagine that, just a table and chair and books? I confess that sometimes that sounds like a fair proposition. Apparently Cosmas received all who visited and let them read what was helpful to them.' Ariosto is wearing a grey smock finger-stained with manure. He is perhaps mid-thirties with thinning hair on the crown but long to the nape, full bearded, a nose hooked sharply toward his lip and eyes pregnant with some as-yet unknown spectral power. Hugh cannot make the man out at all—eyes hawk like, darting everywhere and seeing everything—and yet this appearance of a labouring man. *What is one supposed to say?*

'I had it built for the family,' Ariosto says, gesturing at the back of his three-storied house, and then, as if by explanation. 'It is the difficulty with public servants like my father. He was given a fine villa in Reggio nell'Emilia because he was commander of the citadel. A fine villa comes gratis with a position like that, but when he died ten years ago, I was the oldest of ten children, and we had to make the best of it. Father's affairs were not entirely in good order.' He sighs, and wipes his dirty hands again on the smock. 'Mother likes it here now we are almost finished. She doesn't like dust, but the rooms are all but plastered now, so we shall be happy and content I think.'

Hugh asks, 'You have children of your own?'

'Yes, but they are inside at their lessons along with my own younger siblings, and if we are to have peace, let us stay out here. Our friend Bembo is in the bower; it is his only retreat. I will have wine and olives brought out, and pears, too. We have fine pears here. I hope you approve of my small garden.' His upturned palm moves in a wide arc to lead Hugh's eye. 'It is our first real season, but we have had good crops, and cabbages to make even the emperor Diocletian envious. I find the work stimulates my mind.' He shouts ahead of him. 'Come Bembo, show thyself, your paladin has visited you at last.'

Bembo's head protrudes from the bower, quill in hand. 'Hugh, you have come.'

'Yes, and I didn't expect to find you in such Arcadian style, my friend. Have you become a hermit or a shepherd?'

'I think I prefer your melancholia to your sarcasm.' Bembo looks past Hugh and Ariosto to the house with a wary eye. 'In truth I am forced into my friends Hesperidin paradise by his family's attentions, which are continuous. I don't think I have the constitution for children, Hugh; that is the truth.' A dark thought seems suddenly to pass Bembo's already furrowed brow. '*Madre Dio,* Ludovico, you haven't told your progeny that the real Orlando has come, have you? We shall have no peace.'

Ariosto shakes his head. 'Have no fear, Pietro, *caro*. We will not be disturbed, but I should at least go and change.'

Bembo sniffs. 'Yes, you should. I am sure manure must be turned, but for heaven's sake let a servant do it. You smell like a pig.'

'Please do not change on my account, signor.' Hugh slides onto the bench with Bembo, shoving him slightly in jest. 'The Platonists among us will take no harm from the remembrance of where their food comes from.'

Ariosto laughs. 'I see we shall have a lively discussion. For my own part, I like to turn verses over in my mind while I turn manure, a happy combination. But I will change nonetheless as I have done my work for the day.' He bows and retreats towards the house, shouting back. 'I will return anon, gentlemen.'

'And find some soap,' Bembo calls after him, adding to Hugh. 'He is a fine man and a great poet. And inordinately proud of his dung heap. Now tell me about court. Does anyone ask after me?'

'No.'

'And the duchess? Has the duchess mentioned me.'

'No.'

'Oh.' Bembo's eyes goes defensively back to his folio of papers on the table. 'And does the duke know I am here?'

'*Dio mio*, Bembo, I should hope he has better sense than to admit it even if he does. He will be forced to keep his promise, spill your blood and expose himself as a cuckold and his whole family to ridicule. Now desist from this craving of yours, for it will undo more than just your own inwards.'

'Enough, enough, and so delicately put.' Bembo does a bad impression of nonchalance. 'Very well, I will not mention it again. But tell me how it goes with you, my friend. You obviously survived your journey with the cardinal.'

'I did.'

'And the duke?'

'I like him. He reminds me Felice's husband, though half his age and twice as cultured.'

'Huh, not hard.' Bembo shifts and looks askance at Hugh. 'And he evidently likes you too. I heard that he took you about the city defences and ramparts with his chief engineer. There was much talk of it in the market.'

'Yes, he asked my advice.'

'And?'

'And I gave it to him.'

'Such as?'

'If you are really interested, I said that scarp-backed ramparts are all very well, even with ones as thick and high as his, but many of his curtain walls are too long, and that he needs more bastions for his ordinance and outworks, and triangular bulwarks to stop the enemy laying their batteries too close. I think he knew so already, but was too gracious to say so.'

'And you have been to the palace, I suppose?'

'Yes, we have dined there each night, and last night we took to the adjoining castello for drinks on an upper terrace, looking out over the moat and city skyline. Do you know the one?'

'With the orange trees? Yes, I know it. I can almost see you all hugging yourselves with self-congratulations.' Bembo groans slightly and bites his knuckle, probably remembering all the masques and madrigals he had enjoyed in those places that he would never see again. His eyes suddenly ignite with a delicious lip-licking malevolence. 'You know why they built such a fist of a moated fortress in the centre of the city, I suppose. Many generations ago an angry mob besieged the ducal palace because they were angry with the family's chief advisor and tax gatherer, Tommaso something-or-other, can't just now remember. They demanded his head and the Este family, in a fit of beneficence, handed him over to them to be torn limb from limb. After that they built the castello and dug the moat and built a corridor to link the palace to it. Because they still want their taxes but with all their own limbs intact.'

'Yes.' Hugh pretends not to hear and continues dreamily so as to increase Bembo's irritation. 'And what a goodly number of poets and composers I met there—two in particular from the northern Low Countries, signors Brumel and Willaert. Very fine work, very fine indeed. They said these flat lands are like their own, only with mosquitos.'

'Willaert! I paid that pastey-faced rascal three crowns to set some of my work to lyre music, and I have yet to receive the score. Did he mention me?'

'No. And I suppose you left Ferrara in something of a hurry before he could fulfill the contract, which is what must be expected when you think from below your belt. You've only yourself to blame, and you'll get no pity from me.' Hugh gives his friend another good-natured nudge, but Bembo shrugs it off with a plaintiff's scowl.

'Oh, Hugh, I hate it when you are in such good humour.' He tosses his quill onto the table. 'So you have been exercising all courtesy at court while I have been beset by Ariosto's progeny and dine on pig's trotters. Well good for you, and the sooner we depart for Venice the better. Or perhaps you are now in no hurry to leave. Perhaps you are too comfortable staying with the duke's family.'

‘I have found them most hospitable.’

‘And the duchess?’

‘What about the duchess?’

‘She is still beautiful?’

‘Really Bembo, you are an ass sometimes. Beauty is a very deep thing, and I wish you wouldn’t go on as if we were some wretched Turks choosing a Circassian at the market.’

Bembo bursts into a long guffaw. ‘Aha, you can give it but not take it. She really has got under your skin then.’

‘Desist, Bembo, for the love of God. Desist your folly. It is not worthy of you or her. If you could meet her now I think even you would see that she has changed from the woman you knew those years ago. The influence of some good sisters and motherhood have wrought deeper beauty in her than you talk of.’

‘Yes, all right; there is no need to lecture me. I was just teasing. And in case you think I have been labouring here on my *Chanson de Gest* for Julius about your progress through Italy, you’d be quite wrong. Don’t worry, I have been working at it on and off – while my own work suffers – but I have been at something greater today, I believe. Look at this.’ Bembo draws a heavily annotated sheet of paper from the folio. Hugh quickly glances at the verses;

Doth any maiden seek the glorious fame
Of chastity, of strength, of courtesy?
Gaze in the eyes of that sweet enemy
Whom all the world doth as my lady name!

How honour grows, and pure devotion's flame,
How truth is joined with graceful dignity,
There thou may'st learn, and what the path may be
To that high heaven which doth her spirit claim;
There learn soft speech, beyond all poet's skill,
And softer silence, and those holy ways
Unutterable, untold by human heart.

But the infinite beauty that all eyes doth fill,
This none can copy! Since its lovely rays
Are given by God's pure grace, and not by art.

Hugh mouths the last two lines as a whisper. 'God's pure grace and not by art.'

Bembo holds the page at arm's length and squints. 'These are some lines from Ludovico's new project, *Orlando Furioso* – The Madness of Roland. I think he will dedicate it eventually to the duchess as I did my *Asolani*. I am sure these lines are for her, and I am sure you approve.' Bembo ribs Hugh with his elbow, before continuing. 'I have persuaded him to rewrite what he has already done in Toscana, and he has let me help with stylistic changes. It is a continuation of Bioardo's *Orlando Innamorato*. Read it?'

'Yes, lived and breathed it at one time when I went up to Cambridge, that and the *Mambriano*. Our neighbours the Boleyns had an unbound copy that they loaned me. Anything that mixed the courts of Charlemagne and Arthur was meat to me as a stripling. Made me believe most heartily in chivalry and courtesy, as if a lad needed any encouragement. Probably why I am here now.' Hugh's mind wanders back to the remembrance of such certainties and youthful optimism, such naivety. Boiardo's epic poem broke off suddenly with Italy in fire and flame—the coming of the French: twenty thousand foot, ten thousand mounted knights, monster artillery, scorched earth warfare; tens of thousands of starving families; farms aflame as far as the eye could see, and far beyond; misery, pestilence, refugees with black fingers, roadside graves. Children. Babes. Domesday. Boiardo's world of chivalry could not stand in the face of north Italy looking like a charnel house, like an antechamber of hell. Hugh always found those verses incomprehensible as a boy, jarring as they did with his thirst for an ideal narrative symmetry. But he understands them now. He too, no less than the poet Matteo Boiardo, is a refugee from the collapse of chivalry. He feels that his whole life hangs between that old world with its ideals and courtesy and this new one of brute reality that would rather cradle you in the ugly as real, than insist on a beauty with no basis. Ducats, florins and scudis. Maths, machismo, mercenaries. Pragmatism, realism, simonism. Calculation, control, cruelty. *Why would Ariosto take up such a poem, and at such a time too? Is he another naïve fool? He doesn't look like one. Even Bembo approves of him. What could he hope to salvage?*

'So you liked it. Good, good but this,' Bembo doesn't see Hugh's thousand-yard stare, but rather drives his finger repeatedly onto the paper. 'This is different. As the heirs of Roland and Chretien call out to us across the ages, *Je vous avoue que cet Arioste est mon homme,* I must confess, this Ariosto is the man. I believe he will do for our language what Homer did for the Greeks. It is not finished yet; I know that, yes. But you wait, Hugh, you wait. The *Furioso* will outshine Boiardo's *Innamorato*; mark my words. In some ways I think it could be the equal of Dante's *Comedia.* His star is rising, and these pitiful sufferings he has born in life will make his work even more precious to posterity. And the urbanity, courtesy and piety of the work— You will approve it, I know. Something in my heart burns when I read it, I tell you. There is no brawling and swearing as in the former *fableau* but dignity and prayer. Rinaldo is no highwayman as in the *Innamorato,* but brother to Bradamante. Not a breath of vulgarity to be seen anywhere; it is simply not in the poet, you see. *Cet Arioste est mon homme.* Elbows deep in pig shit, he will save us all.'

For a moment, Hugh feels an intense welling of emotion in his gut and tears forming in his eyes. Like a gaping breach in his chest cavity, every yearning of his youth is suddenly before him again, all he has thought to forget, to supress through cynicism, all the longing for the world to be different and him different in it, for aching beauty, the meeting of sweet desire, for justice, fealty, troth; all the unquantifiable myriad of virtue and joy that lays claim to the lives of all mankind, and yet which would not exist unless enacted against the cold tide of expediency, of prudence. *Will those virtues remain in a new world bent on certainties?* Hugh wonders. *Will Secretary Machiavelli suddenly discover that selfless sacrifice is the surest path to the exercise of ducal power in his new work on political science? Why do all these non-tradables, all these things that matter most to us, that give life meaning, that give us meaning—why do they lie beyond the grasp of that strand of knowledge that is now so prized? Are we going mad or were our fathers mad?* While Bembo thumbs through his additions and corrections, occasionally mumbling the words, Hugh considers the enigmas of the present age and his own personal conundrum. Minutes pass thus.

The crunch of gravel and the clink of glass announce Ariosto's arrival. He is carrying a pewter platter with a bottle of wine, and dishes of olives and pears. He is still turning verses over through his beard as if he has heard Hugh's thoughts – *le donne, i cavalier, l'arme, gli amori, la cortesie, l'audaci imprese io canto*, of women, knights, arms, loves, the courtesies, of daring feats I sing. He smiles when he sees Hugh getting up to make space amidst Bembo's work for the platter. 'My apologies, I had reserved some of the finer pears for guests, but it seems the children have helped themselves. These black spots—' He nods to the pears as he sets the tray down. 'Are a curse, but I have brought a knife so we can eat them without the skins. Will you take water with your wine?'

'With water please.'

'And you, Bembo?'

'What?' Bembo looks up, pointing at the tatty sheet of paper. 'Do you think it wise to compare Lucretia and Isabella to Calandra and Bardelon? This Canto is all awry. What, water with wine? Good. No, keep that water away. Your wine here is weak enough as it is. Water is for washing before mass.' Bembo stretches back for a moment, rolling his shoulders, taking the glass from his smiling host. 'My thanks. I am ready for this. As the scribes of old well said, *tres digiti scribubunt totum corpusque laborat*, three fingers write but the whole body labours.'

The glass goblets are thick with bubbles and a green tinge. While he busies himself cutting up pears, Ariosto explains how all his good glass – a wedding present from his wife's parents – was broken by the children and the rest now locked away for auspicious visits from the in-laws. Hugh takes up his glass, trying to take in the fast apologetic speech of his host without blinking. He brings it before his lips and then, just as suddenly puts it down. 'You will excuse me, Signor Ariosto, but I would like to ask you why you have taken such labours to continue this epic of Roland? How will you answer the charge of escapism in such a cynical age? This fascination with Charlemagne, Arthur, Camelot – the people of today are beginning to call all that "The Dark Ages".'

A cloud passes over Ariosto's brow, as it might a child when called out of a fantasy game. But then he declares confidently, even paternally. 'Because they are wrong, and the former poets were wrong to reduce the material to the trite level they did. And the people of whom you speak? These are the same people who said the age of chivalry was already dead even in the days of Chretie n of Troyes, but they are wrong too, quite wrong. Perhaps they wish it so because they lack fortitude. But they are still wrong.' Ariosto prods the four fingers and thumb of his right hand upon his breast with unaffected candor. 'We all must face disappointments with this world and ourselves, especially ourselves, Hugh, but we must not let those disappointments deceive us. Pear?' He proffers the pear toward Hugh straight off the knife, and he takes it.

The fruit is sweet, but not as sweet as this man's words that offer water in the vast desert of the last few years. Hugh knows something is coming; he can feel it in each throb of his heart as it beats against his ribs. It has been happening all over Italy, as if he is being pursued by some relentless hound and brought to ground. Hugh lets the juice trickle deliciously down his throat as the now animated poet spills words forth.

'To be practical, as the call of the age now seems to be, is the coward's retreat in this conflict of mighty opposites, my friend. Perhaps the world seems dualistic to all practical purposes, but in the very last resort, and from that final heresy, we must abstain. We must, signor, we must.' At this point he fixes Hugh with that falcon stare. 'Despite appearances, one of the opposites contains and is not contained by the other. Truth and falsehood are opposites but truth is the norm, not just of truth but of falsehood also. Every great antitheses—life and death, health and sickness—are not arbitrary and certainly not equal. We must insist, against the tide, that all evils are dead or dying things. That is my work as a poet. Each sin really is a mortal disease, no matter how we dress it up or justify it. I know what people will say. Of course, they will misunderstand me. They will think me decorative. I know that. When my Orlando goes mad, it is for unrequited love, which after all is as good a metaphor for our present cynical age, you know. We desire much that cannot be met here and now. Orlando goes rampaging through the world destroying everything in his path. He becomes not a man but a destroying youth tearing apart a music box to find the music, or cutting open a bird so he can find her song. This too is a metaphor for the madness of a purely pragmatic age too I think. They look for the meaning from within, or down here and so they sink in despair.'

Hugh leans forward, his words hoarse. 'But where does the answer come from then? In your story, I mean.'

'From the outside, of course, from heaven.'

'But how?' Hugh fumbles another piece of pear. 'I mean, how have you written it.'

'I haven't yet, but—' Ariosto's eyes suddenly burn with a prophetic intensity that sends a new terror into him. At once Hugh sees in the man what he could not see before: the fires of creation; the hard, brilliant intelligence; the sharp delineator of character that only a man who has suffered can know and truly portray. 'I will, if God permit,' he replies slowly and deliberately. 'I will have an English knight. Yes, why not? An English knight. What is more unlikely than that? An English knight perhaps from Camelot no less. Yes, I will have him travel to Ethiopia in search of my fallen paladin.'

'What?' Hugh is stunned for a moment. Even Bembo looks up from his corrections and wine.

'Yes,' Ariosto continues slowly but certainly as the picture forms in his mind. 'When I eventually write it, I will have an English knight, Hugh. He will find Orlando and bring him back his lost reason. Not from the earth, anywhere but here. That is the point – at least that is Anselm's point in *Cur Deus Homo?* Our troubles are so deep my friend, our sins so heavy, and we, too tied up in the struggle to think well of ourselves – how could salvation come from the earth? To those who try to do so - well, that is his warning to Boso, *nondum considerasti quanti ponderis peccatum sit;* you have not yet considered the gravity of sin. So, not the earth, but from the moon perhaps. Yes, he will bring an answer from some Archimedean point outside this present order, a place where everything that has been lost on this earth may be found. And you do believe in such a place, Fra Hugh, where all we have lost on this earth may be found again?'

Hugh feels the words enter him, like body blows pushing his bones out of joint. 'I certainly used to.' He gulps. 'And would like to again.'

'Then do so. Without stout knights and fair ladies to believe this gospel of hope the world will grow dark again. Nothing has changed really. It is still east-west, Christian-Saracen, and so on. I want to bring the ideals of courtesy within reach of Christian and Saracen alike, for if we may not eventually all be of the same religion then we must at least learn to live alongside each other with a better basis for peace than the greed of trade.'

Bembo looks up again. Stroking his beard with the quill, he says, 'Saracens too, eh? You really are setting your cap high. Not content with reforming a mired Christendom, you want to reform Muslim manners too. You know – ' He puts the quill down and takes up his wine. 'I was reading the other day about Ramon Llull. Ever heard of him? No, well, you put me in mind of him, Ludovico. He was a philosopher and linguist, born in Mallorca, I think, and served as page at Jaime the Conqueror's court. He studied at the University of Montpellier, then elevated to Seneschal of Perpinya. His first book, *Le Llibre de l'Orde de Cavalleria,* was of course about the principles of chivalry, followed by a moment of religious ecstasy after which he spent his time trying to reconcile the three great religions while living at a Franciscan monastery on Mount Randa. He toured around the Mediterranean, also undertaking several missions to North Africa where he engaged in learned disputations with Islamic ulemas.'

'And?' Ariosto says, some of the intensity dissipating from his eyes.

'Nothing, just that you remind me of him.'

'Ah.' Ariosto's moustache peeks into a broad grin. 'For a moment there I thought you were going to tell us how to reconcile the world religions.'

'What, me? I do not think so, my friend. We say that Christ is the one who was foretold, and the Jews say he was not, and the Saracens say that we are both wrong. There is no concord excepting, as you say, that we agree to differ.' Bembo pinches his nose then reaches once more for the wine. 'That, and that they withdraw from our holy sites of course.'

Hugh says, 'But they claim the same places as holy for themselves.'

'But they were ours first. Simple.'

Ariosto stirs. 'And the Jews before that presumably.'

Bembo is dismissive. 'Oh, I don't know, then. Let them stop being such stubborn infidels and convert to the true faith. Anyway, stop bothering me about it now when I am working on this Canto eighty-four. You have written "Lo! Hercules' daughter, lofty Isabella, in whom Ferrara deems her city blest" which I like, and certainly she will like, but you haven't said anything of her brother the cardinal. He is your patron, Ludo, or supposed to be, and I think you should flatter him.'

'Flatter him? Do you know what he said after reading the first section? All he said was, "Why signor, what a vivid imagination you have." That was all, no gift, no position. I know one shouldn't hanker after the mammon of unrighteousness, but I have sixteen people who need to eat here. Compliment him? What would you have me say? Congratulate him on his eyes?'

'No, leave his eyes out of it – as he did his brothers, if you'll pardon my black humour – but do what that brown nose lawyer Cantone Sacco did in his *Semidius*.'

'His what?'

'His *Semidius*, his book on modern warfare. Don't you remember? He compared his patron to Alexander, Aenneus, Jupiter even. Learn to flatter, *caro*. They love that sort of thing. Though heaven knows, that poor book did not stand the Visconti or the Sforza in much stead when the French came and took Milan. And to think how many books those bastards took back to France with them—seventeen owned by Petrarch alone. What I would give for those books. Where are you going, Hugh?'

'Forgive me, but I must not be late for the Marchesa of Mantua.'

'What! They are still in Vespers.'

'I have things to do.'

'What could possibly take that long? An eyebrow manicure? Have another drink with us, for God's sake. No offense, Ludo, but the days are long enough here.' Bembo proffers the bottle, but Hugh demurs.

'You will pardon me, signor.' He bows to Ariosto.

'Hugh, Hugh.' Outside on the street Bembo catches Hugh up. 'You will remember what we talked about.'

'About?'

'About the marchesa,' Bembo gives a furtive glance at the alleyways.

'What? That she already has children to spare, and he has the French disease from many women – mistresses not included in the marriage contract.'

'Right, you have it. Her desire for her husband's release may not be as ardent as his sister's. Tread carefully with her. Don't tell her too much.'

'I understand.' Hugh pats Bembo's chin and cheek. 'I understand. Now let me go for my eyebrow manicure.'

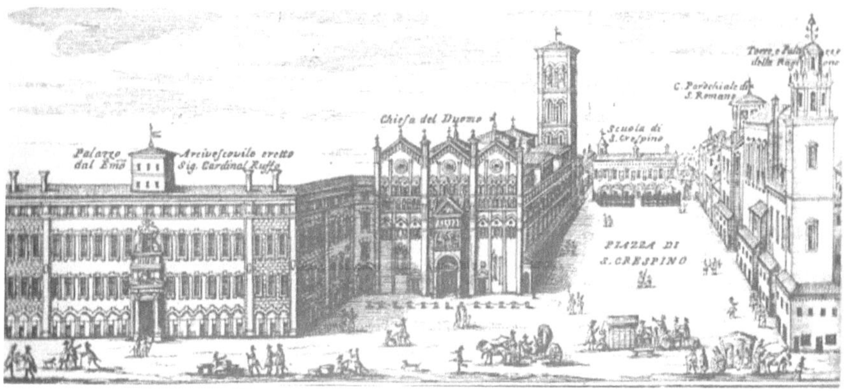

AFTER COMPLINE, 20TH SEPTEMBER, 1509

'So, you want me to wait under the trees.' Wilf, leading both mares, glances across the *Piazza dei Duomo* to a precarious stand of poplars. There is a coolness in the air this evening, and the first of the leaves are starting to curl and fall.

'Huh?' Hugh, dressed in his best black velvet doublet and whitest hose is only half attentive. To their right, either side of the cathedral entrance, two marble lions maul – or cradle – lambs between their drawn claws. Hugh is ignoring them, richly suggestive as they are, at least trying to, and looking toward the entrance of the palazzo where even now carriages, attended by liveried footmen, are arriving in droves. Notable among them is Cardinal d'Este, in red silks and ermine trim, like an overripe cherry gone mouldy. Retainers and petitioners mill about him like insects, and he ignores them all, striding through the archway and past the guards. The guests arrive, not in a steady trickle but in impromptu groups, like leaves blown by the wind. The marchesa's homecoming is an event on many levels, he thinks. First she is a daughter of their own fair city, second, the doyenne of style and taste in all Italy, but then lastly also the ruler of their neighbour and ally, with news of the war – a war which started for the Ferrarese as a church-sanctioned land grab north of the Po, but now begins to blight their waking hours.

'I said, do you want me over there?' Wilf gestures back to the trees.

'Yes, over there.'

'Are you all right?' Wilf pulls the whinnying mare back into place and shoots a nervous glance at Hugh.

'Well enough, Wilf. I am sure we shall be sleeping in our beds tonight and this is just a precaution.'

'I mind not. It's your precautions what's kept us alive. Most of us.'

'You mean Pico?' Wilf had hardly spoken two words about it since Florence.

'Aye.' Wilf sighs heavily. 'Poor mite, he didn't sign up for this sort of work. He warmed to it mind, like any lad with spirit would, but he didn't sign up for it like.'

'I know.' Hugh nods sympathetically. 'And you?'

'Me, hah, what does it signify? I'm old now anyway. Come on, master; get to your own, and mind no duchess turns your head, ot takes itneither.'

LA PRIMA DONNA DEL MUNDO

Thirty minutes later Hugh has ambled through the great hall of the new palazzo, where it is crowded and humid, and up over the bridge that links the palazzo with the old moated castello. He instinctively moves out of doors and props himself against a smooth marble column in the loggia adjoining the courtyard of the orange trees, though in truth it is more a terrace standing above the green waters of the moat, with laden orange trees in pots set about the pavement. He notices a woman beyond the potted trees and near the edge. Another figure is next to her. Hugh squints in the dusk. Its a man. They are both facing away, bent as if whispering. Hugh loosens his collar to temporarily let in some air. The noise of crowds still puts him on edge. The figures remain motionless in the same posture. The noise of street carnival and the smell of grilled foods rise from below. A minute later Hugh is aware of the presence of someone else behind him. Before he can turn he hears the high and somewhat lyrical tone of an older man's voice. 'Ah, standing aloof on the terrace, gazing far away? Augustus watches for omens with the Tiburtine Sibyl.'

Venetian Ambassador Girolamo Donato steps into the lamplight. He is still wearing his black and gold damask doublet, which under the flickering lights, makes him look again like an exotic, if jovial, beetle.

Hugh bows. 'I had not thought to see you here, Ambassador.'

'Nor I you,' the older man says, raising an owlish eyebrow. 'As relations deteriorate, the frontier becomes harder to cross.'

'I will depart soon, I hope.'

'I may yet accompany you. His Holiness has done mauling me, I think.' He gives a sardonic smile and sighs. 'And depending on my audience with the duke tonight—' He motions toward the lone couple on the terrace. 'I may be leaving here within the week myself.'

'I am sure that would be most agreeable to me and to Signor Bembo' Hugh glances in the direction of the couple. 'I did not know that it was his Grace.'

'Well, it is. And the duchess, his sister, I believe. He is a good ruler and she too is formidable and wise.'

'Are relations with Venice not a little strained at present?'

'Oh yes, very much so. But he suffers me as I was a friend of his father, God rest him, and because Ferrara's relations with the papacy are also strained over the salt monopolies. "An enemy of your enemy" and so forth. So.' The ambassador sighs. 'Here we all are, acting in the poor roles given us in a even poorer drama – nay, a tragedy – with a poor first act, a worse middle and God knows what finale. But—' He sighs affectedly again. 'I maintain communication and friendships where I am able. Allegiances, you know, in the Marches must always be malleable for unexpected events can expedite matters in an instant up here, the twinkling of an eye.'

'Yes, I can well imagine that.'

'Have you formed an opinion of the duke yourself? I understand you have rooms at the Schifanoia.'

'I think, Ambassador, that I share your opinion. I am young as he, you know, but I see a prudent man, a capable tactician, perhaps a little too given to the exercise of arms, to munitions and so forth, but hardly a grievous fault at such a time and in such a place. For myself, I like him.'

'Spoken like a diplomat. And the duchess?'

'I have found her amiable, a devoted mother.' Hugh can see the old man's eyebrow flick up enquiringly again and chooses to tack. 'Did you know her brother?'

'No, but I have known many like him. That is the privilege of old age and part of the scourge. The Visconti, Baglioni, Petrucci, Sforza – you see them come and go. I am old enough to even remember Duke Charles le Tèmèraire of Burgundy – and you needn't pretend to be shocked. It is only about thirty years ago; I was probably about the age you are now. They said half of Europe would not have been enough for Duke Charles. He fell at the Battle of Grandson in the Vaud and was only found the next day frozen into a muddy puddle, his head split to the chin by a Swiss halberd and body pierced with many lances, his baggage train despoiled.'

'The Booty of Burgundy,' Hugh says.

'Yes, of course. It passed into folklore. Almost mythic was the plunder the Swiss took back to their mountains, including the duke's solid silver bath. Ah, there is no limit to avarice and pride, Hugh. Remember that. To feed it, is only to increase its appetite. Better to be a modest man.'

'Or a saint.'

'Indeed, or a saint, if there are vacancies, and I suppose there always are. My, what an interesting fellow you are, Fra Erpingham. I expected a soldier, yes, certainly, but not a sage.'

'And certainly not a saint.' Hugh's smile is ironic but wistful. Fra Francesco is in his head these days as much as Vendramin, like the dark and light of the same spectral energy pouring scorn on the current age. Hugh knows it to be a strange movement of the heavenly spheres that has elevated him above his peers to such a place of pre-eminence among them. No one questions that, except Vendramin and Fra Francesco – and he himself, whose sin has nigh blotted out the horizon as if it were a sponge on a canvas.

The ambassador looks away suddenly as the other two figures turn toward them. It is now obviously the duke, broad of chest in voluminous blue velvet and gold chains of office that clink under his thick, square beard as he approaches. To his, diminutive in form, but sure of step comes his sister, *la prima donna del mundo*, Isabella, marchesa of Mantua. As the brother and sister approach the torchlight of the loggia, Hugh sees that the marchesa is not at all as he remembered in Rome, even with the kindness of candlelight. He has read or heard such complimentary tidbits about her person – her beauty, her taste and her learning – yet since seeing her at a distance in Rome, only the latter seems evident now. For there is something in her petit mouth and pert lips that gives Hugh the impression not only of her past hurts, but also the savage possibilities of the tongue within. In her quickness of eye he beholds both the familial pride and the feline shrewdness that put him more on his guard than all the warnings of Bembo.

He and the ambassador fall into a low bow, but the duke rushes to raise them. 'Fra Hugh, by my soul, I missed you this afternoon at the barracks when I had questions and ideas, but enough of that. We cannot talk of war now, or my wife and sister will be ill disposed toward me. I know the ambassador agrees.'

'Indeed, Your Grace, and to see you and your illustrious sister in health, well, I should more gladly speak of music and our former sweet concord before this calamitous League made us enemies.'

'Indeed,' the duke coughs, glances at his sister and back to Donato. 'With regards to the future let us now have some words privily before we dine. My sister will escort Fra Hugh back to the other guests.'

'Surely I will, and the safer I shall feel with a paladin who has no part in our present troubles.' The Marchesa Isabella tilts her head in deference to her brother, then to the ambassador. The diamond and ophir ornaments on her voluminous turban clank like pebbles. They resemble more the turban of a sultan than a traditional tiara worn by her class for such occasions. Hugh is struck by the size of the pearls in the brooch on the front of it and by her earrings. She wears green velvet with a prominent white, dotted, fur sash with a confidence and surety that would make anyone think it was the accepted style of all the Italies. In observing this Hugh cannot but hear the spirit of Bembo's wit whispering in his ear, '*Timoros est hostis eleganter*, fear is the enemy of elegance.' The ringlets that fall from under the turban show almost ginger in the light. Her bosom is small, her hips not so. With her left hand she flutters a fan near her pale cheeks and offers her right as if she would be led – or more likely, lead.

'I would be honoured.' Hugh bows and places his arm under hers. The two other men walk back toward the terrace, and the marchesa tugs lightly but firmly, and they start for the corridor.

At first she says nothing, but after a silence that is awkward for Hugh, she speaks clearly and slowly. 'My beloved sister-in-law, the Duchess of Urbino, has written to me concerning you, signor.' She does not look at him as they move slowly across the enclosed bridge and then through the numerous apartments, where servants and strayed guests fall back respectfully as they pass.

'She is a woman whose praise is not exaggerated,' Hugh says, glancing behind as her ladies in waiting and retainers, bearing the scorpion of the Gonzaga as a livery, exit the first apartment and follow at a discreet distance.

'And who is hard to refuse anything.' Her words are light, almost jocular, and yet Hugh senses the barb.

He waits before answering. 'Indeed, I should believe that to be the very case.'

'She is most attached to her brother, one should say, devoted to him.' When Hugh is too long answering, she continues, speaking faster than before, as if the preliminaries had become arduous. 'It is my opinion that in the absence of her husband, firstly as an object of devotion, and secondarily as a source of guidance, she has placed an inordinate stock in her brother's wellbeing.'

'I see that this might be true.'

'It is true. I know it is. I would not have said so otherwise.' She stops for a moment and shoots him a haughty glance before continuing. 'Elisabetta is no fool and in many ways wise, but certainly she is innocent of the delicate situation here, as are you, as to how our fiefs are balanced in this current situation. I know she has asked you to act on my husband's behalf, to effect his rescue.'

'She has communicated this to you?'

'No, but the lady Emilia has written to me for she shares my concern – my devotion.' She stops again, in the darkness of a doorway between two apartments and looks at him straightly. 'Fra Erpingham, please believe me when I say that no one wishes to see the marchese at liberty more than I. But he is better for now in a place where he cannot lead the field against Venice.'

'But he says he has an ague from the rising waters, and that he fears for his life as winter comes.'

'Yes, so he writes and so let all believe. Perhaps he is in discomfort, perhaps he is not. Men complain at the slightest onset of cramp or fever, which is why childbirth was left to us women. But let me assure you that the doge will not let any harm come to him. He earned his spurs leading their army. The Gonzaga have been valuable allies of their republic and may be so again. But the possibilities of an escape and a chase jeopardise that. I don't care how great your reputation for cunning and boldness, and I don't care how much my sister-in-law wept before you and made you promise. We are not in a knightly romance here, signor. We are not in the Levant even. This is the real world, this is the Romagna, and I will not jeopardise my husband's life and my fiefs—our fiefs—for want of a little patience and fortitude.'

'I see.' Hugh does not know where to look and so focuses past her at the wooden panelling, weighing her words carefully.

'Good. Then you will leave the affairs of Mantua to Mantua,' she says, with such firmness, that Hugh does not know whether she means it as a question or a command.

He fixes her for a moment with an unbending stare. She doesn't need to remind him that he is not in a romance or even the Levant.

He can see that for himself minute by minute, as the monochromatic certainties of Rhodes are yet again complicated by the polychrome complexities of this strange other world. 'I will aim to gratify Mantua and most particularly you, signora, wherever I can.' He knows that it seems to come from between gritted teeth. He cannot help it, or the lingering haughtiness in his own insolent stare as it continues on her.

The whites of her eyes widen for a moment, and her nostrils flare ever so slightly. But then her face falls as placid as it had been, her mouth affecting the slightest possible semblance of a smile. It was a change in her as if her total mental endeavours were now directed on a different course. She breathes in deeply and the smile becomes immediately more evident. 'I knew you would see it no other way. Let us talk no more of it.' She continues to walk. 'You are still bound for *la Serenissima,* I suppose?' She releases her arm momentarily to produce a sealed letter.

'We leave soon, perhaps even with Ambassador Donato.' He tries to avert his eye from the letter. 'He has given me an introduction to Doge Loredan.' *The letter.*

'I would have thought your own reputation would have secured that. The Venetians love a sailor, you know. You will find them more interested than you think. They have been hit harder than they let on, by the loss of the spice trade to the Portuguese earlier this year. In fact, they would love nothing better than an end to this ruinous war and to fill their order books with new galleons for a crusade against the Turks. They'll be the only ones to profit from it. It was ever thus with them.' The noise of the crowd rises as they near the great hall in the new palace. She fans herself now with the letter, looking about the room above everyone's heads from three steps up. Hugh feels his stomach tighten, but even as he makes to disconnect, she holds fast his sleeve. 'I would like you to give this letter to the doge. But take care to tell no one about it and to give it to him only, and of course, to see that no one else reads it. That would hardly be, hmmm, knightly.'

'If you wish it.'

'I do.' She turns so that no one else can see, then lets the letter balance in her fingers, hovering above Hugh's hand. 'I have your word as a knight? It is for the doge only.'

'You have my word.'

She looks at Hugh for a moment, the letter hovers a moment longer while she looks at him with delight. 'Yes, on this at least I can rely. *Adieu, mia cavaliere.*' She hands it to him and then raises her hand. He kisses her emerald ring and then, before walking to the right with her retinue, she says with an air of finality. 'I have enjoyed our meeting. And remember, even a visit to my husband could be ruinous.'

Indeed. Hugh bows. *But to whom?*

LETTER TO RHODES, OCTOBER 2ND

Most illustrious and esteemed Magister,

Grace and peace be yours. I am still alive and en route to Venice, accompanying their ambassador, Girolamo Donato, and their native poet, Pietro Bembo. I have not received any further instructions from you. Please send direct to our priory in Venice, or to the Friars Spirituali, where I plan to visit. My time in Bologna and Ferrara were profitable for the cause, and I believe I have made a favourable impression on those that matter. I also had an audience with the Marchesa of Mantua in Ferrara whose husband was the former gonfalonier of the papal forces but is now imprisoned by Venice. Regarding my last missive, I have seen nothing of them that pursue me and have nothing as yet to report on that knight which I in turn pursue.

Regarding the present troubles: there is no sight of the end of this war, though there is little appetite for it among the northern fiefs and duchies. The league has seen many reverses which only delay matters. The emperor finally came in August with a large imperial army, accompanied by bodies of French and Spanish troops. But I hear that there was again disarray in the provisioning, particularly regarding horses, oxen and mules, and it was weeks before they reached the Veneto from Trento. They laid siege to Padua in mid-September, giving Pitigliano ample time to array as many troops as were still available in the city. The walls were breached, but unaccountably, the emperor did not press his advantage. Instead he desisted the siege altogether by the thirtieth of September and is even now heading north with the main part of his army. I suppose they wish to re-cross the alps before the winter snows block their arrival in the Tyrol.

I cannot but think the Venetians will be amazed that *fortuna* has thus so smiled upon them by this incompetence. The Fuggers will surely worry about the safety of their vast loans to the emperor. Perhaps the League will sue for terms? It is unlikely, for I saw His Holiness in Bologna last month, and he has an iron will, as you know. So it may be that the discord will continue another year until one or other tires.

I attach my usual receipts and accounts. Believe me to be a most loyal servant of the order.

Your servant, Hugh de Erpingham

LETTER TO ISCHIA, OCTOBER 2ND

To the most pious and gracious Duchess of Frankavilla, and her illustrious ward, the Lady Vittoria,

Greetings from Ferrara, and many thanks for your recent letter. You remonstrate with me, lady, that I did not behave gentlemanly enough at court in Urbino, and for this I do owe an apology. I did not bid you farewell when we left that morning, and I did little to seek you out during my sojourn in the noble palazzo of your esteemed grandfather. But be assured I did not seek to avoid you either, as you imply. I will not patronise you with excuses, but suffice to say, my mind was vexed with many matters during my time there, and my departure required haste.

Furthermore, at court I was aware that there were too many prone to find gossip where there was nothing at all. Surely Erasmus was right when he personified Folly to say that she needed not temples and churches built in her honour, for by their behaviour the mass of men and women do show that the whole earth is her church. My withdrawal was partly due to zeal for your honour. In time I hope you will understand this was my motive.

But perhaps I begin to make excuses too readily. My conscience now accuses me that I was also uncomfortable with your constant questions about the state of my salvation, which I confess is still far from certain. Did you enclose these verses particularly to bring light once more into my dungeon? Or do I presume too much, vain man that I am? Verily they do bring hope, as do your prayers. In line three you say we need heaven's light to see the upward path; pray that I may have that illumination now as I journey to Venice, not knowing what evils await – within and without.

Our works are vain, and all our wills are blind.
At the first flight our mortal pinions fail,
Unless in Christ we find our help and stay,
Almighty Lord, whose loving care would show
To us the load of sin and all its stain;

You say here that 'All our wills are blind' and I do not know what it is you mean. Is it that human freewill is blinded generally by sin? Or, that our wills alone are impotent to achieve the divine call to purity? Verily, I think you mean the latter. For I have tried this 'first flight' and have felt 'my mortal pinions fail'. When you found me at Urbino, I was still in an Icarus fall. You write that it is the Almighty's 'loving care' – and not his wrath – that shows 'to us the load of sin and all its stain'. I think Saint Paul says something similar. If true, this to me is worth more than a king's ransom, or the booty of Burgundy. I feel the load, I see the stain; it is ever before my face. So I shall yet hope that – as you write further down – God might 'maintain and succour this my soul by sin brought low'. Further you write:

And though my sins in youth I do confess
Have countless been, and in days of old
The time misspent has caused Thee sore distress,
May'st Thou in pardoning love our guilt enfold;
Whilst I implore in penitence and tears
Thy grace to find Thee in my better years.

In this last canto surely you sacrifice poetic art to preach unto me? Days of old? You must rephrase this, or I will set Bembo on you! But nonetheless how sweet it is to my ears – how like water to my thirst. The thought that better years ahead might be my portion means more to me this cold morning than I can reasonably express. But behind me a voice also whispers and accuses, that it is not 'the sins of youth' so much that will damn me, but sins I am yet bound to pursue on this uncertain path of duty that I now tread. Pray lady, that God will guide this wayward ship to safe harbour. I cannot write more for the courier is leaving at the opening of the city gates.

My debt to you both is more than you can know and more than I can repay in this brief life. If I survive this winter I would be honoured to accept your invitation to the wedding next spring.

I am, as ever, etc

OCTOBER 15TH IN THE PO DI GORO DELTA

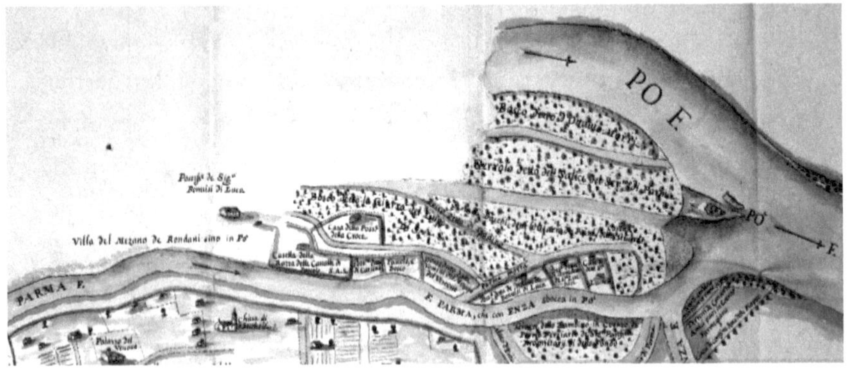

They leave the Po proper upstream somewhere past Berra. The larger river is part of the permeable and shifting frontier of this current war. The grey, green waters of the larger river have therefore become a place where vessels from either side might be fired upon by either side. So their long shallow-draught barge, which Bembo says is little better than a cattle magano, breaks south onto the Po di Goro, idling through swamps and forests toward the small fishing port of Goro.

The river is usually about two hundred feet wide and the surly helmsman who hails from Ostellato and has charged a princely sum, keeps a steady course in midstream and a sharp eye on the banks. The ambassador has an escort of the duke's men, but only six of them, and lightly armed with halberds and cross hilts. Any boat, let alone a shallow boat without sides, is literally a sitting duck. Hugh, sitting with Bembo and the ambassador on broad wooden benches at the stern, keeps one eye on the helmsman and another on the bank. He would have preferred to have gone by night and not with such an ostentatious company. He has heard about this place. They say the same things about the folk that inhabit these marshes as they do about the wastrels that inhabit his own Norfolk fens. These sorts of hellholes are the last places on earth for the outcasts. *Surely only misery and blight are here.* Hugh shudders.

All along the banks it is the same: makeshift landing places, collapsing jetties, ungainly spindles of salt-bleached wood, some rotted thin as the legs of the storks who watch motionless from the mud banks. Heat sears their nostrils.. Acrid odours from the marshes and miasmic vapour from the rubbish dumps near each ramshackle homestead. Gaunt dogs with cankerous sores pick over bones and skin. Behind them, on the hazy horizon lies that vast hinterland of mosquito-ridden salt marshes, canals, maritime pine forests where only the smugglers can navigate, and where only the lawless need live. Nothing grows there but hidden hordes of piratic contraband. It is that half-spoken place where the only duty paid is to the silent poor who take what they can get from smugglers and turn a blind eye to the rest.

To the south of the delta lies the Romagna proper, *le Marche*, ostensibly papal territories but in appearance a disparate warren of petty fiefdoms and estates ruled in turn by nobodies, who rarely die in their beds before being disabused of their dubious gains; before another *l'ultimo* arises in their place to bleed the *minuto populo*. From this impoverished soil come the canon fodder that fuel the fame of Italy's great *condotierre*, those mercenary armies hired out to the highest bidder who, in the case of the Sforza, even occasionally land themselves dukedoms of their own. A man born poor in the Romagna has very little to lose. Ruling from his Rocca at Imola, Cesare Borgia brought some stability to the region on behalf of his father. His chosen method was autocracy tempered by strangulation. But after his ignominious passing, the region slipped back into petty cycles of malignity, vendetta, grief and poverty. All this Hugh hears from the lips of Bembo and Donato, each seeming to delight in outdoing the other in their tales. It seems to Hugh that these places are as much part of a grim fantasy as they are Badlands for Venetians, the place they have been warned of since infancy, the place you'll be sent if you don't finish your Livorno fish stew, or if you carry on telling lies.

Out in the delta and away from the reed banks of the river Hugh feels more at ease. The helmsman's ragged and bony offspring, two sons and three daughters, pull on the bleached oars that propel them away from the land. Bembo is pointing out the different craft that seem to be part of his own childhood memories. 'There is a *topo*. I used to have one of those with my brother. We went everywhere in it until he got a *topetto,* and then I had to row on my own. Look at that small flat-nosed gondola; we call it a *sandalo*. You can go up any shallow cutting in that, go anywhere, even the *palvi* on the lagoon. I used to go with my cousin, also called Pietro, to catch fish on the lagoon in one of those. Ah, happy days they were, searching for *mazzancolle* and *canoce* on the mud flats.' Bembo is standing hands on hips in the fever of his homecoming. He confesses he had forgotten how much he missed his native city, missed the water. As they edge further away from the shore, the small fleets of *bragozetti, bragagna* and *bragozzi*, twin-masted fishing boats from Chioggia, trail nets on one side, their crews talking and singing. What strikes Hugh most is the painted sails, prows and gunwales that seem to him more reminiscent of the art of the Mamaluk Turks of Egypt: geometric designs, clay blues and deep reds, even crudely carved figures, one with an angel another with a dove. As the afternoon wears on a cooler breeze comes from the north across water that twists and swirls from the oars.

The helmsman hales the fishermen when they are close enough to talk. Their accents are so thick, vowels so spongy that Hugh has to ask Donato what is being said. 'He is asking which of them is taking fish to Venice and has space for passengers and luggage. The fishermen are calling to their colleagues in the further boat, the *bragagna*. They say that he is taking their catch to sell at the *pescheria* next to the Rialto. Apparently, his boat has a shallow enough draft that it can even get over the palvi in the lagoon at low waters. He wants to know who we are. He doesn't want any trouble.'

Bembo is not happy about traveling like this to his home city, but the ambassador explains that it is just a precaution because of the war. The helmsmen overhears the poet and says he is welcome to wait for a more comfortable ship, but that is not what they agreed. He will want more money. The ambassador laughs it off; the danger of war erodes respect in the uncouth. 'Do not concern yourself, my friend. It will only be until we reach the blockade of Venetian galleys on the outer lagoon, from where we can send for an eighteen-oared *dispotona*, more suited to your illustrious but unexpected homecoming. Now sit you by me, signor, and tell me more about the days when the gods lived on earth and war was unknown among us.'

'And gentlemen did not travel in fishing boats,' Bembo says, giving a weary sigh, and sitting back on the bench, beret in hand. 'You know, Ambassador, I do believe you are enjoying all this.'

Donato smiles and raises his hands. 'A father so far from his children will suffer any indignity and any means of transport however incommodious, to be reunited with them again. You have a love of your city, which is a good thing, but the love of a parent?' He breaks off midstream leaving it as a question and looking at Hugh. For a moment Hugh does not know how to answer, lost as he is in thinking of his religion's claim that there is fatherhood at the centre of the very cosmos. A world of sons searching for fathers, he knew too well, but the reverse? Eventually he nods and gives Donato the faintest of smiles.

The negotiations are carried out successfully by the ambassador, and Wilf helps the duke's soldiers load their baggage. The fishermen's captain takes payment in florins and ducats, hedging his bets, and seems almost content with the deal after the soldiers leave his boat. Wilf sits scowling in the meagre steerage with Donato's manservant and the trunks. The other three are shown to a bench in the stern among the baskets half full of *shie*, miniscule and still wriggling; *triglie*, a reddish sort of mullet; and *seppioline*, baby cuttlefish. The captain nods at Hugh with a special deference, muttering with approval toward Donato in a thick Veneziano dialect. 'Cavliere di Rodi.'

Ignoring the unpleasant odour, Donato leans toward Hugh, modulating his dialect into Toscana as he knows it is easier for Hugh to understand. 'Our hosts approve of you, signor. They share these waters with the Turks. They sail as far as Corfu for fish. We talk sometimes about the menace of the infidel as if he were far away, but in truth he is just across there.' The ambassador points vaguely east toward Istria and Dalmatia, somewhere beyond the duck-egg blue horizon. 'Beyond the last Venetian outposts they are waiting for their chance to destroy us.'

'That is, if we don't destroy ourselves first,' Bembo says as he takes his seat again. He has been gazing south, right hand shading his brow. 'I feel morose today gentlemen. It is likely the smell of fish, fresh or otherwise. I think I can see Ravenna down the coast. Do you know my father had a statue of Dante erected there, the place of the poet's exile, the place where he died.' Bembo slumps down next to them. 'Poor Dante. My father always said that a true poet, like a true prophet, is without honour in his home town among his kinsmen. It is true. But better exile and ignominy than gain the dubious honours of Ausonius.'

'Ausonius, the poet?' Hugh says.

'Yes, poet,' Donato says, 'but also elevated to quaestor and later consul under Emperor Gratian. Those were times, eh, Bembo? when a poet could rise in the world!'

Ignoring the ribbing and trying to maintain his dolorous mood, Bembo says, 'It was a sign of Rome's decline that he could be lauded thus. His were the sins of Aaron, to cater for the tastes of a debased multitude. His wages were their praise. In a world of such wonders, such as this is, anaemic poetry should be punished with the *strapado* and not political offices. I would rather die in obscurity than become an emperor on such terms.'

'Nobly said, my friend, nobly said.' Donato says, 'For my own part – and I admit my tastes are not as refined as yours – I always liked his verses on the Moselle River.'

'It was the empire's last stand. I think it was you who told me about it, Pietro.' Hugh speaks almost to himself, not thinking about poetry at all, but rather straining to see what he can of Ravenna in the shimmering distance. 'I should like to visit there one day.'

'It was me,' Bembo says. 'The emperor retreated from Rome to establish a more defensible capital on the marshes, not dissimilar to the first poor Venetians who fled the barbarians to the *extremis de finibus*, the ends of the earth, in their turn. Though I always stress that the barbarians within are the greater curse. The world had never known anything as deep and lasting as the *Pax Romana* and yet it fell. It wasn't just outside pressure, hordes of barbarians crossing the Danube and so forth. The great buildings were plundered first by private landowners who used them as quarries for their own estates. Never forget that. The first signs and cause of the decline were private greed. They made themselves very grand indeed while all else crumbled around them. They it is, I say, who are the real barbarians. And here we are so many years later thinking that it could never happen to us, even when the example of Constantinople is before us. Did you know, Hugh, that their last emperor pleaded for years with the wealthy of the city to donate funds for its defence, but they would not. And when the infidels finally swarmed over their walls, and they came and pled with him, his reply was "Go and die with your gold, seeing you could not live without it." So I say again, Rome fell through inner weakness, moral decay, and it fell slowly, like a creeping death.'

Hugh shoots Donato a knowing and humorous glance, but does not interrupt, for he has found that Bembo will often let out gems if you let him rattle on. 'I always remember the words of Marcellinus with a certain dread and foreboding: *bibliothecis sepulcrorum ritu in perpetuum clausis,* surely libraries like tombs are closed forever. It minds me of the Vivarium of Cassiodorus, that late convert, who set aside so many books in Calabria after the Ostrogoths sacked Rome. So many books, but where are they now? Such a library but insufficiently endowed. But how can one make contingency against an apocalypse? I do not feel we are free from the shadow of that, even now.'

'Oh God, please someone get him some food,' Donato says, half in seriousness, and giving the poet a friendly shove. 'I don't think I can take this all the way up the coast. Have we any anchovies left?'

'No, please, I won't,' Bembo says, screwing up his nose as the breeze lessens and the fish odours strengthen.

'You are in an exalted company of naysayers, but I still say you are wrong, *caro*.' Donato slaps the poet's bony leg. 'Hilarianus expected the cataclysm would come in the seventh century, Augustine cautiously suggested the tenth. They were both wrong, and I think you are allowing melancholic humours to influence your learning. Now have an anchovy, or else I shall be forced to sing to cheer you up.'

'My apologies friends,' Bembo says, a mischievous smile creasing his pale face. 'I always considered myself an optimist. I think it is Hugh's influence. That, or the fish.'

BEFORE SUNRISE, 16TH OCTOBER 1509, VENETIAN LAGOON

In the grey light of dawn, and through the shifting mists, Bembo says he thinks that they are near the southern entrance of the lagoon, past Chioggia but not as far as Malmocco. It has been a long and chill night. He has not seen the great stone landings of Palifacado or indeed the spires of the Franciscan friary of San Nicolo much further north on *il Litto*, the long, thin sandbank protecting the lagoon. Hugh peers into the mists, which sometimes clear to reveal a thin black line which may be land but he is never sure. Unlike the seas he sails, these are prone to regular sea fog, particularly in winter. He looks up to check that the ambassador's addition to the mast, the ensign of the signoria, the Venetian Lion of Saint Mark, gold on a ruby background. It is still there, damp and limped, rustling occasionally when the winds whisper to reveal more of the beast. The lion's paw still raised to strike. They too are at the mercy of lions, for the blockade will be near, and they, coming in the small hours may well be taken as an enemy. Hugh grips the cloak about his neck and closes his eyes once more. He must speak to the amiable ambassador before they disembark about his real reason for being in Venice — *Vendramin.*

This ghostly lagoon is a suitable lair for such a phantom. He must get what information he can about Vendramin from Donato. He knows the tack he will take and is thinking about how to phrase it with gentility – rolling sentences through his mind, round and round – when suddenly a shout brings him to with a jump. He opens his eyes and sees a shaft of morning sunlight stream across the sea, casting a long shadow from the sails into the water toward the further mists where Venice is expected to be, like some strange and fantastical land that will only appear to those who believe. He rubs his eyes and shakes his head. He has been sleeping. He turns to see the captain pointing, and shouting comes once more from the mist, then the hollow clank of a bell. Hugh springs to his feet and moves quickly toward the middle of the boat. Now he can see the masts like a forest appearing before his eyes above the fog. Twenty, no thirty, no, fifty ships of the line. A vast floating fortress, and one of the world's greatest navies looms higher and higher until Hugh feels a great lump in the pit of his stomach. He can hear the unmistakable rolling and clank of one, then two, eight pound canon on the nearest ship.

The ensign! Can they see it? He glances upward, it is there. Their own captain is waving. He hears the splash of oars. They are sending us a lighter. Again he hears the clanking of bells, some near the ships, and some far and more numerous, the bells for the office of prime from the myriad islands in the lagoon and from perhaps within the city itself. He returns to the ambassador, who is still seated and still almost asleep.

'Signor, be awake. We are within sight of the fleet. They are sending a lighter to board us.'

'Hmm,' Donato half opens his eyes and then heaves a long sigh of contentment. 'Good, Hugh, good. I was not asleep, but listening to the music of the ducks and gulls. Have you heard them?'

'Well, no.' Hugh strains his ears and makes out the caw and squabbling of sea birds, now rapidly disappearing under the noise of creaking timbers and ropes, oars on rowlocks, the shouting of sailors. He hears no music, just the work of men. *That's a monstrous galley.* Bembo is stretching his legs and now talking to the captain at the other end of the deck. The captain is waving the pennant of his own city Chioggia, a gold lion on red surrounded by a laurel wreath. He does not look alarmed so Hugh turns away and seizes his chance. 'Before we take our leave of you, signor, I should speak about a matter of some import to my order.'

'Really, my boy? Import, eh.' Donato pushes his heels against the boards and rights himself into a sitting posture with attendant groans. He smooths his crumpled, burgundy wool cloak and loosens the brass neck clasp to reveal an area of unshaven neck. 'Say on Hugh, I am listening.'

'It concerns a man of your city, from a patrician family, indeed a knight of our order.' Hugh feels the beads of sweat forming under his beret despite the chill air. This is going to be harder than he thought. He licks his lips and tries again. 'I have been sent to find Marcantonio Vendramin, son of your former doge.'

'Vendramin.' At the mention of the name, the ambassador's eyes open wide. 'He is one of our most revered sons, as I am sure you know. If we could canonise him we would. But I understand he is dead.'

'No.' Hugh searches the grey eyes for any sense of falsity.

'No?' Donato's eye, professes surprise, yet shows some artifice that alerts Hugh's hunter instinct.

'He is very much alive, or at least was when he escape me in Siena this Easter. I have it in my power to reward handsomely a man who could provide information leading to him.'

'I see.' Donato reaches up with his index finger and runs it against the grain of the new grey hairs under his throat. 'I see.'

Hugh presses his advantage, speaking quietly and quickly. 'I will find this man with or without help, but any man who makes my search easier will be richly recompensed. An honest man with so many children has many cares, many receipts. I should rather see the reward go to a man like that than someone less worthy.'

The ambassador looks toward his hands, puckering his lips. He nods slightly but then speaks without looking at Hugh. 'We have spoken much, Hugh, about this life, about our place in the events about us;

what, if anything, we shall be remembered for and so forth. There are few, I think, that can look at their time here and know that they have left the world so much better. But Marcantonio Vendramin may yet be such a man.'

'Signor, I cannot now divulge what I know but – '

'You talk of the Borgia gold, perhaps? My boy, I may have been some years on Crete, but even I know the rumours. Do not destroy a man's reputation for rumours. His family is very great here. People will not take kindly, at a time of already fraught nerves, to suggestions and insinuations.' Donato looks up and raises a wary eyebrow.

'Believe me, signor, I know what he has. I know it for a certainty.' Hugh lets his words and eye bore into the ambassador for a moment before continuing. 'Even now it might be his ill-gotten wealth that wreaks mischief between these Christian states, to punish the insolence of the powerful, the Chigi, the Fuggers. I don't know.'

'But why, Fra Hugh, why? It does not signify.'

'I cannot say for certain, but the words he spoke still haunt me. He means to use that money to bring ruin; that is all I suspect. And I mention it to you that you might help me with a clear conscience.'

'Hugh, Hugh.' The old man's eyes turn paternal, the lines of many creases deepen into a good natured smile. 'I see that you intend good, and I think that in the end you shall do good. But I stand by what I said before.'

'Before?'

'That Marcantonio Vendramin may yet prove to be one of the few men who leaves this world unquestionably better.'

'How can you say that?' Hugh is aghast.

'Because I am an old man, and I know many things that you do not.' And then, with the briefest of smiles, Donato pats Hugh's cheek and rises to greet the approaching boat. 'A good tree bears good fruit.'

ON BOARD THE MARIA ELISABETTA, FLAGSHIP OF THE FLEET

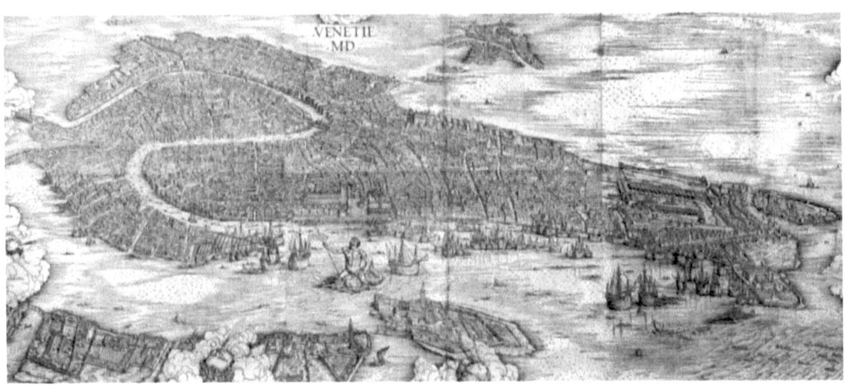

Angelo Trevisan is a man who enjoys his position as admiral. He is, as Hugh sees from the first, a corpulent middle-aged ass of a man, riding high on a noble lineage, like a plate of jellied eggs on a silver platter. He is tall, potbellied with the *belle vivere*, crowned with voluminous black curls and directed by a lazy left eye. He appears from the poop deck in a flurry of dark blue velvet and a broad gold sash, waving lugubrious fingers back and forth with a myriad of orders to men who dash this way and that with fear stricken faces. Hugh notices that most of them make the appearance of activity merely so they will avoid being chided. He also notices provisioning boats arriving alongside the nearest ships, and soldiers and supplies being loaded.

'Why are these men still armed?' Trevisan blinks constantly as the sharp winter light cuts across the deck.

The first lieutenant stands to. 'He is a holy knight, my lord. Gave his name as Hugh Erpingham.' The name causes a general stir among the sailors and marines.

'Erpingham, you say? Gave his name!' Trevisan stammers. 'Spies sneaking in on a fishing boat, and you believed him, I suppose? You dolt.' Trevisan violently pushes his officer away in front of all the men, his bottom lip curled under his upper teethin an expression of both of hatred and pleasure. 'Take away their arms at once.'

For a moment, the nearest sailors seem reluctant to approach. Hugh realises his right hand is already on the pommel of the colhonna. He looks to his left and sees Donato glancing anxiously his way then quickly removing his own seal of office from within his doublet.

'I can vouch for these good men, admiral. I am Girolamo Donato, ambassador to the papal court.'

'What?' Trevisan glances at the seal and back at Donato. 'I see. Yes, I know you. And what have you accomplished with all your soft words, eh? You people will never understand the way these things work. The affairs of state are settled with steel and shot, not fine words.'

'Indeed,' the ambassador braves a smile and continues over the top of the insult. 'And these are my companions, Signor Pietro Bembo, the great poet and citizen of the most serene republic and Fra Hugh Erpingham of Rhodes, the knight conspicuous by his own valour and illustrious by his reputation.'

Trevisan is still blinking and glancing down at Hugh as if he still cannot quite believe it. He is genuinely perplexed for, as a worshipper of mere size and strength, he does not know whether to be appalled that a man of Hugh's reputation should be smaller than he, or indeed, rather happy that he is so much taller. For a moment he wavers but then sneers. 'On a Bragagna, great God.'

'We were anxious to return with all speed. My own embassage requires haste.'

'I bet it does. And what is that may I ask?'

'You may admiral, but it is for Doge Loredan only.'

'Oh,' Trevisan huffs as he begins tucking two thumbs, thick as German sausages, into his sash. 'And them, how do we know they are not spies? Where have they come from?'

'We have all come from Ferrara where we were guests of the duke, and before that Bologna, where we alike had audiences with His Holiness.'

'My God, the very viper's nest. And what were they there consorting about, I wonder.'

'Admiral, I must warn you,' the ambassador raises his head and speaks sternly. 'Fra Erpingham represents a sovereign military order with no part in this war. If his diplomatic status and immunity were to be abused, it would reflect very badly on you if the council should hear of it. His embassage is with the doge, as is mine, and we should alike be granted every courtesy and honour befitting our ancient republic.'

'Really,' Trevisan sways a moment, not quite prepared for the fast repulse. Stupid and suspicious, Hugh thinks, bad combination. He must be from a very fine family to have this job. Suddenly Hugh notices Trevisan's eye widen with a malevolent joy. 'Ferrara, eh. That young duke fancies himself as a big noise in the canon department. Friend of yours, I expect. Well, we're on our way down to teach that double crossing bastard and his brother that they've picked the wrong people to cross swords with. And when I've finished laying waste his pathetic dukedom, his own people will pay me to strap him and his family to my murtherer and blow them in the general direction of Bologna. Friends of yours, are they?' The admiral, still hands on hips, leans forward, his lip curling under his teeth again and his eyes ablaze, as if he knows he can goad Hugh into an incident anytime he chooses. 'A thirty-six pounder would look good up his arse, signor, don't you think? But the duchess? A woman with her reputation, it might get lost up there, signors, might get lost. But maybe you know that, signors, eh, eh? They say not many guests leave her palace without the French disease.'

Hugh sets his jaw and averts his eyes toward the boot straps of the lieutenant, making the strictest agreement with his temper that under no provocation will he disgrace his Order by bundling this cockscomb into the lagoon with a few less teeth.

The ambassador takes up the slack. 'It is very politic of you, admiral, to use vulgarities to test the sincerity of these men, but I can tell you it is not necessary. Do I understand you have orders to open another front against the League?'

'As soon as the sutlers, vintners and the like say our holds have sufficient, and these Albanians and Dalmatians are on board, we'll be off to raise a merry hell.' He gestures with evident pleasure toward the grim faced, soulless mercenaries mounting the plank off a pontoon, shaven heads, scarred, stitched and re-stitched; bills and pikes; cross hilts and bucklers; helmets clanking at their sides; crossbows over their shoulders; blood and money in their eyes. On another plank to their left a quartermaster is counting in supplies for the expedition, announcing each case or barrel as he ticks them off his list, as if they had been guests to a masque. 'Strips of dried beef, twelve cases; salted lamb joints, six crates. Should be ten it says here. Carrots and rutabaga, twenty-two crates. Get them somewhere cool, lads, d'you hear? Somewhere cool.'

Trevisan stretches his collar and glances one last time between Hugh and the mercenaries. 'My stratiotes look hungry, do they not? And they shall have their fill in the Estense.'

TEN MINUTES LATER

In turn the islands loom and pass in the thinning mists. Trevisan is half a mile away now, thank God.

The morning sun, like a golden orb full of strange enchantments, seems to suspend the islands of Proveglia, Santa Spirito, Santa Clemente and Santa Maria di Gratia right above the waters. Cupolas, towers, spires, fastidious poplars and Cypress trees, crenulated brick walls with shuttered windows, and rooves glowing orange in Hugh's enraptured eyes. The outer islands of the lagoon separate on the horizon and float past them. Monks and nuns can already be seen in some places on these holy islands and on the lagoon. Men in sandals and straw hats are fishing with nets, bows and arrows. Hugh has not reached the city, but already he feels it is all a dream: Venice, *la Serenissima*, the most serene, married to the sea.

A bridge between east and west, the city has about a hundred and fifty thousand people of all races—three times the population of Rome. Over a hundred churches and sixty-five monasteries are dotted over the lagoon and the city. So are perhaps as many as eight-thousand brothels which at one time were confined to the Corte Rampani by the *Procuratoria*, but now have spread like the French pox across the city.

As the sun begins to lift the mist like the veil of a bride, and their eighteen-oared *dispotona* effortlessly glides within view of Saint Mark's,

Hugh thinks that he has seen nothing like this before in all his life: the oldest republic on the planet with possessions and lands stretching over most of the known world. All he has known until now is her extremities in the western Mediterranean, but now he has entered her bridal chamber, her *sanctus sanctorum. The pope said that if she didn't exist, we would have to invent her. She is a dream, for sure. Tyre's naval empire disappeared and left no traces, too practical for art, too satisfied for poetry. But Venice, she has endured and prospered.*

Hugh had called her 'the Great Whore that traded on many waters'; he had despised her, at least in his thoughts. And yet at this sublime and soaring beauty—the cupolas and minarets of Saint Mark's, the white marble wharf, the arcades, crenulations and patterned brickwork on the doge's palace, and the great red bell tower rising like a monumental mast above the haze—he feels his heart burn in his breast. No one anywhere in Europe would think of anything other than fortifying their residences and public buildings. But here in Venice, they have made fairy tales in brick and marble for hundreds of years. The cloudless skies gain in colour and strength so much that the waters are transformed from green to azure blue, as if the whole spectacle were part of one pageant in the doge's honour. Hugh observes the faces of the oarsmen, and then the gait of the Venetians who go busily about their morning business on the *fondementa*. But none seems to register surprise. Beauty and goodness are not one and the same. Perhaps this city, this oligarchy masquerading as a republic, this façade, is the beautiful face of a witch. Is Vendramin hiding here? Could villainy dwell with such beauty and not be moved as he is now? It makes Hugh want to be part of it, part of its fabric.

He examines the roof of the palace and the waterline of the sewage sluice from the dungeons. He has studied wood cuts and etchings and subtly made enquiry from people like Castiglione before ever he left Urbino. The Marchese of Mantua claimed in correspondence to be in the dungeons, but it would be more likely to have such an important prisoner away from miasmic vapours in the cells in the garret above the council chambers. *No one gets a ransom for a dead hostage, even a dead marchese. But then perhaps those upper cells are not as secure? Maybe that is why he complained of the rising waters and of a fever, so that he could get higher, and so escape himself?* Hugh knows he will have to request an interview with the prisoner, on some pretext or other, and thus see for himself. He has the marchesa's letter in his breast pocket for the doge, another from the Duchess Elizabetta for her brother. Why do it? Just because she asked? No. It's not that. *I do this one good deed as a payment to the Almighty – save one man, so I can assassinate another.* He feels his doublet to make sure the letters are still there, and then begins to worry about telling Donato about Vendramin. He was so sure of a positive response. Faced now with the monumental challenge of the palazzo and the inscrutable quest to find an invisible pin in a hayrick the size of Venice, Hugh begins to feel weaker by the minute.

As they round the last point of the island known as Giudecca, they enter the tangle of merchant and military shipping: carracks, men of war and even former Turkish *gokes*, mixed in with *megani, braggozetti, topi, topetti* and *gondolas*. A whole world on water. A world without horses. A forest of masts and white sails. A world of reflections. Everywhere the sounds of hammers and saws, the echo of driven iron nails, the slap of oars and the clink of anchor chains. Cattle on board the shallow *megani* are made so somnolent by the gentle motion of their transport that they barely grunt or bleat, but rather look dumbly across at Hugh over the high wooden rails on which their heads rest.

They put in between a Turkish caramusal and a Dalmatian frigate just east of the great piazza, though Bembo is reminding Hugh, they call it a *campo* in Venice, not a piazza. The creak of pulleys and the shouts of stevedores now become more evident. In war time the work of trade and tax go on with even greater vigour. Forget the Rialto; people at this end of the city will buy produce straight from the quay, straight from the boxes. One man is shouting from the quay at them and another newly arrived boat, saying that he will give them fifty ducats for thirty gold florins. Within a two hundred yard stretch a Venetian can buy almost anything he or she wants: beef hearts and truffles, vinegared eels called seppie from Burano, cuttlefish in their own ink, and juicy artichokes; pots with calves' brains, onions and livers in retsina. Barrels of wine are being bought up even as they are being rolled toward the warehouses. There are tables full of dates and bolts of silk wrapped in coarse muslin; men and women, crowing over the *mercerie*; crates with cinnamon, paper ginger, nutmeg, ambergris, musk, attar of roses, gold, Indian diamonds – who needs Antwerp? – Ceylonese pearls, opiates, cane sugar from Madeira, timber from the Levant, salt from Ibiza, which some Venetians favour above the local salt even though it is all the same. Housewives, monks, friars, children and red-capped Jews mingle among swarthy sailors, negro slaves and well fleshed merchants, discussing the weather, price of alum and lead, and the latest news of the war.

Hugh breathes in deeply and from the scent of lemon, bergamot, jasmine and salt water feels that he is back in Rhodes. Will there be any correspondence for him, any orders? As he steps on the quay, he is met by urchins with yellow caps calling, '*Loghetto, logetto, signor. Eccellentissimo.*'

Bembo scatters them with his hand. 'We have lodgings, you rascals. Now be at your work.' He turns to Hugh. 'I assume we have lodgings?'

'For sure; we will stay at the priory.' He turns back to make sure Wilf is seeing to the baggage, and then to Donato. 'Are we free to go?'

Donato looks toward the approaching officials in black woollen coats and black berets. 'Certainly. I will deal with the commissioners. And I will also make a request for an audience for you at the council. My advice would be to secure a gondolier to take your man with the baggage and then get Bembo to walk you there. It is not far. It is a pleasant morning, is it not? Perhaps we shall see you again. You may call on me, Fra Hugh, if you wish. My sons should certainly be gratified to meet you, nay my daughters too.'

Hugh takes the ambassador's hand. 'I am much in your debt, signor. I am sure I shall.'

'Good, good. It is, I am afraid, a very modest house on the *Fondementa San Felice*, just opposite the little *Ponte de Chiodo*. Bembo will show you for he knows he is welcome too.'

Bembo bows and takes the man's arm with a vigour that Hugh has not seen in his companion before.

Later, when they have made their arrangements for the baggage and are watching the lyrical steps of the ambassador tripping away toward the doge's palace with commissioners in attendance, Bembo says with perplexity bordering on admiration, 'You know, Hugh, it is a strange thing to see a public official so impecunious. We used to say that we should entrust power to the rich because they were incorruptible, quite apart from asking by what means they obtained their wealth.' Bembo grins and then allows his face to form something approaching a serious and pious expression. 'As you know, we Venetians are largely wealthy by taxing the labours of others. And, of course, by speculation. That merchant standing so proudly by his silks might well look happy. He'll be asking a hundred ducats and upwards for fifty bolts of printed silk. Many of these spices are sold at a three thousand percent profit. Dear old Donato would only need to invest in a few little ventures to see his family right. But men like that have no stomach for it. They would rather work, I suppose. My father was very much like that. He was a public servant too, a governor. Not glorious enough for me perhaps, but there is a lot to be said for a steady income and the ease of a good name – particularly the income.'

'And the speculators? Did your family never join them?'

'No, I think my father's brother invested a bit in your English wool and made a modest fortune, but we Bembos were more clerical. My father had a special disdain, I remember, for speculators who were growing in number when he was young. He hated all gambling, saw the ruin of it, perhaps feared it might ruin his sons too. He used to lecture me particularly that gamblers and speculators united the worst folly and vice. For, he said, they concentrate their entire interest on chance rather than knowledge, and with all the insolence of an unvarnished egotism, backed opinions that they had no grounds for forming except they were their own or they might fill their pockets with filthy lucre. The rolls of the dice, the stumbling of a horse at the *palio*, the uncertain winds of bringing home our stocks and commodities from the Levant.

He did not trust Fortuna, my father, not at all, almost un-Venetian. He used to warn me about Buonaccorso Pitti. He was almost a byword in our house. Apparently, he lost such vast fortunes that only the princes of Savoy, Brabant and Bavaria could afford to play with him. Papa was wise though; I see that now. His favourite poem was a short one, and he made me write it out many times when he caught me at dice. *O fortuna, velud luna, stau variabilis semper crescis aut decrescis, vita destestabilis,* oh fortune, like the moon, ever changing, eternally you wax and wane, dreadful life. Something, something, *egestatem, potestatem, dissolvit ut glaciem*, poverty and power, it melts them like ice. There are two more stanzas, and I couldn't help feeling sorry for the poet's wife for in truth he must have been a miserable bastard to live with.'

'But he cured you of the urge.'

'Indeed yes. I despise gambling, of course. I know they say that it gets a hold of men, but I can assure you, it has no hold on me, Hugh. I have given it up at least four and twenty times already.' Bembo catches Hugh's eyes to make sure they are reacting with mirth of some sort. 'In fact, I would go so far as to say he cured me so thoroughly that I now suffer the penury of a poet, and if it were not for my good Duchess Elizabetta, I would not be able to even keep myself in hose, let alone quills and ink. And that's the truth. Almost. Bless my soul, it is good to be back in Venice. So many places I must show you. Listen, listen to that, Hugh.' Bembo puts a hand on Hugh's sleeve to stop him walking. 'The bell from the campanile of San Marco. We call it the *Marangona*. Ah! How crisp and clear, like a good wine malmsey, and so different from the clanking of that bell in Florence, which they call the *Vacca*, the cow, and rightly so. It is good to be home.'

THE GRAND PRIORY OF VENICE & LOMBARDY, 16TH OCTOBER

Through the alleys and over many footbridges they make their way toward the *Calle dei Furlani*. Already the women are about with their laundry, hands and words as coarse as their washboards; the scent of pine resin and laurel leaf from their wash water is faint but nostalgic for Hugh. It momentarily transports him back to the kitchen of Erpingham Hall. Will he ever have a homecoming like Bembo is having now?

The women shift their buckets to let them pass. On the edge of the *fondamenta* lye soap and chamber pots sit side by side, the sharp light illuminating steam rising from both. Further along the undulating pavement, Hugh detects more than a faint odour of urine and the woodsmoke of bread ovens. Blue curling smog lies thick in the cool shadows. Castello is that city quarter between the civic institutions in the Piazza San Marco and the great naval powerhouse of the arsenals, though nearer the latter. So the priory is ideally situated in every sense. The walk has seemed less than ten minutes and, what with his companion's chatter, the journey is a pleasant one. Often Hugh's stomach lurches at the site of a Moorish arch or other arabesque feature in the palazzi he passes along the way. He has not seen such things since his captivity, and they form, for a dark moment, a series of memories that he successfully ignores.

The *fondementa* are, in places, very narrow. They almost come to difficulty when a glass blower turns into a doorway to give way but almost clips Bembo's head with the *borsella* he is carrying on his shoulder. After chiding the scurrilous looking lad, telling him that if his glassblowing was as good as his manners then he was only fit to raise eels in a barrel, Bembo procedes with an extra spring in his gait. 'Of course, if he was any good he'd be on the island of Murano just north of here. But their blowers are under oath never to leave the island lest their competitors find out their secrets.'

'And if they break their oath?'

'Ah, well, *vendetta* is an Italian word.' He pivots on one heel on the crest of a smooth limestone bridge and raises both arms. 'And here we are. Observe, please, for as you can see Venice can be a difficult place in which to navigate. So here is the *Rio di San Antonino* behind me; it will take you more or less north to the upper lagoon. The water entrance to the priory is just there.' Hugh's eyes follow Bembo's excited fingers. Seaweed-covered steps rise through a dark gothic archway with heavy oak doors. 'This street is the *Calle dei Furlani* and this is the entrance of the priory by foot.' Bembo then points Hugh toward a fifteen-foot-high oak door at the end of a small courtyard. To the right of the *calle* stand two guards with black surcoats and halberds.

Hugh observes the two young men. He can smell candle wax and notices a feather merchant and stationers office further up the canal on the left where the fondementa is covered by an arch. Numbers of people mill about, but none seem to be watching them. Hugh catches the scent of bread, no doubt occasioned by the opening and emptying of a communal oven somewhere nearby.

'Fresh bread,' Bembo says, licking his lips. 'Are we expected?'

'No.' Hugh leads the way. 'But I am eager to see how we shall be received.'

'If you will wait here, please.' The secretary of Prior Enrico da Mosta leaves Hugh standing on the rush matting in the hallway while he enters an upper salon to speak to his superior. Hugh glances quickly at the peeling plaster on the wall. Like most of Venice, this place has seen better days. He cannot suppress the thought that the secretary seemed agitated and surprised to see him. *My great fame, or something else?* He walks towards the window and looks down into a small stone courtyard where he might have expected to see horses, but then realises that there will be none here. *Chevaliers san chevaux*, knights without horses. It has a poetic, perhaps even prophetic sound to him. But he does not have time to follow through the metaphysical implications, for from behind the door he can now hear the shill whispered exclamation. 'What? Here? Now?'

The voices at once become softer, quieter and faster. Hugh has counted only four armed men so far and has told Bembo to do the same as he waits below in the lobby. He is not sure what if anything Prior da Mosta has heard from Rome or Rhodes, but now he feels his worst fears confirmed. He smooths his own well-travelled woollens, loosens the window catch, in case the need should arise for a swift exit, and waits for the footsteps on the other side of the door. He can hear another door opening, more footsteps and a further set of whispers and shufflings. *What are they up to? I'll walk in and surprise them. No, stupid idea, stay calm. Here they come.*

The footsteps come in twos. Hugh walks back to face the door, feet spread. He pushes the scrip, which hangs from his belt, to left to allow freer movement of his right arm, and then waits. He has nothing to be ashamed off. The footsteps grow louder and more distinct. He rubs his nose, then loosens the cloak he is wearing by the neck chain and quickly folds it over his left arm. *I'll not take any shit from them.* If the rot has got this far, then he'll act in absentia for the magister. He'll not put up with any shit. *They'll not have me in a dungeon. I won't stand for it. I am Hugh Erpingham.* With a stiff inward breath Hugh tries to rein in his wilder thoughts. He cranes his neck, steadying the twitch starting in his right eye.

The door opens toward him but instead of the rush of assassins, or even the pinched face of the secretary, he sees the genial smile of another man in a prior's gown. Thick white hair rolls over a loose cotton collar. From his olive-tanned skin and easy movement, Hugh guesses the prior is not old. Beads of sweat dot his left temple, and thick grey hair protrudes from his nostrils that move as he speaks – which is in

English. 'Fra Hugh, this is an honour indeed. An honour, an honour. You are, uh, most a welcome.' He shuts the door behind him, leaving the terrified looking secretary gazing after them, and then raises both hands as if he might embrace Hugh or give him the kiss of peace. For a moment Hugh is not sure what to do, so he bows.

When he looks again, the prior is folding his hands in satisfaction, his signature smile pushing two round cheeks outward and upward so that his eyes become unreadable. 'I have heard of your visit to Italy, of course, but you must forgive us for any lack of preparation; we did not know you were coming to honour us too. This war makes communication so difficult, so, so difficult.' Broad smile.

'Nothing from Rome perhaps?'

'No, not from Rome, signor.'

'Nothing from Rhodes?'

'No.'

'I am sorry, Prior. I asked Magister d'Amboise to send orders to me here.'

'We have heard nothing.'

'And do you expect shipping from Rhodes?'

'Yes, yes, of course and soon too, usually before the feast of Saint Jude. Perhaps the magister will send word.'

'Perhaps he will.'

'And until then...' He pauses and raises his hands once more. 'Urgh, until then there is much for you to do, no?'

'Yes, Ambassador Donato is arranging an audience with the council.'

'Of course, of course, the council will want to hear what you have to say. The doge, too. Venice will want to see you, signor. You are very respected here, many, many stories of you.' He pauses and then adds. 'And you are here alone?'

'No, I travel with the poet Pietro Bembo and my servant.'

'Ah yes, I know him; he is a Venetian, *si, si*. Very good, very, very good. *Bene*. And he will stay with his family?'

'No, he will stay here with us. If it please you.'

Slight pause. And then again the broad display of milk white teeth.

'But of course, we are a hospitable order, of course, of course. But our rooms are very simple, perhaps he would prefer...'

The prior leaves the words gently balanced on his uplifted palms. Hugh tries to match the affable expression on the prior's face, and then says, 'He will be honoured to take such hospitality as the order may offer.'

'Very well, as you please.' The prior pauses, then glances behind himself toward the door and then to the stairs. 'Perhaps I might show you around?'

They descend the stairs, find Bembo, and all is at once affability and Veneziano at double speed as both Venetians outdo each other with mutual acquaintances and family connections. The da Mosta are an ancient merchant family with explorers and admirals to their fame. Bembo seems at ease with his host, Hugh thinks, perhaps too much. The prior, constantly tucking his hair behind his ears, leads them through the cloister, under another arch and out into a large verdant garden with lines of laurels and citrus trees, shady walks under laden trellises and a large central lawn, sparkling with dew. Hugh breathes the air which is thinly scented with the last offerings of jasmine, bergamot and lemon balm before the onset of the winter. 'Of course to us Venetians,' the prior says, 'the garden is a most precious commodity. We use ours, which as you can see is one of the largest in Venice, for many good how-you-say "parties"?'

He garbles something at Bembo who interprets. 'The prior means for entertaining officials of the republic and foreign dignitaries.'

Hugh nods affably, and keeps a weather eye on the upper windows where he discerns movement. The prior gives up on his broken English and slips back into Veneziano with Bembo translating. Apparently the building bordering the south of the garden is the hospital of Santa Caterina, which the order had extended much, but now ceded to the Order of the Confraternity of Saints George and Tryphon, also known as the order of the Slavs for they were originally from Dalmatia. The prior keeps talking. Bembo keeps interpreting. Hugh keeps watching.

A servant is emptying the wood-ash from the *scaldini* onto the rose beds and dust drifts across the path. Hugh looks closer as they approach. There are many *scaldini,* small earthenware jars filled with coals from the kitchen fires, stacked on a barrow, their corks collected in a separate pot. Back and forth the servant goes, like a pagan priest scattering the ashes of the dead – *momento mori.* The servant does not look up at them, and the prior does not acknowledge him. For the prior's eyes are more often darting back toward the cloister. He looks nervous as hell. Hugh examines the boundaries, beyond the last avenue of fruit trees, for ways of escape should it ever come to it. But the gardens are bordered by the backs of other houses and tenements

The prior leads them over the pavement, back into the cloister and then through a corridor to their private side entrance to the church of Saint John. It is a small basilica in the Italian style, perhaps a hundred feet by fifty, Hugh reckons, a square rather than rounded apse, constructed, like most of the buildings in Venice, of red brick which occasionally shows where the plaster has crumbled at the base to a height of about two feet. The prior sees Hugh looking at it and explains it is the *aqua alta*, when the high tides and onshore winds bring the water levels higher than most of the city's ground floors. 'But we are married to the sea, of course so –' The prior shrugs and grins again, and then leads them about the walls which are hung with banners from various campaigns and memorial stones marking where some of their priory are buried. Hugh lets him ramble on as they do their circular tour. He is not interested initially, but suddenly hears, in an offhand way, the name he wants and does not want to hear.

'Please say that again, Prior, if you would,' Hugh says, eyeing the crudely sculpted relief of a knight holding a sword over his chest on an almost lifesize stone set into the wall.

'Of course, this is the tomb of Fra Bertucci Contarini. It is very honoured, of course, very honoured. He was the son of a widow and became prior here, dying in the year of our Blessed Lord 1490.'

'Yes,' Hugh snaps with impatience. 'But you said something about the great siege.'

'Yes, of course, Fra Contarini is the quiet saviour of Rhodes for not only did he do great work raising moneys for the relief of Rhodes in the days of Sixtus, but of course, he also was responsible for recruiting the greatest knight, uh how do you say, *il piu famoso, celebrato*? Uh'

'Illustrious?'

'*Si, si*, illustrious, *bene*, of course. Fra Marcantonio Vendramin, our most, uh, most illustrious knight. They were neighbours on the Grand Canal. The Contarini are a very old family. Their palazzo is the *Casa d'Oro*, a very beautiful and magnificent palace, I can assure you, signor. Very magnificent and illustrious.'

'And Vendramin?'

'Oh yes, they are a very old family also, like ours is, like de Mosta. For a time Fra Vendramin's father, Signor Andrea, was our doge. A very great man, very illustrious as you say. But of course he did not wish his eldest son to become a knight, any more than a father would wish a son to become a friar. But Fra Contarini persuaded Marcantonnio to forsake his life of ease. Fra Bertucci was a very holy man, and Marcantonnio loved him as a brother, and so they joined together, and together played a great part in the relief of Rhodes. They are the most remembered sons of our priory.'

'Indeed, Prior, and I am surprised that there is no memorial to Fra Vendramin.' Hugh eyeballs the prior before he can smile. 'Of course, some say that he is not dead at all.'

The prior smirks, and shrugs. 'Yes, I have heard this too. But I do not believe it. Fra Vendramin had, how-you-say, *un grande cuore*, a big, uh, great heart. I have met him many times, a very holy man, a great Venetian. It is a sin to speak evil of the dead.' The prior crosses himself and suggests they see their room. Before they can answer or ask more, he leads them out through the same door, and then to the right toward the stairwell. He glances twice to the left into the cloister as he does so and then ascends.

Hugh follows closely with Bembo lagging in the rear. The prior is explaining that the place is quieter than usual for the knights are at the *Arsenale* looking over the commissioning of a new ship. They come to an upper corridor and walk half way down it. The floor is polished terracotta tiles laid on wooden boards, perhaps maritime pine planks of a dismantled ship. It is a very un-English way to mask the rusticity of wood. But at least they creak. Of this, at least, Hugh approves. Always nice to hear people coming. The prior shows them into a cell with two truckle beds, horse-hair mattresses, a blanket, linen sheets, a table, a wax candle, and a faded fresco on the left wall of Saint John of the Cross. The prior wanders to the window from where he can survey the cloister. Hugh joins him just in time to see a shadow pass at one corner, but after that, nothing except the noise of the grinding of large hinges and distant banging of the outer door.

'Someone in a hurry?'

Again the broad smile, the closed eyes. 'Perhaps, er, you wish to change from your traveling clothes? I will send for water.'

'I thank you. Our luggage will arrive shortly.' Hugh continues to stare deep into the prior, but he sees nothing but the face. *He is hiding something for sure.*

18TH OCTOBER 1509, TWO DAYS LATER IN THE BASILICA OF SAINT MARK

The Feast of Saint Luke, the other gospel writer, perhaps a friend of the city's chosen saint, is good enough reason to collect the *magnati* and *grandi* into the den of thieves otherwise known as the Basilica of Saint Mark. Virtually everything Hugh is looking at is stolen: the bronze horses on the plinth above the portico, the gold for the mosaic tiles that cover everything, every jewel on every crucifix. This republic of pirates despoiled Constantinople long before the infidel breached the walls.

'There he is, Hugh.' Bembo's voice is shrill and little above a whisper as the worshipers file in for a view of the doge.

Hugh assumes that is who Bembo is referring to. The doge has indeed arrived from a connecting passage from his palace to a balcony to their right. He is decked in white silk and surrounded by the venerable council members, clad in black, grey beards flowing – though there is no beard on Doge Loredan. It is hard to tell much else about him from this distance through the incense which rises in great serpentine swirls high up into the golden domes. But, in fact, this is not who Bembo is pointing to. Hugh follows his eyes and finger to a man about Hugh's age near a pillar on the other side of the nave. His hair is light brown, worn long to the shoulder. His nose aquiline and pointed, his skin pale, lips full, almost effeminate. His eyes do not move from the man with whom he is in conversation.

'It is the painter I told you about, Tiziano Vecello—Titian.'

'You didn't tell me about any painter.'

'I did, when we were in Florence. I said I should get him to do you a portrait if we ever made it to Venice alive. It was just after we helped tip Don Michelle over the edge, I am surprised you have forgotten.'

'It was a busy day.' Hugh squints through the incense. 'He seems young. Is he good?'

'He is, if I might quote Dante, a "sun among small stars" and well they all know it.'

'You know him?'

'I know them all, *caro*. The men he stands with are all artists. The white bearded men to whom he speaks, the Bellini brothers, maestri of Venetian painting, were at one time his teachers, but now he has his own workshop.'

'Ah, the Bellini.' Hugh watches them for a moment. 'I have heard of them. The one called Gentile was sent to Constantinople as a sign of peace toward Mehmed II. I always thought it a strange offering to appease a man like Mehmed, a gamble.'

'Not really, Hugh. His brother Giovanni is the better painter.'

'I see.' Hugh laughs. 'Heir and a spare! And these others about them, they look like very self-important young men. All painters?'

'Yes, all painters. The one next to him is his older brother Francesco. The sickly looking man next to him is Giorgione, the others Signors Luciano, Lotto and Serinalta are all painters in their own way; I knew them well when I was writing my *Asolani*. Convivial fellows, but Tiziano particularly so. I think they all know he will receive the *la Sanseria* after Maestro Bellini, and so he should.'

'*La Sanseria*?'

'The broker's patent. It is much coveted among the artists and a lucrative position, too: a generous annuity, about twenty crowns I think. Exemption from certain taxes and a further eight crowns every time you paint the doge.

'Nice work if you can get it.'

'And he deserves it, I say, he does. There is something deep in that young man. I cannot quite describe it, but you will know it when he looks at you.'

'And you really think he will drop his brushes to paint me?'

'Certainly he will for me. You forget I am – how would our host put it? – very illustrious in this republic. And besides, he says his days are filled with tedium at present because of a commission for the German merchants at the *Fondaci dei Tedeschi*.'

'You've already spoken to him?'

'Of course. I never know how long we shall be in a place so I have acted quickly. I hope that is all right, my friend. He himself wanted to capture you on canvas as I shall in verse. And His Holiness shall be pleased.'

'I'm sure His Holiness shall.'

20TH OCTOBER 1509, THE CASA D'ORO

The evening is still, like a held breath. The bells for compline have begun to tinkle and clang through the canals. The huge wooden bridge at the Rialto is pivoted open, and a bottleneck of brightly coloured *bragozetti*, *bragagni* and smaller masted craft are all filing out of the market after being loaded with their purchases or their unsold goods: spices, silks, wood, cloth, sugar, olive oil, citrus fruits, almonds, furs, brocades, dyes, alum, transparent mineral salt. Hugh can see some of them, smell others. The bridge timbers creaked as they pass under. He looks into the water and imagines the day two hundred years ago when one of the Vendramin family dived in here to rescue a fragment of the Holy Cross after it had been tipped overboard by a careless priest. There are no floating relics today except cabbages and a rat as big as a dog towing a dead gull toward the farther bank. The many oars of their own barge pull them swiftly beyond the colonnade of the market hall and round the bend where the canal is quieter.

The dark grey waters lap peacefully against the hulls of boats, many at this hour being of the felze variety, that is, having a covered cabin obscuring the identity of the occupants. Privacy, like everything else in Venice, is a tradable commodity. The lantern on the prow of the priory barge swings rhythmically back and forth, and Hugh glances through the thin autumnal mist at the many other palazzi on his side of the boat. One gondolier is singing *Aves* with a boat full of nuns whose white *unsoggoli* are reflected like fluttering doves in the canal.

They are being watched and followed by another boat. There doesn't seem any pretence on behalf of the two spies, and when Hugh mentions it, Bembo does not seem surprised. 'Welcome to Venice, Hugh. It's probably the doge's people wanting to make sure who you are talking to. You can't blame them. Or it may be someone else; Venice is a web of surveillance. There is one set of spies, policemen, judges and inquisitors for ferrymen, another for the prostitutes, another for brawlers, foreign dealers in arms and another for writers and printers. I'm serious. It's a wonder there are not more watching us really. In fact, there probably are.'

Prior da Mosta steps over the boards of the barge and approaches Hugh from behind. He pats Hugh's hand as they approach the Palace of the Contarini on the Grand Canal. Hugh notices that the prior's palms are greasy with sweat, and that his face seems strained with unease. Their presence for this dinner was requested by Alvise Contarini of the ancient noble House of Contarini, etc. Bembo says that they will want to show Hugh off and remember Alvise's brother, a former knight and prior.

'The *Casa d'Oro* is a noble palazzo indeed, Prior,' Hugh says, feigning an easy grace and admiring the gothic tracery in white marble, the high arabesque columns on the waterfront, and the loggia on the second floor where guests are standing with drinks already. As they near, he sees the upper ornament. Those portions still high enough to catch the dying sun are iridescent with light. For a moment Hugh catches himself in disbelief for these external architectural decorations are overlaid with gold. With difficulty Hugh lets his eye move left to the handsome palazzo next door, the one he knows to be Vendramin's childhood home. It is dimly lit inside but there is no sign of life, whether by person, shadow or silhouette. *Is he there, the master of subterfuge? Could it be that simple? Surely not.*

'Please, not *Ca' d'Oro*. The lady of the house, Signora Polissena, is most particular that it be called the *Palazzo Santa Sofia*.' The prior gulps and, joining his hands together, says, 'What a lot of people they have already. I did not know. I hope we are not under dressed.'

Back at the priory, Prior da Mosta had insisted it would be correct to merely wear the black surcoat of the order, fastened simply with a belt. He insisted that the Venetians are most particular about correct customs, the observance of the sumptuary laws and the like. A holy knight, with all humility should be dressed as such. So he and Hugh look just like the image of every woodcut, wood panel and engraving of their order from the last two centuries. It is the type that is important, the symbol.

As it is, everyone seems to assume that Bembo, the taller and more handsomely attired, is Hugh Erpingham of Rhodes, and that the two knights are escorts. No one seems to remember him as himself – the great poet – which Hugh enjoys very much. Young men on the stairs fawn and bow, and the ladies with them titter behind their fans. Servants liveried with the yellow and blue stripes of the Contarini announce them at the entrance of the Piano Nobile on the second floor of the palace. And what a room. Below, the canal was all chill and gloom, but up here – Hugh blinks as the last of the evening sun gives one last benediction through the open doors and obscure glass, bathing the walls, furniture and guests in golden light. The room fully opens through delicate arches into the loggia above the canal. There are, he guesses, about thirty guests, many prelates, two cardinal's berets and many women with twin cornet headdresses like something fashionable many generations before which Hugh has only ever seen in the Flemish panel paintings in Norfolk. The tops of these headdresses have thin silk veils attached. and as their wearers glide about the party they look like masts and sails over a sea of heads.

While the prior is introducing Bembo to the host and hostess, Hugh glances about the room wondering whether such a scene could ever be imagined in England, which of course it could not. These Italians think the English little above the Germans for barbarity. Silks drape couches, richly upholstered in red damask. All walls are covered with a Flemish or Arabesque tapestry, and no table lacks a covering of Turkish rugs, bearing some exquisite design or other. On the tables and in the cabinets are all manner of precious objects like medals, medallions, cameos, some inside open boxes beautifully inlaid with ivory, lapis, and precious stones. To Hugh's left he sees an open book cabinet piled high with manuscripts, mostly bound, many in volumes with Minutius' printer's emblem on the spines. Next to the cupboard, and behind a quartet of lutists, is yet another small floor cabinet with coins, intaglios and vases. In Florence, any display of ostentation is frowned upon, but in Venice they have given up the pretense of such moderation. Honesty is, after all, a great virtue – at least as great a virtue as charity. The poor are honest and make no show of riches, so let us embrace a similar honesty they say.

Hugh's self-satisfied reflections are cut short as the prior introduces him to his hosts with all formality. Signor Alvise Contarini, thick set, heavy lidded, bows only slightly whereby his delicate, spidery wife, Signora Polissena excuses any offence, saying it is his gout. After further pleasantries, Hugh is whisked away by their son Gasparo to a quieter corner.

'Ah Fra Erpingham, what fortune has brought you here, right in the middle of this war.' He is a handsome and earnest youth in his early twenties, beard not full grown and with large brown eyes staring with admiration from an elongated head. He explains that he is a student of the sciences and philosophy, recently returned from Padua University. 'But before the siege, thank God, as I thought I might never get back here or be killed, as indeed some of my fellow students have been.' He takes a large gulp of his Burgundian red and then, glancing wistfully at the ceiling, says, 'And so here I am, ready to dedicate my life to God's service. And the honour of Venice, of course, but it is not so easy. I am a Contarini; all doors are open to me. It is not easy to have so many choices. But then I hear that you are in Venice, and it puts me in mind of my Uncle Bertucci who was a prior of your order, and my breast veritably swelled with an ardor to forsake other paths, and become a knight instead.'

'Do your parents know if this?'

'No, well, not really. Not that I am seriously considering it. I have mentioned something in passing. You know how it is.' He speaks fast avoiding Hugh's gaze by looking absently again at the ceiling. 'Of course they want me to come into the family business, but they have other children, and father is in good enough health. It is just this providence of your coming and that quickening I felt, as if you had perhaps come on heaven's wings during this time of indecision. Forgive me for speaking like this, with such familiarity, it's just that, well – '

'Please do not mention it.' Hugh thinks to ask about what in particular this youth finds distasteful about the family business, and then also what in particular he find so attractive about entering into service on Rhodes. But he does not do so because he already knows the answer. He is talking to his former self, fresh from Cambridge seven years earlier. 'It is not wrong for you to desire a life of purpose and service, honour even. But if I have, as you suspect, come at an opportune time, then let it be to speak to you as I have to my own younger brother back in England.'

Gasparo Contarini sips his wine and nods effusively. 'Sure, sure.' For a moment he looks as if he might burst into tears. Hugh smiles to reassure him, and then, looking into the young aristocrat's half drained glass, says, 'You are an educated and sensible man of rank, in a city that often holds the balance of power in Italy, indeed, in the Mediterranean. So my advice would be this: submit to your parents' wishes and use your position to bring peace wherever you see discord. Become a son of peace; know what it is to sleep under heaven without bloodguilt. There are plenty of people to wage war, in case you haven't noticed.'

Gasparo nods his long head again, his bottom lip turned down in seriousness. 'It is good advice. I thank you, I do. I thank you.'

Hugh asks him about Marcantionio Vendramin, but the young man says that he has never seen him, but for the painting of him that once hung in the doge's palace. Hugh says that he would like to see it. 'You should, Fra Hugh. There is not a knight more talked of for deeds of valour than you, than he. But you will not find it here. Doge Loredan gave it to the Duke of Ferrara on his accession to the dukedom. It is, if

I remember, a very fine portrait and well received by the duke, whom you know is a man of war, too. I hope the doge had a copy made, for we should have the likeness of our greatest sons to inspire the next generation. Perhaps you, signor, should consider a portrait while you are here. We have many fine artists, you know.'

'I thank you, signor. My companion Pietro Bembo has already secured the talents of the young painter they call Titian.'

It is as the last word leaves Hugh's mouth that Bembo joins them with a young cardinal. 'Please forgive the intrusion, Signor Contarini, but may I introduce Hugh to Cardinal Giovanni de Medici.' At once Hugh recognizes the man he had seen a year before on his first visit to the pope's apartments. They had never actually met, but he had been in an anteroom with his sister that day. Colocci remarked about it, and Hugh remembered. And here he is now, exiled from Florence after his brother's fall to Savonarola—Magnifico's son in the flesh, about Hugh's age and smiling genially over the rim of his glass. Hugh kisses his ruby ring.

'I am honoured to meet you, Fra Erpingham. Bembo has been telling me much about you.'

'And telling me of you, Your Grace. We had the honour of dining with your brother in Urbino recently.'

'Is he well? I have not had a letter from him for months.' The cardinal removes the scarlet berretta with white lace trim in order to daub his forehead with a linen cloth, which he carries in his left hand. The velvet beret is carefully sculpted to fit right over his ears. He brandishes it apologetically at them. 'Excellent for a winter's walk on the *fondamenta*, but really too warm for indoors.' He laughs to himself at a recollection that Gasparo, who seems to be on very good terms with the cardinal, presses from him. 'Well, I will tell you if you insist, but really it is nothing. I just remembered my first year here, when my brother and I first arrived. We were grateful to have somewhere to go and very young too. Anyway, we were walking in a narrow *calle* just off the Piazza San Marco, and I was wearing my berretta – for I have been a cardinal since I was sixteen, you see – with a thick black woolen cloak over my shoulders. We were pushed to one side by some drunk ferrymen who insulted me, calling me a filthy Jew. You see, the Jews in Venice are made to wear red berets to symbolize Christ's blood. So in Venice it is cardinals and Jews that share the red berets, like reflections in the lagoon of honour and dishonor. I am sure someone gifted like Signor Bembo could make a pretty quadrille of such a paradox. I am sure I cannot. Venice is a paradox in many ways. Do you know they make the elders of the Jews footrace naked at Eastertide through the streets so they can be beaten with switches by the apprentices? And is it any wonder when the populous believe that some of the fiends are responsible by their wicked arts for stillbirths and those poor children and mothers dead of milk fever, and puerperal fever? But I don't want to talk about them here, rather let us hear news from our friends in far off places. You say you have been in Urbino; tell us news from there. I hear the duke died, poor fellow, but the duchess soldiers on. She is a dear woman. And how is our friend Castiglione? Will we ever get this book of his published? Eh, Bembo, eh? Never heard a man talk so much about a book before it was published. But I like him a good deal for all that.'

Bembo answers to this and several other enquiries. The conversation stays mainly on these domestic, artistic and literary themes until they are summoned to dinner. All the while Hugh cannot but notice their prior is engrossed in an opposite corner with another cardinal, an older man, perhaps fifty, with sharp features and tight skin stretched over them like a new tent. *I know him from somewhere. Rome?* Hugh cannot escape the feeling that he is the subject of their discourse because the two men always seem to be looking his direction. A disquiet in his humours prompts Hugh two minutes later to glance again. They are still looking his way. People always look at him when they know who he is, but there are ways of looking, and you get used to it. Some people want to meet the great Achilles of Rhodes just to say they have shaken his hand, or had him kiss their ring. Some want to give you hospitality, so later they can tell everyone else what sort of august personages they have to feed these days. Others look at you like you just killed their maiden aunt or made off with their savings. It is more the latter that he feels at this moment.

Cardinal de Medici, who cannot but always be bringing the conversation back to himself and his family keeps speaking as Hugh's attention flits in and out. He is trying to imagine connections and motive: the prior of Venice, the prior of Rome, yet another cardinal.

Giovanni bemoans his exile and declaims upon the ingratitude of the Florentines. 'We Medici were always careful not to insult public sensibility like the Albizzi. Why, great grandfather Cosimo even rode a mule rather than a horse. He gave a third of a million florins to the city in buildings, charitable donations and taxes. Imagine that, fifty years ago, too. He was so generous to the Friary of San Marco that the monks protested the amounts. But you know what he said?'

The prior's cardinal is still looking.

'I will tell you, he says. "Never shall I be able to give God enough to set him down my books as a debtor." That is what he said.'

Still looking.

'He also used to say,' Giovanni de Medici continues, '"Do nothing to offend the rich and powerful." They were his words and our family lived by them. We did not ever grasp for power like the Pazzi and Albizzi, but were happy to dedicate ourselves to business and fulfil our duties to the republic when called upon. How Soderini's party ever managed to turn the populous against us I will never fathom. Seven or eight yards of silk will make a new citizen nowadays. It is all wickedness and avarice, and I pray God I may live long enough to see the injustice righted.'

Still staring, and whispering into their glasses. The older cardinal is nodding as if some agreement has been made. His eyes meet Hugh's, and the old cardinal raises his glass. He wants to ask Bembo who he is, wants to go over there and introduce himself, but he cannot get free of this good-natured fool of a Medici, who is now following his discourse on his family's humility by saying, as he allows a servant to refill his glass, that at his brother's wedding to Philiberte of Savoy, they had vast copper coolers filled with the best Tuscan wines, mostly *Trenniano* and *Vernaccia*. 'We celebrated for seven days culminating with a great masqued ball where people dressed as characters from the *Commedia dell'Arte* – Pulcinello, Pedrolino, Harlequin, Brighella. Nothing had been in the city like it. But of course our family were always able to source anything our clients wanted from almost anywhere on God's earth: tapestries, relics, horses, slaves, even painted panels by the friars of Antwerp. The very best. Once my father even received a commission to source choir boys from Douai and Cambrai for the pope's church of Saint John in Lateran. And he did it, of course. We are servants, you see, at the end of the day, all of us.'

Hugh smiles. You cannot blame a man for being an ass if he himself does not know it. Prior da Mosta and the older cardinal are walking to the door. Alvise Contarini claps his hands and announces with a bellicose roar, that dinner is being served downstairs in the hall. Hugh glances toward the loggia. The guests are coming back into the *piano nobile*, placing their glasses on the trays and walking toward the door. Hugh goes out. He has an idea.

Twenty minutes later the guests are still milling about at the tables full of food. A servant offers Hugh water from a ewer so he can wash his hands. He takes it, trying desperately to slow his quickness of breath, all the while looking about for Bembo. The dining hall is lit by a suspended chandelier and wall lights, which reflect from large mirrors on the walls making the effect mesmeric. He sees Bembo in front and politely joins him. In front of him Gasparo Contarini and Cardinal de Medici are quizzing the servants next to the tables on which the hot food steams from terrines and platters. Because of the din from the other guests the cardinal has to ask the steward to almost shout out the dishes and their ingredients. Chicken minestra flavoured with ginger, ground almonds, cloves, cinnamon, sprinkled with cheese, and sugar. Fish pie suffused with olive oil, citrus fruit juices, pepper, salt, cloves, parsley, nutmeg, saffron, dates, raisins, powdered bay leaves and marjoram.

'Did you hear that, Bembo?' the cardinal announces with glee, though never once taking his eyes off the food. He points a chubby finger at a terrine where another servant stirs a red sauce over a brazier. 'And what is this pray? It smells divine.'

The steward replies, 'It is known as *savore sanguine,* a great delicacy, Your Grace. It contains meat, wine, raisins and cinnamon.'

'Enough, enough. You tempt an honest man beyond his limits. Let me taste it at once.'

While the steward is arranging spoons, and the cardinal is otherwise engaged, Hugh touches Bembo on the shoulder. Bembo turns sharply. 'Where in the seven spheres have you been? I thought you'd been kidnapped.'

'I have just been making sure that Vendramin has not been using his family's warehouse to hide the gold.' Hugh straightens his surcoat at the belt.

'You went next door?' Bembo's face drains with alarm. 'You went, you, you could have been seen. What on earth possessed you?'

'Well, of course I removed my surcoat, and the warehouse was unoccupied. It is quite late, you know.'

'But the doors would be barred at this time. Are you mad?'

'Please, not so loud, my friend. I went in at the first floor from our host's loggia. Do not worry, no one saw me. I imagine the family are here tonight. And there was nothing to see out of the ordinary in the warehouse either.'

'I would have thought that was obvious.'

'Yes, yes, I know, but I wanted to be sure.'

'Well, I am glad you were not caught. It would have been very dangerous. We'd have been joining the Marchese of Mantua under the doge's palace.'

'Never mind that,' Hugh says, seeing the prior seated at the far end of the room. 'Tell me, who is the other cardinal seated next to our good prior?'

Bembo looks for a moment and then says, 'Cardinal Adriano de Castello, of course. Did you not meet him in Rome last year? Yes, he was always around the pope at the time you arrived. Well anyway, you should meet him, and I should think he will want to meet you. He has spent time in England and held episcopal offices there, too. Or so I've heard. I only really know him to say hello to, that sort of thing.'

23RD OCTOBER 1509, CALLE DEL FONTEGO DEI TEDESCHI, VENICE

'I am honoured,' Hugh says. 'I hear you have painted the Marchesa of Mantua.' Hugh sits uneasily for an initial consultation with the young painter Titiano Vecelli. They are alone in a garret high above the canal.

'Oh, yes,' Titian says, while thumbing through his charcoal basin. 'And she made sure I painted her twenty years younger too. Which I did, of course. It is a great honour.'

'Did that bother you?'

'No, it was a good commission. I would have done it for free.'

'I meant having to paint her younger.'

Titian shrugs. 'Not really, she was honest enough to tell me exactly what she wanted. It is a help, you know. And as my uncle used to say, a woman confiding her age is like a buyer giving his final price to a Turkish rug dealer.' The young painter draws himself up and turns the corners of his mouth down in imitation of an old man. 'Titziano, he'd say, never trust a woman who tells you her age. A woman like that would tell you anything.'

Titian, nervous, apologetic, moves a pile of papers from the bench and hand brushes the *intonnaco* from it, sending a plume of brown-grey dust upwards. 'My apologies. My current employers are not keen for me to be away from the building, but they will not suspect you.' He opens a shutter of the top floor room where his paints and plaster are stored. His employers are the German traders who live and work in this vast palazzo just opposite the Rialto. Men of Nuremburg, Judenburg and Augsburg bustle and barter outside the door and in the quadrangle below. Commodities from the east are traded here on their way over the Alps, all with a healthy percentage going to the Republic. The Germans live and work here, they do not leave without special permission. It is called a *fondaco*, from the Arabic for warehouse. The Turks have a similar *fondaco* father up the canal. It is busy as ever, even now.

As the shutter opens wider Hugh can hear the traders across the canal hawking their wares. The creak of pulleys mixes with shouts of prices and sometimes applause. The smell of roast chestnuts wafts into the room, and outside the afternoon light illumines the thin drizzle that still falls like confetti. Over the rooftops a sea of chimneys, fluted at the top like half-closed fans, belch out white wood smoke. Winter has come.

Titian gazes through the drizzle north toward the Alps. 'We cannot fresco outside in this weather, and yet we are so tied by our contract that we must not leave for other jobs. It is ridiculous. My family were notaries near Belluno, near the Alps. I wish I had paid more attention to that wretched contract. My father said that I never paid attention as a child, that I always assumed too much. "Tiziano," he'd say. "Tiziano, never assume. Never assume."

'A notary, then?'

'No, he was not a notary, but a castellan in our town of Cadore and the manager of a mine.' He rubs the damp from his fingers over a chemise, which is drawn with frayed strings near his neck. It is already besmirched with paints and dust.

'Did he approve of your apprenticeship?' As he speaks, Hugh is thinking about his own father's disapproval. He was the eldest son who should have recovered the family's name and lands in service to the Tudor king, not sail away to the Levant to please God-knows-who. Hugh re-aligns himself on the stool so that the light illumines more of his face. He has never been painted before. He spent ten minutes in the mirror that morning while Bembo was out, trying to imagine what face he should show. But he gave it up as a bad job long before he reached any conclusion. A man is sometimes the last person to know himself. It is why he goes to confession – and perhaps, even now to an artist.

'No, he did not approve at all.' Titian says absently, stroking his beard and arranging his canvas. 'We fell out very badly because he had many other plans for me. To be a notary like my grandfather and uncles, to walk in the procession of the most honoured of guilds. I wanted to please him, of course. There are so many of my profession who slave all their lives covered in *intonacco,* doing commissions that they would rather not, unknown and forgotten. My father belongs to a generation where the artist might only aspire to membership in the lower guilds, you see. But now, well, what shall I say? Now there is a fresh spirit abroad. A man like Maestro Bellini for example has found renown, and rightly so.'

'I have heard others say that you shall too.'

The young man's eyes glance modestly toward the ground. 'I fear you have found me out, signor. You have made a name for yourself by great valour already, and no doubt the ambition of an artist seems petty indeed.'

'No, do not think it. If honour is earned honourably then there is no shame. Only I would beware that it does not itself become your consuming aim, for I know well that it can beguile an honest heart.'

'Like enough,' is all the artist replies, for now he is sketching carefully with charcoal onto the canvas.

'You do not want me to change position?'

'No. Where you are is fine. Please hold still as you can.' Scratch, scratch, scratch. On every third stroke of the charcoal, the beady brown eyes flicker toward Hugh and bore into his mind. Sometimes the artist smudges with his thumb, sometimes squints. If he is not happy, he grimaces. When he is happy that he is getting somewhere, he continues conversation. 'Have you observed the old capitals on the colonnade under the ducal palace?'

'Yes indeed.'

'Hold still please.' Again the hawk-like look. 'My least favourite is the one showing the seven deadly sins. It is the one I look at most, and if I ever meet someone around there I will say that we should meet under that column. For we all need reminding of what we would rather not know.'

'I will search it out.'

'Please do. Most of the vices are portrayed as women, but Pride is carved as a knight. Isn't that interesting?' Scratch, scratch, scratch. Sharp scratches, sharp incisive glances. 'He is brandishing a sword and with a dragon's head on his shield. I always fancied pride was a dragon of sorts.' For a moment Titian stands and drags his thumb four times over his chemise. 'In truth signor, I am struggling to see you.'

'You wish me to move?'

'No. I mean, that I am struggling to know how to portray you. Not the prose, but the poetry if you like. Your eyes do not seem to rest. They move constantly, your lids lowered as if in disinterest, or shame, or modesty, I cannot tell. I cannot see who you are, signor.' The artist lays a marble white hand on the edge of the canvas and stares straight at Hugh as if he might give an answer any moment.

Hugh retreats further, withdrawing into himself, his secret self. Life in the jaws of the Turk has a way of taking the poetry out of a man's soul. The Turks? *Who is he trying to fool, himself? It is sin alone that lowers the eyelids; it is babes alone that open them wide and keep them so. Can I disclose myself to a stranger when I cannot even fully understand my own self?* Hugh averts his eyes for a moment to where a large chunk of plaster is missing from the ceiling and there is cobwebbed lattice. 'Be content with the prose, signor.'

'But if I paint just prose, I fear I should do God the dishonor of painting a man who has buried his soul. A portrait should declare the inward parts.'

'You may not like what you see.'

'Ah, a cynic.' Titian glances back at his sketch and then to his hand, still resting on the top of the canvas. 'My uncle, who was, as I now see, a very wise man, used to say if you scratch a pessimist, you will find a disappointed optimist underneath.'

Hugh exhales heavily. Two-penny sophistry and semantics suffice only young or shallow men who have not faced themselves in the wilderness. If he were not under obligation to sit, he would gladly walk away. 'Believe me, signor, I have scratched and been scratched already and deeply too, as if by the very tigers of hell and my own nature. And I can assure you, there is only corruption underneath the surface. Be content to paint that and it will be truth enough.'

Titian moves back and shrinks slightly as Hugh spews the words. For a moment he seems not to know how to respond, and his mouth hangs open. Hugh continues to stare with a fixed hatred and loathing at the ignorance of the man before him. But to his surprise Titian holds his gaze and little by little Hugh feels the strength of it penetrate deeper and deeper into the fabric of his being. *God, it is like being with Ariosto.* 'I am sure that you know more of these great beasts of the east, signor. But we Venetians know about the strength of lions for it is our emblem.'

Hugh flinches at the mention of lions. 'Be that as it may, but nothing is stronger than a tiger. A tiger will easily overcome a lion when they meet. That I know for sure. That is what I have proved.' *That is my declaration of despair, you young prick. Fra Francesco can keep his repentance, and you can keep your high-minded optimism. I am what I am. I have dared all, tried all, tried to believe all, but I am what I am. Forsaken.*

The artist continues to stare, sometimes blinking, sometimes adjusting the position of his head, birdlike. The hand holding the charcoal rests on the top of the canvas, and now Hugh sees his index finger is tapping. Suddenly he raises his left hand and waggles his finger as if he were admonishing a naughty child. 'You know, signor, I have heard that too. My uncle, the one I mentioned before, the notary, he once told me the same thing: that if one tiger were to fight one lion, then the tiger would surely win. But he also said, and I believe that it is a saying among the Turks, that if four tigers were to fight four lions, then the lions would win because they hunt together whereas the tiger fights on his own. So what you say is true, but not so true, you know? In the end, it is the lion who is master of the beasts.'

'Lawyers are always full of words.' But even as Hugh begins to speak he can feel an assault, a breach again, upon his inmost person. He shudders for a moment and then rather than rebuff the remark with cynicism hears himself asking, 'And what else did he tell you?'

'Ah, well, the most valuable thing he ever told me, and it was at the time when I was estranged from my father, was that the greatest sorrow and burden you can lay on a father is to believe that he does not love you. Simply that.'

Hugh does not know exactly what happens in the next two or three seconds, but he can feel the muscles in his own face relax, and at the same moment a new look appear on the artist's face, the look of a chess player garnering the pieces after an intricate ruse—not the gloat of victory, but the smile of a man who has found what he was searching for. 'Thank you, signor.' Titian says and at once his hand is back on the canvas.

Scratch, scratch, scratch. 'Please hold that position for me.'

26TH OCTOBER 1509, SALA DEI CONSIGLIO, PALAZZO DUCALE

It is the largest room in Europe, probably the world, for ought anyone knows. Welcome to Venice, the great antidote to your own misguided national pride. Hugh's mouth gapes wide as he gazes up a vault wider than any cathedral – a vault supported by nothing but air. Hugh and Prior Enrico walk reverently across the great Council Chamber, which Hugh guesses is big enough the hold a *palio* in. Vast gothic windows to their right bring in the morning light, flooding the tiled floors, which have the unmistakable smell of fresh wax polish. All the way up the stairs and through the preceding chambers they have walked against a tide of two hundred council members leaving the morning session.

Hugh has finally been granted his audience with Doge Loredan after a week of waiting, and now he feels something in him that would rather forego the privilege.

The Petronilla from Rhodes made dock the day before, but there was no letter from the magister. Was it dispatched previously to Rome or somewhere else when the ship made port at Ravenna some days before? He does not know. The prior did not seem surprised by the news, which is perhaps even more alarming. All Hugh knows is that since the *Petronilla*, arrived, the number of spies watching him has doubled. He counted at least six who followed him to the palace that morning—big lads, some of whom look like they've been knocked about a bit themselves. He told Bembo to leave five minutes after him to follow them, as Juvenal said, *custodiet ipsos custodies*, to watch the watchers. He has the letter from the Marchesa Isabella in his chest pocket. He checks to make sure it is still there. He feels it, and also the thumping of his heart.

'Do not be nervous,' the prior reassures him with another winning smile. 'We knights are greatly respected here. We have the same aims, almost.' He gestures to his right. 'The balcony where the doge addresses the people.' His upturned palm motions toward the small crowd of men gathering near a doorway in the far right corner of the chamber. 'These are the members of the Council of Ten and their special advisors. They await the hour as we do. Let us mingle.'

Most are dressed in the blood-red robes of The Ten, but others are obviously prelates or private gentlemen. Smooth as butter, the prior glides Hugh toward two men in private conference near the back of these loitering *magnati*. The one facing them has a cardinal's berretta and a familiar face. Hugh tries to remember where he has seen him before. The pope's rooms perhaps? The one with his back to them wears a large royal blue velvet cloak fixed over his shoulder. He is a bulky fellow with a good square head, and with one foot raised against the dais.

'Gentlemen, gentlemen, good morning to you both,' the prior says.

'Prior Da Mosta,' says the second man, turning as the prior's silver tones meet his ears. His frame entirely obscures the cardinal behind him, whom he now ignores and fails to introduce. He is perhaps sixty with square shoulders and a barrel chest, amply swathed in blue silk and gold studs. He is almost bald with just two strips of white hair above his ears and two bloodshot eyes sitting well above and behind his ruddy, veined cheeks. 'You're here are you? I hear today that there is some sign of plague in Castello, is it true?'

Da Mosta bows a second time. 'I have heard nothing, my noble lord, and seen nothing.'

'Good,' he says gruffly. 'Bloody war is bad enough, but plague in addition always increases the prices of domestic servants beyond reason. Scarcity, you see. God, you end up having to hire Greeks, Turks or Russians, which I can tell you are always a bad choice. My wife on the whole prefers Circassians, but you know women have little sense in these matters. I always say that Tartars have a more even temper, more biddable, but she will have her way. My father's policy was always, why bother paying a servant ten florins a year when you can get a slave for fifty? Good advice as long as they don't keep dying on you. Anyway, enough of that. You say there is no plague. Good. So what brings you here, Prior?'

'I have come with Fra Hugh Erpingham of our order. He has an audience with the doge this morning.' And then without turning to Hugh says, 'This is Signor Niccolò di Pitigliano, gonfalonier of the Republic's troops.'

Hugh bows his head, a gesture barely reciprocated by the old commander. He steps closer as if he were short sighted. He gives a warm red wine burp in which Hugh can also smell his foul herring and garlic breath. He seems to totter for a moment on the balls of his feet, as if he's been up all night on the bottle, which he probably has. 'Erpingham, eh. Hmm, I've heard of you. I thought you were dead.'

Hugh raises his head and says, 'The reports were vastly exaggerated.' He knows of this man already, a seasoned Orsini condotierre who has taken contracts with everyone in Italy over the last forty years. He is also the one who abandoned his fellow commander and cousin Alviano during the first engagements of this current conflict. Things have gone better for him since then. Due to the incompetence of the emperor's forces and other reversals of recent months, he is now able to hold his head before the council and not have them relieve him of the burden. The uppermost thought however in Hugh's mind is: this is what I might be in thirty years' time.

'Uh,' Pitigliano grunts. 'Well, I heard you were dead, anyway.'

'You forget, Niccolò, it is *de rigeur* for the English to try to outstrip the more civilized nations. Even in regard to death, it seems they are full of surprises.' The crisp words, spoken in a lyrical *Toscana* dialect, come from behind the old man, and from his side appear the grey eyes of another of similar age. It is the cardinal from the *Casa d'Oro*, who, with a genial smile, is proffering Hugh a lean, white hand and a ruby ring.

Hugh takes the hand, kisses the air near the ring, inhales the scent of lemon balm and then withdraws. 'Your Grace.'

‘This, Fra Hugh, is Cardinal Adriano de Castello, Papal Nuncio to England,’ the prior announces.

‘Ah yes, why of course, and the bishop of Bath,’ Hugh concludes, standing upright and tilting his head in deference again with a small nod. This man was a favourite of the late King Henry. ‘We had the pleasure briefly in Rome, I believe. Have you had a chance to meet our new king since his coronation?’

‘No, for many matters of business keep me away; a great shame.’ The cardinal speaks with precision, holding his expression as a mixture of disinterest and inadvertent mirth. ‘But as his father was, so shall he be a good son of the church.’ The cardinal brushes a thread from his scarlet sleeve and sniffs twice. His eyes fall on Hugh for a time as if in a deep contemplation and finally concludes, ‘The queen is a sensible woman. But tell me of yourself, signor, and your great journey around our lands. Have you been successful in your quest?’

‘Quest, Your Grace?’ Hugh holds the cardinal’s eyes. He is not talking about the crusade, that much is for sure.

‘Why, the gathering of pledges of course, to repulse the heathen. I know your own countrymen are eager. ’

‘That is well, but I find yours more eager to kill each other for spoil than defend Christendom.’

‘I think that is unfair,’ the cardinal waves his fingers affably. ‘We cannot speak for the French. I doubt anyone can; they are always *en classe* for the *ars bellum*. But please do not believe that we Italians would not rather live peaceably. Death before one’s time is not highly valued amongst us as it is with the French. It never has been; it's so un-aspirational, so un-Italian, a sort of affront to the *dolce vita*... and worse, in the case of Venice, an impediment to trade. It may be necessary to unite against the Turks, as you say, I am no judge of these things, but necessity has rarely trumped luxury among us, I am afraid. I say that as a confession really. We are too weak to unite, too proud perhaps. We could not in the days of Renzo di Coli, and we cannot now. Disparate republics and duchies, knowing deep down that we are each players in a tragedy, each separately expecting a happy ending. We have no, oh dear, do you have the word, *sistemazione*? No one to bring order from this chaos. We are like that small principality in the alps whose officials did not build a fence next to cliff where travelers were want to stray but did have a surgeon and his boy employed at the bottom. That is us through and through. And of course, it is all made so much worse at this present hour with such an unrefined warmonger in Peter's chair. What can anyone do but defend themselves and pray God that his reign may be – well what can I say? – mercifully short.'

Hugh has already made inquiries since the Casa d' Oro and knows that this cardinal has recently fled to Venice from the wrath of Julius. He's surprised to hear anyone speak so openly against the pope's life. *What did Julius suspect him of, I wonder? What has he done?* Hugh has not only been looking for Vendramin but also the people pulling the strings of Prior Battista back in Rome. Could it be this Cardinal Adriano? Hugh can only half believe it for there does not seem in his face those signs of avarice and pride that he would associate with a man given over to the pursuit of riches and power. The face betrays none but the gentlest intelligence and piety of one who knows what this world is with its folly and so is thereby one step removed from it. Could that be why he fled Rome—he is honest?

COUNCIL CHAMBER, THE DOGE'S PALACE

As Hugh studies the cardinal, Niccolò di Pitigliano adds his own blunt observations, quite apart from the fact that in a few months'

time he might, as a condotierre with Orsini blood ties, be hired by Julius to fight Venice. He concludes his remarks, 'And the bugger owes the doge half a million ducats after his coronation. Typical of a Genoese to invade his creditor rather than pay his bloody debts.' He looks round as the locks on the door are opened. 'Oh, thank God, the doors clank open. I thought we'd be here all morning. Come on Erpingham, follow me and I will show you how these Venetians do things.'

Hugh walks at the commander's side. They are followed by Prior da Mosta and Cardinal Adriano as the various senators and *magistratura degli esecutori*, Venetian senators, file through the door and then left into a high corridor. Each entrance is guarded by a soldier with a halberd held across the door and crosshilt on his belt. 'These soldiers answer to the Council of Ten. These first doors here are their armoury and quarters. These further on are the senators' chamber, then the council of Ten, and finally the senate. My advice is to keep it brief. We all want our lunch. I won't be able to give any reports on the war while you're here so you'll be first. Do not you vex the senate by only speaking to the doge. He has no power and will be merely pleased if no one stabs him during session. Speak to them as a whole, speak to the question, and for God's sake, don't drone on like the bloody bishops do.'

The senators file right to their court and red robed members of the Security Council to theirs, leaving the visitors alone with a clerk who examines his notes as he walks and says nothing at all. As the commander approaches the recessed doorway into the senate chamber, the crossed halberds part. Smooth, dark, polished wooden floors. Coughs and low murmurs from perhaps a hundred grey beards assembled, mostly wearing black, which contrasts with the white silk gown worn by the doge. He is seated on a throne at the center, which though on a dais, is at the same height as his peers, whose stalls are equally raised. The notion of equality is at least enshrined in wood, if not in flesh. About thirty senators sit around the sides in carved wooden seats like monks in a choir. The four are shown to seats on the left near the door by which they have just entered. No sooner has Hugh sat down then the clerk beckons him forward.

A man in a black floor-length gown to the right of the doge rises. 'The senate recognizes a delegation from Magister d'Amboise of Rhodes.' He beckons Hugh closer, but there seems no obvious place to stop. Perhaps the foot of the steps that rise onto the dais? But he has letters to deliver, one from the magister and the other one from the Marchesa of Mantua about her imprisoned husband. He goes as far as the steps, bows to the doge, looks left and right, and mounts the steps. One or two senators gasp, but he continues holding out the letters towards the doge.

'My lords, I thank you for this honour. I present letters of appeal from your brothers, the most holy knights of Rhodes regarding the depredations of the infidel.' With his magister's brother leading an army across Venetian territory he considers it best not to mention the name d'Amboise again. He steps closer holding out the letters, but the doge, now only a few feet away shows no sign of accepting them. He is altogether like a waxwork with a manikin smile and flawless skin fixed in one benign expression as if in aspic. 'I also present a letter from the Marchesa of Mantua regarding her husband, currently under your care.'

Ripples of muttering fan out around him. The clerk appears at his side whispering. 'The doge does not open his own letters. Please give them to me.' The clerk takes the letters and delivers them to the man in the gown. He scowls at them and then passes them to the man on his right who breaks the seals and reads them. He passes the magister's letter back to the man in the gown who passes it to the doge.

Doge Loredan's head turns mechanically to observe the expression of the giver, which is very grave, and then takes the letter. He reads it carefully while the gowned man looks about at his fellow senators and says, 'You are Hugh Erpingham?'

Hugh nods. *Brilliant, we're getting somewhere.*

The doge looks up to observe him intently, his lips tight, his grey blue eyes now intense. When he speaks his voice is cracked and high at first. 'Fra Erpingham, your magister asks for pledges of support, but the Senate will attest we have already made plain to him that we are ready to act the part of Christians as soon as we are free from the oppression of this current pope. We can build ships at favourable rates and arm them too. We will pay our *cruciatae* tax, and supply sailors for a fleet gladly. We will provide safe anchorage at our ports too, of course. We will do all these things for you but we Venetians have the skills and power to help Christendom to survive the terrible onslaught of these heathen? But how can we help when this pope is set on our despoliation? In the days of our fathers, the princes of Europe squabbled while Mehmed overran Constantinople, now alas it is the same. With this war, our hands are tied, but we hope for better days.'

'I see,' Hugh says with more than a little hint of defiance, remembering that before ever the canon smoke had thinned Venice had sent ships to negotiate trade deals with the sultan. 'Our needs are clearly stated in that letter, my lord. We need relief now, for defense, for armaments. If Rhodes falls, you will surely loose Cyprus and every other possession in the Levant. I plead with you to reconsider, for surely – '

The doge opens his mouth to speak, but the gowned man over speaks him. 'It is impossible, signor. Our hands are tied.'

'But, what of the loans we request. The letter details the loans and securities given.'

'Those will be looked at, and we will send answers within the month.'

'Thank you, my lords.' Everything is possible at eight percent. This is Venice. 'Also, I should like to visit the Marchese of Mantua. I have particular requests from his sister, the Duchess of Urbino to see that he is yet in health.'

The gowned man looks at the doge, and then to the other senators. Hugh follows his eyes. The men are variously shrugging and nodding. But then the man with the Marchesa's letter shows it to the gowned man, and with a thinly disguised look of alarm, he shows it to the doge, whispering as he does so.

After reading the letter, and betraying no emotion, the doge says, 'Fra Erpingham, I am told that you accomplish such feats against our enemies that it has almost given faith to infidels; that you accomplish everything you are sent to do; that Fortuna smiles on your every venture.'

'Others are comforted to think so, my lords.'

The doge says, 'I hear you spent some time as a prisoner of the Turks.'

Hugh feels the shiver. 'My lord?' *Where the hell is he going with this? Has the Marchesa betrayed me in that letter?*

'Did you learn anything during your sojourn with them?'

'I learnt that it is better to die than fall into their hands.' Hugh glances from face to face. They are conferring over the letter again. They seem uncertain, their eyes say as much, they keep glancing back at Hugh. Eventually the doge waves the gowned man away, who leaves the Senate chamber in what appears to Hugh to be some haste. The doge says, 'Yes, prison is a terrible place, signor. But what can we do? We have done all things necessary for a man of rank. More than we would expect at the hands of Julius if he had anyone of us in his Castel Sant'Angelo.'

'Thank you.' Hugh says, bowing again, and then replacing his beret.

The clerk escorts him and the prior out. They pass the gowned man coming from the chamber of the Council of Ten. He bows to them briskly but does not speak again.

'I think that went well.' The prior rubs his hands.

'Hmm.' Hugh checks behind them to see whether they are being followed. Something is definitely not right. The web is too tangled here. On Rhodes at least you know who your enemy is, but here there are too many angles, too many interests.

27TH OCTOBER 1509. THE GRAND PRIORY OF VENICE AND LOMBARDY

The priory laundry is a good place for a meeting like this. The vats of boiling water and the crackle of willow logs go a long way to cover escape plans made *sotto voce*. Hugh has found Wilf doing his linen, and no one else is in the pantiled loggia adjacent to the walled garden where everything is washed and dried.

'Are you well this day, Wilf?'

'Aye, sir,' Wilf says, but Hugh notices his sunken shoulders and moist eyes.

'You're upset, man.'

'That's as may be, but it don't do no good blabbing, eh.' He rubs lye soap mercilessly on Hugh's best chemise. Hugh waits; he knows by now that it is all he has to do. Eventually Wilf throws the chemise into the boiling vat and looks up to the rafters. 'If you must know, I was looking out at these trees losing their leaves thinking of home, and how I used to love autumn as a lad, scrumping apples, hedging with my old man, and the like. Then I remembered Pico, and how I used to clip him about the ears when he wouldn't do your shirts right, and then, well, then it got on top of me. That's all, nothing really.' Wilf's eyes turn from the ceiling to the walled garden. He breathes out theatrically and then continues. 'Don't do no good for a man like me to do too much thinking. But I wonder, sir, sometimes what a man's life is, what my life is, why we're here.'

Hugh is taken aback by such a question from a man like Wilf. Has he been drinking? For a moment his own thoughts escape him. If they'd both been standing there naked, he could not have felt more tongue-tied. Hugh feels the glow in his cheeks. 'I, I think we are here to serve Christ and glorify God, like the catechism says.'

'Aye, sir, I can see that for gentlemen like yourself.' Wilf looks round for the first time at Hugh.

'No, Wilf, it must be for every man in his own way if it is true.'

'Aye, sir, I can see that and all. I serve you as you serve the church, and then in the end we're all serving God in some way.' Hugh is about to answer when Wilf continues. 'But sir, I'd be a mite happier like, if I knew for sure that you were really serving Christ; like, if *you* knew it, sir.'

'Wilf?' Hugh's stomach tightens. It's another ambush.

'Well, sir, don't hear me wrong, only since we've been here, we've faced a few villains who probably thought they were on God's side, too. So how do we know?'

'Because we obey the teaching of Christ and the church.'

'Tell me to shut up if I speak amiss, but the pope is the head of the church, and we heard that priest at mass on Sunday denounce the pope as a warmonger and worse. So how do we know, sir? I'm not saying I should get an answer, only, as I say, I'd be a mite happier if you could tell me that you and me was on the right side—that all this is for something.'

Hugh flounders for moment. 'Well, it is. It is. Put your mind at ease on that point.' He ignores Wilf's raised eyebrows and says, 'And if you've had enough, you just need to say. There're plenty of boats for Yarmouth from here that'll take you home.'

'All right, all right, there's no need for that; I was just asking. Not as young as I was. Not as young as you neither. But I'll stick around until I'm sure you don't need me, which will probably be never.' Wilf grins. 'How are you doing anyway?'

'Well enough, I suppose.' Hugh glances furtively back along the path.

'Oh, aye.' Wilf puts the lye soap on the stone bench and wipes a hand on his apron. 'What's up then?'

'I am going to visit the marchese tomorrow, but –' Hugh hesitates.

'But what?'

'It's the senate. When they read the letter from the marchesa, their countenance was not the same towards me, and it causes me unease.'

'You should have read that letter before like Signor Bembo said you should. You trust too much; that's your problem.'

'You're the first to accuse me of that.' *Perhaps I'm becoming a saint after all.*

'Yes, well, never mind your knightly ideals, you should listen to your friends, too. So what's to be done?'

'We need to make plans, move some of our stuff out of here. Do you know the little island of San Pietro just beyond the *Arsenale*? No, well go up there today.'

'Will I need a boat?'

'Yes, for the luggage, though the island is connected by a wooden bridge. There is a small boat yard behind the Campo San Pietro; it is very quiet there. You will meet an old man called Timero who has two sons. Store our baggage, and make sure you are not followed. If you suspect you are being followed, come back, and we'll go again tonight.'

'And your shirts?' Wilf says, picking up the fuller's club and jabbing at them in the steaming vat. 'They'll hardly be dried. This is your best one.'

'I value my neck more, and yours, of course.' Hugh is about to go when he remembers the other letter. 'Oh, and a curious thing happened. Someone slid a letter under my door last night. Didn't see anyone creeping about, did you?'

'Last night? Not that I remember, but there's all sorts goes on here. Sooner we're out the better. What did this letter say then?'

'From the magister and looks genuine enough. He seems to have had all my letters and says that he is dealing with Prior Battista in Rome and that I should not get involved. Then there is message written on the outside in another hand that warns me that my life is in danger, as if I didn't know that, and that I should have a care not to travel anywhere unarmed. It must have come with the ship that put in the other day, but Prior da Mosta said there was nothing for me.'

'I don't trust him,' Wilf says. 'He smiles too much, like a bloody dog that's after your dinner. And if you want my advice, which I know you won't take anyhow, then I'd say we should bloody well slip away now and forget your bloody marchese. The rich have always got someone else to look after them, but who's gonna look after you if things go tits up?'

Hugh lays a hand on Wilf's shoulder, something he can't remember ever doing, and says half in jest, 'I've got you, haven't I?'

28TH OCTOBER 1509, ANTICHE PRIGONI

The new prison cells are in the garret above the palace, and there is talk of yet more on the further side of the *Rio Canico Palazzo* which could be joined by a bridge over the canal directly from the court. But the old prisons, called the *Pozzi*, or the Wells, are on the ground floor on the east of the palace courtyard. That is where Hugh is heading on an overcast Tuesday morning by himself, almost.

He is glad to leave the men following him at the gate, all four of them. More than once he has only narrowly resisted the urge to wait in an alley in order to do them some harm. They used to travel in two sets of two, but now they are made up to travel as one. It is curious Hugh thinks, that in a city of spies they will work together. *Perhaps they will have a guild one day.* Hugh crosses the courtyard behind two soldiers. He lifts his hood against the rain and notices that he is being observed from an upper balcony by other men, one possibly the gowned man from the senate, though he cannot be sure. *I hope,* he thinks, *that they are not expecting a jailbreak today. I am here to observe.*

The old prison block is not as large as Hugh expects, perhaps fifty feet square bordered by two alleyways that lead directly onto the canal that runs alongside the palace. The alleyway in which he is standing has large iron gates heavily guarded. The prison windows are set high with iron bars, and over one facing the courtyard are the words, 'The Marchese of Mantua'. *Ah,* thinks Hugh, *they want to show him off to a frightened populace, like the Persian king who captured Valerian and kept him as a horse mount so he could say that every time he took to his horse he stood on the neck of an emperor of Rome. I wonder,* he broods, *if the marchese died whether the Venetians would not have him stuffed and placed somewhere in Saint Mark's as the Persians did with Valerian?*

The warder, a swarthy old rascal who looks to have Moorish or Berber blood in him, has Hugh frisked. He licks his thick lips when he sees Hugh's twelve-inch boot daggers. 'Oh now, my good signor, I shall keep these for you. Very nice they are, and sharp, too, I see. Prefer the old *bastinado* myself, jailers' best friend.' The brute nods to a switch of peeled hazel leaning against the wall. 'Don't look like much, signor, I know it don't, but I tell you it makes the toughest of these men like children, so help me God, it does.' *So refreshing to find a man who enjoys his work.*

Hugh is busy counting the exits, the guard posts and the general layout and so only vaguely responds with an 'Oh yes.'

'That's right, my noble lord, our way here is to wait for the first sign of arsiness from the prisoners, if you'll pardon my language, signor; this job don't leave a man much time for cultivating fine speech. Anyway, as I says, we wait for them to step out of line, and they all do, mind, they all do. Then we ties them upside down and gives them their first taste of real pain on the soles of their bare feet. After that you just have to show it to them, and they is like babes, signor.'

'Yes, I can well believe it.' Hugh's toes curl, and a shudder passes through his whole body. The Turks favoured foot whipping for it didn't affect a prisoner's ability to row their galleys. Ulcerated, pustulous sores that leached and stung for weeks at a time. God, the pain. Cankered wounds fed on nocturnally by rats. Waking hour by hour to find them at you. Nightmares even when they weren't. Without the salt water in the bilge he'd have been a dead man long since. Hugh shakes the thoughts from his mind. 'And the marchese?'

'Well now, that marchese is a hard case, I grant you. A brave man to be sure, but they always say lords like yourselves are made of a different metal. I confess we don't get many of them sorts down here in the old prison, so right honoured we are to have a real marchese, that I can tell you. They say that he is one of the most famous knights in Europe, that he even led our armies to victory when he was a young man.' The warder removes a large ring of thick iron keys from his belt and leads Hugh from the alley, past the guard room on his right and left down a short, dark stone corridor toward a single door. Hugh steels himself against the smell of sewerage and damp. Green mold is visible on each wall like a tideline a foot from the floor. 'Aye, it's what they say, but you wouldn't think of it now to look at him. Mind, I've given him the bigger cell, seeing he is nobility, and in recent weeks one or two of the signori have sent him luxuries, so he's happy enough.' The warder uses his key to unlock the door, then his shoulder to barge it open on its awkward hinges. 'Good morning, your lordship. I have that visitor to see you.'

Hugh lets his eyes adjust to the light. Two high and heavily barred windows illumine a small desk with a burnt out candle on it and some loose papers. A chair. Straw. A privy bucket, covered with a wooden lid. A shelf, two books, three scrolls, some unfolded letters held down by a clay cup. And then to the far right a raised stone cot in deep shadow, where a man is propped up on a horsehair blanket and wrapped in another.

'You may leave us.' A hoarse voice croaks from the shadow.

'Right you are,' the warder says, returning to the door and giving Hugh a nod. 'You let us know if you need anything, sir. Just bang and someone will hear you.'

'Thank you, warder.'

When the door is safely locked and the warder's heavy steps retreat out of earshot, Hugh says, 'I am Fra Hugh Erpingham of the Knights of Rhodes.'

'They told me who you are.' His voice is defiant, and yet Hugh detects a hint of weakening when the marchese follows with, 'They said you might bring news from my sister.'

'She received the news of your condition with great distress. I happened upon her soon after she read the letter from your wife.'

'My wife, hah,' the marchese says with venom, throwing aside his blanket and kicking out his legs. As yet Hugh cannot see his face because of the shadows.

'Your sister fears for your health and knew I was travelling to Venice, so,' Hugh pauses as he can see the marchese moving so as to get up.

'So she sent you to help me.' Two boots slide down onto the straw, followed by the body of a short man in a crumbled velvet doublet and stained velvet hose. They are or were light grey-blue. He is just another old man in torment with pallid skin and foul breath. The marchese shuffles forward, sniffing and wrapping the blanket about his person. As he approaches the centre of the room his face comes under the light. Snub nosed, bug-eyed, long hair and unkempt beard, and the swellings of tertiary syphilis on his neck and cheek. He is something much less than the vision of chivalric splendor that Hugh witnessed when he saw him last, galloping up Bramante's spiral ramp. Hugh bows notwithstanding and tries not to show how much he pities him. He wouldn't do that. The marchese looks up high to his left to a small grate and then back at Hugh, whispering. 'And what help can you be, knight?'

Hugh whispers back. 'My lord, I will take you from here and restore you to your family.'

'Hmm,' he sniffs with bitterness and hugs himself. 'That is very gallant of you, signor knight.' His chuckle turns into a throated cough, and Hugh sees signs that his eyes are tearing up. 'Of course, I know who you are, the great knight. I used to be jealous of you; can you believe that? Well, believe it. And for that reason I will not waste your time.' He glances up once more at the high grate and whispers, 'I have come, shall we say, to an arrangement with some senior men here with regard to Mantua, myself, and the leading of their armies dependent on certain contingencies. I cannot tell you more, still less expect a man like you to understand the decisions that someone like me must make on occasions, the weights and balances, counterweights and so forth. Only believe me when I say that for now I am in the safest place—with these, generous bastards. You can tell my sister that.' While Gonzaga coughs deep and long, Hugh tries to piece together what this might mean. *He's done a deal with them, of course, but for what? While he is a member of the alliance, his own fiefs are secure so long as the battlefront is this side of Mantua. But supposing Venetian forces gain the ascendency? Supposing they push right up to the Gonzaga lands? Ah, then he is safe by his agreement with the most serene republic. Clever.*

'I see.' Hugh absorbs this realignment with a series of blinks. He is not sure how to feel; relieved at the release from his duty? But also put out that the pragmatics of Italian alliance-making has made him look a bit thick. That is, of course, if he doesn't get killed. He nods and gives what must sound like a weary sigh, for Gonzaga gives the beginnings of a grin.

Nodding subtly toward the grate Gonzaga speaks in louder voice. 'And so you find me with the unenviable job of writing up my own campaigns without a secretary.'

Hugh turns to the table and observes the papers and inkhorn. The marchese leads him over to them and slumps into the chair. 'I need more ink and another reed or two to continue, but I have got as far as that day, fourteen years ago, on the banks of the River Taro. It is the day they will all want to read about.'

'Indeed, my lord, they say it was your finest day, a day of great glory.'

The marchese sniffs modestly at the compliment. 'The French were heading north. They were like nothing we had ever seen. Unstoppable. Fast like we could not believe. In truth, we were no match for Charles's artillery and cavalry. They were beyond our metal. You know, I suppose, that we *condotierre* had perfected a different style of warfare, but this, this—' Gonzaga gestures toward the papers—'So short and ferocious, our losses were enormous, almost unspeakable. They tore into our ranks, then continued north, while hundreds of their camp followers came onto the field with axes and knives to hack apart our wounded.' He leant forward to retrieve and examine his reed, rubbing his stubby thumb over the point. 'Still, by some strange twist of Fortuna, at Fornovo we fell upon them almost unawares. The river was swollen, I was unhorsed in the charge -

'You led the cavalry, who was commanding the wider field?'

'Men need to be led, I was, I was, was needed to lead.' Gonzaga says all this rather too quickly, his eyes resolute and his lips suddenly tightening in defense.

Ah, Hugh thinks, *la gloire*.

'It was fierce work, I can tell you, and quick too. I nearly had the king, but as I say, I was unhorsed and other aspects didn't play out as I had planned. Blasted *Stradiote* went for the spoils and not the king, confound them. But we did get their baggage train. Yes, indeed, we did get that much. And that evening, I found myself in possession of a sword and helmet that had belonged to Charlemagne, a piece of the holy cross, a sacred thorn, a vest of the holy virgin, a limb of Saint Denis and—' He glances up at Hugh with a lascivious eye— 'A most interesting book with pictures of naked women in various postures.' His chuckle turns once more to a retching cough as he tosses the reed back on the table. When he recovers, Hugh can see other ghosts in Gonzaga's glazed eyes. He stares toward the pages he has written and shakes his head. 'Our losses were enormous. You know, signor, they say that remembering and forgetting are their own kind of walls and bars, and it is true. I wonder sometimes if we will be remembered at all. I built a great church in Mantua to Victory and struck a medal with the words *Ob restitutam Italiae libertatem*, for the reestablishment of Italian liberty. But we never achieved any unity for Italy. We are still as divided as ever, as you see, and as all Europe sees. Maybe if I had captured the French king, who knows? Yes, I saw that look in your eye just now. Maybe I should have held commanded from higher ground. But it was a victory of sorts. Mantegna did me an altarpiece; me kneeling before

Our Lady of Victory - looking young and pious. I think maybe even I was back then. Maybe its how I will be remembered. Sometimes I think that the artists and poets we employed, the ones who made the world beautiful, will be remembered ahead of us who had the dirty work of keeping it peaceful with sword and lance. Perhaps that is as it should be. But enough musing.' Gonzaga leans forward and presses himself onto his feet, gathering the blanket and turning his eyes back to Hugh. 'You should be going. Perhaps you could tell them that I need some more ink and things, and wine. God, if someone could get me some *Vernaccia* or a half decent Burgundy, I'd pledge my finest mare in payment.'

'I will have my man bring what you need, my lord. There is no need for pledges or payment.'

Suddenly Gonzaga's eyes come aflame with a new purpose. He draws close to Hugh, and after glancing one last time toward the grate, moves him by his arm toward the door, and whispers 'Quietly now. I will tell you something else for your own good, by way of payment for my sister's trust in you. They knew you were coming to rescue me, I heard them saying as much. It was in my wife's letter.'

'She betrayed you?' Hugh had been warned about *la prima donna del mundo*, but even so it takes some believing.

'No, you fool, she betrayed *you* to them. Of course, she is happy to see me punished here, and perhaps I have given her good reason.' He coughs some phlegm onto the blanket, and Hugh supports him. '*Le querrelles des femmes,* the quarrels of women, eh, but she knows of our deal with Venice, and she is acting for Mantua and her family. Do not blame her.'

'But she already had the letter for the doge written before she knew of my intentions.'

'But I suppose she only gave it to you when she was assured of them? Eh well, knight, it is possible to be overly chivalrous, you know. Got yourself stuck, as the French have it, between *un marteau et une èclume*, between the hammer and the anvil. Better look to yourself now and make plans to disappear. When you have brought those small items.'

'Will they arrest me now?'

'Perhaps, but perhaps they observe you and apply for the warrant today. Then tomorrow they arrest you. Perhaps. That is what I heard. And if they do take you, then remember: you heard nothing from me.'

'My lord, I thank you for this warning.' Hugh looks deep into the bulbous eyes of the marchese.

'Ah well, there are few parts in this life in which a man can take pride, signor, few parts. You came here and risked your life at the behest of my sister. I cannot betray her honour as I have my own. Bloody Venetians can have my body, but not my soul, damn them. If you see her, tell her that I've forgotten none of what she said to me. But now get you gone.' He shakes Hugh's arm in a firm grip and then says loudly. 'And I shall look forward greatly to your largess. My very great thanks. God speed.'

PALACE COURTYARD – FIVE MINUTES LATER

The warder seems reticent to give Hugh back the two basilard daggers. That is the first clue that all may not be exactly well. Hugh is counting out some gold Zecchino coins for the marchese to have writing implements and wine, and adding a few sixteen soldi pieces for the warder. At this point Hugh is standing inside the prison block at the guardroom right at the door by which he entered the place. The clink of coin distracts the warder while Hugh examines the left corridor, which is lined with four cells and then a door into the other alley. A boy is going through it with buckets of excrement. Perhaps the shite goes out on the hay-barges like in London, perhaps the iron gate to the canal is open at the other side of the prison block. He trains his ear to the right, beyond the door into the alleyway outside. Low coughs. The tightening of leather gloves. The clink and tap of steel. The scuffing of more boots on the pavement than could be made by the two guards that had previously been standing by the canal gate. As he drops the last coins into the warder's hand, he can see it shaking. A bead of sweat on his forehead and pupils dilating. 'My knives warder, if you please.' Hugh can see them on the table in the guardroom.

The warder looks momentarily toward the door. There is another twitch in his eye. He pulls himself up to his full un-slouched height and with an arrogant smile says, 'Thing is I quite fancied them for myself like.' Seeing Hugh's eyes on them, he moves his bulk to block Hugh's vision, planting his legs wide apart with the sort of leer that says, "Come on then if you think you're hard enough. I'm the man who makes marcheses cry for their mothers."

'I see.' Hugh says, looking one last time to see a shadow growing on the doorstep to his right, and then left to see the adjacent door closing behind the lad with the bucket. Think. Think. I need my weapons, and I don't want this oaf arousing the whole palace guard. 'You will see that the marchese gets his ink.'

'He'll get it all right.'

Hugh tosses an extra last coin for him to catch. As the warder's eyes follow the coin midair, Hugh kicks him in the groin. Thud. The man's face contorts with an agony that evacuates all the wind from his lungs. He doubles, then falls helpless to his knees. Hugh springs past him and takes back his knives. It's not like having the colhonna, but he can do more with two of these than most men can do with a cross hilt and buckler. As he glances around the door, the first soldier enters the prison. Hugh pulls back inside the guardroom. *He's not seen me, but he'll call the others. Big breath. One, two. Go.* Hugh rushes through the doorway and sees the soldier bending to examine the warder. Big mistake. He kicks his head so hard with his heel that it sends the whole man bodily across the corridor, slamming against the far wall and falls unconscious.

Hugh sprints the length of the corridor and catches the oak door behind the lad with the buckets. The lad looks round at Hugh with wide eyes, but Hugh is already squeezing past him into the light of the second alley to the canal. *Not going back to prison. No one will take me. Is the gate open? No. Locked and guarded. Damn.*

Hugh tucks the knives back into his boots and wraps his cloak over the white cross on his black velvet doublet. He needs another exit, another plan. Everything on the ground floor will be guarded and that is where they will expect him. *Think, think.* He walks casually from the door and through the broad alley back into the great courtyard around which the palace is build. He can hear shouts from inside the prison as the party of soldiers find their comrade. *The courtyard, exits, stairs on the far side. Too far.* He rounds the corner and sees another flight of ceremonial outdoor marble stairs that rises to the floor directly over where he is standing. A loose procession of council members are walking in that direction, and Hugh slips in behind them. It is a fifty-yard walk in full view of all the windows and all the other guard positions. The council members do not turn or register his presence. They round the corner and start to ascend. *Come on, hurry up.*

Hugh pretends to examine something on his sleeve as if perhaps he had a meeting with the senate while all the time taking stock of his orientation. He will be entering that same upper corridor where he was two days before. The top of the stairs are guarded, but that is where he is going. The soldiers do not even move as the signori pant their way up the last steps and straight away across the corridor to the next flight. Hugh slows down to examine his options. *I could jump into the canal from a first floor window, or into a boat. Hmm, possible, but risky – a wet man is easy to find.* He looks to the left and sees the domes of the basilica. Saint Mark's. Of course. The senate's private balcony where he saw the doge the other day. *They must have a link to this palace. It'll do.*

He can hear shouts in the courtyard and the sound of many boots. Quick. He peels left and walks swiftly toward the basilica. Two more soldiers, clad in the scarlet wool surcoats and liveried with the golden lion of Saint Mark. Two hundred yards. *Come on.* Each are wearing a distinctive metal helmet with the point beaten back, and each carry a *falcione*, a modified halberd, where instead of the spike there is a large, slicing knife with a returned hook on the back of the blade so as to be able to lock that of an opponent.

When he is within twenty feet of them he smiles. 'San Marco? Basilica?'

'Yes,' one says, stepping forward and raising his hand. 'But it is only for the senate.'

'I must get to mass, for that is the Angelus bell, no?'

'Then you must see a clerk. You cannot enter here.'

'Oh, I see, the clerk,' Hugh says, nodding his head in acceptance but not slackening pace for now he hears many boots on the marble stairs. 'Can you point me to the clerk's office please.' *Closer, closer.*

While the soldier uses his right hand to point to the courtyard, Hugh takes hold of his *falcione* and shoulder shoves him in the chest, sending him flailing backwards. The other soldier is barely able to level his weapon before Hugh descends on him with a series of swift steps and side cuts which fell him, clutching at his own inwards as they spill like tripe on the Istrian marble. The first fellow is now up and moving behind him with a cross hilt. Hugh whirls around just in time to parry the blow with the butt of his *falcione* and counter with a nice cut to the guard's smart red surcoat. Not deep enough, though. 'Come on, you bastard,' Hugh snarls in English.

The soldier retreats a few steps, then sweeps his left foot back in a fighting stance. He has the scars to show that this isn't the first fight he's been in. Hugh can see a group of six soldiers nearing the top of the stairs. It is his arrest party. This will have to be quick. In some ways he'd rather do this with the basilards because the heavy Brescian steel in the *falcione* make it top heavy and unwieldy for this sort of work.

The guard is coming for some more. Hugh switches the ends and parries again with the butt end. Jab, jab, jab. The man is quick, moving in and out like a bee, looking for Hugh to misstep, looking for the opening, an overbalance. Hugh gives him one intentionally, and he comes in with two steps. His mistake. Hugh sidesteps, parrying the blade to the left with the butt and returns one slash to the shoulder and one fatal stab to the chest. The guard drops to his knees, looking at Hugh in wide-eyed agony. Hugh sees the first of the soldiers on the upper corridor. Time to be elsewhere.

He darts through the doorway and down a corridor to his left, which he knows is bringing him alongside the southern transept of the basilica. He can smell incense already, freedom. *I'm not going to prison, not ever. I'll kill them all first.* At the end of the corridor is one set of large double doors of highly polished teak. He rushes up to them. He can hear Gregorian chant from the other side. *Good.* He pushes one open swiftly and slips inside. To his surprise, the doge and senators are all sitting with their backs to him, on their private balcony, gazing towards the multiple golden mosaic clad domes, all moulded smoothly as if they were in some subterranean chamber of an ancient Greek god. They do not hear him above chants from the choristers and deacons, so he secures the doors quietly, using the *falcione* as a prop. *Now what?* He starts to walk slowly to his left. This is a dead end, unless you can jump or climb down. He has less than a minute. He reaches the end of the back wall and so walks down past the rows to the front, reverently as if he might be the bearer of a message. He reaches the balcony. Most of the preceding rows are now looking at him. The doge turns and stares, at first vacantly and then with widening eyes of recognition, bordering on blind panic. The doge glances for moment to the man on the end of the row next to Hugh.

Hugh follows his eyes and immediately recognizes the gowned man, who no doubt organized the warrant for his arrest. The man stands in an instant, takes hold of Hugh's cloak, and hisses, 'You are arrested. What are you doing here? You are a spy. Help, help! Seize him, all of you.' He fumbles with his left hand somewhere toward his belt. *An eating knife perhaps? Bad idea.* Hugh head butts him twice and resists the urge to throw him over the balcony. Killing inside churches is something that, as far as he knows, only the Scots and Italians have sunk to. Michelotto was an honorable exception, and besides even Michelotto was technically outside the church on the roof.

The bloodied senator falls back towards the doge as Hugh glances over the balcony. The wall returns north to a balcony on the south of the nave. It is only a few feet away. Great thundering blows are being laid on the doors, and the senators at the back are doing their best to remove the *falcione. I could jump it.* They all begin to shout, and the monks below them falter in their offices. From the corner of his eye, Hugh can see them pointing up at him. And then another senator grabs at Hugh. Others crowd in. Hugh pushes his last assailant at them and mounts the balcony rail. The senators recover and surge forward, but Hugh leaps before they can pull him back.

Through the incense laden air the void passes below his peripheral vision. He lands heavily with his upper arms clasping the stone banister and his legs flailing against the slippery mosaic surface. He pulls himself up and over the stone parapet as the first of the crossbow bolts glance from the pillar to his side. Dragging himself beside the pillar he hunches down to avoid the volley and catch his breath. The soldiers are shouting that they will skin him and warning the devout Venetians below to be on their guard.

Hugh stands for a moment longer, until he hears the crank of the crossbow mechanisms. He pushes away from the pillar and sprints down the corridor directly above the south ambulatory. It is not a feast day, and the upper basilica is mostly empty. No one tries to stop him, and soon he is skidding to a halt at the entrance of the final stairwell. Taking the stairs four and five at a time Hugh emerges a few seconds later in the long church porch, where Byzantine saints in mosaics look disinterestedly out of the great outer doors in the piazza. A crowd is already pouring out of the church in terror. Hugh points wildly back up the stairs, saying in as good a Veneziano dialect as he can muster, 'Quick, escaped prisoner.'

Some young toughs unsheathe their swords and dash past him up the stairs. Hugh steps through the crowd and approaches the outer door with cautious steps. *Breathe, gently breathe.* He sees no soldiers left; no soldiers right. *Just breathe and walk.* He has got to get far away from this place. He looks across the campo north, towards the small tower where the clock is chiming ten. He lingers, then glances left to see some guards running out of the carter's entrance to the palace. They are still looking back into the courtyard, probably wondering what all the shouting is about. *Oh no, not them.* The men who have been following him that morning are under the colonnade. He counts three. They start toward the crowd, moving swiftly but not running – their right hands under their cloaks. *They've seen me. Shit.*

Hugh crosses the square, passes the clock tower and enters the maze of narrow streets, alleyways, tunnels and bridges that crisscross the city like a labyrinth. He's heading north, as far away from the trouble as he can. The narrow alley lays a thick shadow on him, like the comfort of a witch. He must get to Castello, to the priory. *No. Too dangerous; it'll be watched.* He must get word to Bembo, Wilf. *Later, that is later. First I must lose these spies.* Hugh glances behind as he crosses a bridge over the *Rio delle Procuratie.* They are still coming, and there are four of them now. *How do they do that?* He waits until he is out of sight and then runs, avoiding peddlers and beggars, old mothers and barefoot girls with bread baskets on their heads. A corner, a wall, a bridge, then another. Up and over, on and on. Sweat down his back. Lungs aching. Demons talking. *I won't let them take me again. No more chains. Please, God, no more chains.*

He bursts into a small piazza alongside a church and reads the sign: Santa Maria Formosa. He's not been here before. *Which way now?* He runs down the side of the church and across the back wall, glancing each way and panting for breath. The spies emerge from two separate alleyways to the south. He doesn't believe it. *How did they just converge on this place?* Hugh walks away up the piazza toward the far corner, gathering his breath. *Calm down; walk slowly. There are only four. You can take them if need be, but not if you're already knackered.* When he clears the corner of the last building and enters the alley, he begins running again, crossing bridges and taking turns and counter turns, all the while suspicious that he is veering to the west but never sure. The city is quieter the further away from the center. He stops on a bridge after three or four minutes to listen for his pursuers. They have the advantage of knowing the outcome of each *calle*, each *fondementa.* They know where to take short cuts, but that doesn't mean Hugh can't cut back and outwit them. It's like being seen from above. It's like been pursued by God. It doesn't mean he couldn't pick them off. Another bridge. *Shit. Where the hell am I?*

Hugh stills his breath to listen. To his left he hears someone filling a pisspot in a room above him. In another house someone is arguing with his wife. He glances up the canal. It bends to the left where he can see two further bridges. He is about to turn the other way when he feels a shiver down his spine. He turns slowly and sees, between the lines of washing, an old man, standing still as a heron, clad in a black woolen cloak on the further bridge. Hugh squints for a moment. Is this the man I've searched Italy for? *Why does he stand like that, so confident, so resolute?* For a tantalizing moment Hugh tries to penetrate under the hood that shadows the man's upper face. *But surely to God - that nose, that chin, that grey beard—I recognise that. Where? The ladder in the Domus Aureum in Rome? My God, is it really him?*

Hugh slams the balustrade and bellows, 'Vendramin. Vendramin you bastard son of a devil, I'm coming for you.' Hugh dashes into the alley, pushing past two old women and looking frantically for the next connecting route to the right. He finds it, and runs the hundred yards to the *calle*, edging carefully up to the corner. *Slowly now.* After all, it might be a trap. Hugh crouches catlike and removes the knives from his boots. In the silence he cross examines himself. *Was it him, really? How can you know when you only half saw him in Rome?* When he hears nothing, he launches round the corner like a demoniac and down the last leg toward the canal bridge. But when he arrives, there is no one. Hands on knees, gasping for breath, he blinks through the sweat running in his eyes. *Where is he?* The long, straight *calle* is empty. The man can't just disappear. *It was him; I know it was.* Hugh tries again to imagine the soldier that stood at the entrance to Pandolfo Petrucci's salon. The bristly, white beard, rough cut below the chin is all he can recall. Hugh slams the side of his fist into the balustrade. *Damnation, he was just here. Wasn't he? Where now?*

He looks up to see two of his pursuers running down the alley. He turns to escape, but the other two are behind him. When they see the drawn knives, they pull back their cloaks and rest their gloved hands on their cross hilts. They draw closer until they are at the foot of the bridge. They are not impoverished gutter snitches, but well-heeled men with a military vigour and bearing.

'Hey, big man,' one says, raising his unshaven chin. 'What is all this with the knives.' He sounds Venetian.

Hugh stands sideways, leveling a blade at each pair of men. 'Why are you following me?'

'It's Venice, my friend; everyone is following someone. You mustn't cause any trouble, signor. That would be no good.'

'Who's paying you?'

The man scratches a bristly neck and squints. 'Well now, that is a question, isn't it? But see, I'm not paid to tell you that—only to follow you.'

'And to fight me?'

The spy smiles with the sort of morbid delight known only to those who have forgotten simpler pleasures. 'Say, if you set upon us or if you goes somewhere you aren't supposed to go – well...'

'And where would that be?'

'Ah, well, that would be telling. But we'll let you know sure enough, and don't worry, signor, we've heard you're a slippery bugger so we're prepared for trouble.'

Hugh looks the other way. 'And you two, who's paying you?' When his question is only met with a sullen expression, Hugh glances between both sets of men. 'You don't have to tell me, I know already, just saw him on the bridge.'

'Did you now, signor? Well, good for you.'

'You can tell him from me that I will find him, that he can't hide forever from me.' *Yes, you can smile all you like, you bastard. If it wasn't four on one, I'd cut that smile off your face.*

But Hugh can't but notice a momentary shadow of perplexity furrow his brow. The spy nods his head and opens a way for Hugh to pass him. A distant peel of bells is matched by others much nearer. The spy looks up. 'The bells ring to alert the districts of an escaped prisoner. I think you'll be getting on with your business. Don't need to mind us, signor. We'll keep our distance.'

Hugh looks about in the windows and doorways. He's out there somewhere, watching. *Damn my luck, being so close to him finally but having to escape Venice at the same time.* Hugh ignores the spy who has opened the way for him and turns back north down the *calle* through which he arrived. The spies move aside as Hugh draws near. He eyeballs them, but neither flinches as he passes. Ten paces on Hugh hears once more the soft patting of their steps behind him.

What does all this mean? He cannot compute why Vendramin wouldn't have him killed. Is he being recruited? God's oath, he'd rather die first. He takes a left, then another. If he can just find the northern edge of the city then he can work his way back to the Castello district. *No*, he chides himself, *they will be waiting for you*. He must send a message. But how, with these idiots following him? Hugh keeps walking, what he assumes is, north. But soon he feels that he should have come to the northern edge by now. Twenty minutes pass. He crosses some larger canals and eventually comes to a triangular piazza where four *calli* converge. He sees red-capped Jews, and then some soldiers, who are checking people as they cross a large bridge. More Jews. He must be near the Jewish quarter, too far west. *Damn. Damn it. I knew it. Too far west.*

'Cavaliere di Rhodi', the soldiers are shouting to some angry weavers who are annoyed at waiting to cross the bridge. Hugh makes sure his badge is covered by the cloak. He slips along a *fondementa* to his right under some low balconies. What if the spies tell the soldiers? They mustn't find him.

Five minutes later he is still walking fast and wondering what to do, when he sees a name that he recognizes, *Fondementa San Felice*, and then a sign written on a crude wooden board with peeling white paint, *Ponte de Chiodo*. His memory flickers. Ambassador Donato lives here. He said he lived 'opposite the bridge in a modest house'. No kidding; modesty in this neighbourhood means it has more plaster than bare brick. He does not slacken his pace, but when he hears someone tuning a lute from an upper window, he knows. *That is the house. Now let's lose these others.*

At the next corner, Hugh starts into a run, then doubles back and back again until he is where he started at Signor Donato's bridge. He crosses it quickly and knocks at the door.

A young woman opens almost immediately. 'Signor?'

'The house of Signor Donato?'

'*Si*, signor.'

CA' DONATI, FONDEMENTA SAN FELICE, VENICE

'Hugh my boy, how good of you to visit. Take a chair.' Signor Donato is by now, in Hugh's mind, the father he should have liked to have had. The hall smells of rosemary and garlic. Someone is cooking, and above him someone is playing the lute he heard from outside. Hugh can see his own hand shaking, so he keeps it behind his back, but bows so as not to give offence. The hallway is dark, but as his eyes adjust he sees a cupboard and table piled with folios. Hugh steadies himself by placing his hand on the table. It is worn at the edges with ruts and woodworm decay. The clay tiled floor, wooden beams, the panel paintings of flutists are similarly well-aged and peeling with easy contentment. Through an open door in the cupboard, which still has the key in, he sees familiar ornaments and glassware that he recognises as the work of Greek islanders.

The ambassador, dressed in a loose cotton chemise and a long woollen nightgown, draws Hugh away from the parlour and into his study. He is stooped and hobbles heavily. 'Come away from there or the women will not be pleased, for they're preparing a modest feast – you are invited, of course, if you wish to come – but they would not have you see them covered in flour and so forth.'

'A feast,' Hugh says, partly stunned.

'Indeed, a man I knew has died, a university friend, a great musician, a man with such a voice, a tenor. Ah.' The ambassador sighs as if he might even cry. 'Each time I return I find an old friend has passed on. The loss of friends is like a tax on old age. Some have been gone many years. I wager they're all up there now, harps and clouds. Probably wondering if I've gone to the other place. Do say you will come, to the feat I mean, not Hades; the family will be so pleased, and we are having my favourite, *Fegato alla Veneziano.* Say you will come.' The ambassador smacks his lips to his fingers. '*Bellissima*'

'I will be delighted,' Hugh says, glancing fertively out the small window as he sits in a wooden chair with a faded silk cushion. *This will be as good a place as any to disappear until dark.* At his feet a black cat rests by the fire, and all about the shelves are piled high with books and papers. He sees the *Fioretti* of St Francis and *Il Poverello* laid open on a table with many straw markers inserted between the pages.

'Now my boy, you look hot. Are you well? I hope you have had no trouble with the young men of the neighbourhood?'

'No, not at all.'

'Or the soldiery? I heard the bells sounding for an escaped prisoner.'

'Yes.' Hugh watches Signor Donato's forehead crease with an expression of enquiry, or irony, or foreknowledge or something. *Does he know?* 'I saw the soldiers at the bridge just down there, but well, forgive me, I am just hot.' Hugh moves his legs from the fire and loosens his collar.

'Signor Bembo not with you?' Donato lingers by the door, fingers caressing the handle like some instrument yet to be mastered.

'No. But I would like to send a message to him if I may.'

'Let me call my boy Filippo. You will find paper on my desk here. Perhaps some wine?'

'Yes, thank you.' Hugh moves immediately to the desk and takes up the reed and ink horn. He is still trying to catch his breath. Donato leaves the room. Alone now, he can still discern the imprint of the words in his mind, *I am not going back to prison.* It is like an echo getting fainter, losing power to control him. He examines the backs of his trembling hands as they reach for the paper and reed—these hands that have shed blood once again. *The shadow of Cain.*

He is brought to by the voice of Donato. 'Filippo, Filippo dear.' The boy, being summoned, comes down the stairs with a jump. In the corridor his father tries to admonish him for the clatter, to which Hugh hears him answer. 'Papa, I jumped the last seven steps, that's two more than Michael did at my age.'

Hugh looks up from his feverish writing as the lad enters. He is about ten, not tall, but well dressed – better than his father – in dark blue, silk britches and a matching doublet. The lad says, 'You are Fra Erpingham whom Papa told me about. I knew you would come.' The lad bows generously, pretending to doff a cap that he isn't actually wearing. 'I am very honoured to make your acquaintance, signor.'

'And I you,' Hugh says, rising and bowing in similar fashion. 'Your father says you might oblige me by running an errand to my friends.'

'I will, sir, and I'll do it quicker than my older brother, for I can run, sir, very fast. I wish to be a knight one day, then you will see. I can be very brave too, like you, sir.'

'I see, Filippo.' Hugh sits and finishes the note. He will meet Bembo and Wilf at the boatyard. 'You know the first thing is to obey orders?'

'Yes, signor.' The boy stands wide eyed and almost to attention.

'And to obey you must listen carefully.' Hugh drips wax on the note and seals it with his ring. He is trying not to drip any excess on the myriad pieces of paper that cover the desk on which are written musical scores and notes on arrangements for voices.

'I can do that; I can listen very well.'

'Do you know where the knight's priory is in Castello?'

'Oh yes, signor. I have been to mass there with Mama, many times, perhaps a hundred.'

'Do you know the dovecote high on the wall to the side of the church?'

'Oh yes, signor, I do. Michael and his friend threw stones at the doves, but I didn't because Mama says Saint Francis taught us to be kind to God's creatures.'

'Very good for you, lad.' Hugh checks the wax has hardened, blowing it one last time, then stands to hand it to the him. 'This is your first commission for the knights of Rhodes. It is a very important commission. There is a window just below that dovecote. My servant will be in that room. I want you to wrap this note around a stone and throw it through the window. Do you think you can do that?'

'Yes, sir, I can throw just as good as Michael, even though he's two years older. I'll throw it through the window.'

'Good lad. The knights have many enemies, so I don't want anyone to see you do it, you understand?'

'Yes, signor. I will wait until it is quiet. No people.'

A creak of the study door hails the arrival of the ambassador. 'The wine is coming. Is everything to your satisfaction, Hugh?'

'Yes, Papa,' Filippo says, brandishing the letter at his father. 'I have my first commission for the knights of Rhodes. Can I go now?'

'Yes, my boy, but perhaps you should take the back alley, eh?' Donato glances significantly at Hugh. 'And don't forget your beret either, and to conceal the note.'

'Yes, papa, of course.' Filippo dashes out of the room.

His father calls after him. 'Go the long way north via the church of San Giovanni and San Paulo. And come straight back the same way.' Donato gestures Hugh back to the fireside and then peers from the small window which looks over the canal at the front of the house. He slumps into his desk chair. 'Don't worry, Hugh. I don't need to know anything. I didn't expect you'd keep out of trouble long. It is an uncertain time for the republic; people are unsure about their survival. We, all of us, tell ourselves the old, old lies that we are immortal, that we cannot be defeated, cannot be removed. But Venice must face her mortality as we all must. Our history is not all glorious, as you know I am sure, though others forget with regularity. But we have survived the Hun, the plagues and even our successes. The mark of Cain was both a judgement and a mercy from the Almighty. Never forget that my boy. One day Venice will fall, maybe not this time, but another time she will. This is not a pleasant thought to her, as indeed old age is not pleasant to any of us. I had the idea that I should grow old in a country villa where it was always summer, with my grandchildren about me, but now I realise I shall properly die of a palsy on my own in some hostel or inn in the service of the republic. I could have been rich as a governor if I had taken bribes, but my wife would not let me. You know women!' Donato waves a dismissive hand, then gestures to two small trunks beside the desk. 'I am to leave again to find Julius and stand before him once more. Strange to say the other young aristocrats are not queuing up for the privilege. I think the council delight in sending a man who would be worth nothing as a hostage. They always bid me farewell with a sort of relief, as if they won't ever have the bore of doing it again.' He smiles a weary but wily smile.

A maid with a long, sallow face enters with wine. 'Thank you, Maria. Just set it down my dear.' She does so and leaves them without a word. Donato pours the dark red vintage into a clay goblet and offers it to Hugh.

'To your health, Ambassador,' Hugh says, 'and to the wisdom of old age.'

'Yes, to old age. God help us' He raises his goblet a little. 'Not so bad when you consider the alternatives, I suppose.' He takes a long draught then places the goblet back on the desk. 'We shouldn't jest, my friend.' Donato twists his neck left then right, his face scrunched up in pain. 'If age imparted wisdom there would be fewer old fools like me about. No, my boy, wisdom doesn't show up with age. Age usually comes by herself, uninvited. And even if I really have learned everything by now, I'll be a merchant's monkey if I can remember the half of it. But enough of this, I want to know about your country, the people and music.'

For an hour they talk thus, Hugh of his home, his family, his county, the customs and usages, the music and dances he remembers. Later on, Donato gets Hugh to talk about his time at Cambridge and the move to Rhodes. Hugh is aware he is speaking without the least agitation, even when he comes to the subject of his captivity and some of his later troubles on being ransomed.

'It was a very long time before I could talk as I am now, signor. My servant asked me yesterday whether I was truly serving Christ when so many others are so mistaken.' Hugh looks demurely into his goblet. 'And I did not know how to answer him. My own servant turned sage. I pray, but I hear nothing. I feel sometimes like I am losing my mind. That I have not only chosen a wrong path, but that the right one is forever lost to me.'

'You know, Hugh, we have a saying in Venice: as long as you can be disappointed, then you are still young. And you are. Young, I mean—young enough at least to remember the ideals you pledged your life for, young enough to recover. The instinct was not wrong, only the application perhaps, or the world. Well, of course, we know the world is wrong. But we must not make it easy for the devil by giving in, eh, eh? Do not sink in despondency, my boy; your answer will come; I am sure of it. Success in most things depends on knowing how long it takes to hold fast. When it is dark enough, you can see the stars. I think I know how you feel Hugh, but remember the Mark of Cain was –

'A judgement and a mercy.' Hugh mutters the fragment that had lodged in him from a few minutes before.'

'That's right.'

'But which will it be?'

'For you and me Hugh? Who can tell? The end will show it. But remember withal that only God can give a man his true name.'

Hugh is rubbing his wrists and casting his eyes about the room, torn between the man he would be and the role cast for him by others. 'I think I saw Vendramin today. I chased him, but could not find him.' Hugh glances to see whether Donato is surprised or not. He is.

But then, almost as quickly, a distant mist seems to fill the ambassador's middle vision, and he whispers, '*Filii aspiciens ad patres*, sons seeking fathers.'

'Pardon?'

'What? Sorry, I was just thinking, you know.' The ambassador comes to. 'Thinking that you may yet find him, and that you should not be afraid. I think you and he are of the same cloth, the same tree, if you like. Both marked, if you take my meaning.'

Hugh looks into his hands. 'You mean him and me?'

'I think I do, Hugh. I think I do.' The older man begins to run his fingers along the edge of a music score. 'I know, for example, that you think that I have information about Vendramin that I am withholding from you, that you are expected to use every means to fulfill your commission, and yet you do nothing to me. My eyes are dim, Hugh, but

I can see something of what you are really looking for. And I think you shall find it anon if you go on as you are.'

'You are kind to speak so, Ambassador.' The cat rolls against Hugh's foot. He leans forward and tickles it behind the ears, saying without believing it, 'And perhaps you are right.'

'Of course, I am. If only my own children were like you, but you'd better use your breathe to cool your soup than tell them their business. Old men can give very good advice because they can no longer be bad examples. They all want to be musicians, every last one of them – apart from Filippo, dear boy. Can you believe it?'

'I can believe that they have caught your love for beauty and harmony.'

'Then perhaps they should be ambassadors too. It is easy to play a lute, to write melody for flutes, to make a harmony with three voices. But to make harmony between mankind, to make them sing as one—that is a task only for Sisythus. I believe there are norms for musical harmony as there is for political concord, but some men's ears are closed. They want all the world to sing their ugly song. It is monstrous. So maybe not ambassadors, but perhaps notaries, for at least they make money. My great concern is that they do well for themselves. I fear I have ill equipped them to face this uncertain future. I shall not be here forever.'

'You are a good man, signor. I attest it.'

The ambassador bats the compliment aside, 'at my age, a man is like a peach; he goes sweet just as he is going off.'

'You are not so old, signor,' Hugh says, laughing so as to humour the crumpled faced Venetian who has just discovered a wine stain on his chemise.

'I'm sixty, Hugh, sixty next month.'

'They say you are only as old as you feel.'

'Which is a lie, thank God.' Donato rolls his shoulder back with a grimace. 'But to be honest with you, I don't feel sixty. Mind you, most mornings I don't feel anything until midday, which is when I take my siesta anyway.' He raises his goblet again with a huge grin, then drains it. 'Ah, so here we are, all despondency and gloom. Do you know what we need, Hugh?'

'No.'

'Entertainment and food, *pia verba*, loving words, entertainment and food.' He claps his hands and stands unsteadily. 'Come on now. Let us frighten the women and cause some trouble. If a man is to be head of his house, let him have at least that pleasure. Do you know, Hugh, when I was growing up, we were not rich. And the sumptuary laws did not permit many delicacies. But when I was out of sorts, my mother would make me what was then called "roasted game pie". Hah!' He stamps his right foot and claps his hand, giggling like a child. 'And what she didn't put in that pie: pork, almonds, eggs, dates. All the things we were not allowed. And nobody knew. I think I enjoyed it all the more because eating it was getting rid of incriminating evidence.' Donato walks to the door and eases it open, bending his ear to the crack, and then whispering. 'Signora Donato and I have found over the years that if any of the children is out of sorts, then usually food will remedy the situation. Hmm, I can smell a fish dish, can you? It is *Bisato su l'Ara*. Come, come.'

Hugh checks the front window again as he rises. But there is no sign of the spies.

He follows Donato through the dark passage into a spacious dining room where a twelve-foot table is spread with a white linen cloth and many dishes. The doors at the far end are open. Through the steam that pours from a kitchen, four young women enter with aprons and flour besmirched faces. They do not see their father at first, nor the distinguished visitor. But their mother, who follows them, suddenly does. She shrieks, 'Donato' at her husband, almost dropping her dish of tortellini. The daughters, ranging in age from around fifteen to twenty, curtsey, put their dishes on the table, then follow their mother out of the room with shrieks and giggles.

'Come back, come back, my fair daughters of the Veneto. Alas, alas Hugh, but is almost impossible not to love someone who makes you *Bisato su l'Ara*.' he says with comic resignation after the door has slammed and the steam evaporates. 'They will come back when they have made themselves beautiful no doubt, but for now let us feast our eyes on these and make sure they taste all right. Hmm, take a spoon and try this garlic-flavoured ravioli. Delicious. And this liver sausage. Try some; go on. They will not disturb us now, I fancy. We can only keep one cook and a maid. This is not usual, and she would not want you to think it, of course. How proud women are, and how ill marriage to me has served her, poor woman. She was from a better family than me. Come eat. On Crete we had guinea fowl every Thursday, and lamb on Sundays; other days, spiced veal, boiled veal, pork jelly, partridge, turtledove, peacock. Good lord, I took it all for granted, grew quite stout. But now my poor wife makes do with more boiled eel and beetroot. But not today, for today we remember my dear friend.'

Hugh lets his spoon fill with tortellini. His hand is still trembling from exhaustion, which he only feels now as the wine relaxes him. 'Tastes very good.'

'Have a little more. You look like you could do with a little something. This is my wife's family specialty: pudding rice cooked in milk of almonds served with sugar and honey, or maybe – I don't know – even some *pincchitato* made from pine kernels. It is very fine. Once for my birthday last year she had the cook give little jellies made of almond milk, coloured with saffron and modelled to look like animals and human figures. I was indeed a happy man, a king with my children about me. But we lost that cook, which is a pity. I think we were not decent enough for her, even though we paid what she asked, but still this is Venice: if you want a friend –

'Ah,' Hugh says with a smile and an attempt not to dribble the ravioli. 'Like Rome, is it?'

'Exactly. So you've heard.'

They say in unison, 'Get a dog.' And then they both laugh as if there was no trouble in the whole world.

FIGHT AT THE ARESENALE

Hugh sits motionless inside the blackened *felze* as the gondola rocks this way then that. He is being poled quietly through the narrow canals. Slow and vulnerable, like a sitting duck. In the end he did not stay for the meal, and Donato did not press him. Filippo brought a message from Bembo. It said they should leave *before* dark. *Why?* He now thinks, *why so early, in daylight?* He glances through the lattice in the *felze* door and sees a *sandalo* laden with red apple skins which they use here for dying flax.

They pass a deep, black alley, where the sound of thumping boots on stone flags sends shivers through him. He hates confined spaces. He hates having such a small field of vision. He hates being poled by a gondolier he can't see. *Suppose he already knows who I am, suppose he leads me into a trap? There is probably a price on my head.* Hugh uses two jittery fingers to loosen his collar. The demons of fear gnaw at his mind. He rubs the sweat off his palms and glances again out the window as they veer right onto a new canal. To his left a huge red brick wall rises thirty feet above him. He twists his neck to see the crenulations: the great *Arsenale* of Venice. This vast walled city on the northeastern edge of Venice builds and services the finest ships the world has seen. A legion of wharfs, warehouses, dry docks and a forest of masts lie behind that wall. Hugh traces the mental map he has made from his wanderings in the neighbourhood. The *Arsenale* stands between him and the little island of Saint Peter's. The gondolier will have to cross in front of the *Arsenale*'s main gates, which are always heavily guarded. Other canals further away could avoid the front gate but to say something now would surely arouse suspicion.

Hugh clasps the handle on the door. The door's black paint has been chipped away and a thousand greasy hands have polished the bare wood that shows. He takes a deep breath and sets his face. The alleyways resound with shouting as they come closer to the workers' entrance. Men's voices bark orders. The relentless beating of hammers, the creaks and groans of capstans and pulleys bring back a thousand memories of Yarmouth, Tilbury, Rhodes or Gallipoli. The smell of burning pitch, like Hades, wafts from over the wall. Hugh shudders. He looks through the opposite window. Women are talking on doorsteps. They don't seem to be taking alarm. *Come on; just get there.* They turn a corner of the wall, and as the boat comes round he can see the great bastioned gates two hundred yards ahead of him. Workers pour out over a draw bridge that blocks their waterway. The soldiers, distinguished by their red doublets, are armed like the two he killed at the palace. The blades of their *falcioni* glint in the pale afternoon sun. Four, six, ten of them. Three of them have cross bows. He swallows hard and releases white knuckles from the door handle. *It's as good a time as any to pass them. No one suspects us.*

The seconds pass slowly, a minute is like an hour. Sweat beads on Hugh's brow as they approach the workers' gate. 'How much longer?' he asks, trying to sound indifferent.

The gondolier says they are not far, but they must wait for the workers bridge to be raised.

A moment later their craft scrapes against the *fondementa,* and Hugh feels the gondola rock forward as the gondolier steps off. He passes Hugh's window, pulling his hose and hailing the workers, one of whom he seems to know. Hugh leans forward, tapping his finger on his knee in time with his galloping heart. *Come on, get back in.* Hugh hears the greetings between his gondolier and the other man. They talk about a cousin who is ill, about the price of doctors and how they don't expect him to survive. They pause. Hugh places his ear to the lattice. One coughs and asks what the other has been up to.

He says, 'Nothing, just work. I am poling a gentleman to Saint Peter's. You?'

'Just work,' the other says. 'Building a new galley for the knights of Rhodes. A beauty. But I don't know whether we'll be on it tomorrow. They say one of the knights has killed people at the palace, tried to kill the doge even. An Englishman.'

'An Englishman?' The gondolier's voice betrays alarm and trails off into a whisper. Hugh waits. Three seconds pass and nothing. He eases the lattice door open and peers out. Both men are walking towards the soldiers as if they had the devil after them. *Shit.* Hugh slips his boot knives under his cloak. He lurches forward and steps out onto the *fondementa.* A hundred yards to the guarded gate and two hundred to the alley at the corner behind him. Which way? To look for a route round another way will only waste time. *Whatever I do I must cross the wooden bridge over the large canal that links the Arsenale to the lagoon.* He has to go straight at them. It's the only way.

Hugh walks swiftly after the two men, shouting out his best swear words with a little extra French to add texture. 'Am I to be kept waiting all day, you son of a horse gelder? You wander off and am I suppose to pole myself?'

The gondolier looks round in alarm. His friend looks to the soldiers who are thirty yards away. Hugh closes the gap with great strides and a further torrent of abuse. Mustn't give them time to load those crossbows. The gondolier wavers, glances toward the soldiers, who have begun to look. Hugh holds up a coin. 'Come here and get your sixteen *soldi,* you lazy whoremonger, and I'll walk the rest of the way.'

It's not going to work. He's turning away. Twenty yards. Hugh sprints towards them. He must either get past them to the bridge round the corner, or else slip into the *Arsenale* through the gate using the workers as cover.

The gondolier shouts, 'This man is an Englishmen, like the knight who tried to kill our doge. Help us.'

Immediately, the soldiers eyes widen and their hands fumble for their weapons. No more talk. Hugh rushes level with the gondolier just in time to see a cross bow levelling in his direction. The gondolier tries to catch hold of Hugh's cloak, and Hugh, in turn, takes hold of him, using the man as a pivot as the crack of the crossbow reverberates off the high walls. Hugh spins his partner a hundred and eighty degrees until they have exchanged places. The bolt enters the gondolier's upper arm without a sound as Hugh tears away, knives in hand.

'Get him, men,' a captain shouts. 'Take him. Ready.'

The first two soldiers push past the workers with crosshilts levelled, one of them six feet in front of the other. The first soldier lunges straight at Hugh with one thrust followed by a series of jabs as if he had been a farmer goading a heifer. Hugh moves forward on the third jab, catches and parries the blade with his knives, and then elbow-shoves the man to the side. The second tries to catch Hugh off balance with a high cut. But Hugh spins about, catches the descending blade between his two daggers, pushes his blade up high, and knees him in the groin. The soldier crumples and Hugh shoves him aside.

The workers scatter as he runs at them. *Ten yards to the gate. Ten yards.* He discerns another three flashes of red in his peripheral vision as others soldiers barge their way towards him. It is too close quarters for *falcioni,* and they are hampered by the knots of panicked workers, who are now shouting in confusion. Two soldiers manoeuvre to block Hugh's final dash for the opening. Hugh shoves a worker at them, and as he sprawls forward they lower their *falcioni* so as not to injure him. Hugh, who has barely slackened his relentless advance, springs over the fallen man. He stumbles against the right hand soldier, and they both go down. He head butts him and rolls off him just in time to avoid the stabs of the second man. The eighteen inch blade passes through his cloak between his arm and ribs. He doesn't feel any pain, but he knows it has caught his torso by the angle. Hugh throws a dagger at him before he can carve or stab again. It lodges deep in his upper thigh and the soldier immediately releases one hand on his weapon to grasp his leg. The one lying on Hugh's left is flailing for his belt dagger. Hugh catches his right arm, rolls him over and head butts him again. Some of the workers are making grabs at Hugh, but he kicks and punches them off. He then scrambles to his feet, snatches the *falcione* from the injured soldier and charges toward the gate with it held aloft like a lance. A final pathway clears and he mounts the bridge, driving one soldier clean off the other side and into the dock.

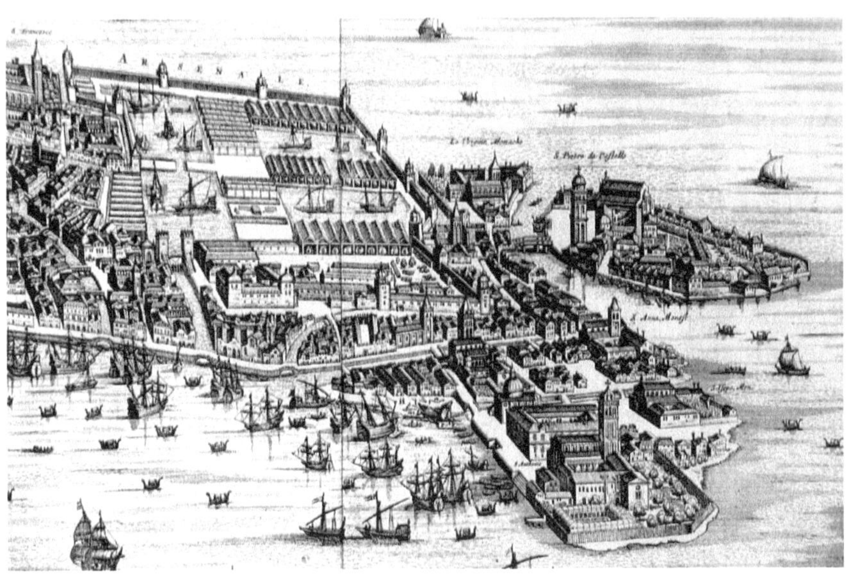

Workers, as yet unsuspecting, are still crossing the bridge. Hugh weaves amongst them. A crossbow bolt splinters a post in front of him. He turns right when through the gate and sees another wooden bridge spanning the larger canal. He dashes along the worn wooden boards. *Crack.* Another bolt whistles behind him. *Crack.* And another passes in front of him and lodges with a thud in a schooner moored thirty yards from the wharf. This is close work. A quick sideways glance shows Hugh the rest of the place. A dock stretches perhaps a thousand yards to his left, bordered by warehouses, some without doors, some open and with the prows of boats protruding from inside.

The dock is partitioned by a bridge in the middle with thirty or so vessels of various sizes moored to the quay or to pontoons. Perhaps a hundred workers are gathering at various points to see what the shouting is about. Hugh is not heading toward them, but east along another wharf, between the southern boundary wall and a three-storey barracks. As he passes into the alley Hugh drops the *falcione* and slides his remaining dagger up his sleeve. His right side is wet with blood, but not hurting. *Flesh wound, thank God.*

He emerges at the other end of the alley, but here the dock is much wider, and the industry more concentrated. Great wooden pontoons and galleys are pulled nearly horizontal to the water. Attached to their masts are great creaking ropes connected to capstans the size of wine vats and operated by ten men each with eight foot poles. The masts almost touch the warehouse rooves. Below the quayside, on the pontoons that run around the far side of the ships, billowing fires belch plumes of black smoke—fires that heat the cauldrons of tar. Men are ladling the burning tar on the hulls where other men with rakes and paddles work it in. Hugh has seen it before. They do their own ships in the dry dock on Rhodes. They keep the pitch aflame while working it into place so that it runs better. He can feel the heat already. *Eyes front,* Hugh reminds himself. Sailors and admirals, quartermasters and victuallers, shipwrights and sutlers line the wharf or walk to and fro on it.

The smoke creates cover for Hugh. When it is thick enough he runs, but when it clears he walks purposefully, passing galley after galley, all the time looking east in the hopes of seeing the leaning campanile of Saint Peter's. It's a distance off yet but if he could just see it he would feel more confident about his direction. But the wall is too high here.

The smoke clears in front of him, and he sees more warehouses six hundred yards away at the far end of the dock. Half way down, talking with robed officials, and surrounded by his four spies, is the same man he saw earlier that day on the bridge. *Is it Vendramin at last? Has he seen me?* Hugh doesn't know. *Surely not.* At the first glance he thinks he can see an eye patch, but the next time the smoke clears he has turned his head, and Hugh cannot see. More smoke covers him for three seconds, oily and pitch black. A bell rings behind him, and he hears shouts and boots coming in the alley. *The soldiers.* He runs through the smoke for another ten second then turns. Three men with crossbows, others with swords.

He needs cover. Two bowmen take aim. Hugh jumps from the quayside six feet down onto the pontoon that shudders under him. He races to the far side of the galley out of view. Two bolts embed in the tar-blackened hull behind him as he goes. He runs past the men tending the cauldron and past one with the ladle. He ducks under the ladder where another nearly drops a bucket of tar on him. On and on to the prow of the ship where the smoke is less thick and he can see the next ship thirty yards in front. He looks up but he cannot see where Vendramin is standing now, if it is him. If he keeps going maybe he'll come right under him. The clatter of boots on pontoon boards tells him that the soldiers are closing in. He runs toward the next ship, its hull dripping with burning tar. A young lad, standing on the gunwales with a smoothing paddle shouts at Hugh as he runs forward. In front of him the red heart of the fire under the caldron pierces the gloom and stench of tar. Even as he enters the blackness two shapes take form, and two of the spies from earlier rush toward him, blades drawn.

'You'd better come quietly,' says the first.

'Certainly,' Hugh says, raising his hands and drawing closer to them. When he is within a few feet he lowers his hands as if offering them for manacles.

The first spy comes close. 'That is good for you, signor. Nice and easy.'

The second spy moves to the side. 'On your knees, Erpingham.'

Hugh looks straight ahead, keeping each man in his field of vision. The first moves in to shove Hugh down. Huge mistake. Hugh reaches over the top of his arm, locks it, then uses all his strength to throw him at his friend. The second man stumbles but recovers quickly. He waves the blade in Hugh's face. 'No you don't, Erpingham.'

But Hugh had retrieved his dagger. He parries the blade with it, and follows through with a swift right hook to the spy's jaw. The soldier reels backward, and Hugh plunges forward again into the smoke, past the cauldron, past the flames, the knots of workers who don't see him coming out of the blackness, on and on.

Behind him he now hears again the clatter of more boots on the pontoons. He jumps onto a ladder going up on the hull. Overtaking a young lad with a bucket of bubbling pitch, he yanks it from him and lets it fall to the pontoon. Workers scatter from it, and the first soldiers to arrive slip and burn themselves. The others ascend after Hugh. The lad moves ahead quickly, and Hugh is soon standing high up on the almost level surface of the ship's gunwales. Coming up a ladder twenty yards along the side of the ship are the other two spies. Hugh looks around, the tar-men stop but don't otherwise seem to pose a threat. Some of them are using ropes attached to the rigging to give them stability on the curving hull. He can see now the campanile of Saint Peter's through the smoke and above the tops of the warehouses. He looks at the quayside, but there is no sign of the old man. The masts, stripped of yardarms are pulled over so far by the capstans that they overhang the warehouse rooves, which form the southern wall off the *Arsenale*. But it is too far to jump. I'd go through the pantiles and break my neck. The two spies are now running his way, and behind him he sees three soldiers on the ladder fixed to the gunwales adjoining the poop deck. Swords to the left and right and a wall of fire and smoke between. Almost poetic somehow.

Can he jump through the smoke, over the pontoon and into the dock? *Probably but then they'd have me for sure.* He must fight it out. Hugh grabs a rope from one of the tar men with his left hand and holds his knife in the other. As the spies come on quickly, but unsteadily, Hugh runs and rappels himself away from the hull, mid-air over through the smoke in an arc. He sees and feels the flames at his boots, tastes the tar in his mouth. For a split second he emerges into fresh air and sees the dock and the further boat sheds. But then he enters the smoke again, descending between the two spies, knocking one of them over the gunwales, where he is left clinging for life on the rail. The other spy, the captain who had spoken to Hugh only hours before, moves back to give space for his crosshilt. 'Give it up, you fool. Come quietly.'

But Hugh crowds him, leaving him no room to deploy. He forces the spy's blade downward with his dagger. When the spy is overbalanced, Hugh stamps on the blade, and drives him over the gunwale with three hammering punches to the head. The man collapses over the edge, but saves himself from the drop by folding his arm about the guard rail.

Hugh stands over him, and raises his foot as if to stamp the man to his death. 'Where is Vendramin? Where has he gone?'

The spy, unshaven and panting in terror, looks back and forth from the drop to Hugh. 'I don't know.'

Hugh slams his heel into the man's forearm. 'Liar. He was just here. I saw him.'

'What? Here? I don't know.'

Hugh kicks him again, and his arm weakens. Hugh bends down, brandishing the blade in his face. 'Wrong answer. Now tell me where he is or where I can find him, or I will stick this through your left eye to encourage your right one to tell what it has seen. Now tell me.'

The spy looks up at Hugh through the growing welt in his eye. 'I swear, I don't know. I swear it.'

By now more soldiers are coming at him from the other side. Hugh can hear their shouts and the clatter of steel. He grabs the spy's crosshilt from under his boot and turns to face them one at a time. The first, he confuses by throwing the rope at him. After that he is a blur of sword and basilard, parries and thrusts, kicks and head-butts, bobbing and weaving, slicing and punching, sending the soldiers this way then that over the edge on the waterside. He can hear a captain barking orders for the crossbowmen to make ready. He can see them through a break in the smoke. He grabs his rope and lowers himself down the hull out of sight just as the crack reaches his ears.

One bolt hits the rail, two whistle overhead. His feet scrabble on the tar beneath his rapidly heating boots. Flames lick his ankles. He looks at the rope, then up at the rigging and mast. The mast. Hugh pulls himself back onto the gunwales and climbs on the rigging. He climbs ten feet up in full view of the quay where a crowd is quickly gathering. The soldiers hand-crank their crossbows for another shot. The dockers jeer and shout abuse at Hugh. He hasn't got long. He climbs further and further until he is directly above their head. He sees the soldiers placing their bolts, and so slips over the edge of the rigging, dangling for a moment until he is aligned to drop onto the mast. The mast is more steeply inclined than he thought and so he starts to slip back.

Crack. The first bolt whistles past his left ear. He takes hold of some loose tackle, to steady himself. His fingers reach inside a rotten wooden pulley and he yanks himself into an upright position. Thick though it is, the mast is little cover. The other soldiers are running to his right to get a better shot, cheered on by the dockers. Hugh runs up the main, the residual tar on his boots giving him traction. He reaches the crow's nest and gets his leg over it as the second bolt whistles and glances off the mast near his right leg. He gets the second leg over, falling unceremoniously against the top mast and once more grasping at ropes and pulleys to stop himself falling the sixty or so feet onto the quayside. The top mast is lashed to the trunk of the main mast. The top yard arm has been removed, but the ropes and pulleys that hold her are all in place and tethered to the six foot square platform which Hugh now hides behind. He chances a look back over the edge of the crow's nest and immediately hears a crack from the last crossbow and a great shout of delight, then dismay, as the bolt pierces the underside of the nest.

They are cranking again. Hugh looks up and down the quayside, but there is still no sign of Vendramin – only the view of Saint Peter's Istrian marble campanile like a pure white marker for him to aim at. Hugh examines the ropes that connect to the pinnacle of the top mast. They must be unencumbered if this is going to work. *This one will do.* He starts to cut through it with the dagger.

The soldiers are repositioning themselves, and are now right under him, pointing up. Hugh cuts feverishly through the rope and takes hold of the end. He looks at the roof of the warehouse, then at the length of the rope, and the angle of the mast. *I need to be higher.* He slips the dagger back into his boot and pulls himself forward with the rope. Crack. The first bolt passes clean through his cloak. Too close. He keeps going, hand over hand, hand over hand. He blinks the sweat out of his eyes. *Is this far enough? No, a bit more. Shit.* Crack. Another bolt thuds into the mast tearing off a splinter of wood. The dockers groan and start pelting Hugh with rocks. Hand over hand. A stone hits his arm, another his head. *Better than a bolt.* Hand over hand. He looks again; the roof, the rope, the angle.

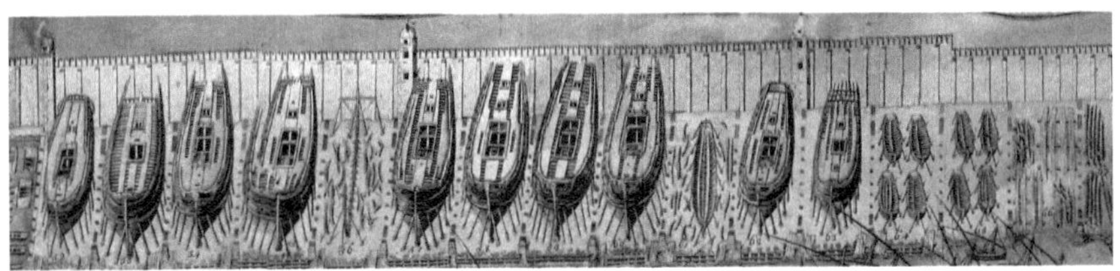

One last look down, and he sees a soldier taking aim. Hugh takes a deep breath through gritted teeth and pushes sideways off the mast, clear of the other ropes and pulleys. The air passes his eyes and hair, his stomach heaves as if he is in freefall. The stone pavement rushes upon him, the faces, the hail of stones. But gradually too he feels the weight on his arms, growing unbearably as he starts to come up and around. His legs flail, and he closes his eyes because of the pressure on his arms. When he opens them again, the crowd has gone and in their place he sees pantiles. Up and up. They pass under his feet. The ridge tiles. *Quick.*

Hugh releases his grip and falls arse first onto the far side of the roof, hits it like a sack of turnips and bruises his coccyx something awful. 'He cries out as he tumbles and rolls down the roof. After two turns he rights himself and skids to a halt near the far edge. He waits to catch his breath, chuckling and groaning by turns. He has actually done it! And everyone chasing him will either have to get somehow on the roof, or else go all the way back to the workers gate.

Hugh peers over the far edge of the roof into the street below. As he does so, his nose catches the acrid stench of the tanneries that line the *fondementa. Good, but how do I get down?* Hugh wanders along the roof, looking for hand holds or even jumping points. It is about forty feet, with a canal directly below. At one point he skids on bird muck and nearly slips over the edge.

No sooner has he recovered himself from the precipice, then he hears the clatter of pursuers on the roof. They must have had ladders.

He runs a hundred feet then turns back to see marines with billhooks running along the ridge tiles and shouting at him.

The rooves in front of Hugh, which are now two hundred yards from the further extent of the southern side of the *Arsenale*, do not look like they have been in use for some years. Stuck away in the far corner of the complex, the beams have sagged where whole sections of missing tiles have let water in. The men on the ridge move with the agility of yardarm monkeys. They are shouting that he has nowhere to run and that the admiral says they are going to flay him alive. Hugh does the best he can, avoiding the sags, and damaged sections, but the sailors are gaining on him. The nearest of them runs down the roof towards Hugh. It is a section that looks all right, but it gives way under him. Without even a cry, he plummets out of sight. At first the other pursuers stop and shout for their mate, but a moment later Hugh hears them redouble their efforts with curses and oaths.

All the time Hugh keeps as much as he can to the lowest part of the roof which is over the wall head. He is perilously close to falling and so needs all his concentration to keep upright. What he will do at the end of this warehouse roof he doesn't know. He had hopes of washing lines spanning the gap, but it appears the admiralty keep them clear. *Very sensible.* The marines come opposite him and level their billhooks in his direction. 'Nowhere to run, you *bastardo inglesi*. Nowhere to run.'

At the turn of the building Hugh sees the adjoining canal of San Daniello which runs north-south along the eastern perimeter of the *Arsenale*. Coming round the corner he spies a twenty-foot, flat-bottomed shrimping boat with a mast reaching eye level with him. The shrimper has gathered the sails in the hull and is poling himself up the canal, singing tunelessly with a flagon of wine at his side.

The marines on the ridge tiles are now level and even ahead of Hugh. The first of them heads down the corner purlin of the warehouse to cut Hugh off. Hugh keeps one eye on the point of his billhook and another on the mast as it comes closer. Should he get his dagger out, or run faster to make the jump? He can't do both.

They close further, the billhook twenty feet, the mast thirty. Then fifteen to twenty. Then ten to fifteen. *To hell with it*. Hugh brushes past the approaching hook and leaps from the hip tile. For a moment he is weightless, flying mid-air with the green water far below him. His legs keep running, and his hands flail wildly for the top of the mast as he approaches it. The nearer it gets, the more he begins to regret it. It rushes on him and slams into his cheek like a fuller's club. He wraps his arms and legs round it, but his legs keep going. He has imagined the boat rocking a bit then righting itself. He would then slide down to the deck.

Hugh looks back to see the marine with the billhook fall from the roof into the canal with a high pitched scream. He looks east to the white campanile and sees the buildings in front of it rushing forward. The boat is going over onto the east side of the canal. At least it's the right direction. The drunk shrimper is shouting, the mast is splitting in its socket, and the soldiers on the roof are screaming. The boat is still moving north even as it capsizes, and they are coming level with a narrow *calle*. As the boat tilts more, so the speed of Hugh's descent slows. One. Two. Three. The tip of the mast scrapes the edge of the corner building, splinters and snaps. The mast goes down into the alley with Hugh on it, falling through two washing lines before he sees the pavement ten feet before his boots.

Hugh glances across at the shrimper whose hull is filling with water. The poor man looks back at him in sheer terror. Hugh laughs in relief and releases his grip, dropping to the ground. The mast immediately springs back up, catapulting various articles of wet undergarments skyward. Hugh leans against a wall clutching at his arm while dusting himself down. The bellicose shrimper has now joined the soldier in the canal. It is a vision to savour for sure, but savour on the run.

Hugh darts into the alley and after a few turns emerges on the Canale di San Pietro. He crosses the wooden bridge, looking occasionally behind him and walks swiftly to the back of the church where he finds Bembo and Wilf waiting.

'What happened to you?' Bembo says, rushing along the small jetty where the boat is tethered.

'Never mind now. I'll tell you later. Just get this boat going.'

'You're bleeding,' Wilf says from the boat.

'I'm alive; that is all that matters. But we must go now.' Hugh glances toward the boatman and his son who are taking up their oars. 'Fast as you can to Torcello.'

IN A WHEAT FIELD ON TORCELLO, TWO HOURS LATER

'So what now?' Wilf tightens the bandage around Hugh's chest with a series of unsympathetic tugs.

'We wait for Bembo.' Hugh winces with pain and glances saint-like toward the campanile of the seventh century basilica. It rises from an ethereal mist that gathers like a blanket over the small island as the autumnal sun wanes in the western sky. This is where Venice was born, where those poor sods fled from the barbarian Huns—Torcello, doomsday-refuge from the horsemen of the apocalypse. Not four, but forty thousand horsemen. Inconceivable almost. That is what Bembo told them as they were skulling up the brackish creek, relieved to have escaped the city unmolested. Now they seek refuge from their pursuers on the same island as those first Venetians did theirs.

Hugh sits on a trunk, looking across field and salt marsh. Thirty thousand souls lived here before the lagoon silted and the malaria decimated them. It is hard to imagine it now. He can see a few farm rooves. Most of the fields have wheat awaiting harvest. If as many as fifty people live here now he would be surprised. It's like a ghost town – an omen perhaps – and here at the centre is a grand Byzantine basilica, the former seat of a bishop, standing silent witness to nearly a millennium of shifting sandbanks and fortunes.

'Wait for Bembo.' Wilf repeats Hugh's words and tugs one last time on the bandage before tying it off. He's always sullen when hungry.

'Yes, we wait, Wilf. He'll find someone to feed us, and then take us across the water to the north.' Hugh pulls his shirt down and twists his new, stiffened torso back and forth.

'The last bloke could have taken us to the mainland.' Wilf bristles and tugs violently on the leather straps that secure their trunk. 'He'd a dunnit for us, no extra charge, neither.'

'But I didn't want him knowing where we were going. He lives too near where I was last seen.'

'Maybe, maybe,' Wilf says, 'but we could be nearing an inn or a station right now, instead of sat here on our arses waiting for a man I can't believe you still trust after all he's done. He could be talking to anyone. Bloody swamp rats these Venetians.'

'Well, they haven't done for us yet.'

'It's 'cos you've got the devil's luck, master. That's what it is.'

'Yes,' Hugh says mechanically, absently, easily. He glances toward the colonnade of arches on the baptistery a few hundred feet away adjacent to the basilica. They are elongated like the Moorish arches and slowly being swamped by the fog. How many were baptised in there? How many emerged from those waters saying they would serve heaven before they ever knew how impractical heaven is? *The devil's luck? That is what I am afraid of.*

PART III - PARA BELLUM

THE CITY OF A THOUSAND HORIZONS. 30TH OCTOBER 1509

Asolo is Bembo's idea – his idea of paradise, but also a refuge in this instance.

He is a favourite there, a celebrity. Bembo drones on about it as they mount the hill. He's written a book here, a book actually set here. The visit will give them a chance to appreciate it—the book, that is, and he supposes, the city even. Plus, they'll be fed. Besides, it is the pearl of the province of Treviso, the city of a hundred horizons. Everyone loves him here. Just wait and see. They'll be all right. It's a peach of a place.

And so it is. A small hill town on the edge of the Veneto, in sight of the Alps. They won't stay long, but they can freshen up, have food, launder their small clothes. What could be more pleasant?

Hugh is already suspicious as they ascend the road from the east and pass the remains of the Roman aqueduct. A plume of dust is rising from the plain twenty miles away—a lot of dust. It's an army. *Shit.* Wilf gives Hugh an I-told-you-so look as if Bembo might have betrayed them and Venice had sent their entire infantry and light horse after him. *Idiot.*

For one thing they are approaching from the southwest, Vicenza. The pope? The emperor maybe, but not Venice.

Bembo has not seen it. Or is he pretending? Whichever, he is declaiming on one of his heroes—the rogue *collectore* Poggio Bracciolini, son of an impoverished apothecary, who became a notary and then chief manuscript collector for Niccolo Niccoli. Taking lugubrious and theatrical strides, Bembo waves an olive sprig as he chatters on. 'Dear Poggio was a convivial fellow, intelligent and resourceful, not above bribing monks in German, Swiss, and French monasteries in order to procure rare treasures for his master. He brought many lost masterpieces to light from those *scriptoria*, and in one dank dungeon, at the base of a tower, he found Lucretius *De Rerum Natura*, and a history by Ammianus Marcellinus, and a book of cookery by Apicus. Oh, and something by Quintilian, though I cannot remember what. He also spent time in England, Hugh, but found it very painful, I am afraid. He said that you English spend at least four hours at the table, and do nothing but eat and drink. He says, and we have no reason to doubt him – well, not much, anyway – that he was obliged to bathe his eyes in cold water so as not to fall asleep. But, persistent fellow that he was, Poggio managed to recover ten of Cicero's discourses in a monastery'

'Bembo.' Hugh says pointing across the plain.

'I think it was something on education. What?'

'Over there.'

But Bembo is striding hands on hips in front of them. 'In a minute friend, I am nearly finished. Where was I? Oh yes, Lucretius. What a discovery? What a survival. I imagine there are those who wished it had remained hidden. But if an idea, however fanciful is worth telling, then it is also worth setting forth in verse.' Bembo turns, his face flushed with the exercise, and his voice breathless with the remorseless hyperbole. He is such an ass. 'Do you know, Poggio sired fourteen illegitimate children by various mistresses, but married late in life to an eighteen-year-old Florentine. Yes, I know. And with a large dowry which he used to build a grand palazzo, which he filled with those children, and in which he wrote his great lament. Not bad. Not bad at all. What is that?'

Bembo's eyes are now squinting and his mouth agape. '*Dio mio;* it's an army, Hugh.'

'That's right.'

'They are marching on Asolo. We must warn them.'

'I think they will know it already, but let us make haste all the same.'

THE COURT OF THE LAST QUEEN OF CYPRUS. AN HOUR LATER

They are standing, together with a number of courtiers, upon a terrace of Caterina Cornaro's modest palazzo on the southern edge of the town. The ground falls sharply away through gardens and olive and chestnut groves toward the plain where the spectre of destruction looms larger by the minute. The Lady of Asolo had built something grander three miles away outside the village of Altivo, but that is now aflame, swarming with the infantry. She is thick-set, mid-fifties with a small pointed nose and beady blue eyes. Her plump fingers clutch at the dark brown silk around her waist and thumb her long string of pearls. But she does not speak for she has seen the destroyers at work many times already.

How she became a queen, and then lost her kingdom was well rehearsed by Bembo on their ascent. Another good daughter of St Mark, she had been married to James II of Cyprus at the age of fourteen. The king died shortly after the marriage. Many suspected a Venetian plot. Not unlikely. Already pregnant, Catherine ruled as regent, but in reality, the island was run by Venetian merchants. Her infant son died before his first birthday, again a Venetian plot was suspected. Fifteen years later the republic forced her to abdicate, and she was given Asolo as a sovereign possession in compensation.

A young man attends them in beige livery, breathless and agitated. He informs the queen, after a perfunctory bow, that it is Cardinal d'Amboise at the head of a French army, and that the castellan says she must come to the Rocca with all haste.

'Must?' She says reeling about on him in anger. '*Must* is not a word to use with princes, boy. And why do you not lower your eyes in my presence? I should have you flogged, but for this present crisis. Be gone with you, and tell the castellan that a queen's place is among her people and in no wise to save herself.'

When the servant has left she turns to Hugh. 'And you, signor, what would you advise me?'

'Majesty,' Hugh bows and keeps his eyes lowered. 'Pray tell me what resources you have?'

'A citizen militia of two hundred, the Rocca on the hilltop behind us, and three small canon.'

'Even with stout hearts that would avail you about three hours against a man like d'Amboise. Even the Rocca would fall in a day or two. The old walls are no match for this new French artillery.'

'You think I should surrender?' Her eyes widen, and she tilts her head imperiously.

Hugh lets his eyes meet hers. 'I have met the cardinal. Let me go to their camp under a banner of truce and seek honourable terms for you and these people.' Looking down once more, Hugh can hear the whispers erupting around the edges of the terrace from various courtiers. These over fleshed, long haired poets and prelates know little of war and show little sign of warming to the idea anyway. Honourable surrender has a decent sound to it. The mute sounds of their approval are suddenly covered by the rustle of taffeta. He feels the queen's hand on his elbow, raising him and then drawing him to one side.

Her face has lost a measure of its dread aloofness. 'Without any resistance? I understood that the knights never surrendered.'

'Against the infidel, yes. But here, in a place of no strategic significance to Venice? A place they have not thought fit to garrison even? Half the city will be slain, my lady. Remember Volterra: the blood lust of an army can be uncontrollable.' *I should know.*

The queen's shoulders slump slightly, and she turns back to face the terrace, the abyss. 'You will laugh at me. But I have read so much about those brave women who showed true *nobilita* and did not surrender their cities, but kept them for their husbands, who were active abroad. I always thought that I should like to be the same. But now I come to it, I see you are right. The sacrifice, the vast numbers that should die of the common people – not just the fighting, but the pestilence and starvation that will follow – and I cannot bear it, at least not without a very good reason.' She turns back to Hugh with a look of fixed resolution. 'Very well, Fra Erpingham, I will give you this commission. As a holy knight and a non-combatant in this war, I send you to obtain what terms you can. Remembering that I stand in a unique relation to France on account of my former husband. These people are not to be molested. If possible, only a small detachment of the French soldiery should be garrisoned here. There will be no looting. I will return to Venice under my own pennants and banners, my retinue bearing arms.'

'I will try my upmost.' Hugh kisses the offered ring.

'You may take Signor Bembo with you. See if his charm works on the French.'

THE CAMP OF THE FRENCH

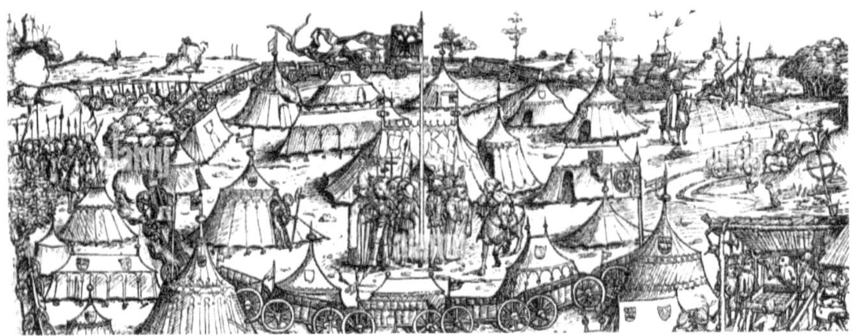

The Vesper's bell is sounding in the villages of the plain as Hugh, Bembo and the queen's retinue approach the outskirts of the French camp. Vespers? You'd think that these people would run a mile when they heard the French were coming. But instead they ring their bells and pray, showing they have balls as big as a doge, and shaming their enemies who should be praying too, rather than pillaging other Christians.

The French are spread like locusts either side of the road just before the village of Sant'Apollanare, at the foot of the hill upon which Asolo sits. On the way down the hill Hugh has been counting their banners, marking their ordinance. He guesses at about six hundred lances, which is about five thousand foot soldiers, then another two thousand Gascon and Swiss infantry, each under their respective woollen banners that sag listlessly in the calm of the late afternoon. Bills, halberds and pikes litter the sky like a temporary forest. Officers run all about the lines, barking orders for the preparation of the camp. Great teams of oxen, and some horse teams also, are advancing with the latest in ordinance: great canons, French calibre of course, and steel shot – some doubtless courtesy of the foundries at Brescia, good Italian engineering used on their own people. And beyond them? The great mass of camp followers: tradesmen, tapsters, sutlers, women and farriers. And with them Hades himself rides in the vanguard with his captains, contagion and pestilence, close behind. Most feared is gaol fever. It came from Spain at the time of the Borgias – bowels voiding continuously, raging fever and head pains, listlessness, delirium, red rashes and sores that canker and putrefy. In the successful siege of Granada the Spaniards lost three thousand men in the action, but nearly six times that to the fever. Hugh knows a camp that has it; the smell of gangrenous flesh is distinct. He can even feel his bile rising at the thought.

They are taken by an armed escort toward the centre of the camp where d'Amboise is seated on a throne, surrounded by young captains and a couple of older generals with white beards. Behind them a royal tent is being erected. The smell of horse manure, saddle leather and oil are thick about them. Under his scarlet robes d'Amboise wears a highly polished harness embossed with two fighting horses as if he were a new Alexander. Above his head the banners of France and the d'Amboise family unfurl. His own arms show a line of three *fleur de lys* on a mid-blue field with scarlet and ochre strips bellow. His face is greyer than when Hugh last saw him in Konstanz, but even so he looks pleased and then surprised at Hugh's sudden appearance.

'Am I mistaken, or is this Fra Erpingham of Rhodes? *Mon Dieu*, it is you. Take note all of you. My brother puts great stock in his abilities.' D'Amboise points a weary hand at his young captains. They glance at Hugh and then at each other in astonishment, but one captain more so than all the rest. He seems to stare with more interest and knowledge than the others. He is about Hugh's own age, perhaps younger, in finely blued yet unfussy plate. His hair and beard are raven black, curly and cropped short. His rich, brown eyes belie some intelligence, but also jealous hatred. Hugh marks it, but is quickly drawn back to the cardinal who continues to speak. 'This is one of my brother's knights. He's the one who slew a thousand Saracens with the jawbone of an ass or something. Not much to look at is he? What are you doing in the way of my army, young knight? You're a long way from home.'

Hugh bows and speaks toward the ground with due deference. 'I am here following the orders of your most illustrious brother – '

'Yes, yes, money for your crusade. We know all about that. But here? Now? Speak man, speak.'

Hugh stands upright. 'I am here at the behest of the Lady of Asolo, who has sent me to solicit terms with Your Eminence.'

'Terms?' The cardinal proffers an impatient hand and takes the sealed scroll from the queen's hoary old chancellor who is still in the process of bending his aged limbs. The cardinal leans forward and snatches it. He tears it open and reads it with astonishment and picking out phrases. 'With banners, and arms. Only a small garrison to be billeted in the city. My word that there will be no plundering. Fair terms for her, signor, fair terms, indeed. All authorities from Xenophon attest that "it is a law established among mankind, that when a city is taken in war, the persons and the property of its inhabitants belong to the captors." What can she exchange, pray?'

'The city, Eminence, with no loss of life.'

'Loss of life! What possible threat could they be to us?'

Hugh gestures at the hillside behind him, raising his hand up and down between the town and the castle that crowns the summit. 'They have ordinance, and an elevated situation. They have the Rocca and a well-trained militia who have prepared extensively for this conflict. If they are to be despoiled then they will make sure that every footstep you advance will be at the greatest cost they can inflict.'

Not entirely true, but Hugh can see the Frenchman pause, and so continues with velvet glove. 'Come, Your Grace, have you seen the place? It is more a hilltop village than a city. You hold Vicenza; Asolo is of little consequence. Do not spill unnecessary Christian blood here, and do not let the city be pillaged before winter so that children go without bread, lest they cry to heaven against you.' The cardinal's eyes narrow at the mention of Christian blood. Hugh softens the next appeal. 'Winter will soon be upon us, I say. You may have the glory of the city at no expense, only let the lady keep her honour. Let her request and the blood ties of her husband to your monarch's royal house find clemency with you. To be magnanimous in victory is, after all, the mark of a true knight.'

The cardinal raises a hand for Hugh to cease. He glances with a raised eyebrow towards his officers. They are all nodding. All except that one young captain who still stares at Hugh.

The cardinal drags his right index finger lightly over his top lip before he speaks. 'Very well. We will graciously agree to these terms on account of the lady's peculiar standing in these affairs and because of our clemency. Let that be so noted by all. But let her first grace us with her presence tonight at dinner, here. You may attend also, Erpingham. And who is that? No, not you, the other one.' D'Amboise points past the old chancellor to Bembo.

'Signor Pietro Bembo, at your service, Eminence.'

'The poet? Very well, you may attend too, but no one else. Our dining tent is modest.'

CARDINAL D'AMBOISE, TWO HOURS LATER

The dining tent is anything *but* modest—sixty feet long, draped with silk hangings, Flemish tapestries, six large chandelier and many servants in the D'Amboise livery. The chief officers are present but no other women save the forlorn lady of Asolo. The cardinal bows to the last queen of Cyprus, who is dressed in all magnificence: a lavish vermillion silk gown, with gathered sleeves, richly embroidered with pearls. The cardinal's knees creak audibly; it is not often that he does this. The queen proffers her emerald ring in his direction, but not near enough for him to reach. He pauses, shuffles forward with ill grace and a grunt, then kisses it before finally rising.

D'Amboise squeezes out a malignant smile, and says by way of retaliation. 'Your majesty is not wearing her crown.'

'I have placed it long ago at the foot of Christ in our cathedral, as your king Charlemagne once did his. We shall all give account, Your Grace.'

'Indeed. Commendable. So we shall.' The cardinal presents her to his officers with a slow gesture of the hand. 'Gentlemen, may I present her majesty, the queen of Cyprus.'

'And Armenia, and Jerusalem,' she adds while looking steadily at the young men before her.

'Titular queen,' D'Amboise adds quickly, his mouth tightening as if he had tasted something unpleasant and was about to spit it out.

'All offices in this world are titular, even the office of cardinal, Your Grace. One day we shall give account. All of us.' She glances from one officer to the next. 'I trust you will remember that, in your dealings with the people of Asolo. Shall we sit, Your Grace?'

While they are being seated, Hugh outlines in his own mind all that he has heard. *She is queen of Jerusalem - the city of peace.* In her person, even more than in his or the knights of Rhodes, is embodied the relic of the crusader states. *See how she sits. See how she is resigned to her fate. What does it all mean? What has she learnt that I have not?* Hugh allows the servant to push his chair in. D'Amboise' travelling dinner service is all silver, apart from the cardinal himself and the queen who eat and drink from gold tableware. There is no glass, the French are too practical to have half of it smashed on the rutted roads, which, in their case, are roads which invariably lead to victory. He allows himself a half goblet of burgundy and soon realises that the young captain with the curly hair, now being seated opposite him, still eyes him coldly as he takes his first draught. *Who is he? Just one more son of Aeneas or Hector?* Italian history is run through with the progeny of vagrant Trojan émigré princes. *But no, he has the crest of Aragon on his doublet buttons. And why the stare? I do not know him. Perhaps I have killed someone he knows.*

Hugh leans back on his chair and lets the wine run around his mouth and cheeks. Servants serve artichokes from a terrine. D'Amboise is complaining how hard the outer leaves are. After a few pleasantries, to which the queen makes barely a comment, the cardinal lets the conversation fall to war. Pushing the half eaten artichokes aside and landing his fists on the table, arms straight, he says that the rapaciousness of Venice, of whom the queen has been as much a victim as any, must needs be suppressed by the only means left, if they will not heed the commands of the church. 'Besides,' d'Amboise continues, taking up his gold goblet and sitting back in the same throne-like chair he had been on outside. 'The ancients all attest, Heraclitus for a start, that war is "the father of us all, the king of all." And Plato, that war is "always existing by nature." And where would the other arts be without it? Eh, signor Bembo, eh? What poetry would we have? What sculpture? What painting if not for the arts of war?'

Bembo, who sits opposite Hugh and next to the young captain, lays his own wrists on the table with an expression of evident delight, his chance to exhibit to such an august audience. Hugh would kick him if only he could reach. 'You are right of course, Your Grace, the relationship is a singular one. Great conflicts have indeed called forth great virtue in the arts. As Virgil says *arma virum que cano* and so forth, I sing of arms and man. Aeschylus, so great a poet, did not wish his epitaph to be his plays, but only to be that he fought at Marathon. Even the Greek gods show forth this great paradox, this tension. Apollo, for example, is supposed to be the god of wisdom and intellect, yet he is known by his arrow and bow before the lyre. And Athena is more readily identified by her shield and helmet than her shuttle, yet the ancients looked to her for wisdom in conduct too.'

'There, you see? It has ever been thus,' D'Amboise adds with nonchalance. 'We are the same as they.'

Bembo catches a foul glare from Hugh. 'Not quite the same I think. We are both plagued by war, no doubt, but the Greeks also had a love of it that we, I mean we Romans, never had. We say that we were born under Mars and suckled by a wolf, but really, our exercise of war was, I fancy, more practical than poetical. We fought for expansion, to spread *the Pax Romana – pacis imponere morem,* to impose peace, and so forth. We never fought for the glory of the thing, as did Greece or Egypt. We never fought as Menelaus did, crazed for sweet human blood, or as Ajax, claw mad for the joy of war. Our poetry was of the objects of battle and domestic concerns. We were ever farmers and not soldiers in our hearts.' Bembo raises his goblet and gives one of his cheeky, if nervous, grins.

'Thank you, signor.' D'Amboise leans forward virtually onto the table top. 'That explains so much about the national character.'

The grin quickly evaporates from Bembo's face, and his mouth hangs agape at so sweeping an insult.

'And yet,' Hugh says, his mouth parched. 'And yet, these Italians have given us some of our most illustrious knights.'

'What?' d'Amboise barks. 'More illustrious than the English, you mean? Not hard, I should think.'

'I was thinking rather of Marcantonnio Vendramin.'

The cardinal's head cocks backward in astonishment, his eyes becoming wide with amusement and incredulity. 'I should think Vendramin's latter actions regarding the Borgia gold call into question all we were led to believe of his former valour. It is perhaps best in that regard that we let sleeping dogs lie.'

Hugh has been keeping an eye on the Lady of Asolo, who betrays no emotion at the mention of the name. He is even more surprised when the young man opposite him breaks forth in one of the Spanish tongues.

'*Yo os digo que es muerto uno de los mejores caballeros del mundo.*'

His eyes are on the table and only raised toward Hugh when he has finished speaking. Hugh in turn looks steadfastly at him. He did not understand it all but garners quick enough that man has praised Vendramin as a great knight. *Well, well. He has met him.*

D'Amboise snaps his fingers. 'Come, Fernando, Latin or French, if you have something to say. If, that is.'

The young man turns to the cardinal. 'I was saying that we cannot know enough of the circumstances to form such opinions as would ruin a reputation such as his.'

'I see, I see. Well it seems plain enough to the rest of us, but you are free to believe what you will. I say that Italians have become corrupted by ease, as Sallust said, and that it is divine providence that ordained the *ars bellica* be mastered by the French – on behalf of the church triumphant, of course – rather than by her enemies. You may despise us and fear us by turns, but we are the hammer of God at this hour. No doubt about it.'

The queen looks across the table at Hugh, her lips pursed in anger, her cheeks red, eyes defiant. Hugh can now distinguish between the Italian and French officers, for the latter are nodding deferentially toward their commander and chief. The young captain Ferdinand however, rises from the table, bows in the general direction of the queen and cardinal. 'You must excuse me, I am out of countenance this evening.' And with that he walks from the tent.

D'Amboise feigns not to notice, but rather raps his right knuckle three times on the table as he continues. 'I say again, what Sallust said is true enough of Italy: valour begets tranquillity, tranquillity ease, ease disorder and thence ruin. Venice has raised its head against the church; it is the beginning of ruin for they divide all Christendom. But not while I live and breathe. Augustine says that if an anointed prince says a war is just, then it is so. Venice and her territories stand against Almighty God and his church. We fight with God. God wills it.'

More nods and grunts of approval from the French officers. D'Amboise summons one of his retainers and whispers something while looking at the tent door. Hugh marks it well when the servant's eyes widen slightly. He nods, and leaves swiftly. Looking back around the table, Hugh notices most of all that the captains, even the older condottieri, seem to hold a passive expression, as if no one has ever thought it worth their while to stand up to this man. He looks back at the cardinal, now cleaning his teeth with a pick. "God wills it." *What a peacock. I wonder if, in his mind, God has the temerity to hold an opinion other than the king of France. This prick could doubtless find any number of other justifications to vindicate an opposite course in the morning if it suited him.* Hugh almost snorts. Should he say something? Was it for him to criticize at the table of his host, particularly when his host happens to be one of the most powerful men living? All the hairs on the back of his neck bristle, and a shiver passes down his spine.

Just as he is condemning himself and everyone else for cowardice, the queen speaks into the abyss of silence, her voice clear and certain. 'Your Grace's study of the ancients is truly commendable. Perhaps you could correct me then, for I fancy I have read in Thucydides that men never go to war for the gods or omens, but rather for honour and self-interest. Do you think that is so?'

'Yes, perhaps he said that,' D'Amboise snaps, eyeing her contemptuously. 'I dare say the pagan Greeks were no angels. But you cannot apply the same rule here. The Italies have descended into disorder, and you can all thank God that we French possess the martial strength and Spartan discipline to bring it back. No question. No question at all.'

Is she silenced with that? Hugh looks around. *Will Bembo say nothing? The brown nose.* Hugh clears the dryness of his throat with a sip of wine. His hand trembles on the goblet. He puts it down quickly and gives a mall cough. 'If I remember aright, your majesty, it was in that same book that Thucydides speaks of the divided nature of the Hellenic world—democratic leaders trying to bring in the Athenians, while oligarchs brought in the Spartans. Even the words and expressions of the day began to change.'

'What?' the cardinal barks back. 'What the hell are you talking about?'

'The terms of usage, Eminence, even they began to change in the historian's lifetime.' Hugh looks up at the chandelier so as not to be cowered by the older man's obdurate stare.

The lady follows Hugh into the fray, saying quietly but firmly. 'Yes, I remember the passage. He said that what had formally been called a thoughtless act of aggression was now called martial courage. The idea of moderation was just another way of hiding unmanly character and cowardice, so they said. To seek to understand the dilemma from various standpoints became the hallmark of a man unfitted for action. And anyone who held violent opinions, who had a fanatical enthusiasm for war, was to be trusted. Truce breaking was justified as legitimate self-defence. Anyone who showed the slightest caution was immediately suspected as a traitor. If I remember aright, and I am sure you will correct me, the historian tells us that the decline in the Greek character was entirely traced to that time. And thereafter, the plain way of looking at something, which was the mark of a noble nature, was ridiculed and soon ceased to exist. And from then on, no man trusted his neighbour again, as they fell under Spartan tyranny and never recovered.'

Up until this point d'Amboise, probably not wanting to confirm her points, had not interrupted. But as her last words trail away, he mutters, 'Bollocks,' in a low whisper and raises both index fingers from the table. He speaks with a glacial clarity. 'May I remind your majesty that we have graciously acceded to your terms – terms by which we benefit little – and that your majesty should accordingly show due gratitude, and not a wanton lack of respect toward her benefactors. As a woman, I cannot perhaps expect you to understand the power of our ordinance, but suffice to say, many more impolitic remarks and ill-judged comparisons and I will be more than willing to show, that even from here, down on the plain, we could level your chief buildings without proceeding a step further.' His voice rises in volume and speed until the penultimate point where his knuckles once more rap the table top.

Following the breathless silence in which Hugh sees Bembo shoot him a nervous glance, her words are still clearer. 'As a woman, Eminence, you will forgive our feminine insistence that the only active power in this universe is the power to create, to nurture and to love. Lifeless and dead things destroy. A fire-ship might destroy a whole fleet but have no power. A cankered corpse may spread pestilence enough to destroy a city, but it has no life. I have ruled a whole kingdom, once, long ago it seems. And as of this afternoon, I have also ruled over a city, whose people I have carried in my heart. And I can tell you, that to ensure the piety and happiness of one body of people, and productivity of one fief, the upholding of just laws, requires the whole life of a prince. Do you not agree? And yet what have we done, but exalt in our writing and in our customs the prince who thinks he can, by some alchemy, increase his power by invading his neighbour's city. Whereas he has done two cities' worth of mischief rather than one city's worth of good. He forgoes the real power to do good in order to multiply those subject to him, to multiply them like flies, and no wonder for Beelzebub is his god.'

'You are right,' the cardinal concedes, as he looks into the gold goblet, perhaps at his reflection. But then he looks about his captains as if addressing them. 'We cannot expect the fairer and more angelic sex to understand the choleric humours of men. It is our natures, I fancy.'

'I do not believe it, Your Grace. You do yourself disservice. I knew of a woman from one of our villages, delicate and fair to behold. But she was found drowning her own baby. Yes, gasp all you want, you men. A woman can sin and kill as easily as a man. It later transpired that the child – which was conceived out of wedlock, and born in secret – would have prevented her from an advantageous marriage if it had been known. Was she fulfilling her nature? The magistrate had her hung for murder and rightly so. But if we are mere pawns of our humours, driven on by the heavenly bodies, without free will to act and face God, then let us have done with justice and magistrates altogether. And I will tell you something else as well. I knew a poor innkeeper in our city who was as choleric as any I had ever met. One night a fire was kindled in his kitchen that consumed the place. But what do you think? He repeatedly ran back into the flames to rescue everyone who lodged there. And the next morning he died of his burns. He did not give his life because of some fine point of theology, or because he feared prosecution, or because of any special relationship he had with those lodgers, other than they were his guests. He was fulfilling his nature as a man made in the image of God. Not as a saint, I say, or our notion of one, but as a true man. He exercised a power to save, to preserve or give life – the only real power that there is – unlike the selfish princes of our age who expect the guests to pay and sacrifice their lives too.'

D'Amboise smiles so that the creases around his eyes obscure his obvious irritation. Hugh knows the look; the cardinal is caught between the imposition of being lectured at his own table, and the ignominy of showing it and thus causing further damage. 'You have expressed yourself forcefully, madam. We French admire that. But I think you will agree that the balance of power between great states is vastly more complex than you can be expected to know. A garden needs sunlight, but also the shears, *non*? Maybe our natures do differ after all, but we are alike in the same boat.'

'And all sea sick too,' she mutters.

Again the cardinal feigns not to hear but speaks on. 'Howsoever, decorum forbids that we discuss this further.' The cardinal rises, placing his hands on his hips. 'I see that the second course, some venison sent from the Marchesa of Mantua's estates, is being brought in. Let us enjoy it and have no more talk of war tonight.'

Hugh, nods absently. *And let us hope the venison is not laced with canterella poison.* He looks toward the canvas curtain by which the Spaniard left. He should very much like to interview the man about Vendramin, and tonight could be his last chance.

TEN MINUTES LATER

It is not altogether easy to excuse yourself from such an august dining tent, particularly when the other soldiers are not sure whether you are a guest or a prisoner – and you are not even sure yourself. But Hugh uses the soft power of his celebrity with four, young Angevin guards to go unaided toward the latrine. The night air is thick with dew and the scent of turned turf. The guards look up from their brazier and point toward the place, but as soon as he is out of the light of their fire, Hugh looks for any tent nearby with the ensign or pennant of Aragon. Even in this low light, the red and yellow stripes are easily discernible, and he finds it quickly, just a hundred yards down the first avenue of tents.

Two men stand outside, one not much more than a boy. As he nears he can see that they are servants, glancing back every few seconds at the tent, a two-pole affair, forty feet long. They are nervous about something. They do not see Hugh approach and jump when he salutes them *sotto vocce*, asking for Signor Fernando.

The older servant is wringing his hands as he replies in the Roman dialect. 'Yes, yes, but you cannot go in, for he has visitors. Cardinal's orders; they say they mustn't be disturbed.' The servants look askance at the tent entrance once again.

Hugh immediately images it is a woman, a whore perhaps, but as he listens he can hear the low, urgent voices of angry men, followed by muffled thuds and groans. Trouble.

He shoves the servant aside. 'Go get help.' He steps up to the opening. Through the crack he sees two men and Fernando. One is holding while the other applies the punches. Fernando has a split lip and swollen eye. Without waiting, Hugh pushes the curtain aside and walks straight at them, like an idiot. 'Enough,' he bellows. No sooner have the words left his mouth than Hugh feels an iron band of arm muscle clamp his chest.

'Captain, we have company.'

Hugh smells the garlic, stale wine and women raped during their monthlies—rights of conquest, so called. These animals aren't picky. Hugh struggles, but the brute is big enough to have him off his feet altogether. The pressure feels like a bull is sitting on his chest. Hugh assesses what is available: camp bed, trunks, armour stand, rush matting, lamps. The others turn and look at him. They are rough types with crumpled noses, well scarred and knocked about, more fingers than they have teeth.

'C'est l'anglais,' says the one holding the young Spaniard, in a guttural French.

The one throwing the punches spits. 'What you want, English? English want a broken face, too, uh?' He raises his shovel-like hands, clenches them into a fist and slams it into the Spaniard's temple. Fernando doesn't cry out but merely falls limp, head hanging like a rag doll. 'Chevaliers de Rhodes, chattes chouchoutées.'

Hugh curses himself for walking in without checking the other side of the entrance. That was his mistake. The man holding Hugh now brings his head nearer to make a purring noise in his ear. That is his. Always nice to know you're not the only idiot in the room. Hugh smashes his head back twice with all the force he can muster. He is aiming for the nose, but the loudness of the crunch tells him that he has shattered the oaf's jaw. Hugh bursts the grip easily this time, and thrusts his elbow backward to wind his assailant. He crumples like a babe.

The others look up in surprise. Maybe they'd have observed some civility due to Hugh's station, but now he's knackered their mate's face, they seem to have forgotten their manners altogether. They drop the Spaniard like a sack of oats and come full tilt at him. Big lads, used to dirty work. All Hugh's weapons were surrendered before dinner. The first thug crashes into him in a flurry of fists. Hugh twists to avoid getting his face rearranged and in so doing sees the armour-stand again. The helmet. A glancing blow on Hugh's chest propels him in a spiral. His hand reaches for the helmet as he spins out of control, belly first into a pile of small chests and one large trunk. He has it. Finely etched with a handy rim, a sharp ridge on the crest and the visor, it's as good as a buckler. Hugh springs up, wielding the helmet in a great haymaking arc hard into the brute's temple. *See how you like it, Francoise.* The Frenchman's head twists as the clank of steel on bone rings out. He staggers and tries to refocus, but Hugh brings the helmet up at him with a swift backhand. The rim slices clean into the man's jaw, and he flails back.

The third man overpowers Hugh before he can get his balance. They fall back into the leather packing cases. Hugh is underneath, struggling feebly against the weight, winded and faint from a knock to the head. He sees the glint of steel. *A knife. Shit.* He grabs at the man's wrist, one hand then two, but the other is too heavy. The knife is coming down on his upper chest in steady, inevitable increments. He's hissing like a kettle. *Too heavy.* The red veins in eyes, the sweat beading on his brow, the grimace turning into a smile as Hugh's strength gives way to the crushing weight. The blade enters through Hugh's wool doublet, glancing the button aside and passing silently in. 'Argh.' Hugh cries out, lamb-like almost. The blade is cold on his skin, and then a moment later a searing pain curls his toes. He tries to scream but has no more breath. The point passes into his flesh and rests square on a rib. The rib compresses. He feels it bend, an inch or more. *God help me.* The Frenchman shifts his weight slightly to realign the blade. Hugh gasps. Suddenly a dark form looms above him. *Is it Death?* He hears a thud and feels the Frenchman ripped from him to the left. The knife tears at the flesh of Hugh's chest but goes no deeper. The dark form descends on them from the shadows. It is Fernando, come to himself, and now wielding a Spanish sword with swept hilt. He plunges it three times into the chest of the man he has kicked off Hugh, who squeals and writhes like a pig as he is driven into the ground by each new thrust. On the third he does not rise. Fernando turns to the other two men and finishes them off with the same treatment, cursing and spitting blood on them by turns.

He suddenly wheels around, blade black with blood in the candlelight and raises it against Hugh. For a moment he sways on his feet, the blood from his burst lip streaming down his chin and neck. 'I should kill you too, Erpingham.' He levels the blade momentarily between Hugh's baffled eyes. It moves left, then right, from eye to eye as the man sways. Fernando mutters something uncomplimentary about the cardinal's mother before sinking to his knees, where he stays for some moments, panting.

Hugh uses his right hand to push himself into a sitting position, and his left to put pressure on his chest wound. It will need stitches. *God, that was close.* He breathes out a long, shuddering breath. The night is turning stranger and stranger. 'Why kill me? I don't understand.'

'Because you make love to my fiancée.' Fernando looks through his one open eye, which bulges with rage.

'Your fiancée?'

'Don't act surprised, you English dog, or I will run you through. Do you hear me? I will run you – ' He breaks off in the agony of exhaustion and despair.

'Me? Why? Who is she?'

'Letting her send you poetry, leading her on. Don't think I don't know.'

'The Lady Vittoria?'

'Don't used her name or I swear.' His voice breaks. 'I swear – '

'She is your fiancée?' *Puppy love. God deliver me.* Hugh lets his head collapse back in laughter.

'Why are you laughing at me? I will kill you.'

'No, no, wait.' Hugh recovers his composure. 'Her aunt allowed it. They only wanted me to help her. Most of her poetry is pious, or about you.'

'Oh, and she just wanted to let another man read her intimate thoughts. I suppose you think I'm stupid just because I am young?'

'Don't be such an ass. I just told you, her aunt supervised what was sent. It was not done in a corner.'

'I see, and what made them choose someone like you?'

'Because, I am a soldier, like you. She wanted my help, so that she might have your approval the more. It was that simple in her mind. Though for my own part I felt that I was of little help. Indeed I felt the help was all one way.'

'What mean you by that?' Fernando lets out another pent up breath, but still keeps the blade steady.

'That her poetry was oftener the healer of my own soul, than my advice the mender of it. In the heat of battle we oft forget what is important and what is not.'

'I see, and there was never a word of love between you? Ever? You would swear on your honour to it?'

'I so swear. There is nothing between her and me. Do not take offence so.' Sensing that the present danger has passed, Hugh lies back down with a heaving sigh. 'After all I have just rescued you. You should be grateful.'

'Oh.' Fernando lowers the blade and sinks back onto his heels. 'D'Amboise is a madman; he thinks he is king of all Christendom. If you disagree with him about anything, he has you beaten into submission. The French are animals.'

'He's not going to be happy about this.' Hugh cocks his head in the direction of the corpses.

'He won't mind when he sees my face, but I will let him save his by saying that I caught them robbing my tent. He will know, and I will know. That is all that matters.' Fernando drops his sword and fingers his swollen eye. 'I am sorry to have threatened you. I misunderstood. Are you hurt?'

'I would have been dead if it were not for you. So the debt is amply repaid.' Hugh's gaze is met by the young captain, and they both smile. 'So, you are Fernando D'Avalos. You are a lucky man. Vittoria is a noble hearted woman. She will make you a fine wife, of that I am sure.'

He smiles and casts his head down, still obviously uncertain of Hugh. 'I know it. I have been such a fool to doubt her. I believed her lady-in-waiting. She is jealous perhaps. Oh, thank God it isn't true.' Fernando gasps and lets out a sigh of exasperation. 'Thank God. How I long to be out of this war. There is no honour here. Bloody French. God, I hate them.' All at once he looks at Hugh. 'But tell me how you came to be passing my tent.'

'I came to ask you about Vendramin.'

'Vendramin? Why?'

'I am looking for him.'

'But he is dead. Years ago. Well, that is what I heard. I don't believe all that about the gold. He would not steal.'

Hugh straightens up, putting pressure on the chest wound again and wincing. 'When did you last see him?'

'Oh, at my aunt's court on the island, five, six years ago. A long time ago anyway. He was there with some Franciscans, and I was not allowed in. I was maybe fourteen then and remembered being very angry about it. I liked him. He taught me some good tricks with the sword. He would tell me many things, many stories. Why do you ask?'

'Because I have seen him. And I know he has the gold because he told me he had it.'

'What? Why? I don't believe you. I won't. It can't be true.'

'I was hoping you might answer that. He was last seen with your illustrious aunt. The gold was buried in a cave nearby, then it disappeared.'

'How can I believe you, signor?' He tilts his head slightly, then mumbles. 'I suppose you want it for the knights.'

Hugh ignores the question, but says, 'Answer in the hypothetical then. Humour me.'

'In the hypothetical? What would a noble man in this world do with a fortune of gold? That is a good question. But you are asking the wrong man. Have you asked my aunt, the duchess?'

'She was not inclined to tell me, so I did not pursue the matter.'

'She loved him, I think. I expect she thought you'd been sent as an assassin.' When Hugh does not answer, Fernando says, 'Oh, I see. You are. Then I pity you, signor.'

'Pity me, why? Because Vendramin has outwitted everyone else in Italy? We English are sly bastards too, you know.'

'No, not that, but because you have been commissioned to fulfil such an ignoble and unknightly deed.'

'I think you judge too swiftly. Vendramin withholds the means by which Rhodes and Christendom may be saved, therefore to return him to the path of duty and to return the gold is more knightly than you allow.'

'God needs this gold to save his own? You make him sound like some pagan deity.'

'Martial politics requires us to be more than a little pagan on occasion.'

'And now you sound like d'Amboise. I had been given to believe you were a knight of unsurpassed valour and virtue. It is what Vittoria tells me. I do not believe the mob or popular tales, of course—ass's jawbones and all that. But I believed her, and I confess I was more than a little jealous.'

Hugh closes his mouth. It would be like answering a younger self. Hugh reclines uneasily against the baggage behind him. Fernando gazes at the corpses. For a fleeting moment their eyes meet before each drifts away to his own private thoughts. Two versions of himself seem to be colliding, exploding like the stone and lead balls of a lantern round from a canon, tearing at the fabric of his mind, his being, every part of what he had thought or had dreamed himself to be. He can always think of a comeback; he was always a cocky runt. But that is not the point, never is. He doesn't want to justify himself anymore—fig-leaves of words that vanish in the air. What he wants now is what all normal, unwarped men want in their best moments: the true path, the way to live without constant internal contradiction, the *eudaimonia* of Aristotle. It is not that he thinks D'Avalos has married the angels and demons of his nature any better than he has himself. D'Avalos does not yet know of what metal he is, of what he is capable. *God, I envy him. God, I pity him, too. Idealism is the correct province for youth. Its not to be despised, but neither is it a place for grown men to hide. There must be a realism more real than that of the pragmatists, and an optimism more solid than the idealists, of that I am sure. If I can sense such a desire within me, then surely there will be a food to meet such a hunger - or else it will be the first appetite there has ever been with a coreresponding satisfaction.*

And, of course, there is Fra Francesco of Assisi. Hugh used to find a cynic's comfort in that everywhere he looked he saw only hypocrites like himself. Where he hungered for giants, he only found pigmies growing on this mortal coil – mere escutcheons of vice and concealed hatreds. But then—these Franciscans who speak of God as if he really were love; these men who live among the poor as if there really were a world hidden from our eyes. *I lived with them those few weeks, didn't I?* Either they are better liars than Hugh can credit them, or they are mad, or else true men, living amongst those of us too far down the road to hell to see what they see. And they see something. *Francesco says even I, post res perditas, after being lost, might yet be a saint.* 'Perhaps he is mad after all.'

'Pardon?' Hugh comes to himself and sees d'Avalos gazing at him intently.

'I was lost in thought for a moment. I think that I am growing faint.' Hugh reaches out and lays his right hand on d'Avalos knee. 'Thank you for rebuking me as you did. Your life will bring you many temptations, but always remember that your initial instincts in this regard were never wrong. But enough of this, I need to see a surgeon.'

16TH NOVEMBER 1509. LETTER TO RHODES

Most Illustrious Magister,

I write to you on the Feast of Albertus Magnus, from the noble court of Mantua where we are treated as honoured guests of the marchesa, or as they verily refer to her here, *la prima donna del mondo*. I am recovering from a small wound to my chest, and have been enchanted by the diplomat Niccolo da Corregio who says that he met you in Avignon some years back. But to my report in general I now come.

I was able, as per my last missive, to use my friendship with the Venetian ambassador to pass the naval blockade on the Venetian lagoon and gain access to the city. I stayed at our priory there but grew to distrust the prior. I have no solid evidence against him, though I mention it for I was followed everywhere I went.

I was able to make a search at the Casa Vendramin, but found nothing. I would have made more searches at other places, but I was unexpectedly ambushed by soldiers in the doge's palace. I killed some of them in order to preserve my own liberty. I hope this does not jeopardise diplomatic relations with the republic, but I did not trust that softer negotiations would avail, and so acted accordingly.

During my escape through the city, I was followed by what I assumed were the prior's spies. However, I also saw a man that I would have been ready to swear was Vendramin himself, but now I cannot be sure. I saw him in daylight last spring in Perugia. It was fleeting and even then he was in disguise. Yet there was something in this man's face – a man I saw for a moment on a bridge – that brought some flame of remembrance to me. Perhaps this was intuition, or premonition. I cannot know now, but I mention it, for I saw the same man once more at the *Arsenale* on that same day, and this may be significant.

We escaped the Veneto with great difficulty, via the small city of Asolo, where we were able to mediate that city's surrender to your brother and the league's military officers. Cardinal d'Amboise was magnanimous in victory, you may be assured. During these negotiations I interviewed the nephew of the Duchess of Francivallia, Constanza d'Avalos. Fernando d'Avalos serves as captain of a detachment of horse from Naples. He last saw Vendramin at her court on Ischia with a delegation of Franciscans. There was, you may remember, a friary directly above the cave where the gold had been hidden. So I was suspicious, of course. I am invited to the island of Ischia in the spring when this same captain returns to marry the lady Vittoria Colonna. If need be, I can use my visit to resolve this matter, but I will need your express order if I am to use *modica coactio* with the duchess, for it could cause diplomatic difficulties with Spain and Aragon if it were discovered.

But long before that, I am bound once more for Ferrara. I have learned in Venice from Gasparo Contarini that the duke of Ferrara, who favours my opinion on ordinance and other matters, was given a portrait of Vendramin five years ago. It was painted by Titziano Vecello – who makes excellent likenesses, I can assure you. If I can see this painting, fix this man's face in my mind, then I am sure it will aid me in my quest.

And this brings me to the war. News comes of reverses almost daily, and we hear the canons oft when the wind is in the north, which it was two days ago. Gonfalonier Pitigliano returned to the offensive shortly after I met him in Venice, and he has been busy. The Venetian forces under his command have defeated the remaining imperial army, recapturing Vicenza, Este, Feltre and Belluno in the last few weeks. As I write, he besieges Verona, but with the winter coming on I am doubtful that he can succeed. Even so, they have shown a high hand.

So I am bound for Ferrara but with no great relish, as we hear daily the depredations wrought in the countryside by the mercenaries under the command of Venetian admiral Trevisian. I met him too, at the naval blockade on the lagoon and can quite believe all I am hearing now. When lands and cities change hands with such rapidity as they do here, one would have thought they would be more circumspect about rapine and pillage. Many more will starve this winter than have found themselves on the wrong end of Dalmatian and Albanian lances. But I digress.

Let us hope that with such a strong position, Venice may again go to the negotiating table. I have great faith in their ambassador, who has been dispatched to Rome, and may even be there already. I do not know Signor Donato's orders, but he is an able and humane agent, whose company I have benefitted from most especially. Most people of good will wish an end to this madness. The French horse have eaten much of the standing grain north of here. It will be a hard winter for many. Will there be a settlement made before Christmas? It is hard to say. The pope has invested much and gotten little in return. We will see anon. And I will write when I know more. I am sending duplicates of this letter on several ships to ensure you receive it. I enclose no accounts for we lost some of our baggage, including our copybook, while fleeing Venice.

The instructions enclosed separately for the Medici bank are from Signor Bembo. The meagre subsidy is for the mother of our late servant. Everything is explained in the requisition, but I mention it so that it might be a matter of honour to be speedily dealt with.

Yours faithfully, et cetera

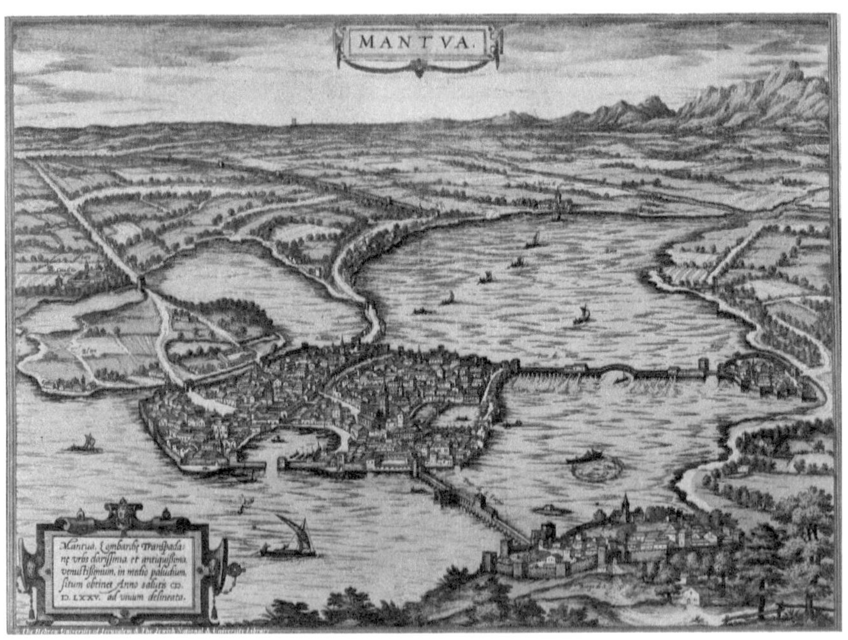

PALAZZO SAN SEBASTIANO, MANTUA. 26TH NOVEMBER 1509

Hugh unfurls the map and savours the odour of vellum, dust and must. He gazes intently on the birthplace of Virgil unrolled before his eyes, Alberti's new Rome, blessed Mantua, queen of cities.

Hubris is a Greek word, not imported to Italy with the Corinthian capitals and everything else. The map shows a bird's eye view from the east. Maps help no end in a flat country because you can never get high enough to get the sense of the place. This one shows the grey Alps in the top right corner much nearer than they really are. Hugh smiles. If they could just entice the hills to come a bit closer, perhaps this place really would be Virgil's Arcadia after all.

He sits huddled in the chill-marble Room of the Crucible. He's glad of his winter cloak. The cube-like room is twenty feet across with a pure white vault centred on a fresco of a golden goblet in a fiery crucible. *Tried by fire.* He knows how the goblet feels, but he doesn't feel particularly golden himself today. His trials and privations have no outward appearance of unilineal progression toward sainthood, but he still has hope that they are not totally without some hidden narrative. That is one step up from total despair, but at least it is something, and more than he had eight months before.

He involuntarily shifts his feet, trying to circulate the blood. He could wish for a fire in this room today for the easterly winds are blowing hard across the golden reeds of the marsh. His chest wound is healing faster than a chill he took on the journey south from Asolo, where the rain was incessant and the roads often impassable. There are fires upstairs but not here, on the ground floor, where this afternoon he is trying to understand the city and its environs. This is partially out of a general interest and partially – as ever – in case he ever needs a plan of escape.

He unfurls the vellum on the left corner. It is bleached and crisp from too much sun – not something they worry about back in England. Casting a quick eye over it, he sees he is a fair way up river, perhaps two days ride, from Ferrara. But Mantua is not on the mighty Po itself, but rather a few miles north on a smaller tributary called the Mincio. This river balloons into a brackish lake that curls around two islands, linked to each other and the mainland by a system of bridges, causeways and sluices. The further island from the shore is the walled city of Mantua, with fine bastions and two good fortified harbours, packed full of flat bottomed *magani*, like the one he travelled in from Ferrara, and a few other sail boats that remind him of the wherries of his native Norfolk broads.

To the west of the city Hugh traces with his finger a defensive wall between the Mincio and the Po. That is one big wall. They were serious about keeping the northern barbarians out—all those Hunnish Franks and Burgundians with their bloodlust and ambitions. A fair prize Mantua would be, a jewel among the thousands of Italy. But you'd have to get past the Gonzaga first, and it's not for nothing that their insignia is the scorpion. Here, amid the dreamy spires, cupolas and turrets; amid red brick palazzi and churches ancient and modern; amid harbours and wharves crammed with luxuries from across the world; Isabella Gonzaga, the self-styled first lady of the renaissance, sits amply as queen. Like a spider on a web, she knew the moment Hugh and Bembo entered the Mantua territories. They were made to come as guests. *Made.* Bembo must be celebrated in paint, and the poet in turn must celebrate Mantua and her queen in verse. Or else. And Hugh, why was he here? She hasn't spoken directly to him about Venice yet, about her husband, or what passed between them in the letter – or how Hugh managed to get out alive, even.

Hugh has tried not to be impressed with this place. He wanted to say afterwards that it was like a slice of faux-Rome stuck out on a malarial swamp. He wanted to pay the marchesa back for that letter of betrayal by saying the whole place only has a veneer of style, all fur coat and no knickers. But he grew to admire the place notwithstanding. It is hard not to when Mantua is everything the English dream Italy to be. It is why the English are half mad these days to pull everything down that isn't *Italianate*, as they call it. Spires give way to domes, pointed arches to round or square, dark rooms for light, war for peace, poverty for wealth, prose for verse, poachers to poets – on and on, up and up until there will be no one to empty the bedpans. Hugh smiles. Even so, it is hard not to feel like a half-cultured barbarian when you're being escorted through the ducal palace. When you see how Andrea Mantegna painted, even a decade ago, you just want to hang up your brushes.

The marchesa would not countenance their sleeping at the ducal palace. Why? Because she has just built a new palazzo on the southern island beyond the city walls right on the water's edge. It is her retreat from the pressures of the dark, gothic court, the wagging tongues and miasma of the city. This is her own little *delizia*, built in the *au courant* classical style, simple, confident, understated in decoration. Soldiers are scarcely seen here, much less lawyers, notaries and the like. You don't have soldiers in Arcadia, only semi-clad shepherds and voluptuous shepherdesses. There are numerous African and Moorish servants. Corregio told Hugh that the marchesa has them sought out from the markets of Venice to Constantinople, as black as possible. The upper floors are given over to the tutors and poets who instruct the young Gonzagas from prime to sext. After the angelus bell the next generation scatter to the stables, mounting on various sizes of palfrey so they can go hawking and indulge in other forms of field sport.

This they did barely a half hour ago, shouting and running like calves let out of winter stalls. Hugh has been undisturbed all this time, but now he hears the sounds of slippers on the marble. A pang of guilt rushes upon him, and he quickly rolls the map up. *They will think me a spy, going through these maps which detail their defences.* He walks quickly to the open shelved wardrobe and places the map inside, then walks toward the door.

When he reaches the door and looks to the further doorway of the room he is entering, Hugh sees that it is the marchesa herself, standing there, quite alone in a pale green velvet gown and fur stole.

'Fra Erpingham, I thought you would be with your friend the poet.' She fingers a loose ringlet above her right eyebrow, then walks to the centre of the room with small, floating steps. She bows as if they were about to dance a pavan together, which they probably are, Hugh thinks.

'He has gone again to your archives at the ducal palace. Verily I think he could live there if you let him. Castiglione has already boasted much of your collection.'

'There is none like it. Frankly, I am surprised that our dear ambassador does not spend more time in his native city. What has Urbino that Mantua does not? Stuck up there in the hills.'

Hugh maintains his face. He would have answered 'love'. But he will not temp the enmity of a woman known for her recalcitrance. He approaches cautiously, though not so nearly the centre, and bows. 'Who can say, my lady?'

A draft of icy wind comes through the doorway from the loggia behind her. On the northern façade of the building, the loggia – so cooling in summer, so unwelcome now – is enclosed by an arcade of unfluted marble columns with Corinthian capitals. The acanthus leaves are exquisitely carved and polished. Hugh shudders inwardly and suppresses the urge to rub his hands like a money changer in order to warm them. The ice queen seems unmoved.

Pleasantries accomplished, the diminutive green tyrant raises her eyes heavenward and circles the room with deliberate steps. 'How auspicious that we should meet in this room of all rooms, signor.' She metes out her words with each step, as a fishmonger would lay out slabs of cold, grey mullet. 'I had wanted to talk to you before now, but life is what it is. I have much to do in my husband's absence.'

'He is well.'

'What?' She stops her procession for a moment and looks at him with uncomprehending eyes.

'Your husband.'

'Oh, him.'

'An ague or distemper of the lungs perhaps, but tolerably well under the circumstances.'

'You saw him then. Did he give you any message for me?'

'We were interrupted.' *Better not say any more than that.*

'Ah, I see. Interrupted.' Her words echo in the icy white vault. 'I will not play with you, signor. I can see that you are an intelligent man, perhaps even a survivor, like me. I will be frank with you. I knew when I met you in Ferrara that you would not rest until you had fulfilled the request of my sister-in-law. She is a gentle soul, the sort that ignites knightly ardour. I knew that, of course. But as I told you then, it is best for Mantua that my husband stay where he is for now. And I always get my way.'

'The letter.' Hugh folds his arms.

'Indeed, delivered by your own hand. A second Uriah, if you like. It was snot personal. Indeed, I am sorry for your sake, but regret nothing. My allegiance is first to my family, my children, to Mantua. We have great souls here in Mantua, but we are a small power. To protect the balance of power is not easy. I said that it was auspicious that we meet in this room because I caught sight of the device repeated on the vault and lunettes.'

Hugh glances up to see a porcupine with a crown resting above it. 'I cannot read the inscription.'

'*Comminus et eminus*, from near or far. The device is not ours, but French, though God alone knows why they chose a porcupine and not an ox or a butcher's cleaver. But we have chosen it, as we have chosen the scorpion. Come near us, and we know how to sting you, but even far away we have ways of launching our quills.' She stops pacing and faces him abruptly. 'I hope the doge was fair with you. It was not my intention that you should be hurt.'

'They are at war, my lady. War makes public officials more than ordinarily scrupulous in the execution of justice. In truth, I did not wait to find out.'

'Good, I am glad. *Vae Victis*, woe to the vanquished. Then all is well, no harm done? Good, then we are friends. Will you take my hand?' She proffers an emerald ring for him to kiss.

He lingers long enough to let her know that he doesn't quite view it that way and then says, 'Marchesa.' He bends once more to kiss the ring, savouring the smell of rose water on her marble-cold fingers.

When he stands again, she is smiling with pert lips. 'Good. My husband will see all is done for the best. You need not have risked your neck to rescue his. All is well.'

Ah, not so quickly, my lady Lillith. Hugh takes a pace back. 'You make it sound like he has no will in all this.'

'He is in bonds. What in heaven do you mean?' Her eyes burn with indignation. 'Of course, he is passive, for once.'

'His person is bound, certainly. But not his mouth or his great reputation as a gonfalonier.'

The Marchesa tilts her head back imperiously and glances down her nose with increasing alarm at Hugh. 'What do you mean?'

'What I mean is this: I might have rescued him if he had not already formed a prior agreement with his captors.'

'With his captors!' Her shrill shriek shakes the vault.

'He judges that the Italies will soon grow tired of their fruitless efforts to despoil Venice and begin to regret that they invited the French to spread their power east. He has accepted an offer to be gonfalonier of a Venetian force once more when that occurs.'

'It has not occurred. It will not occur.' The Marchesa's fists are clasped to her side as she stamps her right slipper on the marble. 'He does not know what he is talking about.'

'Venice judges it to be the case. For myself I do not know, of course, but your husband judges that they are right. And as you say, keeping the balance of power is such a delicate business.'

'You have been our guest for two weeks, and you only mention it now? Oh, men!'

'My apologies, I assumed you would know.' *Obviously the quills of Mantua do not reach that far*, Hugh is tempted to say but refrains when he sees how the Marchesa's eye narrow and harden. To placate her, and so that the anger does not become directed at him, he continues. 'He did not ask me to tell you. I suppose he expected you would understand he had acted for the best of his family and Mantua.'

'For the best? by exposing us as the most southerly of Julius' enemies? I suppose you thought it was all very fine while you were entertained here at San Sebastiano. But I tell you something –'

At these words she stops, and from her eyes Hugh can see that her mind is changing direction, and working on something new. It is for the briefest moment, but when she continues her tone is less shrill, more measured, and therefore more chilling. 'Yes, I will tell you something about Saint Sebastian, for he was from these parts, you know. A captain in the Praetorian Guard and a great soldier like you are, I suppose. He thought he would help his fellow Christians by meddling, but he was found out, and Diocletian had him shot through with many arrows. And thus he is always shown in our painting, but he did not die that way. He was rescued by a woman called Irene who nursed him to health. They say you have come back from the grave, too—the great knight who was slain but who now lives. The Turks cannot kill you, nor Pandolfo Petrucci, nor that commander from Florence – what was his name? Don Michelle or something. It is fine, very fine.' Her false mirth turns swiftly to menace. 'We women are not afraid of blood, signor. We see it every month. We can nurse, and give life as Irene did. But we can just as easily take it away. Men cannot bridle their lusts as we can. Sebastian was puffed up with his own resurrection and thought to lock horns once more with the emperor. Can you believe his pride? He got his head beaten in with a cudgel for his impudence. Not a public and glorious martyr's death after all, but the ignominious death of a fool, bludgeoned until his brains spilled forth far away from the historian's eye. I often wonder how many meddlesome fools die that way. Such a shame, such a waste don't you think?'

Hugh's eyes meet hers. She is a d'Este through and through. She will do whatever it takes to maintain control. If they lock up their own siblings, how much more would they dispose of an errant knight whom she felt was making a fool of them. 'I cannot speak for Saint Sebastian for I do not know enough about the matter. But what you say is true: we men are prone to vanity and many vexations that afflict us and thereby the world.' Hugh thinks of how he might assert his position as the ambassador of a sovereign order, for he feels she might call for the guards at any moment, but every new formulation of words sounds weaker than the last. So he finishes his reply, rather dumbly with *world*, and waits.

'You say that you are on your way to my brothers in Ferrara.'

'That is my intention, by your leave.'

'I think you should go quickly. What with Trevisian's Albanians despoiling the countryside it would be a shame if something should—' She pauses. '—happen to you.'

'Thank you, my lady,' Hugh says with a courteous bow, thankful at least that he will not be carrying any letters from her again.

SANT'AGOSTINO, HALF A DAY WEST OF FERRARA. 28TH NOVEMBER 1509

Bembo and Hugh have come out of their way south to avoid the skirmishers, but the bastards are everywhere. Outside the town of Sant'Agostino six Dalmatian marauders jump them from the long reeds, bold as brass as if the Estense has no army to defend its byways. Stirrup to stirrup Hugh and Bembo see them off and kill three outright at the first charge. The others disappear into the reeds.

Bembo is exceedingly pleased with the rout, for he has slain two of them. Wilf is less happy having the punctured corpses next to their trunks and food, but Hugh insists that they get burial. Although he will never marry, he knows he will leave behind many widows when he goes. It weighs on him, and he hangs his head in meditation as they approach the town gate.

It is late afternoon, and the constable is hesitant to open to them. He recognises the blue stripes of the Dalmatians and sends for the castellan. 'How do we know you are not spies? How do we know you are not bringing plague corpses to our town? The gate is shut. We have no food for strangers either.'

'I am Fra Hugh Erpingham of Rhodes. I have letters from your duke, from even the Holy Father. We have come down from Mantua where we were guests of the court. Send a man out and you will see. We killed these men when they ambushed us.'

After almost a minute's pause, the constable speaks again. 'It is not our policy to open the gates after the waning of the light. I will not be the one to open our gates and risk disaster, signor. Go to Ferrara if you will.'

Hugh sighs. *Saints preserve us.* 'What is your name, porter?'

Another interminable pause. 'The castellan is coming.'

As he finishes speaking, Hugh sees a cloud of dust on the horizon behind them and hears the clatter of hooves. A cavalcade of two hundred horse approach. The ground shakes as the ensigns of Ferrara come into view on the bleak skyline. The castellan calls for the gates to be opened, but Wilf cannot get the mule to move quickly enough. The mounted troop hasten at the sight of the gates, and Hugh moves calmly to the rear to halt them, while Wilf's curses are drowned by the bucking and whinnying of the mares as they scream to an ungainly halt. The crimson captains are enraged.

One of them shouts with a raised lance, 'Get this tinker's cart out of our way or we will drive him into the ditch.'

Hugh doffs his cap. 'Forgive the beast; it is old and has travelled far.'

'And so has the mule, fair captains of the Estense,' Bembo adds with a flourish.

A few laugh, but the angry captain points his lance at the dead Dalmatians then back at Hugh. 'And who are you, hospitaller, who travels with the corpses of our enemies. Give your answer carefully, for we are not to be humoured when so many of our enemy are abroad.'

'I am Hugh Erpingham, knight and ambassador of Rhodes, friend to your noble duke.' Hugh gestures back at the corpses, but does not take his eye off the lance. 'These men we killed when they ambushed us about two miles hence.'

'How many were there?' the captain asks.

'Six, but three retreated to the marshes, and we were not inclined to follow.'

'That is correct.' The captain revolves the lance slightly so that Hugh can see that it is freshly blooded. 'We picked up the others. Two we have left for the pigs, one we have brought with us for the cardinal to question.'

'The cardinal?' Hugh says, feeling the humours unbalance deep in his gut.

'Yes,' a voice behind him says. Hugh turns and sees Cardinal Ippolito d'Este in full harness and crimson cloak, standing next to the castellan on the city wall. 'How nice of you to come to me, Fra Erpingham, just as you promised you would. Captain, I would that you bring this man to me in the inner prison along with the captive. The knight and I will interview him. We have much to discuss.'

'Very well, Your Grace.'

CARDINAL D'ESTE, TEN MINUTES LATER

It is even worse than Hugh had thought: a temporary torture chamber—temporary but with every accessory a devil could wish for. Thinking he has nothing to hide Hugh has let himself be stripped of weapons, even his boot daggers. Now chained to a wall, he realises that having nothing to hide is not necessarily a virtue in times like these.

The other prisoner, lit by three torches, which are the only light, is a lean Dalmatian. He is no more than a boy, and has already been softened up; most of his teeth have been knocked out and his left eye is swollen shut. He gazes wildly between Hugh and a corpse whose head still remains conflated in a head-crushing tourniquet – bladder and bowels voided through ripped and ragged hose. The smell is terrible as it is familiar. The Dalmatian is babbling in his native tongue like a baby, then praying *Pater Nosters* in Latin. He knows this is the last room he will ever see. He had his last meal without even knowing it. The prayers run on and on.

It suddenly seems a poor thing to Hugh that man can't pray his last prayers in his own language. This man will have sins to atone for. War doesn't make any man a saint, but by all accounts these *Statioti* of Trevisian have been savage beyond the natural in their bloodlust. Hugh endeavours to engender some pity for the lad in order to take his mind off his own predicament. Bembo and Wilf probably think he is dining in a different part of the castle. Hugh shifts his position and feels once more the manacles gnawing at his wrists and ankles. *The cardinal only means to frighten me. Shit. It's working.*

The heavy olive wood doors lurch open, grinding on their rusty hinges and scraping the flags, as the cardinal enters. He wears fine calf-skin gloves, glinting harness but has shed his cloak. He looks at Hugh, fingers his fringe effeminately and gives a brief smile. *The door is closing. The way out of the underworld is closing.* Hugh feels his bowels loosen. The door wafts the smell of roasted pork towards him from a small brazier to his left. A pair of iron tongs and pincers rest near the embers with torn flesh attached. Tools of the trade, and the smell is definitely not pork.

The cardinal claps his hands twice, once in delight, and the second time like a man getting down to business. 'Ah, my sister sent me word that you were coming. I looked for you on the road but could not find you, and yet here you are. It is like destiny.' The cardinal twists about like a serpent uncoiling as he continues to speak. 'Do you like my little room? One has to make concessions when travelling, but in a time of war there is so much opportunity. I know you of all people understand Hugh – you don't mind my using familiar terms, I hope? I feel we understand each other, or at least we shall. My collection, my hobby if you will.'

He pivots with hands raised, palms up, gesturing to leather, iron, spikes and all. 'The Dominicans of Spain call them the "weapons of virtue". I like that, don't you? Truth is a very great virtue, and we must have it after all. You, signor, battle with your weapons of sword and buckler, and I with mine – my, er, weapons of virtue. They are not all as effective of course. The hanging cage and the spiked coffin are more often useful as storage for the other items when traveling. Each play their part – each of my weapons: the saw that cuts you slowly into two pieces, the finger-stretching tourniquet, the bone breaking pendulum, the seat of pins, the long needle that perforated the devil's moles, the iron claw that shreds the flesh, the red hot pincer and tongs, the whip with the knife at the end, the pillory, the gaff, the ball that swells and tears the mouths of heretics and the anuses of pederasts. Ah.' The cardinal sighs deliciously, then lets his palm caress the cheek of the corpse within the head-crushing tourniquet. 'This man was a very well-to-do banker. Yesterday, that is. He said he could wait no longer for the money I owed him. I think he forgot his manners. The dead are far more polite, eh Giacomo, eh?' He pats the sunken cheek again and then says, looking sharply at Hugh. 'The dead will always wait for you.'

Hugh tries to speak with nonchalance. 'I am on my way to see your brother. He has shown me great favour, you know. I do not think he would approve of this.'

'Hah, my noble brother disapproves of much, of that you may be sure. And our father even more so.' The cardinal folds his arms, his face spiteful, resentful, and injured. 'But you will find he and I are one, two sides of the same ducat. In the east they believe that there must be a balance of light and dark, kindness and cruelty. And I have long thought that they understand more than we do. But we are quick learners. Take me, for example. With practice I have come to understand much. But why do I tell you this? Only that you should know that I understand you, my friend. For we, both of us, are soldiers. We both have ascended in prowess in our various spheres of battle. That is good and proper, and it is right that it should bring us pleasure and honour. With experience we come to appreciate the weapons that perhaps we once despised. Take this iron gag for example.' The cardinal retrieves a dull grey brace with a tongue plate on the inside. He deftly fits it to the struggling prisoner, securing it tightly at the back with a speed that sends a new shiver through Hugh. 'I used to despise the gag because I enjoyed the sounds that a man could make when he had too. But even this bored me after a year or two. You cannot imagine what it is like to be given everything you want all your life. Every pleasure dies on you, every new sally forth into delight makes one numb as before. When I put my brother Giulio's eyes out with a bodkin, I felt such an exquisite power that I had not sensed before. It is he that I have to thank for all this really. It was so easy, too.' Without warning, and with a curled lip, the cardinal draws a small eating knife from his belt and plunges it two inches into the prisoner's swollen eye. 'An eye for an eye, my young friend. You shouldn't have come into the Estense to plunder, should you?' The man bellows into the gag, great gruff grunts like a wounded boar, as the cardinal withdraws and examines the blade in the torch-light. The soldier thrashes back and forth, eventually curling forward in long heaving sobs. 'It will not kill him. Another inch maybe, but you know that don't you my brother. I expect you have done it many times to Saracens and the like.'

Hugh looks to the floor. Blood drips in a pool under the stool. 'I have killed more men than I can count.' Hugh's voice is hoarse and dry. He clears it and then continues. 'But I swear I have taken no pleasure in it.'

'What? Really? Surely finding pleasure in serving God is a knight's meat and drink?' His voice is now shrill, bordering on the hysterical. 'I don't believe you. We are the same, you and I. Let us have no pretense down here. Let us have no show of hypocrisy. That is what I love about a place like this. There can be honesty. So let us be as we really are. The truth will set us free, Hugh.'

Hugh remembers the Turks he slew on that galley in his purple rage. That was over a year ago and yet the memory of the slain is still with him – not the faces now, just the decks and gunwales scarlet with gore. The faces become one face in the end, which is no face eventually. Was that his memory? It seems like another man. Was there pleasure in slaughter? No. Perhaps he did look to escape the drowning melancholy by action, to cut himself as with the knives of the priests of Baal. Then come alive again, to feel again, something, anything. Perhaps, but there was no pleasure in the act itself. *I may be worse, but I am not of the same cloth as this demon.* He must bring this demoniac to his senses. Must do something. 'My lord cardinal, I am a knight and an ambassador of Saint John. And I can tell now – '

'Don't. Please don't. Don't spoil everything. I want you to observe. I want you to consider. You are a sensible man, I fancy. You know how serious I am. You know what I want. Let us not be hasty. I know you will tell me anon. But first let us indulge a little. Where shall we start? *Where. Shall. We. Start?* Tongs or pincers?' The cardinal locks his jaw and speaks with an exultant delight as he places the tools deeper into the embers of the brazier. 'God, I love these.' While they are heating up, the cardinal moves the victim's chair directly opposite Hugh. He then stares at Hugh, with great beads of sweat running down his forehead and licking his lips. 'I want you to watch, signor. I want you to remember that his insignificant passing will not be in vain because it will put you in remembrance of your duty.'

LATER. ONE HOUR, TEN HOURS?

Hugh's head is swooning, swimming, reeling. One man's agony and another's delight fuse in his mind in abhorrence but also act to unhinge his own reason somehow. Hugh is blinking back the madness. The cardinal's eyes have gone from his victim, to his 'instrument of virtue' and back to Hugh every five seconds. For how long? He cannot say. *Is their time in hell?* His heart is racing, and his humors are in such flux that he has lost all sense of it. He keeps forgetting to breathe, to hold his bladder, to stand. Every time he sees the cardinal's eye he wants to say something, but he cannot. His throat is sand dry, his limbs cold with sweat.

The Dalmatian soldier hangs limp in the chair, lacerated, perforated, burnt. Dead.

The cardinal stands back and takes off his right glove. It is deeply stained. He lets a white finger delicately caress his own brow and arrange his fringe. He smirks and says, 'Well, I would have expected a young man in the flower of youth to last a little longer. But there you are. You get the idea.' He replaces the glove and unfastens the iron gag. The victim's head hangs limply forward and when the gag is removed, various bodily fluids spill from inside it. 'Let us begin, shall we.'

Hugh heaves. 'What, why?' Heart racing so fast now that his knees are buckling. *God no, please no.* As the cardinal approaches, Hugh strains his head further up the wall. Staring down his own nose, he can now see where men's teeth have worn into the tongue plate. 'Look, I will tell you everything I know.' The cardinal pauses, and Hugh tries to wet his mouth and continue before the spell is broken. 'I think that I saw Vendramin in Venice, but I could not get to him. Wait, wait. I made a search of the warehouse under his family's palazzo. Nothing. Wait, wait please, I barely escaped Venice with my life.' He sees the cardinal's eyes lower toward the gag. He is losing interest. 'I learnt that a portrait of him was given to your brother some few years ago. I have come to see it, to be sure. To be sure if it was him or not – the man I saw. Then I will know what to do next. That is all I know, I swear it.'

The cardinal smiles benignly, but it quickly shrinks from his face. 'You disappoint me, signor. Really you do. I can tell you are holding back, but I will not ask you again now. For first we must have some purgation. *Non? Oui?* Of course we shall. Just hold still while I fit you with this. Wouldn't want to hurt you.'

Hugh strains at the shackles. 'Please, I am an ambassador of Rhodes.' He has virtually no movement in them. 'I beg you, by all the rules of honour, of war even.'

'The rules? Ah yes, *the rules*, of course. My own view, which I have most honestly held for a long time now, is that the rules are best seen as a web. They catch the smaller insects in them, and that is necessary. But the larger animals, like birds for example, pass straight through. And there perhaps is the difference between you and me. You cannot pass through the web. But you are surely on it, are you not?'

Hugh strains again until he feels his hands will tear away at the wrist. The only part of his body that he can move is his head. *It is my only chance. There is no way this devil will let me out alive now.*

The cardinal reaches up with the gag. Some of the Dalmatian's wiry brown hairs are lodged in the tightening mechanism. The cardinal tries unsuccessfully to free them with his gloves. His attention is diverted for a moment. It is all Hugh needs. He lunges his head forward far enough to break the bridge of the prelate's nose while he is looking downwards. D'Este immediately drops the gag, and reels backward into his last victim. He puts out a hand wildly to stop his fall, but it plunges into the brazier. He topples with it toward the straw with a high-pitched scream. The scream stops abruptly as his head hits the far wall. A dull wooden thud, and the room falls strangely silent. Hugh gazes dumbly as the body sprawls on the straw, surrounded by a smattering of fresh coals. Smoke begins to rise from the straw, and after a minute, a flame, but the body remains still.

Without the incessant monologue of bile coming from the cardinal's mouth, Hugh has space to think again, almost as if a spell has been broken. He plays through a few scenarios in his mind. The fire must be sufficient for the guards to release him and for them to ring the bell. *I will have to wait as long as I can before I cry out.*

The room fills with smoke, and flames lick at the boots and legs of the cardinal. Still he does not move. It would be good for this creature to boil in his own juices, but I'll be damned if I am going to go with him. The smoke descends lower and lower, thicker and thicker. Hugh coughs. 'Fire, fire, the prison is on fire. Save the cardinal. Save Cardinal d'Este.' That is the last thing he remembers.

ALFONSO D'AVALOS, THE NEXT DAY

'He's stirring. He's coming to, Marchese.'

The voice is distance, above him. Hugh opens his eyes briefly and blinks. Looks like a church dome above him. A temporary hospital? Incense, bees wax polish. Gunpowder. Hugh coughs and blinks again. His throat and lungs burn like hell. His head aches and pulsates. He is surrounded by Wilf, Bembo, and a surgeon wiping blooded hands on an apron. The fourth man, the one they call 'Marchese', he cannot see.

The surgeon peers with a peculiar sneer, as if disappointed. 'He's all right, is he? We'll need his bed.'

Hugh hears the sound of heavy ordinance booming like thunder, and suddenly remembers. The dungeon, the pincers, the screams, the smell. A riot of panic seizes him. He grabs Bembo's arm. 'The cardinal?'

The other man, the marchese, still out of view to Hugh, answers. 'His Grace is still unconscious.'

'He has some nasty burns,' the surgeon says, examining a black finger on Hugh's right hand. 'But he'll probably live.'

'Calm yourself, Hugh,' Bembo says. 'Everything will be all right. The city is under attack but not a full siege.' Bembo's voice relays an overtly intense earnestness and is rather louder than necessary. 'I have explained to the marchese that we are heading for Ferrara, and that you are a favourite of the duke. The marchese here will vouch for you until the cardinal recovers.'

Hugh blinks and looks from one man to the other. 'Forgive me, Your Grace, my eyes are still recovering from the smoke.'

The marchese bends forward over the bed and into Hugh's vision. Hugh blinks, then strains to see a young man with honest eyes and broad jaw approach the bedside, still cradling his helmet. When Hugh adds the black curly hair to the general shape of the face, he knows he has been saved by Ferdinand Francesco d'Avalos – Marchese of Pesaro. 'D'Avalos, thank God. I thought you were assigned to the French.'

'That became difficult after your visit to the camp, signor. So I am reassigned here among the noble Ferrarese and sorely glad to be rid of the French command. And glad also to return you the favour. Signor Bembo has explained that the cardinal's grievance with you is a personal matter. If the cardinal recovers – well, if he does I will tell him I have sent you to his brother. And I will write to the duke if necessary. The duke is not like his brother, as I am sure you know. You will be sent under armed escort just as soon as we drive these Albanians and Venetians back. We expect reinforcements tomorrow. It will not be long.'

'I thank you, my lord. Words cannot express my relief and gratitude.' Hugh turns his neck and sees Wilf wiping tears from his eyes. 'Wilf?'

'Thought we'd lost you this time, master.'

LETTER TO RHODES FROM PONTELAGOSCURO, NEAR FERRARA. 16 DECEMBER 1509

Most Illustrious Magister,

I write in haste, entrusting myself to God, and this brief missive to the honourable poet Ludovico Ariosto who has promised that if I do not survive the Venetian guns or the caprice of Cardinal d'Este, he will make sure it reaches you.

I came to Ferrara from Mantua, but fell into the hands of the cardinal at the town of Sant'Agostino. He knows what we seek, and I only narrowly escaped with my life because of a prison fire. I have been warned that he has just now arrived in Ferrara and that his wrath against me is as terrible as if I had been a Venetian.

I am currently in the duke's forward military camp one mile north of the city. We are pinned down by a barrage from Trevisan's galleys. We have counted no less than seventeen ships of the line, all of which are shielded from our ordinance by the high banks of the Po River. The Venetians have dug a fine gun battery on the levy, and we have kept them busy, though the duke will not let his larger guns be brought from the city in case they are captured and the city compromised.

The depredations of the Venetian forces here have been truly unimaginable, and I will not waste ink trying to express what cannot be written. Almost the entire country is laid waste, and more *bouche inutiles* are daily pouring into the city with tales of woe, 'useless mouths' in a city where food is already scarce. It is a dangerous situation and cannot continue long without calamity. Ass meat has already become a delicacy, cats disappeared weeks ago and efforts have been made to kill falcons and owls. No wheat can be had, and the price of an egg has risen to ten *soldi*; a rat, thirteen! The last runner who made through to us with a message told me that he saw a man being beaten in the market for trying to sell a barrel of wine for ten crowns. We are not under direct siege, but you would think they were.

It seems that Admiral Trevisan will attempt nothing against the city for it is too well defended, but has busied himself in the softer warfare of killing farmers and their families in order to goad the duke out to him. It is a cowardly war, and the Albanian and Dalmatian *stratioti* have proved themselves worthy of such a debased action. That such atrocities should come upon the common people at the hands of their Christian countrymen – that generals will not prosecute open and manly warfare in the field or on the open sea – shows that we have sunk to a level beneath the heathen. The duke upbraids himself for investing so much in the city and not fortifying the river towns better, but in truth who could prepare against such cowardice from a neighbour? It has no parallel among the cruelest tyrants of Asia. We are undone.

Notwithstanding, and though many advised against it, the duke, who is fully aware of the risks, has sallied forth with a small force, for he is too much a knight to stay behind the walls while his people suffer. I can see his standard even now from my tent. It is pierced by many holes and has been remounted ten times or more. But we are still here. He hopes his standard will draw the skirmishers away from the villages to meet him in the open field. But I fear that he looks for honour where there is none.

All this means that I have not been able to see the portrait of Vendramin at the palace as yet. But I hope to, if God spares me, just as soon as matters reach a head here, one way or the other.

Until then I am, etc.

THE VALLEY OF ELAH, 21ST NOVEMBER 1509. THE DUKE OF FERRARA'S TENT

They say that 'water is the life blood of battle'. In ladles maybe, but not when it falls from the sky in buckets as it has this last three days. The grey clay gets on everything, into everything. Grey skies, grey mud, grey hearts. Water trickles down the centre pole of Alfonso d'Este's once lavish tent. Drips as big as peas fall every other moment on the maps, or tinkle into the silver terrine on the table.

Hugh can still see the duke's standard through an opening in the tent. It flaps like forgotten washing under the torrential deluge. He has just stepped into the tent uninvited. His intention was to resolve this standoff, see the Vendramin portrait, and then find Vendramin. But...

He shakes the water from the fringes of his cloak. The commanders of the Ferrarese soldiers have finished their breakfast, and they give him little heed even though he is dripping head to toe and bursting with a new idea.

Hugh searches their faces to find someone to ask him where he has been. But nothing. They are stone silent. These last few days they have been pinned down by Venetian guns. Trevisan anchored the bulk of the fleet gunwale to gunwale across the river like a bridge, and then had his engineers raise a great, square defensive earthwork on the Ferrarese side where he has mounted his biggest guns. It is a fine elevated position from which they not only can protect the fleet, but also harry the duke's men. The duke's plan to draw the skirmishers back from the city has worked – rather too well and too swiftly. The marauders are descending on them from every quarter, and wait like a pack of jackals while their numbers grow daily. Poor visibility means the duke cannot communicate with the city by flag. His commanders tell him that it is their last chance to retreat to the city before they are outflanked in the rear. And the duke slumps disconsolately back, his hands gripping the arms of the chair, his curled bottom lip brooding into his beard. The joints of his armour creak, as does the chair under him.

He doesn't want to give up their position. Hugh can see that, and the duke said as much yesterday. He doesn't want to abandon his redoubt and the defended gun platforms with their all-round fields of fire. His men have spent the last three weeks building these, and they will take some beating. The redoubt itself is state of the art: in the French style, low, wide, reinforced with gabions. Let the bastards swarm on them if they want, the more the merrier. He'll give them a taste of his lantern rounds. They make a hell of a mess at fifty yards when they explode with stone and lead balls. If only these vermin and horse-gelders would come a little closer. That is what the duke wants – a fight, some pay-back – not to sit here on his piles being talked into retreat by his late father's generals.

The duke casts a weary but vexed eye about the table and then upward to the outer circle of retainers and sergeants. Hugh feels the eye rest on him and remain.

'Well, Fra Hugh, what would you do? I suppose you'd say the same as them?'

'My lord?' Hugh stares for a moment, a little stunned, but he quickly collects his thoughts as every eye falls on him. He understands and knows the weight of command, but not the peculiar weight of the father, the husband, the ruler of a multitude.

'Do you says we should bugger off to the city and let Trevisian carry the field?' The duke rests a knuckle under his nose, and then clenches a fist with it and erupts. 'God's oath! When they are so close, and we can hardly touch them. Damnation.'

'My lord,' Hugh says, stepping closer and avoiding the hoary looks of the commanders who don't trust him. 'My lord, I have just been this night beyond the enemy line and seen the river.' Hugh's pulse races and his throat is dry. 'It has risen at least eight feet. It will surely rise more. Even if the rain should stop today, the river will continue to rise.'

For a moment the duke looks uncomprehendingly at Hugh. If it had been anyone else, he might have derided him for speaking in riddles. But he knows this Englishman is canny, and moreover a master gunner. It has got something to do with the canons. 'The ships,' he blurts out like a schoolboy. 'The ships, of course. The river is raising the ships above the levy. When will the hulls be in range of our guns?'

'It's hard to be sure, but by this evening,' Hugh says. 'Or tomorrow certainly.'

'No, it will not do, I say.' A slack jawed captain with long white whiskers and dull grey eyes, shakes his head. 'What guns have we here that would do sufficient damage before Trevisan weighed anchor and got away? We should not risk becoming their prey just for a mere gesture. We risk the duke's person. You, my lord, hold the balance of power in this region. If you die, the pope will swallow this fief. You must not risk it.'

'You are right, old friend.' The duke stands and rests his hands on his hips with a heavy sigh. 'It would be a wasted opportunity with the ordinance we now have, but if we were to bring up more from the city, then that would be another matter. God, nature, Fortuna, whatever you call it, has given us this moment, and we cannot waste it for want of a little valour. I would rather summon my largest gun, the Lord's Own Devil, from the city and die here while giving Trevisan a taste of death, than retreat and live to seventy in shame.'

'But my lord,' the old man pleads again, pointing a finger toward the south. 'Even if we break their lines behind, they will regroup and seize our canons on the way back, and then use them against us.'

'What Erpingham?' The duke turns a hungry eye on Hugh. 'You look like you want to say something man. Spit it out, come on.'

'There is truth in what the venerable captain says. We need not risk sending a great force against the soldiers that cut us off from the city. Leave your strength here. Let them defend your person and this position. I, myself, will pass through their lines via the ditches. They will not see one man in this weather. I will take your orders to the council. Give me a small detachment of men who know the land round here. We will take note of the enemy encampments and instruct the gunners on the north wall of their locations. We will hit them from the air then ride through them back here with the guns you need.'

'Folly and madness,' the old captain barks at Hugh. 'A man who by his own confession has just been visiting the bloody doge! How do we know he wasn't delivering messages to the Venetian forces? He says he's been beyond their lines to the river. By whose permission? Perhaps he had a rendezvous with Trevisan.'

'My permission,' the Marchese of Pesaro says, while revolving his silver goblet on the table, and gazing carefully into the contents as they swill. He chooses his next words carefully. 'He went on my instructions.'

'Marchese?' The duke looks approvingly at him, and then at the others.

'The Englishman and I agree, but so that there is no misunderstanding, I should be given this commission and not him. My lord, one of my vintenars says he knows all the farms here about. He says he played in every dike and culvert as a boy. The honour should not go to a foreigner, I will lead this expedition. I have some local men in my company whom I can trust also. Give me this commission, my lord, for the honour of my father's house. I will bring the guns safely to you, even if I make a bridge of the *Canale Bianca* with my own body.'

'Very well,' the duke says. 'Yes, very well. I will give you a list of what ordinance we need. And you, my guest, are you willing to go with the marchese under these terms and to be subject to him? You need not for our sake.'

'But for my own sake, I shall,' Hugh says. 'My honour has been impugned, and I must prove myself an honest man. The knights by oath are not permitted to take to the field against another Christian nation. But I am one man, not an army, and this rapine and slaughter of farmers and children is not an honourable war but murder and desecration. They say these Albanians are little better than white moors, perhaps they are. I will help you answer that outrage if these good men agree to keep my part in it secret afterwards.'

Nods of approval. Easy bit done.

TWO HOURS LATER, THE *CANALE BIANCA*

Hugh is wondering why he bothered to change his wet clothes. The rain is horizontal, and he's waist deep in grey dike water again and passing the enemy lines near the *Canale Bianca*. It runs off his felt beret and down his neck. The marchese is in front, and Wilf is behind; wouldn't trust his master again into the hands of degos.

And now he is complaining in earnest. 'Cold as a witch's pap.'

Hugh turns and gives his shivery, grey-lipped smile. 'Stop your bellyaching. Who'd have thought a good old Norfolk boy would ever complain about water.'

Wilf is about to reply when the marchese signals them to lie low. Across the canal Hugh sees a sentry approach the canal to pee. But he hurries back through the puddles to a guard tent on the edge of their camp, cursing like a German. D'Avalos was right; there couldn't be better weather for slipping past a mercenary army. Those men don't care, surrounded by trees and bushes. They know Italians don't fight in the rain. Why get wet unnecessarily when it takes three days to dry your woollens? D'Avalos signals them to move on.

They cross the canal and move quickly into another dike, stepping over a bloated cow but glad for the rushes that protect them from view. They reach the corners of the field, taking a series of right and left turns. They surprise a sheep, but it does not bleat for its fellows, probably because there aren't any left. It trots away from them towards a ruined pump mill, whose sails and timbers have been scarified by wind and fire. Five minutes wading later, the marchese turns with a grin and says, 'This is the dike that will take us straight to the city.'

Hugh nods and glances over d'Avalos's shoulder. The dike stretches away south into the storm bent reeds and willows. Beyond that? The Porta Padua and Ferrara. Survive that far, and he'll maybe have the pleasure of facing the cardinal again.

One hour later Hugh is wearing Bembo's clothes and seated next to a fire in Ariosto's house. It's like a dream. The open fire and leek broth do little to ease the shivering cold deep in his bones. He can feel his feet again which is a start. Wilf, fully recovered and dutiful as an old bloodhound, keeps an eye on the street from an upstairs window in case Ippolito sends some of his retainers over. It is possible that the cardinal doesn't know that Hugh is inside the city. The marchese is dealing with the council and has ordered Hugh to lie low for the afternoon. Even if they consent and act swiftly, it will take until evening to ready the cavalry, foot loons, gunners, mattrosses, and oxen.

By late afternoon Ariosto returns from the piazza. Bembo and Hugh are still hunched about the fire. Ariosto stamps his winter boots in the hallway and calls for a maid to take his cloak. He enters rubbing his hands. The rain has finally stopped, and it appears he has run all the way home for he is quite breathless, and his eyes and cheeks are alive with the exercise. He gives them a description of the preparations worthy of an epic. 'I saw the six thousand pound murtherers all in a line being harnessed to teams of oxen, and many smaller guns mounted on wheeled carriages – some cast in iron, some in bronze. But those murtherers, Hugh! Thirty-six pound shot will make a mess of Trevisan's galleys. God, I hope so.'

'I suppose,' Bembo says, rocking back and forth slightly in his chair, 'that it is not hard to be a closet canon enthusiast when you live in Ferrara.'

Hugh smiles and says, 'When you have the pope at your back and Venice in front, you need to be able to punch above your weight in times of crisis, which this definitely is.'

'Hush, both of you. I will tell you what I saw.' Ariosto throws his cap on the walnut table and draws his hands across the air in front of his face like a conjurer. 'Oh Bembo my friend, you should have seen it. In the hour of battle, the men of Ferrara, pouring into the piazza, pennants flapping, the cavalry assembling, gunners, their mates and mattrosses carrying out last minute drills for loading the guns – all in the Almain fashion – labourers, carters, farriers, smiths, joiners, carpenters, wheelwrights, coopers – a blaze of activity. God you should have seen it. What a sight. And huge carts carrying vast sulphurous barrels reeking of brimstone and death. Each man giving his all, his very best. Banners, banners everywhere – most glorious. And women fussing over the food supplies for their men. People embracing. Children crying, girls with garlands. It will all be watched from the walls, I dare say – Troy sending out her champions. They say the marchese gave a fair speech, and the duchess spoke well too. They were saluted in the council. All is under preparation. Venice has challenged, and Ferrara will answer. I want to ride out with the militia, with you, Hugh.'

Hugh uncurls slightly, lets his hands feel the flames. Then he shakes his head. 'My friend, you have a household that depend on you. Let others have this honour.'

The poet's eyes are unmoved. 'They say Aristophanes himself wished his epitaph to be that he fought with the hoplites at Marathon, and not that he wrote his comedies.' He gestures suddenly toward the door. 'Words, words, fine words, Bembo. That is our trade – ideas, sentiments. But what is that compared to one moment of true action, one second of glorious sacrifice?'

'My good friend.' Hugh speaks before Bembo can give the sarcastic reply that he can see already forming on his lips. 'Be content on this day to do what those lusty young men cannot do: immortalise them and your duke in verse worthy of their valour.'

'Yes,' Bembo says, 'and hopefully worthy of a victory too. In your *Orlando Furioso*, you might add something in canto forty to that effect. It would please the duke to be thus immortalised in a personalised mythology.'

At that moment, they are interrupted by the poc-cheeked maid.

'Excuse me, master. A boy has brought this message and is waiting for a reply.'

'Thank you, Mary.' Ariosto examines the note. 'It is for you, Hugh. It has the duke's seal.'

Hugh takes it and from the scent of orange water knows immediately from whom it comes. He breaks the seal and scans the three-lined message. 'It is from Duchess Lucretia.' He hands it to Bembo. 'She wishes to see me at the hospital.'

Ariosto dismisses the maid, and looks warily at him. He joins Bembo and looks at the note. 'A trap from the cardinal?'

'No,' Bembo says, 'this is undoubtedly her hand. And scent.' Bembo looks up, slightly abashed. 'Well, it is not something a man forgets easily.'

Ariosto takes the note, smells it and examines the script. 'She might be in league with her brother-in-law. The temporary hospital is at the Monastery of Corpus Domini – the far side of town and very near the cardinal's palace. Should you risk it when you are so close to rejoining the army for battle?'

Both men look for Hugh's answer. He leans forward for a moment and gazes into the flames. 'Perhaps you would be so kind, my friends, to attend with me. We can go armed. You could wait within earshot perhaps?'

They nod. Ariosto beams from ear to ear. Perhaps he will see some action after all.

The streets are thronged with people. They see the marchese with a detachment of horse, their riders wearing a royal blue wool doublet and a scarlet sash. If one is to die today, it is best to be well dressed. The four of them pass before the duomo, Ariosto leading, Hugh, Bembo and Wilf behind.

Hugh feels Wilf's hand on his shoulder. 'Is that the cardinal's carriage, master?'

Hugh looks to the opening into Palazzo Nuovo. The crest is unmistakable—red brimmed hat and red rope-work around a quartered shield with white falcons. It is the carriage he travelled from Bologna in. Sweat breaks out all down his back. Soldiers stand about it in the cardinal's livery. Is he in it? Is he watching me? Or is he in the council chamber? Images of the iron gag and the head-crushing tourniquet insinuate themselves into his mind, but he steels himself, and says quietly, 'Keep an eye on it, will you?'

They approach the duomo, its wet marble shining in a sharp burst of white winter sunlight. Hugh observes the two great carved lions on either side of the western portico. One – *Ippolito?* – has a decapitated calf's head between its paws. But the other cradles an unscathed lamb. *Alfonso?* He'd never noticed the lamb before. It brought his mind back to Florence's escaped lion who captured the child, but then let it go unharmed. It gave him a sudden feeling of hope. *Irrational? Perhaps. But I have come this far almost in one piece. Maybe I shall find what I am looking for after all.* He spent the rest of the short journey thinking what, exactly, that might be.

Approaching the convent on the *Via Contessa*, they see lines of biers come to take the dead for burial. Some are attended by mourners in black woollens, others leave quietly with nothing but the sound of the cartwheels on the cobbles. Soon after they are passed by the first bier, Bembo – never the most naturally empathetic man – falls into a detailed account of the funerary customs of his boyhood Florence.

'Like everything else in the republic, entering the great sea – as we call it – is heavily regulated by the Signoria. Two candles are allowed at the interment, or torches, but no more than thirty pounds of wax between them. It is republican equality regulated by bureaucrats. And the candles must be extinguished immediately after the service and returned to the dealer, who is not allowed to sell candles that weigh more than fifteen pounds – which includes paper and candle ends. Yes. So there you have it gentlemen. And any fine incurred is put into the *opera*, a fund for building repairs.'

They are passed at this point by an opulent *beccamorti*, the funerary undertaker, leading a pair of black mares with black peacock plumes on their foreheads and two finely carved caskets on the bier behind.

When the mourners of this party are out of earshot. Bembo carries on prattling. 'And in Florence, the *beccamorti* have their wages fixed at a maximum of eight *soldi.* I don't think eight *soldi* would do for that fellow, would it? And the mourners must all wear black, loosely stitched so it can be used later for making clothes. The widow is not to receive from the heirs either a gown, a headdress, a girdle or petticoat, but only a skirt or cloak lined with taffeta. And only two courses can be served at a funeral dinner. I don't supposed the rich obey, but it must save most people from feeling they ought to spend half the estate before they find out who's got what.'

'Here we are,' Hugh says, looking up at the high red brick walls and licking his lips with trepidation. 'Wilf, wait here by the main entrance. If you see the cardinal's people or any of his retinue, then come find me.'

They pass the gates and walk the short distance across a courtyard into a leafy cloister. He glances about but sees no one out of place. 'All right, my friends. You wait here. If I need you, I will shout.'

Ariosto grips his arm, eyes full of feeling. 'God speed, Hugh.'

Hugh looks deep into the poet's eyes. He would die for the truth, would Ariosto.

Hugh walks to the half open doors of the convent church. For a moment he leans on the entrance of the hospital before entering, resting his hands on old red bricks, blackened by centuries of tallow smoke. The nuns are using the main church for the overflow of the sick and injured who daily come in from the surrounding countryside. The smell of incense mixed with the odours of a hospital – the sacred and profane – for a moment give him pause. He steps down the three worn, marble steps from the cloister side door. He glances back once more to his companions in the upper world of light, before descending into the twilight of the dying.

His senses are immediately sharpened by the faces he sees as he steps carefully past the pallets and mats where each hunched form tells a story of woe. The floor is strewn with wormwood and meadowsweet to combat insects and evil humours. He sees two quiet, lean nuns dicing herbs on a table to his left: lovage, thyme, sage and dill, artemisia, betony, plantain, comfrey, southern wood, hyssop and henbane – blessed henbane for pain relief. A hospitallier should know the whole armoury of his original calling. But Hugh only knows them because his mother trained him to know. The knights have long since abandoned their ministry of life to become God's pirates. He remembers himself on a pallet of straw, just like these poor souls, and it doesn't seem like yesterday. When he arrived back in Rhodes after his ordeal with the Turks, he was in need of pain relief. And on Rhodes, the monks kept a special pain relief in great flagons: lettuce juice, bryony, hemlock and henbane, bound with vinegar in a wine solution. But there is some deeper pain that no compote or infusion can relieve. He breathes in suddenly with a deep shudder at the remembrance. The smell of thyme and hyssop mingle in his nose with that of human waste. And the sound of plainchant mingles likewise with the groans of agony. This veil of tears, these shadowlands, are fuller of contradictions than he can articulate. If there were time, he would call Ariosto down to escort him now as Virgil escorted Dante, for surely a poet is what is needed here.

Where is she? Hugh casts his eye to the further recesses of the church, from pillar to pillar, to the parts of the aisles that he can see. There are no soldiers thankfully, many nuns, but no finely dressed lady. He hears a shuffling in the doorway behind him and turns to see an apothecary coming down the steps laden with two bags of medicines to sell. He wears a tall hat trimmed with fillets, long fur gown, shabby and threadbare so that no furrier could guess which animal had provided the skin. Hugh steps aside, suspecting fleas. The man has the lips of a gourmand and the chin of a prelate. He looks hungrily at the mass of suffering humanity, and limps swiftly past Hugh without a greeting, making straight for the nuns at the table. A burgeoning market. It must be feast or famine for his sort.

Hugh walks unsteadily toward the crossing, passing a surgeon at work in a small cubicle made of drapes hung between pillars. The surgeon is using some goose billed forceps to extract fragments of shot from an unconscious woman who is breathing heavily and bleeding more so. Hugh forces his eyes away and suppresses the rising bile. The forceps remind him of the cardinal's instruments of virtue. He walks on and sees a nun packing the deep shoulder wound of a young peasant with honey and cobwebs. She chides him. 'And don't you pick at it, or it will fester and mortify.' A man with a grey face and depressed skull fracture slumps with his back against the pillar – waiting for the ferryman.

When he reaches the chancel crossing, Hugh glances to his right, and there in the south transept he sees her. If not for her golden hair cascading down the back, he perhaps would not have recognised her, for the duchess is simply clad in a royal blue gown with a white apron over the front. She is facing away from him, talking to a tall, young physician who, even in such a place and at such a time, is effecting all elegance. His beaked mask is tilted back high on his forehead, which itself tilts further back as he laughs at some joke. The hollow cackle echoes from the vault. His capacious black robe is trimmed with squirrel fur and bands of scarlet. Perhaps he is just arriving, or going. What a cockscomb he is, fingers monstrously be-gemmed with rings like an Asiatic tyrant and gilded spurs like a knight. Well spake Petrarch when he derided this type of physician as a mere observer of other people's maladies. Hugh knows the sort too well. They inspect the water and excrement with a puckered brow, feel the pulse from which to recognise the forces of nature, consult their colleagues and after much discussion agree to the remedy, which is usually cabbage as a general panacea. And if perchance the beverage is effective they never cease to extol the cure. If not, they blame the patient.

As Hugh approaches, the duchess turns and says in a tone both surprised and delighted, 'Fra Hugh, you have come. Good. May I introduce our new court physician Maestro Manetti. The good physician has left the palace at my behest and offered himself to the sisters who tend the sick.' And then without taking her eyes from Hugh. 'Maestro, this is the man I told you about.'

They bow and once the peacock physician has recovered his mask – for it had fallen back over his face – he points down at Hugh's hand.

'You know, signor, that a short hand is a sure sign of cold humours. Bartolomeo Cocles says so, and we cannot have a better authority. But a long hand with short stiff fingers, like mine you see, denotes a phlegmatic with much courage.' At this extraordinary remark, the man smooths the edges of his thin moustache and lays his fortuitous hands upon his hips.'

'Ah, you see,' Lucretia says with a girlish clap, 'how Antonio has something to say on all subjects. And how he brings all the newest learning from Padua University to us. Today, he is scandalised that our surgeons are still cauterising wounds here with burning oil in the Spanish fashion.'

'Indeed I am. Da Vigo is all very well for yesteryear, and I dare say good enough on barbarian Germans and the French. But let the civilised nations have no more scaldings when we know a wound is far better irrigated with wine and then closed with neat stitches and a balsam dressing. There are no doubt a few that need as much here.'

'Please don't let me keep you from your work.' Hugh bows his head deferentially.

'What me? No, I shall come back tomorrow with my bags. But today I will be there on the wall to watch the militia riding through the lines of these damned *stratioti*. The duchess tells me that you will be with them.'

'I will do what I can, maestro, small fingers and cold humours notwithstanding.'

'Huh,' the physician says, nonchalantly, folding his arms. 'Can't say I would busy myself in someone else's war. But all luck to you. I'll be here tomorrow to clean up the mess no doubt.'

Hugh resisting the urge to say what he is thinking, bows and says, ever so politely. 'I hope I shall not have need of your services.'

'Yes, I see. Well then, until the morrow, Duchess.' He bows to them both and replaces his beaked mask before moving through the lines of his coughing and groaning countrymen without breaking step. Some reach out to him, but he cannot see them from behind the mask.

Hugh immediately feels the full gaze of the duchess. Her sapphire eyes seem more iridescent in the half light of greys and browns. She waits until the physician has fully departed before saying, 'Do not think too ill of him. I remember what it was to be so young and full of nonsense. He must be encouraged first, then we shall see to his character.' She giggles suddenly and catches her mouth. 'Quoting Cocles as if we'd never heard of him! Our old physician, rest his soul, always worried my husband that any lady with short hands and long fingers, such as I and most women have, would be in peril during childbirth – as indeed most women are already. I thank God that I have been delivered of both boys and girls without incident. I have always come to this convent for the births, and the sisters have been good to me – as I think I told you when we met last. And if, God forbid, I should take harm—' She folds her arms so that Hugh can see the hairs standing up on them. 'Then one day I shall return here again to this church to be laid with my husband's ancestors. And if I grow to be an old maid, wearied of this life and its luxuries – which is possible, I think – then I shall enter this place as a sister and die a penitent at a goodly age, full of years and good deeds.' She raises her eyebrows at him and flashes a pert smile. 'What say you to that, good knight?'

Hugh grins and bows his head slightly. 'Then I shall say it befits you well.'

'Ah,' she says, wagging a slender white finger. 'You can mock – though less than I deserve, perhaps – but you see, I am in earnest and already under the orders of the mother superior. These poor, poor people.' She loses all her coyness for a moment, as she casts a baleful eye across the transept floor where thirty pallets are laid out. 'Sister Agnes said I should come here two mornings a week to minister to the sick, and at first I disdained the thought. And then my pride told me what a small price it would be to gain the honour and love of the people. It is shameful, I know. But now...' At this the duchess crouches to lay her hand on the shoulder of an old woman wrapped in a grey woollen blanket. 'Now I see that God has sent me here for my own good. The real treasure in God's world are his children.' The duchess's lily white hand caresses the grey hair of the woman, who is waking from a sleep and beginning to give a toothless smile. 'There is a pleasure in the species of love and service that no one ever told me about before I came here. These poor people.'

'So you see,' the duchess smiles at her ward then stands, dusting off her apron. 'I grow pious almost despite myself. Do you know that the fanatical monk from our town who went to Florence—I mean Savonarola, of course—could not for all his reforms, change the laws regarding jewellery, or low cut dresses, or curls, ringlets, silks and so forth? The Florentines would not have it even though they were in a frenzy to burn books and paintings at his orders – before they burnt him at my father's orders. And yet, just yesterday after being with those happy sisters, I could quite willingly have taken the veil and never worn finery again. But for my dear children, of course, and my husband. I have learnt well to find joy in my children, but to find it among the poor – that I did not expect. I tasted a happiness, a freedom even, that they enjoy, the like of which I had never seen before. They will never be known as you and I shall be known, in chronicles, in books. But I think that is because God loves them too much to burden them with it.'

'I...' Hugh pauses, wondering what exactly he can say to all this. She speaks so fast, always grasping for meanings, and with every sentence compelling him to understand her. Is this really why she called him here? 'I am sincerely honoured that you have shared this with me.'

'I cannot tell whether you are teasing me. A man like you perhaps cannot understand us. You embraced lady poverty so long ago, perhaps you have forgotten.'

'I would not say that, my lady.'

But she ignores Hugh's limp protestation with a wave of the hand, a good humoured rendition of her nurses and governesses. 'When I was growing up, my nurse always said, "Oh Lucretia is made of such fine flax, she will easily get a spindle and distaff to spin gold with it." I was trained in every luxury, though my education was very modest – there was no thought I would ever become a nun so no one saw the point. No. Lucretia would become a *donna di palazzo*, and everything I underwent was toward that end. For me it was always "*Portatura,* deportment, Lucretia, *portetura.*" And, "Don't run, Lucretia, and don't dance so vigorously, Lucretia. Remember the woman of Florence who was engaged to the duke of Sterlich. She danced so vivaciously that she fell and broke her leg, and so the duke was no longer willing to marry her." And always, always, always, "Too much make-up, Lucretia; it is a crime for young ladies to wear so much", to which I would always rejoin that it was a greater crime for old maids like her not to wear any. "*Chi imbianca la casa la vuole appigionare,* he who whitewashes a house wishes to let it. Modesty my child, modesty." All their good intentions and good advice were lost on me. But I see you grow weary of my silly recollections and begin to wonder why I asked you to come here in the first place. Come and we shall speak over here.' The duchess walks softly toward the one side altar that is in the furthest corner of the transept and kneels on the lower step. Hugh lingers at the step for a moment and then, not knowing what else to do, follows suit.

The duchess is not praying or mouthing prayers, but rather staring intently forward, as if formulating her words. Hugh remains silent for some moments before she speaks calmly. 'I wish to ask of you a favour today. That is why I called you here. You ride with our cavalry and militia to reinforce the duke's garrison beyond the walls. The physician does not know why you do it, perhaps you do not fully know, but I do.' She glances up at a wooden crucifix, buttons her lip during an intake of breath, then continues. 'God sent you in answer to my prayers. Tell me, signor, how did you find my husband? Did he seem well to you? Did he seem well supported?'

'As well as any prince might be,' Hugh says. 'He seemed well to me, under the circumstances. He carries a heavy weight, of course.'

'Of course,' she adds. 'But you did not sense anything untoward in the camp?'

'My lady,' Hugh stammers uncertainly. 'I am not sure what you are asking me.'

'I will be plain. I fear for his life. Yes, from the Venetians but more than that. I will not play with you. You know of whom I speak. He would renounce his red hat as soon as that if he could replace his brother. That is why he has returned now, when he was supposed to be defending the border towns further west. He means to use this military action to his own advantage. Perhaps he will secretly send assassins out today with the militia – it would be easy enough. I don't know, I just don't know for sure.' She inhales deeply, but then holds her breath as if she were keeping back her soul with her teeth. Eventually she releases it in a rush, and speaks. 'I am telling you because you are from the outside. I know my husband trusts you, and so do I. I also tell you because a certain marchese speaks very highly of you, and tells me that my brother-in-law was not able to kill you at Sant'Agostino. Just like the Turks could not, Petrucci could not, nor Don Michelle – yes, I know about him too. I believe that God has preserved you for some great purpose.'

'Duchess, really. You must not –

'You are still alive, aren't you?'

'Perhaps it is the devil's luck.'

'No, it is angels, signor, and *grace Dieu*. Are you the first sinner to seek redemption? Listen to me. I know you men think that we women have weak reason. But call it woman's intuition or prophecy, whatever you will, I know that you, signor, are marked with special favour. Perhaps it is many years away, I cannot say. But what I do ask, is that you watch over my husband during this battle. My children need their father, but more than that, Ferrara needs a lord who can act not just wisely, but well. The balance of power here is delicate. The wrong duke could bring misery on many thousands. So promise me you will stay close to him during this action. I will not ask more of you than that.'

'Well, I...er.' Flattered to the gunwales, Hugh is trying to see through the smog. She talks so fast that he has trouble layering his own thoughts and responses. He hears himself agreeing, as if he almost believed her prophecy that he would be preserved, and then catches himself. *What am I thinking? What am I saying?* Six months ago, he was certain he was damned, and no one could persuade him otherwise. Is he now to believe he's a favoured son at the instigation of this fair duchess? Back in Assisi he tried with all his might to believe Fra Francesco's free salvation, and even then he thought it empty as a pardoner's promise or a witch's pap. And now, at the words of this modern Magdalen, he is ready to believe that a tolerated sinner might be raised to a son with purpose. Divine justice would surely be impugned. It would not be just. *I will not be taken in. The universe must be just, or there is no sanity or hope. I will not be flattered into a position where the whole cosmos of scoundrels can not only get off scot free, but then also share in the governance. It is just too monstrous.*

'Fra Hugh?'

'My apologies. My mind was far away. I will do all you ask. And perhaps there is something you might arrange for me in return.'

'And what is that?'

'I would very much like to see a certain painting that your husband was given by the doge.'

'The one of the knight of Rhodes, by Titian. I remember it, though I'm not sure where it is hung, if it even is. What was his name? Ah yes, Vendramin. Yes, I will make enquiries.'

'Discreetly, if you would.'

'Discreetly? What an enigma you are, signor. Are all the English so easily repaid?' She laughs, then says, 'Don't answer that. I will pray for you from the moment you leave the city until I hear our trumpets. God speed you.'

FERARRA, THROUGH THE PORTA PADUA

Seeing Bembo and Ariosto waving from the crowd as they pass, Francesco d'Avalos leans across to Hugh in his saddle, and says, 'I do not know your friend Bembo well. I understand he is highly thought of, and certainly he seems to have a mind of information.'

'Not all of it useful,' Hugh shouts back, fending off the laurel garlands that are thrown their way by the daughters of Ferrara.

'Indeed,' the marchese says, laughing. 'He told me just now that the Nestorians have a certain prayer—I suppose it is more a spell—against artillery. A prayer to *anathematize all the expulsions from the engines of war and all the balls of the guns of our wicked enemies*. Can you believe that?'

'That he told you, or that it is true? Yes, I can. He told me the same thing this morning while I was trying to sleep. I think it is his way of saying that he will be praying for us.' They are the throw-away comments of men with other things on their minds. Hugh surveys the trail of garrons and knock-kneed palfreys behind them, many skittish of the noise of the crowd, some bucking and whinnying in terror. Not a great sign. The big guns haven't even sounded yet. To make up for their inauspicious journey in, D'Avalos and Hugh are both riding fine boned stallions—one black, one dappled grey. They belong to the duchess, and this too pleases the crowd. He's also been given some fine Italian plate that used to be the duke's when he was younger. He must have been a big, barrel-chested lad even then. Hugh could almost get his hand inside. It's thick as bull hide, and Hugh feels warm for the first time all day. He glances up at the clouds and is glad that it's not a midsummer.

Hugh's eye catches Wilf's uneasy stare. He is astride a sturdy cob, about fifteen or sixteen hands. He wouldn't hear of staying but wouldn't say why either. Hugh knows. Wilf, wearing his own leather jerkin and a shiny new Almain rivet, has a cross hilt and buckler on his belt and an English bill in his hand. *God knows where he found that in the duke's armoury. No one else has one or is likely to have one.* Apparently the armourer said he was welcome to keep it. Wilf says he'll show 'them degos' merry hell just as soon as he gets close enough to them. For a man handy with a pike staff – and Wilf certainly is – the English bill is the next level in efficiency.

Beyond Wilf's stoic brow, Hugh observes the hobilars, archers, water carriers and the baggage train. The light cavalry look all right but the militia less so. Farmers and craftsmen bent on vengeance are no match for men trained to obey unerringly when the shit kicks off, which it is about to. He'd feel happier with a tenth the quantity of Swiss pike men. They know their business the Swiss. Rumour has it that Julius is so impressed with them that he is commissioning a new Swiss guard for his own person.

Hugh turns back in his saddle, gives one last nod towards his friends and then looks straight ahead across the plain. It is almost one direct road to the duke's camp, with the enemy between them around the Canale Bianca. The plan is for the cavalry to pincer the enemy positions, and then the militia will come in a line behind and clean up.

'VAE VICTIS' - WOE TO THE VANQUISHED

The cavalry draw up on the edge of a squelching field, hooves sinking six inches into the clay sod. The foot loons follow their flags and form in battalions behind, right and left. The teams of horse pulling the lighter guns are clawing the stones on the road heading north, and behind them teams of oxen pull the devil's larger toys and bellow under their yokes. Some are still coming through the gates. D'Avalos gives the nod, and a lad to his right waves a flag towards the angled bastion behind them. A moment later the barrage begins: the great thunderous boom of Ferrara's guns, and then far off, the falling of the devil's rain in the woodland copses and farms where the enemy are dug in. Hugh is used to their song and can name each calibre just from the sound. Even so, there are more firing this afternoon than they possess on the whole of Rhodes. Flames and smoke belch fifty feet from the walls. Stone balls streak across the horizon in long, black lines of destruction. Somewhere out of view to Hugh, the Venetian forces, who thought they were hidden from view, will be getting a nasty surprise. *Not long now.* Hugh reins in his steed. The stallion is either nervous or claw mad for battle. It is hard to tell at this stage. Hugh feels the blood pumping and his lungs heaving. He is a mix of both himself, and he knows it. He glances along the line of snorting, steaming horse flesh, and among the lieutenants, captains, condottieri, and other officials. It is there that Hugh sees the cardinal's standard and a group of knights under it. *I'll have to watch them too.*

Ten minutes into the barrage and D'Avalos gives the order to advance. They start at a trot, lances raised, visors up. Hugh looks back at Wilf. 'You all right?'

'Ayes will be when I'm out of this country.'

Hugh sets his reins and wonders if there was ever a man more unfitted to leave Norfolk. He turns back again and smiles, saying after a moment, 'I thank God for you, my old friend.'

'Aye, master,' Wilf says. 'Well, then.' But that is all he can say before fixing nervous eyes straight forward.

With each field crossing, the pace increases. The cannon behind them fall silent as they canter within view of the farms that they had passed that morning. The late afternoon light casts long shadows from the red roofs and trees. Some of the trees split under the cannon fire, some sunder altogether. They break into a gallop and bend right behind a stand of poplars. When they emerge on the far side, Hugh can see that they are now within striking distance. In the shadows of the woods men run in disarray. With the silence of the guns to their rear, they now hear the sounds of the wounded and the commands of captains: knock, draw, loose. Hugh gets one glance from D'Avalos as he checks the line. 'Go, go!' he shouts. *Right,* Hugh thinks. *No messing; visors and lances down, stirrup to stirrup, hit the bastards hard. Come on, boys. Come on.*

The whistling black hail hits them like hornets. The enemy has crossbows, and they're coming straight at them. Then a flash, a boom, a barrel of smoke and the two six-pound guns open straight at the Ferrara troop. A ball passes through the chest of a officer who has ridden ten feet in front of Hugh's right. He slumps forward but does not fall for another furlong. Hugh can hear more screams to his left and right but cannot see who has been hit. What matters now is driving the bastards from the woods. What matters now is momentum—keeping the pace no matter who goes down. What matters is— *Shit, shit.* Two bolts glance off Hugh's chest. He almost laughs. *I'm all right. Good old Italian plate.*

The trees loom. The Albanians are retreating from the edges and back to the farm buildings. They'd better be good runners. Hugh passes the first poplar and jumps a trench. D'Avalos is to his right somewhere, and he can hear Wilf swearing behind him. His horse tramples one man, and his lance pierces a second through the joints of the shoulders. The man falls as the horse thunders past, and Hugh manages to relevel his lance to catch a hulk of a man with a crossbow whom he pins to a tree. The lance shears at the end, and Hugh can only use it one last time on a swarthy captain in whom he leaves it. As he is reaching down for the colhonna, he sees hundreds of *stratiote* in retreat along the meagre earthwork. The guns of Ferrara have done an admirable job of softening up these foreigners. There are already dead and dying men near the farm. It will be a massacre for sure when the militia get here in a minute. Lances everywhere are giving way to cross-hilts.

Wilf pulls up alongside Hugh. Hugh searches left then right. D'Avalos is up in front. 'Quick, Wilf, onward.'

Hugh digs in his spurs. They press the enemy back to the canal, hacking like men possessed. The marchese' courage borders on recklessness. Twice he races ahead into a body of the enemy with only his signalman and his personal retinue. By the time he sees the *stratioti* swimming across the canal, Hugh is sure the field is theirs. They press on left, back to the centre, back to the bridge that will take the canon over the canal. In the woods, it is an ungovernable scene of carnage. The militia are pouring over the earthworks and hacking at the surrendering, the wounded and the dying. The screams are deafening. The gun placements are overrun. The bridge is in sight across one last field. The rest of the cavalry already occupy the position and are now signalling for the guns to be brought up.

It's a hell of a mess by the bridge. The mud is crimson, spilled guts everywhere, perhaps three four hundred men and many writhing horses. Hugh surveys the scene as they canter towards the five standards – one being the cardinal's. He is not there himself, Hugh is pretty sure of that. But even so he feels more than a little unease as they cross the field towards them. Left and right, the militia are finishing off the invader. Twitching carcasses, grotesque, contorted. The stench of ruptured intestines, spilled like tripe in the mud. Hugh can feel his bile rising. There will be no prisoners. Even trained soldiers are nearly ungovernable when the red mist reaches this level, when the blood lust of the most peaceable farmer turns into that of a raging animal. They have endured a lot these last months. They do not know that this brief revenge will add little solace in the long run. Look at them, Hugh thinks, as his horse passes behind the water wagon. *Many of them are killing for the first time. It is in their eyes when they stop to take the ladle for water. The last time they did something simple like drink, there was no blood on their hands. The Shadow of Cain.* One young tough in the tan doublet, hose, and livery of a paid infantrymen bursts into loud sobs and drops the ladle back in the bucket. Another archer of middle age, not a soldier, is leaning head down against the wagon, retching and sobbing by turns. Some are jeering at them, looking to the mounted knights for approval. But Hugh would rather be that man voiding his guts – for at least he still has heart enough to feel the horror of it all – than be the finest knight in Christendom, which some idiots think he is already. Others are cheering and shouting, many are still killing and searching the corpses.

As Hugh passes toward the standards, he can see that the more forward thinking captains have secured the Venetian baggage train, which will contain the plunder from many a town and village, many a church and farm. Teams of horses are already taking the loot back to the city, before even the trumpets are sounded. Among the centenars – those who command the brigades of one hundred – it is first come, first serve. As many private fortunes will be made this afternoon as have been lost at any gaming table in the Veneto.

D'Avalos' party draws close to the other brigade. Hugh remains back slightly as they talk, visor down. The cardinal's man, built like a privy and resting a double handled axe over his saddle says they should secure the bridge and get the guns over under tight escort. 'We saw more *stratioti* up river heading this way. My scouts will confirm the number soon, but I advise that we move fast while we have the advantage.'

The marchese agrees and has the trumpets blown. As the standards are raised and the infantry rallied, D'Avalos turns to Hugh. 'They can strip the dead on their way back—if they survive that long. Right now we have work to do. We are less than a mile away, but there may be resistance up ahead. Are you hurt?'

Pulling his visor up, Hugh comes out of his thoughts for a moment to reply. 'No, thank God. This plate is munition quality.' He taps his breastplate with a grin. 'I was just hoping after all this that the river really has carried on rising. It's been dry all afternoon, you know.'

'Oh, don't you worry. My man told me that the Po is fed by the Alps and the great lakes. It takes weeks to stop rising after it has started. When it bursts its banks, it can take until spring before we see the land again. So don't worry. Let's get back to the duke and see his smile.'

'I'm right behind you.'

THE DUKE'S CAMP. THIRTY MINUTES LATER

The commanders attend the duke on the earthworks, looking north toward the enemy gun positions.

'They probably expect we've got something for them by now.' The old condoiterre with the long white whiskers – the one who was so pessimistic before – is now pacing on the edge of the redoubt and shaking his head. 'They must know we're coming after all that gunfire. Your brother's general—' He looks at the cardinal's man Manozzi with the doubled handed axe. 'He says we have another army of Dalmatians coming down the river behind us. We should take care. We may be trapped. We may give Trevisan just what he planned to get, and then all the sacrifice of our countrymen will have been in vain.'

'I do not think so, old friend.' The duke is stroking his beard with one hand and holding the knot of the sash that secures his blue velvet surcoat. Under it he is wearing full armour. Hugh admires the blueing and etching on his gauntlets which would make the finest armourers of Greenwich jealous. 'No, I really do not think so. They have not yet disbanded the fleet. I see nothing amiss up on the levy. What I do see—' He turns to the marchese and Hugh with a cunning grin. 'Are carriages with my best field gun and enough shot to blow these bastards back to hell – which is where, by God's grace, I will send them all. You have done well, all of you. You have proved your salt and made Ferrara proud. But I would rather die here with you all, my brothers, than see those ships escape my wrath. If I cannot protect the people of the Estense who look to me for protection, then I am no prince worthy of the name. We may be nothing to Venice and her mighty empire, but we will give them a bloody nose today that they will never forget. D'you hear me, all of you? A bloody nose, by my oath.' The duke, eyes full of fire, raises a shovel-sized fist and purses his lips in a menacing way, then summons a young man who is holding a scrolled map. He rolls it out on another servant's back. 'They think we're coming for their earthworks, but their whole bridgehead will crumple, will be of no use whatever, the moment we hit their ships. By the immortal gods, boys, with the range my Devil has I will fire those ships so completely that the bridgehead will lose its reason to exist. You understand? They will abandon it like rats to get to their ships, only their ships will be sinking.'

He steps to the side of the servant so everyone can see the map and then points his finger at it. 'We bring up our big guns, here, here and here. At that angle, we can hit the flotilla from all sides. I begin to see their masts above the tree tops even now. Look!' Hugh follows the duke's finger toward a tangled-looking forest of masts on the horizon. 'We have no time to dig them in and pray God we may not need to. I will order the gunners to find what cover they can. Speed is the thing. General Manozzi –'

'Yes, my lord, I will stay at your side as per your servant, the cardinal's instructions.'

'As will I.' It is the older whiskery condotierre that speaks.

'I see, very well.' The duke's eyes betray a slight disorientation, but only for a moment. When he recovers he turns to the Marchese of Pesaro. 'Well d'Avalos, you have well-earned your spurs already this day. But I have one last commission for you.'

'Anything, Your Grace.'

'I want your brigade to assist the infantry and the lighter guns into positions here and here, right in front of the enemy gun placement – under their noses. I want you to distract them and draw the Venetian fire, and when they collapse – which by God they will when we start sinking their galleys – lead your horse and infantry and overrun their positions. No quarter asked and none given, is that clear? These bastards will pay. Even Trevisan – especially Trevisan – though no one will want to ransom him after this anyway. Are we agreed.'

'With my life, Your Grace,' D'Avalos says, bowing.

'You others? Are we clear?'

'Yes, Your Grace,' they agree as he turns and looks at the twenty or so men surrounding him.

'Are we agreed,' he repeats gruffly, and they grunt and nod replies, some with bloody oaths. 'Good. Well, go and tell your men to get ready, and have the artillery officers meet me in my tent just as soon as they get here. Don't let them unharness the oxen even – we have work to do.'

The men disband, and Hugh is left for a moment with the duke and the servants, the fire in the duke's eyes slowly being replaced with the doubts of a leader on the verge of battle. He approaches Hugh with an uneasy smile. 'Do you really think we can do it?'

'Yes, I believe you can.'

'But will they hold to their positions?'

'The Marchese of Pesaro will. His men will follow him, I am sure.'

'He is a good man. Keen for glory.'

'But full of honour too. He is a man you may depend on.'

'Yes,' the duke says absently. 'Yes, he is a man to watch certainly. Would you like to go with him again?'

'No, Your Grace. If it please you, I would like to stay at your side for this next action. In fact, even if it please you not, for I have made a promise to do so.' Hugh coughs and gives a knowing grin. 'To a certain lady of Ferrara.'

'Really?' The duke's eyes widen for a moment, and he grins back. 'And I don't suppose this lady has long, blond hair?'

'Indeed she does.'

'How was my lady?'

'She is well, and spending her mornings at the hospitals with the sick.'

'Oh, please God, not more piety!' He says and for a moment looks like any carefree husband exalting over the wife of his youth. 'She will be canonised 'ere long, and then I shall never see her.'

When the next salvo of laughter subsides, Hugh says gently. 'She worries about you and has made me pledge I will keep you safe.'

'Women worry too much. I will be behind the guns. The Venetians will be doing all they can to retreat.'

'She does not fear the Venetians, Your Grace.' Hugh catches the duke's eye with a meaningful and earnest stare. The servants are still folding up the map. Hugh looks from him to them and back again.

'I see. Yes, I see. Then I thank you again. Yes, I see.' The duke's eye falls thoughtfully toward Hugh's breastplate, and then a look of surprise opens up his face. '*Mon Dieu*, is that my old armour? Yes, I'd recognise it anywhere. I haven't seen that, much less worn it for ten years.'

'The duchess insisted, I'm afraid.' Hugh says, shamefacedly.

'Nonsense, nonsense, you are welcome to it. Who better than you? How does it feel?'

'Ample.' More laughter.

'And heavy, too, I'd say.' The duke points at the marks left by the crossbow bolts. 'And I see you have added your own etching. Very fine.'

'Crossbows,' Hugh adds, looking down.

'Ah.' The duke straightens and slaps Hugh's shoulder. 'This thick

Brescia plate—can't beat it. The last time I wore that was when I was sixteen in a tourney, and jousted against my brother.'

'Did you win?'

'Oh, yes. Ippolito was not made for that sort of thing.'

'Then I pray you may do so again.'

The duke absorbs the comment as if someone had just awoken him and put vinegar on his tongue; blinking, swallowing and finally nodding. 'Yes, I see. They are strange times.' His face changes again to one of mirth. 'Well, you are welcome to the armour with my thanks. You will grow into it with age, I should think. Do the English get barrel-chested as we Romagnans do?'

'I hope to live long enough to find out.'

'Hah!' The duke deals Hugh another slap on the shoulder. 'Good, now let us go to meet the artillery officers; give them some real work. We shall fall on those dogs like the wrath of God.'

THE DUKE'S GUN BATTERIES, TWO HOURS LATER

The Albanians and Dalmatians come on from the rear, some in a fury to recover the spoil their countryman lost early that day, some just to get back to the ships. If any of them make it back, they might consider themselves to have experienced a miraculous deliverance. But even then, only as sprats that have jumped from the pan into the fire. And what a fire. The duke's ordinance is like the wrath of God unleashed: fire, steel, stone, fractured timbers, splintered bones. The *stratioti* that come at the duke's earthworks are torn apart by his lantern rounds. They scream themselves to death all through that night with none to aid them. Those who went for the ships are harried and overrun by the marchese whose cavalry sunders their lines and re-crosses them thrice, cutting them to ribbons. The dike is so full of their slain it is said that the horses no longer have to jump but can walk across on the bodies. As night comes, a new fog descends over the low lying fields adjacent to the mighty river—canon fog, the smog of gunpowder, the death-belchings of over a hundred canon. It lies in horizontal strips across the land, hovering like an acrid shroud to hide the dying from heaven's eyes. The wailing is incessant. A dying man is calling for his father, hour upon hour. Hugh is listening. It is the cry of all creation.

'Well, Your Grace. The river has indeed risen as if Neptune himself has elevated the Venetian fleet before our guns. Let us drink your health.' Manozzi's face is light red and orange in the light of a nearby cauldron of burning oil. Around them the night is sporadically made day at the flash of the canons. They go off almost every second; the noise is terrible. Beyond the horizon the conflagration gains in intensity, and flames rise up the masts toward heaven, as do the screams of the dying. It is a sort of warfare by proxy, the canon balls replacing battalions and lances, delivering death at a comfortable distance. The Lord's Own Devil thunders from a redoubt three furlongs away, such a range as Hugh has never seen. It shakes the very ground under their feet. The duke is ecstatic, hand on hips and saying at every blast, 'You wait, you wait; she is barely warmed to her task.' The cardinal's other officers are about him, and Manozzi's retainer offers wine to the duke as if in celebration. Hugh looks at the cup, at Manozzi's eyes, at the eyes of the others. *The cup. Will they poison him? Bloody Italian cowards.*

Hugh steps forward. 'We should not celebrate as men who take off armour, Your Grace. Indeed many ships have been fired, but some are even now breaking away. I have counted five.' *The cup.* Hugh sees the duke take it from the retainer. *Shit.* Hugh hastens to him, and takes hold of the duke's arm. 'We must press the advantage and take the light guns onto the bank. There is no time to lose, the horses should be hitched now.' Hugh takes the goblet and pours out the wine in a lavish and defiant gesture. 'I pour it out for you as David poured out the water from the well at Bethlehem. Let the duke have vengeance on his enemies first.' Hugh catches Manozzi's eyes, which are burning with rage, or fear, or both. Hugh lays an easy hand on the hilt of his carrack sword. *If he tries anything, I'll open him up, the blackguard.*

'By God, yes,' the duke says, taking up his helmet. 'The Englishman speaks what is right. The fires of hell are doing their work for us now, let the light guns be brought up to the bank, and we will make sure none of these bastards escape.'

Thirty minutes later, the same ensemble are galloping along the high river bank inspecting the carnage. Trevisan's flag ship is one of the five attempting to limp away. She is missing half a mast and listing to starboard. Hugh shouts across to the duke. 'She is taking on water, no doubt about it. She won't make the sea, much less Venice.'

The duke leans back in his saddle. 'If he makes it back to Venice, they will hang him for this humiliation, I swear it. This will go down in the chronicles. Look at it, the flames are half a mile high.'

Hugh looks toward the conflagration that was once a flotilla of galleys large enough to be anchored side by side and form a bridge across the mighty Po. D'Avalos has overrun their earthworks, and the duke's flag is established about the flames and bodies of the dead. Their last defence was a brigade of pikemen. But D'Avalos' infantry breaks them apart with kerns and long handed axes. Hundreds of men are swimming from the ships and many skirmishes are apparent along the banks. The archers pick them off from the high ground. The duke pulls up his horse in a clearing among the willow, where he can survey the scene. *When does a battle become a massacre?* A rider comes from behind them with dispatches. The duke turns the paper so that he can read it by the light of his enemy's burning ships.

'D'Avalos is victorious over their bridgehead, God be praised.' He reads down further, then squints. His face turns to a grimace. 'He says he has taken many prisoners. Some of the cowards surrendered when they swam to the bank. I said no quarter.'

'He has disobeyed a direct order, Your Grace,' Manozzi says, as his horse strains its neck to the grass, and he yanks it upward with severe force. 'He should be court marshalled.'

Before the duke can even answer, Hugh laughs. 'My lord, I pray you would not take such counsel. D'Avalos has done valiantly, and to be magnanimous in victory is the hallmark of a knight.'

Manozzi rises in his stirrups and points his axe at Hugh in a rage. 'Do you, a visitor, tell the duke his word means nothing?'

'The duke spoke naturally as a man that puts on armour. Now he sees that God has given him victory, a very great victory. The field is yours this day, Your Grace, but know also that the marchese has hazarded his life at every hour for your honour. Many victories have been obscured with the taint of massacre. Let not that dishonour come near your door.'

'You hear that general? Erpingham of Rhodes calls for clemency – him, the scourge of the Saracen. Very well,' the duke says decisively. 'We'll send word back to D'Avalos that he has done well by me. Tell him also to capture the flags of the enemy and bring them to my tent before dawn. Tell him also that our light guns will see to the escaped galleys and other boats. And send word back to the city, and to the duchess of what God has wrought here and that we shall have great celebrations when the army returns.'

The messenger turns his horses head. 'Aye, Your Grace, I will do all that. Long live, Your Grace.' And then he digs in his heels and disappears into the trees.

'Celebrations,' Manozzi says with a thin guffaw. 'Pity we won't all be there to see them.'

A strange silence follows in which the duke's further comments are lost to other senses that come alive. *What did he say?* The air is suddenly a crackle with a heightened sense of danger. Hugh feels a shiver as he looks around at the faces of the officers in attendance. They are all the cardinal's men, and they are now alone and a long way from help. *How did this happen? Where are the rest of the duke's escort? This is Manozzi's doing. Look at him smiling and checking that there are no witnesses.*

Hugh urges his horse closer to the duke's. Eight against two are not good odds, but they are increased if he has a brute like the duke at his back. The mare nudges forward, but Hugh suddenly finds himself pressed by two knights. One reaches for his reins. Other knights are already moving on the duke.

'What do you mean?' the duke says.

Manozzi rises in his stirrups. 'What I mean, my noble lord, is that that while you have been goose-footing about these last months, your people have starved, even the members of your own infantry. So this will be their victory and not yours. And all this bollocks about giving quarter to the enemy confirms it. Your father would turn in his grave. You are not fit to govern a hen roost. You will have been murdered by the Englishman, who in turn was himself executed in the act. Come on men, to your work, damn you.'

Two knights close on the duke and secure him for the third who will do the deed. Hugh feels a sledgehammer blow from behind that lands on his helmet and glances off his shoulder plates. *You'll have to try harder than that you bastard.* Hugh digs his spurs into the flanks and then the underbelly of the mare. She breaks and rises up like a dart, pulling the man holding Hugh's reins off his horse. Hugh lurches forward and barges the knights surrounding the duke, hitting one horse in the flanks and unseating the rider. The knight near him is trying to insert a long dagger between the plates of the duke's armour, just under the arm. Hugh unsheathes the colhonna, just right for this sort of up-close, dirty, Italian cloak-and-dagger stuff. Hugh brings his carrack sword down in a full arc onto the knight's gauntlet. The knight's arm goes down, and his own body leans with it. Hugh grabs the crest of his helmet and pulls him down with a series of yanks. An idiot is still reigning blows onto Hugh's back without much damage, and one of the unhorsed knights is trying to pull Hugh down too. *I'll deal with you two later, but first the duke.* Hugh slashes the hams of the horse in front of him, and it rears up, sending its rider skyward. Then it lashes out with its back hoofs which catch the knight who had been tugging at Hugh's leg. The second kick caves in his helmet and sends him backward into the dark without another noise.

But now that the duke's sword arm is freed, it falls to swings and blows. The duke sends his blade into one man's groin. Another he hammers with such fury that he almost servers his head, notwithstanding the chainmail. Manozzi waits for a weak moment then moves on the duke, deals a blow to his front that glances from his chest and cuts into his stallion's neck. The horse goes down and the duke with it. Manozzi steadies his horse then moves it forward, his axed raised for another blow.

Hugh reels about and jabs his blade through the visor of the knight whose been using him as an anvil. It slides into his eyes with a sickening ease and he shrieks. *That's how you do it, cockscomb.* Another knight is onto Hugh with a crosshilt, but Hugh catches it in the rings of his Portugese sword, twists it out of the man's grip and drives his own blade between the plates of the other's armour under the left armpit.

Manozzi's second blow falls on the duke's shoulder as he struggles to his feet. He collapses under it. One like that to the head, even a head like the duke's, will end it. Hugh digs his spurs in once more and urges his stallion across the small parcel of land that separates him from the old general, trampling down two knights on his way. Manozzi's helmet swivels to see Hugh coming, and he levels the blade in a back-handed arc level with his neck. Hugh can't see much through his visor, but he can see the axe, glinting orange and red as it gets bigger and bigger. He bends back on his saddle so that he is almost lying on his mare's hind quarters. The axe swooshes past his eyes, and scrapes the brim of the visor. But as soon as he can see the orange clouds again, Hugh springs up and strikes the over-extended torso of the general. His blade finds a sore piece of flesh in the arm though not deep. Hugh withdraws and wields his blade in a full circle above his head, bringing it at Manozzi's neck.

Hugh hears the collar bone crunch under the chain mail. The general bellows in pain like an stag in rut. But even with his left collar bone splintered Manozzi lurches back up with a powerful right cut. It catches Hugh on the right arm and chest and sends him clean off the back of his horse. His head hits the ground, but his left foot remains twisted in the stirrup. Even as Hugh is falling, his mare spins about and drags him unceremoniously in a half circle until he is once more under Manozzi's axe. The general spurs his stallion forward to trample Hugh.

Hugh sees the hooves rise and fall at his head, but his whole body suddenly shoots to the side as his mare drags him away in her terror. She barges past two other horses, and Hugh's back bounces over bodies. His sides catch trees. His body is also thrown under the mare's back hooves. One catches his chest, crushing the air from it so that he cannot even cry out for the pain. All is black in the track through the willow thicket. The mare brakes into a full gallop, hooves beating the ground in an endless thunder. Hugh's sword is long gone, and so are his gauntlets.

The last thing Hugh remembers is a crack to the side of his helmet from a tree trunk, then blackness. When he comes to in the dark, the horse is gone, but his foot is still attached to the broken stirrup. His lungs rasp for air. He feels the breastplate, collapsed inward from the horse's hoof and crushing his chest. The guns are still firing, and above the canopy of trees the skyline is red as Hades.

The duke. Shit. Hugh pulls up his visor and struggles to his feet. He can't hear anything. *Which way, damn it, which way?* He tears the helmet off and discards it. The sound of steel on steel comes from behind him. He swivels unsteadily, recovers his balance and staggers in the direction of the sounds. Twice he stumbles, once he falls in the dark, but eventually he arrives back in a clearing that is bathed in the reds and orange of the flaming skies. Four horses stand dumbly to his right. In the center, a lone knight, axe in hand, stands over another – which is headless.

No! Hugh charges with a roar and leaps on the assassin from behind. They tumble into a heap. Hugh hoped to have the advantage on Manozzi because of the collar bone, but he is surprised to be so easily repulsed when they are on the ground. First he gets an elbow in the face that almost sends his jaw from its socket, then the other man casts him off easily like a miller tossing a bag of oats. He's as quick and strong as a twenty-year-old. Hugh has barely enough time to recover himself into a crouch before the other has retrieved the axe and is raising it for an easy blow. It is only then that Hugh sees the knight's helmet.

'Wait,' Hugh cries out, hands raised. 'For God's sake. Wait.'

'Erpingham! Hah! Erpingham!' The duke draws himself up and gasps. 'Thank God, Erpingham. Thank God you were here.'

'Are they all dead?'

'Yes, they're dead all right. Finished them off while they were down,' the duke says, offering Hugh his bear-sized gauntlet.

'Are you hurt, Your Grace?' Hugh is tugged up by a strong arm.

'Hurt? No, but I would have been if I'd faced them alone. You are a mean little scrapper, signor, if you don't mind my saying.'

'Not so bad yourself,' Hugh says, standing unsteadily and rubbing his jaw. 'They are your brother's men, are they not?'

The duke smiles. 'I don't think so. They are a faction of our army. Military coups are very common. Manozzi would rather I had let him control the army as he did under my father. I knew he hated me, but I never thought he'd stoop to murder.'

'But they rode under your brother's escutcheon?'

'My brother commanded the western force for this war. But he didn't trust Manozzi one bit either.' The duke supports Hugh under the elbow. 'No, my friend, do not think my brother has set his sights on the dukedom. He aims his guns higher than that, by Jove. Now come, let us saddle up. I don't want to miss seeing Trevisan sink, the evil swine. Can you ride? *Dio mio*, what the hell happened to your chest?'

'Your wife's mare trampled me.'

'Anything broken?'

'Not sure. Hurts like hell.' Hugh grins half-heartedly and says, 'Good old Brescia plate, eh?'

'Hah!' Another hearty bone-shaking slap from the duke and Hugh might not recover. 'At least it fits you now, eh? God's oath, I like you English.'

EVENING OF THE 22ND DECEMBER 1509

Addendum to Hugh's dispatch to Rhodes

Magister,

By *grace dieu* I have survived another chapter of this war to add yet one more addendum to the bottom of my last letter. God has spared my life and that of the duke's meagre army, whereas at least two thousand of the Venetian force are killed or drowned and many taken prisoner – Albanian, Dalmatian and Slavonian.

On the night of twenty-first instant, the feast of Thomas the Apostle, the high waters of the Po brought the enemy galleys up to the level of the embankment. Many ships were sunk, including fifteen galleys, and other supporting vessels captured. Their admiral and some galleys tried to escape, but the flagship sank three miles downstream, and Trevisan escaped north. He will surely be tried for negligence, as the bulk of his fleet was moored together at closed quarters as if it were a pontoon. The scene at the river this morning was truly terrible: myriad corpses waxen and glistening in dew, stiff and crooked. It will be a good year for grave diggers.

There is also news from the north about further Venetian reversals. Your brother's army has forced Pitigliano to withdraw to Padua once again. With a more secure foothold in the Veneto, the allies hope to strangle Venetian food supplies. These two calamities may indeed force the senate to sue for peace before the New Year. We shall see anon.

This afternoon Duke Alfonso d'Este entered Ferrara in high style, and I was beside him. In his train, much booty, munitions and over sixty flags of the enemy. The duchess with her maids of honour were dressed in white with silk garlands for him. The court and the jubilant population lined the streets. Tonight we dine at the palace, and there the duchess has arranged for me to see Titian's canvas of Vendramin.

So I will finish this letter finally tomorrow, when I have made my plans, and dispatch it via Ravenna with all speed.

CASTELLO ESTENSE, FERRARA, EVENING OF THE 22ND DECEMBER 1509

Bembo and Wilf bid Hugh adieu on the last corner before the castle. The compline bell is sounding from the priory opposite, but so too are other bells across the city that have been ringing all day. Revellers line the streets. The duke has distributed wine by the barrel, which is about all that is left. Part of the town will no doubt be outside the gates, stripping the slain and salvaging what can be found. Many others are in the chill alleyways staggering on empty bellies and Trebbiano and other vintages which they have consumed by the gallon. Butchered horse, mule and ox are being brought in from the field of battle and roasted in the town squares. Some hug and dance in long lines. Other sit and weep with relief, or grief. Still others gather around braziers and tell tales of the battle, which is already passing into Romagnian folklore.

Bembo takes Hugh by the arm. 'I am sorry we can't escort you. You look rough and, God, you smell awful.'

'Our host's physician was thorough.' Hugh says shifting uneasily in his chest bandage.

'Thorough, and predictable.' Bembo replies. 'These Byzantine compotes of Bythinian cheese and honey may be standard prescriptions, but it does nothing for a man's general aura. For God's sake, keep away from the ladies. They will think the dead have arisen.'

'It is not the women I have come to see.'

Bembo nods. 'I know, the painting. I wish I could come with you, *caro*. Do you trust the duchess?'

'It is not her I am worried about.' Hugh glances across the street at the Castello Estense, a monumental square fist of stone in the centre of their city of adoring subjects – surrounded by a moat just in case. From where he stands he can see the windows of the dungeons just above the water. *Whatever else happens in there, I am not going to let myself be taken by the cardinal. I'll not be joining his brothers in the dungeon here or anywhere else.*

Hugh takes the silver cup from Wilf. It is laced up in a velvet scrip and will be a small commemorative gesture from Rhodes to Ferrara. 'Just make sure you are ready to leave when I return.'

He crosses the cobbles not looking behind him, only up at the brutal bastions and machiolated battlements – forked like the devil's horns. People are already milling on the orange tree terrace which is half way up the façade, and near the bridge which connects the castello to the new palazzo. He enters under the portcullis and is saluted by the guard. They know him by now, know him by sight. He's hard to miss with the white cross of his order as a livery on the chest of his best black velvet doublet. *Il Cavaliere di Rodi,* is what they call him, touching the brims of their helmets as he approaches. They do not know what part he played in their temporal salvation, and Hugh has asked the duke to keep it that way. The last thing anyone needs is a diplomatic incident with the Venetians or anyone else when they are so close to resolving this ridiculous conflict. He nods to the men and crosses the drawbridge. Others are coming on horseback and in carriages so he moves quickly through the central courtyard and to the entrance. It is lit by torches that crackle and send a trail of thin smoke into the night sky.

He goes up the stairs and into the salon. The place is packed. Two hundred perfumed bodies mill in a double height salon lit by a thousand beeswax candles. Most of the grandees will want to say they were here, one or two of the more impecunious will be more interested in having something different than radish stew to eat. He glances about quickly for any sign of the cardinal's red berret, but he cannot see it. *He won't try anything here,* Hugh tells himself as his eye travels quickly from head to head. It alights for a moment on the duchess at the far end near her husband who is taking the Marchese of Pesaro by the arm and brandishing him about like a trophy. The duchess sees Hugh, and breaking off from the ladies she is talking to, beckons him. When he is just behind them, she separates her friends and leads him forward with a slender hand. She is wearing a golden silk damask gown, magnificently traced with pearls and encrusted at the bosom with clear gems. Diamonds? They know how to dress in Ferrara. Her famed hair, Venetian blonde, fall in streams about her slender neck like a cascade of sunshine.

'Fra Hugh Erpingham, ladies,' she says, leading him before her friends. 'The first knight of Ferrara.'

'My lady should not say so.' Hugh bows and tries to think of something clever to deflect the comment.

'I don't, my husband says so – says you are the *forza magiore.*' She curtseys, along with the two other ladies who raise their eyes with a coyness that flushes Hugh's cheeks. 'I believe we have more to thank you for than we can say, signor.'

He adjusts his beret awkwardly, and then gestures toward the duke who is nearby. 'To see your dukedom safe from marauders and your husband in health, is thanks enough.'

'Ah yes, but there was something else you wanted was there not?'

'My lady?'

'The picture. I haven't forgotten, you know. He is, ladies, a man easily satisfied. He only wants to see a painting of an old knight of his order, and he will be happy.' The women titter into their cut glass punch cups. Lucretia pouts at Hugh's uncertain smile and touches his hand with a small smack. 'Don't look so offended when I tease you. Fancy; a man who will slay a thousand Saracens and not take a little teasing from the ladies. I have forgotten nothing, and I have arranged my servant to take you to it.'

Hugh bows. There is a lump in his throat, God knows why, and when he looks at her again he cannot find any words.

She looks askance at him. 'What? You would see it now perhaps? Before you have even taken a cup of wine?'

'Yes,' is all he can say. He feels like a guilty child. Why? Why should he? *God, I must see that picture.*

The duchess turns to a negro servant behind her. 'Take this man to see the picture I showed you. Do you remember the picture, Puncinello? Yes. Take this man to see it. Remember that you will need torches, for that part of the castello will not be lit tonight.'

The duchess turns back to Hugh. 'You have to repeat things with them. My sister-in-law sent him from Mantua as a gift.'

'Thank you, duchess. I will return anon.'

'Yes, and when you do, promise me that you will have some conversation for us. And promise also that you will dance with the lady Francesca. She thinks you English are very, what did you say?' Lucretia touched the arm of her crimson-cheeked friend, and then says with merriment. 'Ah yes: intriguing. So come back quickly to us and be intriguing.'

Minutes later he might have been in another world. There are no other guests on the upper floor. Some servants run about; guards sneak a quick drink brought them by a sheepish maid, but no guests. The lower corridors are lit, but after two flights of stairs Hugh is glad of his torch. Punchinello is almost impossible to age – somewhere between twenty and fifty. He says nothing but at each corner or new ascent, turns and gestures with his torch. Hugh's stomach knots as they reach the end of the long landing and Punchinello points at the door. Hugh's heart begins to beat wildly. Is this it? He glances from the window to his left and reckons that he is entering a corner apartment in one of the four bastions.

As the servant opens the door, Hugh feels sweat beading his brow and his hand quivering with anticipation. He gestures for the servant to go first, and they pass into darkness. The air is damp here, musty with the scent of ages, decay and neglect. Furniture, covered by dust sheets, appear under the torch's flickering light. *What does a duke do when all the gifts are more than he can use? Now I know. Nice problem to have.*

Hugh is suddenly brought out of his thoughts by the smell of garlic. *Garlic?* He slips his eating knife from his belt in a trice but just as suddenly feels the dull buzzing thump of a cudgel on the back of his head.

AWAKENING SOMETIME LATER

My head. Aching, throbbing, stiff. Throat parched. Heat.

Hugh opens one eye, then two. He is sitting on a chair, hands tied to the chair arms. The room is aglow with a large fire that crackles and hisses as woodworm-rotten picture frames flare in the hearth. Above it; an elaborately carved marble mantle oscillates orange and hades red before his eyes. Lamps are being lit to reveal a room thirty feet square with a high ceiling, and filled with stored furniture under sheets. At first he cannot remember where he is, but then he sees Punchinello sitting on the floor, tied and gagged on the far side of the fire.

Hugh squints grimly into the blaze, willing himself not to hear the voice he fears. Ippolito d'Este. He needs a plan. *Come on, Hugh, look around, get creative: the fire, broken picture frames, painted panels and half burnt maps. Poker? Poker!*

Hugh's mind freezes as he sees a red hot poker protruding from the grate onto the hearth. His bowels loosen. Another 'weapon of virtue'. *Get a grip Erpingham. Breathe and focus.* He hears the shuffling of boots on the bare boards behind him, two, no three pairs. Whispers and murmurs. They don't know he's come to. The cords bite his wrists. They've done a tidy job. *Shit, how could I have been so stupid?* He shifts his weight to test the chair. It is not one of the big carved oak or olive wood chairs of yesteryear but one of the slighter chairs of a lady's boudoir. His body breaks out in a cold sweat with his heart ripping at his ribcage. Punchinello's eyes shift and grow wide with alarm. Boots approach from behind, one foot scuffing as if dragged.

A hand cuffs the back of Hugh's head. 'Come on, Erpingham, wake up. I remembered you wanted to see the painting, so I have had my men wait for you to come. So much easier, so much more efficient, and we must be efficient even if we can't be good.'

The cardinal, in scarlet robes with an odour of rosewater, shuffles past Hugh and carefully eases himself awkwardly into another chair by the fire. He is missing hair from the right side of his temple where he was burnt. The skin is flaking orange in the fire glow. *Good. I hope it hurts,* Hugh thinks. The cardinal bears the tell-tale cut on the bridge of his nose where Hugh butted him, and there is still evidence of bruising. No wonder he hasn't been attending parties, even without the flames he'd look like one of Signorelli's demons from the duomo at Orvieto.

'My brother will throw nothing away; my father was the same.' He pauses to flutter a gloved hand past his face. 'Always clinging to the past, as if there were pleasure or honour there. Holy mother, look at all this rotting, woodworm-ridden rubbish.' His face strains with disgust, as if reaching for something, and then relaxes with a new thought. 'Why, it could have been given to the poor.'

'I've heard that before,' Hugh mutters. The Judas plea for charity, never to an individual but humanity as a whole, has ever been the last retreat of the resentful scoundrel. His eyes dart back to the fire place. *The poker. Shit. I need a plan.*

'What did you say? No, don't bother repeating it. I don't want to hear anything but what you were about to tell me in Sant'Agostino. Oh, I haven't forgotten, you see. How can I now my face and leg are burned?'

'Hope it hurts, Your Grace.'

'Oh it does, and you will pay,' the cardinal shouts, slamming his fist on the chair arm, so that small trails of dust drop vertically like orange gold dust to the floor. 'You will pay,' he repeats definitely and slowly. 'With your pain – pain before the end. I hope you know that, you insolent villain.'

'And I hope your hair never grows back, and you will never forget crossing me.' Hugh smiles as the cardinal's eyes and nostrils both flare in a mix of rage and incomprehension.

'Cross you? You! Why are you smiling? What could a man like you smile about? An idiot who walks into a trap twice?' People like you give imbeciles a bad name. Holstein, hit him for God's sake. Someone hit this idiot.' Hugh hears swift and heavy boots behind and feels the flat of an enormous hand smash his skull. The chair starts to go over, but another hand rights him. His ears ring then whistle, but he shakes himself conscious.

The cardinal laughs and says, 'The only thing to say about English mediocrity is that at least you are always at your best.'

Hugh raises his eyes again to where he had been staring before. That dust, falling in ten, twenty individual fairy threads from under the cardinal's chair arms is not household dust. It is wood dust, fine as flour. Hugh lets his fingers run on the arm and spindles of his own chair. Tiny holes perforate the woodwork. He looks again at the cardinal's chair. Yes, it is the same one. They are sitting on the same chair exactly. And both are riddled with woodworm, eaten through like the cardinal's soul, and brittle, ready for breaking. Hugh starts breathing hard and doing a roll call through his muscles and joints. He leads the heel of his right boot to follow the spindle under the chair until he reaches the thinnest and weakest point. He then brings his left boot forward to brace against the raised hearth. He applies as much pressure as he can, but stops short before the chair moves and arouses suspicion. *Damn.*

'Now I finally have your attention.' The cardinal leans forward with a leer of anticipation. 'You will tell us what you see in the picture and then everything you know, or I will introduce this poker into your rectum, and cut your barbarian English heart from its miserable chest. Holstein, the picture, come on man, the picture.'

A lugubrious, apple-faced German suddenly appears in Hugh's right field of vision, the unframed canvas clutched in his mammoth hands. 'The picture.'

'Yes, Erpingham, the picture,' the cardinal says. 'I trust you to see it and tell me what you know. And maybe we can be friends. Maybe I will give you a job.'

The German angles the canvas so that it catches the blaze of orange light. It shows a man in harness and black surcoat, the white cross of the order on a black woollen cape over his right shoulder. His thick, grey beard is cropped square, dark hair turning white near the moustache. Hugh searches the eyes, the nose the lips. When was it painted, six, seven years ago? He has a carrack sword and points his gauntlet toward a rather fanciful rendering of the defences of Rhodes under siege. He has a wily, hawk-like appearance. *Do I know him?* He cannot say.

'Well, who is it?' the cardinal snaps. 'Come on, Erpingham. Have you seen him? Is this the man from Venice you saw?'

'No,' Hugh says, with a pent up, exasperated breath. 'No.' He desperately strains his eyes, racking his memory, trying to make the eyes fit the Venetian and a thousand other men. The white beard, the noble brow, the leering eyes, the proud Roman nose. 'No, it's not him. Damnation, after all this.' Hugh slumps back in his own chair, as if there had been no cardinal, no henchmen, no poker. He can't believe it. He risked so much just to get here, and it is all for nothing. Perhaps it will come to him in time. But there is no time. *There is something in that face, but there is no time.*

'You are telling me that you have never seen this man. Oh dear. Are you sure? I ask you to reply with care.' The cardinal casts a sideways glance toward the fireplace as an alcoholic would a bottle. *The poker.* His mouth is slightly open, and his tongue lingers at the gate. 'Of course they say that no one can find Vendramin unless he wants to be found. People say all sorts of stupid things like that. But a man with that sort of fortune cannot disappear. I have my people making a most careful search, and we shall find him. But if you have nothing else to tell us then we must part company. Holstein, Brabus, hold him.'

At the command Holstein walks with one stride toward Hugh, so that for a moment his bulk blots out the heat of the flames. Hugh feels an arm from behind putting him in a neck lock and squeezing to secure him but not to strangle. Now or never. Hugh kicks with his right heel on the spindle, and now, with Brabus as a backstop the spindle cracks and splinters. He twists his head and bites Brabus' arm – teeth cut through the cotton shirt and deep into the flesh. Holstein grabs Hugh by the chest with his left hand and draws the other back for a right hook. Brabus screams with pain and tries to tear Hugh away by the ear. *Bastard.* Hugh forces himself to his feet slightly. The chair is raised a few inches off the ground. Holstein's fist is coming. His ear will come away at any moment. *Now.* He crashes down hard once, then again. The chair legs spread and give way. He plummets to the floor, pulling the assailants with him, and lashes out with his feet. It is only a partial victory; his hands are still bound to the upper chair, which is still very much intact.

The cardinal is shouting, 'Hold him, you buffoons. Hold him!'

Hugh receives the punch, which thankfully doesn't land squarely on his jaw, but rather glances from his temple. In the haze that follows, Hugh releases his teeth in Brabus' arm, what is left of it, and Brabus releases Hugh's ear. Holstein is bent over Hugh, ready for another blow, so Hugh kicks Holstein's feet from under him, and the giant collapses onto Hugh like a falling oak. The extra weight flattens the chair. A result of sorts. The brute will still crush him.

Holstein pins Hugh down by the shoulders and shakes him so that his shoulder blades are ground into the floor. 'Stay still Englishman,' he says with a guttural dialect, followed by a number of what sounds like Saxon curses. Hugh looks past the beast's shoulder to see the looming shape of the cardinal brandishing the iron. The glowing tip illuminates his maniacal eyes. 'I think we should quarterize his insolent tongue first, make it swell so that it fills his mouth. Brabus, stop playing with your arm and hold his bloody mouth open.'

Hugh sees for the first time the drawn visage of Brabus, middle aged, scarred with remembrance and sin. Lifeless, heavy-lidded, grey eyes which stand still like two millstones that have forgotten the motive power of wind or water. His hands press Hugh's skull and jaw like a vice, prizing his mouth apart. The cardinal stands over Hugh with a diabolical fervour and wide-eyed gaze of triumph. He angles his wrist and leans over the back of Holstein in order to insert the poker. The point comes within six inches until Hugh can see the tiny sparks of wood ember burning off it – until it starts to blur and the heat be felt with each gasping inhalation. He lashes with his free left foot. It scrapes the floor, nothing. He stretches it out and finds the edge of the fire surround. He pushes and jerks himself away, an inch, maybe two.

The cardinal shouts. 'Hold him still, will you.'

Holstein tries to reposition his knees, to use one to suppress each of Hugh's. By so doing he causes the cardinal himself to move to the left, and within reach of Hugh's foot. Hugh kicks out like a man fighting for life, and shins the cardinal with the second kick who shrieks, then drops the poker on the German's neck, before falling backwards out of sight. The German's flesh gives an audible sizzle. The vice like grip suddenly disappears as the German shakes the poker away and grasps his neck. He growls and hisses in agony. With his now freed left hand Hugh quickly retrieves a spindle and drives it upward into Brabus's eye. The man falls back with a blood-curdling yell. Hugh shoves Holstein off him and reaches for the poker. But just as suddenly Hugh feels the German's weight again. He's cursing into Hugh's ear. *You've seen the poker too, have you, Fritz?* Hugh butts his head three times into Holstein's nose. *Too late Fritz. Too late.* Hugh drives the poker hard into the soft beer gut and it burns its way in and in and in, until his inwards hiss on the point.

Hugh rolls Hostein off him, and the German thrashes and squeals in a circle in front of the fire. Hugh stands quickly, poker in hand. Brabus is kneeling with both hands over his eye. Hugh fells him with one kick to the head, and then lands two blows on Holstein with the poker that knocks him senseless.

He turns in the direction of the cardinal, who is just getting to his feet and drawing a knife. 'I'll give you anything you want. You won't get far if you kill me, Erpingham. You know that.' The cardinal crouches forward like a feral cat, right hand stretched forth with the knife, twisting and rotating like a serpent. 'Work with me, and I will share it with you. Think of it, Erpingham. Think of it.'

Hugh's eye momentarily catches a new glimpse of the canvas, which has fallen on the floor and whose contours are now picked up in long shadows cast by the fire. Vendramin is looking at me, he thinks. He glances back at the cardinal's knife. He chances another look. What are those two shadows near his nose. *Titian has dabbed two blobs of paint next to the right nostril. Two moles. Two moles!*

A flash of movement, white hand, scarlet silk sleeve. The knife. Hugh jumps back and raises the poker.

'What did you see just then?' the cardinal says with a shrill whisper. 'I saw something then in your eye, you great and infamous liar. What did you see?'

Hugh feels his mouth opening wider and his gaze fixed firmer in astonishment. *The moles on his face.* 'It's him!'

'What? Who's him?' The cardinal lunges in a fury. 'Tell me, damn you.'

Hugh smashes the delicate wrist with the poker, and the knife falls to the floor. He brings up the poker with a swift backhand swipe that connects with the cardinal's temple. The cardinal sprawls backward across his chair in a heap on the floor. Hugh bends again to examine the canvas, heart pounding, chest heaving, hands sweating. *It is true. Its him all along!* Hugh sits back on his haunches. *I don't believe it.*

Suddenly running footsteps sound in the corridor. Guards shout. The cardinal screams, 'Help me. I am your lord cardinal. Help me, guards. Break down the door. Murder. Murder.'

Hugh jumps onto the cardinal. You don't have to be a skilled diplomat to know that you don't kill cardinals in Italy, or anywhere else, though God knows this one deserves it. Hugh punches him and rams his head four times on the floor until he is silent. Did they hear? The footsteps come right to the door.

They begin to thump at the door. 'Hello? We heard shouting. Open up in the duke's name, open up.'

Hugh looks around. The canvas—no one must see it. He throws it onto the flames, and looks around. This is a dead end, no other doors. The duke's men won't take my word, perhaps even the duke won't. Hugh casts a baleful eyes about the place and then sees the white eyes of Punchinello staring at him out of the darkness.

More banging on the door. 'Open up or we'll break it down.'

Hugh walks across to the servant and ungags his mouth. 'Don't be afraid. I won't hurt you. You serve your mistress well, don't you? Yes, and she doesn't want any harm to come to me. So tell me, Punchinello, how do I get out of here? Is there a way?'

The servant swallows and nods towards the shuttered windows. 'There is a balcony.'

Hugh doesn't wait to find out where or even say thank you. He hears the shoulders against the locked doors. He runs to release the shutters and climb through the window. The air is biting cold, but oh God, how good to be cold and not in front of that fire. Behind him the doorway crashes open. There is no time to do anything but run. He can see the balcony below the window. It runs around the turret and follows as far as he can see along one side of the *castello*. Directly below it, the moat shines silver under the full moon. He runs down it, round the tower, and along the mossy slabs adjacent to the corridor. He looks back. He cannot see the guards, but he can hear the shouts of the men on the outside as well as those running back inside to head him off. He needs a plan. Again. He sees a white statue on the marble wall a hundred feet in front of him. It is a worn and deeply veined marble lion with a raised paw. *The mercy of lions.* He shoves at it, the icy stone numbing his fingers. Nothing. Hugh presses his shoulder to it and braces his foot against the wall. The brittle crystals begin to prick and freeze his cheek. At a shove, the statue rocks back once, and then Hugh heaves it over the precipice and down silently toward the moat. The splash sends a white spray thirty feet in every direction, and the deep boom reverberates off the surrounding buildings like canon fire. People celebrating on the streets quickly flock to the moat and point at the turbulent waters. Three guards appear on the edge of the tower. He crouches but keeps an eye on them from the parapet. They stop running and start shouting and pointing to the disturbed waters below.

A man shouts from the street, 'Someone jumped from the castle, a rich man perhaps. Fetch lanterns. We will rescue him and get a reward.' More people run from the tavern. The guards disappear back through the window.

Hugh moves around the balcony keeping low and walking softly on the balls of his feet. At the further tower he expects any moment to have the other guards appear, but there is no sound. He looks over the edge and sees, further down the tower, a pantile roof which runs down to the terrace of the orange trees, the floor where the guests are gathered. *I could do it.* As he approaches, guests gather at the edge of the terrace, some pointing to the water. Egged on by the street crowd, a chivalrous braggadocio is stripping off and preparing to jump in. He shouts out his name, Deano Vittelli, so that the watching grandees will know who to thank. But, worse for wear, he ends up falling twenty feet into the water with his chemise still half over his head.

If Hugh wanted a distraction, Deano is a gift from heaven. He slides over the balcony and eases himself onto the hip of the roof. It is shallow, and he is able to walk down quietly with one hand on the wall to steady himself. He crouches on the near edge of the tiles, just a ten foot drop away from the terrace. On the terrace guests are shouting and pointing. An old blustering count hobbles out on gouty legs right under Hugh's nose and says, 'What's all this fuss then?'

They will turn and see me. It is now or never. Hugh drops down behind the old man, and falls forward onto his knees. When he looks up, he sees a number of guests are staring at him, including the gouty count.

'What pestilence is this?' the man says, and then exclaims. 'Why it is the English knight. Did you trip on a loose paving stone, or is it the punch? I thought the English could hold their drink, friend.'

Hugh stands, and bows low enough to catch his breath. That done he rises and says, 'Exactly so. Please do forgive me, I grow tired and clumsy. It is time to retire perhaps, excuse me.'

He bows again, then turns on his heels and walks swiftly down the corridors toward the *Salon d'honeur*, arranging his clothes and hair and checking for blood. He can hear the duke making a speech and so does not enter, but rather, takes the corridor to the right which leads to the stairs. The soldiers on the ground floor will know surely. But will they know to look for him? Has the cardinal recovered? Has Punchinello told them? He nears the bottom of the stairs and crosses the drawbridge towards the soldiers. They are already stopping a couple from leaving. 'Our orders are that no one can leave until the intruder is caught.' The couple turn back and pass Hugh without a greeting. Hugh glances through the arch that faces the moat where the idiot Deano Vitelli is being shouted at by the duke's bodyguard. Apparently he is under arrest. Hugh approaches the guards.

They nod deferentially as he comes near. 'Evening, signor. I am afraid there has been a disturbance, and the duke's bodyguard have ordered we keep the guests in. For your safety, signor.'

'Well, duke's bodyguard, eh? The ones with the yellow hose. The ones that look like hens. I am flattered by their care for my safety, but as I can see that they are even now arresting this dangerous malefactor – the town drunk – I think I may go home without harm.' Hugh looks at them carefully. It is the same men that greeted him when he arrived – *Il Cavaliere di Rodi*. 'Gentlemen, I need my bed, and I am prepared to fight all four of you to get to it. So what is it to be?'

The captain, looks at the others. The one nearest the brazier snorts. 'Chicken's legs. Good one signor.'

'Well,' the captain says, 'We know there's no harm in you, signor. You enjoy your sleep. We've seen enough fighting for one day.'

Hugh nods and walks through the arch unmolested and into the darkness. When he is past the first corner, he darts like a hare toward Ariosto's. If they want to get out of Ferrara, it must be now. When the cardinal comes to, all hell will break loose. It is a long ride south to find Vendramin, but this time he knows exactly where to find him.

CHRISTMAS DAY 1509, DORMITORY OF THE SPIRITUALI, ASSISI

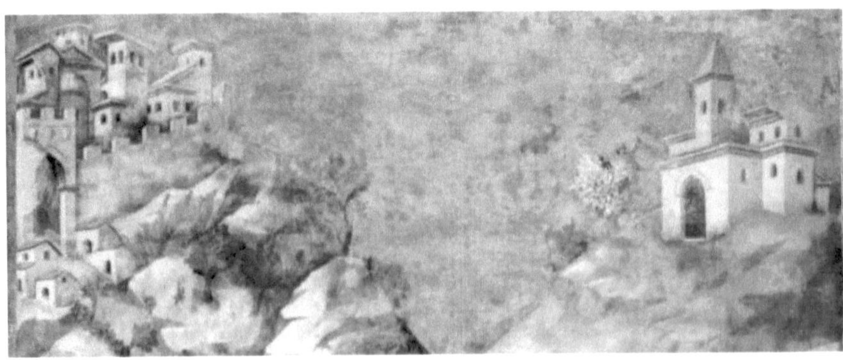

'Why didn't you tell me?' Hugh collapses in an exhaustion before the pallet of Fra Francesco i Bisognoso – Francis the Needy. *Very poetic. How could I not have seen it? Everywhere I went there were Franciscans. I must be going soft.*

Hugh examines his sleeve, covered with dust and mud from three day's hard ride, torn by brier and thorn, heavy laden with rainwater and sweat. His fingers are even now blue with frostbite, his legs numb under him. Wilf and Bembo will hardly have reached Florence with the baggage by now. It is better that way. *They mustn't know. No one must know*. Hugh leans back on his knees and gasps for air. He has a fever of cold, some ague of the chest.

Vendramin, the leper, the penitent, the Franciscan, lies before him, huddled in the same grey, tattered blanket that he was wearing the last time they were together at that terrible parting. The toast of a hundred ballads, the subject of a thousand searches, the richest man in Europe, the one who could finance the fate of Christendom and beyond, is here on a straw pallet. The world rushes on in Bologna silks and chamois gloves while he lies here in his coarse woollens and bandaged hands. All the time he has been tending the wounds of lepers and becoming one of them.

'Why?' Hugh repeats, trying to catch his breath. 'Why did you not tell me?'

They are alone here in the infirmary with only the sound of the wind in the rafters and the occasional purring of the doves in the cote on the gable wall. Vendramin is propped up in a half sitting position, his head hanging forward slightly. He opens his eyes for a moment and looks steadily at Hugh. 'You know why.' He coughs the fluid from his lungs. 'And if you have finally come to kill me, then you'd better be quick. I am not long for this world in any case.'

'You were dying last time, too.' But even as he says it, Hugh can see the man's face is as grey as a November sky. Near the two moles next to his right nostril, the veins spreading across the cheeks are like black ivy. He is dying.

'Be quick about it,' he rasps again.

'Is that what you think?' Hugh replies.

Vendramin raises an eyebrow, and when he speaks next, it is with more vigour and hope. 'You come here in harness, fully armed. I know they sent you to kill me, well I am weak enough now. What do you expect me to think?' Vendramin rests his head and closes his eyes. 'I failed with you, Hugh. That is the truth. You came to me for help, and I failed to lead you to God. I had not enough of Christ myself to share with you. I failed God and you, so it is just I should pay. Do it now if you want, but make it quick.'

‘I see, you can’t be a saint so you’ll be a martyr,’ Hugh scoffs. ‘Well, let me tell you. I’m dressed like this because I am fleeing a cardinal who would have killed me just because I am the only one who claims to have seen you.’

‘There are so many cardinals, most made dangerous by boredom. But you didn’t tell him anything? Good. I am flattered.’

‘I didn’t know anything. Not until a few nights ago when I saw Titziano Vicelli’s painting of you.’

‘Ah, so you were in Ferrara then. Ah, and with Cardinal d’Este. He is an evil man. And you didn’t kill him. That showed great restraint.’

‘How do you know I didn’t?’

‘Because you said he was chasing you. But he is not the cardinal you should fear. He is a mere flea bite compared to the other one.’

‘Which one? Damn it, tell me. Who could possibly be left?’

‘I don’t know who he is. I didn’t know when I spoke of him in the tunnels of Siena, and I don’t know now, not really. I have my suspicions, but I don’t know. All I do know is that his spies call him the White Cardinal. Make of that what you will. They say the devil himself appears as an angel of light. But he’s clever, this one, that I do know. And he’s been searching for me from the start. Not blundering about like Petrucci, Michelotto and Cardinal d’Este, but quietly. As I say he’s a clever one, and he’ll have been watching you, make no mistake about that.’ Vendramin turns a weary head toward Hugh and stares at him again through heavy lids. A cracked smile surfaces like a drowning man coming up for the last time. His lips are purple and blue, his breathing heavy, arrhythmic. But there is still fight in those eyes. In the odd moment they blaze like those of a young man entering his first battle.

‘So Hugh, you are not going to kill me after all. Huh. That won’t please them. I suppose you’ve seen enough in Italy to make you question everything. Are they still butchering each other in the north?’

‘Yes, though there is hope Venice will sue for peace now.’

‘Hah,’ Vendramin snorts. ‘Julius had enough blood, has he? And what about you? Do you still think the gold and the Greek Fire will help you to establish the kingdom of God?’

Hugh shifts sideways so that he can rest himself on the edge of the next pallet. He draws a defensive arm across his aching midriff. 'They might.'

'Spoken like a true knight. You know, there was a man of my generation from Genoa – very ambitious. This man I knew well. He was a sailor, like you and me. And like you and me, an optimist, a humanist, an idealist even. He was not a knight, but he was pious like you. You get the picture, no?' He pauses to give a rasping cough. 'Well, he once said the same thing to me. No one would help him in Genoa, but the King of Spain did, and they gave him ships. He set off on a great quest like you have, though his was much nobler than yours, I think. He was going to convert the heathen and make his sovereigns wealthy beyond the reach of avarice. And with that gold the holy city of Jerusalem would be freed from the Saracens. And everyone would be happy.'

'Columbus?' Hugh says, 'You are talking about Columbus?'

'Of course, I am.' Vendramin scowls and coughs into a shaking fist. 'And you know very well how that gold has corrupted the Spaniards and financed their wars – wars even against fellow Christians. And the Indians have been slaughtered and abused, and if that were not stench enough, now has grown across these oceans this trade of slavery that cries unto heaven. So you tell me, if that is what Satan can do to a young man with good intentions, what can he do with those who by greed and violence are already his own? Tell me that. So yes, I have taken the last of that gold from Columbus' rapine before his death, and with it only good will come. Not one *scudi* will be spent on weapons of war.'

'What then? What will you do with it?'

'Not what we *will* do, but what we *are* doing. We are distributing it among the poor, bit by bit. One day wars will cease, and until that day comes, we obey Christ and live as children of tomorrow.'

'But where? How?'

'I'll tell you because I suppose you'll guess anyway. And I'll tell you because now I can see that you are a child of the light after all. You won't betray us.'

'You are sure of that? I've given you no pledge. Maybe I won't kill you, but I've said nothing about this gold.'

'It is all one. You will not betray God, that is the point.' Vendramin's eyes ignite with a celestial fire that turns Hugh's inward parts into liquid, like wax before a flame. 'Oh thank God,' Vendramin exclaims, gazing to the rafters. 'Thank God. I see now that I didn't fail with you after all. You will walk free, Hugh. Yes, I will tell you about the gold. I have entrusted the gold to the only people who have renounced property, the Brothers Spiritual. It is they who are distributing it slowly throughout Europe and beyond. Alms houses, famine relief, new institutions and communities of brothers to serve the poor. Schools, farms, learning, change. The meek will inherit the earth one day, Hugh. It may be a thousand years away, but Christ will finish the rule of the mighty when he returns – all those who have ploughed with the devil. Either way, we must all give account before his judgement seat, and my conscience is clear in this matter at least.' Vendramin leans slowly back, taking deep breaths and nodding to himself occasionally. His face is angled toward the tiles, his mouth open slightly, breathing with a faint rattle. After a pause he says, 'So, you are not an assassin after all. What are you going to do then, when you've finished feeling sorry for yourself?'

'I don't know.' Hugh covers his eyes with icy palms. 'I really don't know. Go back to Rhodes, I suppose, seeing that you will not help us against the enemy.'

'Our enemies are within, as you very well know. Listen to me, Hugh, listen to me, for God alone knows this might be the last time I speak with you. You took me as a confessor once, so heed me now. Francis went long ago to Egypt and spent a whole week with the nephew of the great Saladin. They talked long about these things. The sultan would not be converted to Christ on that occasion, but in one week Francis had exerted a greater power over the eastern menace than all the armies we had sent over the previous five hundred years. Francis returned to the crusader camp with an offer of peace. Yes, peace, and there could have been a lasting peace between east and west if Cardinal Pelagio had not preferred the glory of arms. You are still young, Hugh. Do not think that you must always repeat the mistakes of your forebears.'

'I am foresworn, as are you.'

'Ah, it sounds noble but watch that sophistry.' Vendramin waves his hand as if brushing away flies. 'Your first allegiance is to God, to conscience, to do the right you see. He will not ask more than that. A brave man may repent a rash allegiance if his reasons are honourable. It is to God alone he must give account. Saint Francis disowned his own father before the bishop of this town, before his family and townsmen. He stripped himself of the very clothes on his back and gave them to his father before them all, and walked away naked. Francis needed something bigger than bolts of cloth and columns of coins, he needed to be consumed by something eternal. And you and I are the same Hugh, we cannot live for these small pleasures, these petty idolatries and blasphemies. If the whole world with all its riches and wisdom stand against Christ's words, then so much the worse for the world. I saw that my oath to the knights and the pope was not a true one. People say that if you have made your bed, then you should lie in it. But I say, that if my bed is fouled then I will wash my sheets and make it anew.'

'And them, us, your brothers in arms?'

'I do not condemn those who have not seen the things I have seen, but neither will I live and act day after day against my conscience. I condemn no one. Our founder's greeting was always, "May the Lord give you peace" and so that is my life now.'

'I see.'

'Do you know, the last miracle Francis performed was to reconcile the bishop and podesta of this town here of Assisi. So I curse no one. Instead I have spent my last years helping others find the peace that God alone can bestow. And isn't that what you want, Hugh? Isn't this why you came here to Assisi, the place where men come to learn what they once knew? Isn't it what you've been searching for all along?' Vendramin has strained his lungs to the end of the sentence, and now he bends forward in a series of ghastly coughs.

Hugh struggles up, shuffling forward on his knees. He shakes off his gauntlets and places his right arm round the convulsing figure. 'Stop, for God's sake! Stop. You have spoken enough. Yes, yes, of course it is peace with God that I have searched for—peace with myself, with the universe. I told you that already. Now rest, you fool. Stop talking.'

When Vendramin finally stops coughing, Hugh lays him back slowly on the pallet. He smells of old man's sweat and cankered wounds. He touches the monk's feverish brow with the back of his hand. 'You need a physician. You need to be in a warmer room. This place is damp; its miasmic.'

'No,' Vendramin croaks, and waves Hugh away with a feeble wrist. After a pause he says, 'When Francis was old he grew blind, was covered with sores and afflicted with malaria. The physicians used red hot irons to try to heal his eyes. Physicians! Poor man. He was the only one in Italy that could actually see.' Vendramin sighs and turns his head to Hugh. He raises a tentative hand, covered with fresh bandages and with it pats Hugh's cheek. 'I regret many things, and one is that I never fathered a son. No. No. Let me speak, Hugh. Let me speak. I suppose dying men have always said foolish things like this, but it is true.'

'Did Francis?'

'No, but *he* was a saint.' Vendramin attempts a feeble smile and the faintest wheeze of a laugh.

'And you are not? When you said I should be.'

'You will have more time, my lad, I hope.' Vendramin's grey eyes are fixed now and unblinking, his words no more than whispers. 'You know, Francis' last words were "I have done what is mine; may Christ teach you what is yours to do." That is what I pray for you my son: that you will find what is yours to do. God has a purpose for you in this world. Maybe you will take holy orders, I do not tell you what to do, but maybe you will. And if you do, remember the young poet of Emperor Frederick's court who renounced the world to follow Francis. Francis called him Pacificus. For a man looking for peace, as you are, it is a good name. So I mention it, but now I grow tired. We will talk anon.'

Vendramin turns his head away from Hugh and seems almost

immediately to be asleep. His breathing is laboured but regular, his chest rising and falling like the purring of the doves.

Hugh sinks back slowly onto his haunches, still kneeling. The lower edge of the harness digs into his thigh. The offer is there for him, he can sense it in the stillness and unemotional quiet of that upper room. The offer to unbuckle his armour. For the first time he feels the offer is not presented as a duty. It comes with neither threat nor promise—just the choice, and the knowledge that the effects either way will be incalculable. He may yet create a real future in this present moment by what he does, or does not do. It is momentous yet unemotional. His mind, for once, moves without the impulse of craven desire or clamorous fear. *Am I free to refuse? It doesn't seem like much of a choice that way. Am I really free at all?* Hugh glances at the back of his hands. He feels freer right now than he has ever been. Necessity may not be the antithesis of freedom after all. He gazes up toward the rafters and examines the dust particles illumined by the sharp afternoon light. He does not know if this is his real self or a mirage. But perhaps a man is most free when, instead of the endless manufacture of motives, he finally says, 'I am what I do.'

Hugh reaches up with his hands. Reaching up was what Vendramin told him to do in the tunnel. He fumbles with the shoulder strap, unfastens the worn leather from the buckle and eases the harness over his head. He places it on the bed behind him, surprised by how heavy it is, and how light he now feels. The wind gusts outside, and a dove's white feather blows in from under the shutter. It lands near Hugh, and like a child he picks it up. *La colomba della pace,* the dove of peace. 'Providence with irony,' he says quietly and then smiles. *Not exactly a bird in the hand, but it's a start.*

They do not speak properly again that evening of the things which Hugh wants so much to discuss. Time is a thief, each grain a reminder. Hugh stays long into the night, but the old man is growing too tired to engage. He has Hugh talk instead about Rhodes, or Venice, or England. But every time Hugh speaks for more than a minute or two the leprous friar starts snoring. And then, in the small hours, the old man –

stubborn old fool – asks to be laid on the floor in his blanket. It is in imitation of their founder, who had done the same. Paulo helps Hugh move him. He then seems tranquil, and resigned for what is to come, does Vendramin or Fra Francesco, whoever he is – God alone knows a man's name. Paulo even utters Francis' own words as each of them take one of the dying man's hands: 'In the end we must have nothing, except for Christ, who is enough for us.'

And then the remaining darkness passes as it did before, in cycles of awkward speech and sleep. His last words in Hugh's hearing, although it seems as if they are not spoken actually to him, are from Francis' most famous prayer. 'Lord give me true faith, certain hope and perfect love.' These words he repeats, as if to himself over and over, lips blue, breath and life ebbing like a slow tide over the saltmarshes of his native Veneto. After a minute Vendramin pauses and in the lull that follows Hugh asks him if there is anything he needs.

He simply replies. 'I am not afraid, Hugh.' And then after another long pause. 'But my feet are cold.' And then he starts reciting his prayer. Fra Paulo says that he will keep vigil. 'Go to bed, Hugh. I will wake you if there is any change.'

Hugh turns back one last time before descending the stairs. *Good Lord. There lies Marcantonio Vendramin, son of a doge and the most honoured knight of his generation. Europe will not see many like him in the next thousand years.*

The worn stairs creaked under Hugh's feet as he goes gently down for the last time. Still in his ears those whispered words as if they came from each stone. 'Lord give me true faith, certain hope, perfect love.'

Thus chivalry becomes romance, romance becomes poetry, and poetry prayer.

LETTER TO THE GRAND PRIORY OF THE KNIGHTS OF RHODES, ROME. 25TH DECEMBER

My dear Prior,

It is the season of Christ's epiphany, a time of rejoicing and a goodly reminder that redemption has come to the most unworthy of God's servants. I will not labour the allusion further, my good Prior, suffice to say what better time could there be for an unworthy servant to redeem himself in his master's eyes, too.

You have often bespoken yourself with boldness in my presence with regard to the divine power which guides the affairs of earth. You moneyed Florentines are alike in this weakness. You think heaven will fall in behind your pragmatism like a lackie. And I have oft chided and reminded you of your folly, and now look: at the end of all your failed schemes Erpingham is on his way south to Rome as I foretold. It is God's will. That is right. He returns to the city this very Christmastide and all your past failures can be undone, if only you do not fail this last time.

And mark you this, Prior, even your follies and unbelief have worked to achieve the divine will. For look, Erpingham has robed himself in honour while in the north. Yes, that is right, the Battle of the Po. It is not known as yet, but verily it shall be hereafter, that at Ferrara his actions were in large measure the whole cause of success in sinking the Venetian fleet. And my informant also tells me that he dealt with justice towards the duke's brother, Cardinal d'Este, for the dog that he is. For that scoundrel is no true prelate but a fiend drunk on the dark gods of the blood. Before my time is out, we shall have more of this judgement upon the corrupted hirelings, by God we shall.

But anon, Prior, to the immediate business. Erpingham left Ferrara in such haste that it can only mean one thing to my mind: Vendramin. He had privily been asking to see the portrait of that rascal given some years ago to the good duke, and it was only after seeing it that made he hence with great speed. What can that mean, except that he recognised the villain's face?

As I said all along, it is in Rome that he will eventually find his destiny. Be ready for him. He will bring us Medusa's head, by the immortal gods, andwe as Titans shall lay waste the earth. The sword and the spirit together. He my white knight, and I, his White Cardinal.

Be wary of that apostate Julius now more than ever and be ready to do your duty. The man who has brought this at such speed must be rewarded with ten ducats and lodging for one week. See to it therefore and execute your orders with faithfulness for I follow hard on his heels. Yours, etc.

NEW YEAR'S DAY, 1510 – ROME

Hugh hoped to enter the city privily, but the soldiers guarding the Porta Pinciana – earnest men – have his name written at the top of a long list of people Julius wants to see straightaway. Much to Bembo's chagrin a squad of four surly fellows are dispatched to see they do not get waylaid.

'I wanted to visit the baths,' Bembo says. ' God, I've been dreaming about it all the way down from Nazzano. We're hardly fit to see a padre, much less a pontiff. And I am chilled to the bone. Hey you, did you hear me? I want to visit the baths. Are you deaf?'

The captain, the only one of them to be mounted, does not bother to turn in his saddle as he leads them down from the Orsini church, *Santa Trinita del Monti*. 'Our orders are urgent; that is all I know.'

Hugh shrugs inwardly. *Does it matter?* He looks at the flat grey sky, which is letting forth a thin drizzle. He made the rendezvous with the others at Orvieto. Bembo has been in a state of irritation all the way down the long Tiber valley to Rome. Hugh won't tell him anything about Vendramin. What can he tell him that will benefit him and not endanger him? *What will I tell Julius? And does it matter now anyway?* Hugh is in a pious mood and has been since Assisi. Wilf has laid his harness out every day for travel, but he won't wear it. *Where has all this striving got me? Has it added one cubit to my height, or advanced the course of good in the world? Look at the birds; they do not reap or spin, or gather into barns.* Flocks of starlings chirp at them from the branches of maritime pines all the way down the hill. *Francis always said birds were children of the light. Look at the green of those pine needles. It is as if nature were attempting green for the first time.*

The captain leads them the direct route straight down the scrub bank in front of the church. Bembo says that the pope wants to have steps built here one day. The captain mutters that each successive pope since he was a boy has promised steps here. Hugh can spy a dust cloud across the rooftops. It is the new Saint Peter's. They are still shifting the rubble. To its right, Hugh shivers to see the Castel Sant'Angelo. *Screw things up with the pope today and that could be my new permanent residence.*

He turns in his saddle to point it out to Bembo, and as he does so his eye is drawn up the bank to the west. There, alongside the terrace wall of the Medici villa, is a small cavalcade, no more than six horses, and at their head is a man that bears a striking resemblance to the man on the bridge in Venice. The five riders sit upright in their saddles, their bearing military. They are soldiers, no doubt of that. They look straight forward without moving. They are under orders. But the man at their helm? He leans forward, resting his elbow on the horn of his saddle. Even at two hundred yards Hugh can see the same white goatee and shoulder length white hair. Is it the White Cardinal? For a secretive man he shows himself readily enough. *Has he followed me all the way from Venice?* Many times Hugh has sensed he is being watched. *Or perhaps he works for the Venetians, come to punish me for what I did there? Whoever he is, he must be a clever bugger to slip across the lines of battle.*

'What is it now?' Bembo says, reining his horse in tightly as its hind quarters slide on a muddy corner of the path. 'You turn round to tell me something, and then you gawp as if you've just seen a ghost. Spit it out. I am not in humour today.'

Hugh gestures with his head. 'It's them. Do you recognise him at the front?'

Bembo squints with disapproval as he turns. 'No idea. It's a popular viewing point. Perhaps he is a painter.'

'With five soldiers behind him?'

'Oh, well, perhaps a poet then.' Bembo gestures at their escort. 'It is quite the fashion for us to go everywhere these days under guard. We're dangerous men, you know.'

OUTSIDE THE STANZA APARTMENTS. MID-AFTERNOON.

Like everyone else, especially those who are urgently summoned, Hugh and Bembo have to wait for hours to be seen. The *comedia* of bureaucratic torment is overseen lovingly by the twin papal masters of ceremony: Johannes Burchard and Paris di Grassis. During the first hour it is the one, during the second it is the other, like a pair of garden birds feeding their young. When they open the intermediate doors and walk down the corridor to invite the next plaintiff, their persons exude the scents of rose water, amber and mirabolan. Hugh might take exception to the treatment if, firstly, he were not in such saintly humour; and secondly, if there were anything else he could do without causing a diplomatic incident; and thirdly, if he were not in such good company. It is like a meeting of old friends. The reluctant Venetian ambassador Girolamo Donato takes Hugh warmly by the arm.

'So you got out in one piece. It is well. It is well, my boy.'

'Have you been here long?'

'Long? I practically live in the corridor, on hand for a mauling at any moment. Dear Burchard has this special stool sent for me every day. I am practically part of the furniture. It sends the French ambassador into fits, but we can't help that. Not much we can do about the French.'

'I see,' Hugh says, staring apprehensively past the other ambassadors, who are keeping a healthy distance from Donato, toward the doors of the pope's new apartments. 'And His Holiness?'

'Ah.' The old Venetian smiles and retakes his stool. 'His Holiness has just been to mass, and that always makes him irascible, recalcitrant, obstreperous and worse. And to top it all, it is the feast of the circumcision.' Donato crosses his legs with a discomforting raised eyebrow. 'One begins to have sympathy with Jewish children. I don't think Julius will be happy until he has gelded Venice completely.

'So it does go badly for Venice then,' Hugh says.

'Yes, we have had some reverses in the Polesine and elsewhere.' Donato looks about to make sure that no one is within earshot. 'But the pope is driving for a treaty that Venice cannot abide. He wants so many towns back, so many thousand ducats in reparations for the army, before he will offer absolution to the senate and lift the interdict. I can see what will happen, Hugh. If you load the mule too high, you get no grain. The senate will make some promises, offer deferred payment, and then abscond at the earliest opportunity saying it was made under duress. I know them to a man. It is what they will do.'

'I see, so you must wait it out.'

'Yes, until I have authorisation. But it will not come quickly. And in the meantime I wait with my friends.' Donato gestures at the turned backs and raised winter fir collars. 'Ah, Hugh,' he sighs. 'If you really do follow the course of an ambassador – which I do not suggest for a minute – but if you do, I say, you will quickly learn that half the real business in Europe is done in corridors like this one. I suppose that is why they are called the corridors of power, not the thrown rooms.'

The architect Sangallo, who has been there since they arrived, is talking with Bembo – or rather being lectured by Bembo is full of disgust at the young know-nothings who, even here in the *Urbs Aeterna*, crave Tacitus and say they are no longer satisfied with Sallust and Livy.

Catching bits and pieces, Hugh hears Bembo congratulating Sangallo for his Ciceronian virtue, displayed supremely by such an active public life in the service of the state. This takes over ten minutes while poor old Sangallo is barely permitted to do more than stroke his turkey neck and look longingly at the stairs.

He is rescued when Michelangelo appears from the apartment *en route*, he tells them with a smile, to see Giuliano Leno the papal chamberlain to collect five hundred ducats. Poor man travelled all the way to Bologna last month to petition the pope for this payment. 'The chamberlain is a tight bastard. Bramante and Raphael get everything they want, but I have to chase the pope half way around Italy in mid-winter so that I have enough for me and Michi to buy the plaster and bread.' In his hands he carries the small cartoons of the creation of Adam. He unrolls them at Sangallo's request. God is shown in Zeus-like grandeur, leaning forward across his cloud, surrounded by cherubs and stretching his finger out. Adam, who to Hugh's eye is every bit as heroic as Michelangelo's David sculpture and very alike, reclines with his arm outstretched as if he were being offered a grape.

Powerful, they says, majestic, a bold new representation never before seen in Italy. They complement Michelangelo with murmurs and gasps of approval, and he offers to buy them a drink later if they will search him out. Sangallo encourages them to take him up on the offer. 'It's not often that Buonarotti is buying. Indeed, it is not often that he eats.'

As Hugh's eyes follow the two Florentine' heads descending the stairs, he sees the thick black tresses of the Madonna Felice Orsini, wife of the Lord of Bracciano. She is not ascending to the upper apartments of her father the pope, but rather talking to a servant at the bottom of the stairs on a lower corridor. Hugh, looks past Donato and observes her for a minute, her sage green silk gown, simply ornamented with panels of damask and a lace collar. She has the fullest lips of any highborn woman that he has seen north of the Mediterranean. On a woman less worthy they might be construed as common or licentious, but on her they bespeak a deep and tender passion. As Michelangelo approaches, she moves aside to let him pass, greeting him warmly. It is only then that her eye catches Hugh's with a mixture of surprise and delight. When she has bid the others *adieu*, Felice ascends the stairs with grace, and Hugh descends to greet her.

'Signora.'

'I am glad to see you, Fra Hugh, and to see you in health.'

They meet in the center, and he kisses an olive smooth hand, which smells of orange water and civet. Hugh steps back and apologises. 'Rude health, I am afraid. Your father's summons did not permit time to do more than remove my riding cloak and boots.'

'Hah, where my father is concerned, that is usually the case.' Her face changes from the peevish smile to a somber eyed seriousness. 'But that means that you have just returned from the north? Were you near Ferrara?'

'I was near enough, my lady.'

'And so you heard what the duke did? It is truly marvelous. My husband is quite enamored and wants to commission three new canon. Where we shall find the money, I do not know. I have just secured another grain contract with the good chamberlain, but that will hardly cover such an expense. But let us not discuss war now. Are you in town long? You will dine at Monte Giordano, I hope. My husband will be here for another week at least. And I know he will desire your company, as do I.'

'I should be honoured.'

But even as the words leave his mouth, Hugh hears the nasal announcement of Paris de Grassis. 'Erpingham. Erpingham of Rhodes.'

THE STANZA APARTMENT

Hugh is announced quietly, almost as an afterthought. Having done so, Burchard and de Grassis fall in reverential whispers in the left-hand corner of the room. Swallowing hard, Hugh can smell the plaster from Raphael's fresco of the school of Athens. The pope, face ashen like the winter skies, stands beside a central table overspread with maps, not for war, but for Saint Peter's. He does not look up. Angelo Colocci, the pigeon-chested, horse-headed secretary, is sneering at the plans from one side. The architect Bramante and Bishop Egidio da Viterbo are on the other. In the far corner, under the archway to a connecting room the private papal secretary, Sigismondo de Conti, is in deep converse with the banker Agostino Chigi. They are all spending the money they hope to get from Venice, and the tax revenues from the fiefs they hope to acquire. *Good luck to them.*

Eventually the pope drags his heavy knuckles from the plans and places them on his hips. He looks across at Hugh for a moment and then to the others, saying, 'Very well, we all know what we're doing. Good. Off with you. You too, Burchard; I'll ring if I need you. I want to speak with the English knight on my own.'

They file out only too willingly through two different doors. The pope sits heavily at a desk under the window, then turns the chair sideways in a series of unceremonious jerks. That done, he raises his right leg onto an upholstered stool, cursing old age and letting out a long sigh. He screws his nose up like a shrew and inhales deeply. All the while his sunken, hungry eyes remain fixed on Hugh. Julius then raises his hand slowly, and Hugh approaches to kiss the ring.

'Holiness,' Hugh says simply and stands back.

'Well?' the pope snaps, his grip suddenly tightening on the arms of his chair, his eyes kindling with anger. 'What of it? What have you been up to in Venice? I know what you've been up to in Ferrara by God – hear you bloodied the nose of that little shit of a cardinal.' His jowls crease with pleasure at the thought, then he adds, 'Don't worry; I can protect you from him. Mind, if you'd killed him that would be another matter. So, what have you found out for me?'

'I can only tell you what I told Cardinal d'Este.'

'Oh, he wanted to know about the gold as well, did he? I knew he had ambitions. He's a little shit that one, a shit in a silk stocking, and they're thick with the French, the d'Estes. So, what did you tell him?'

Hugh shrugs. 'That I made a search of the Vendramin Palazzo and warehouse, made enquiries.'

'And you found nothing.'

'Neither the gold nor any trace of him, the gold or the Greek Fire.'

'Pah.' Julius drives his palm onto the chair arm. 'Will you swear to it?'

'Upon the Holy Rood.'

'Would you now?' The pope rubs his ring on his top lip, and muses. 'Would you indeed?'

In the pause that follows, Hugh can feel the sweat break out on his back and brow. He has held the pope at arm's length for so long, trying to admire the tiger's stripes while avoiding its claws. He can no longer resist the inevitable. *If I tell him the whole truth, he will surely tear up every Franciscan friary from here to Paris.* Hugh feels his cheeks begin to blush crimson and his heart pound like a beast in his chest. *Why does he keep looking like that?* 'Your Holiness, I will swear to it. I found nothing in Venice and furthermore, I have no hope of finding either now. That is what I am going to say to my superiors. I have failed. That is what I will tell them.'

Julius lingers a moment more and then sighs. 'Well Erpingham, that is too bad. I know you tried for us, and by the looks of your face, you tried harder than most of my people do around here. Bloody laggards all.' He sighs wearily. 'And as things have turned out, we shall soon have enough ducats to cover the war anyway. Venice has come to her senses after the victory at Ferrara. Mind you—' The pope sucks in air in a whistle. 'I can't say that I am not disappointed. But let us not grumble, for as the saint said, "Holy poverty confounds cupidity and avarice and the cares of this world." Heard that before my son? No? It is Saint Francis.'

The air suddenly prickles around Hugh's ears. *What does he mean? Why is he looking like that? Does he know?* Hugh struggles to suppress the urge to run by squeezing his hands as tight as he can behind his back.

Eventually, after what seems like an age of staring, Hugh blurts out a guilty sounding. 'Holiness?'

'Hmm?' The pope's right eyebrow rises sharply. 'It was the Saint of Assisi, that's who it was. I suppose you know I started out as a Franciscan. It was my first vocation. Good people, the Franciscans. I think that if the reins of government had not been conferred on me, I would have been just as happy distributing alms among the poor. Do you know what I mean?' His eyes burn for a moment with an unfathomable fire. 'But each has his gift from God. You are a man of the sea. Of course, my people were fishermen, you know, and I'd have been happy with a fisherman's life too if I had not been called to holy simplicity. But there it is, each has his gift, and we should be grateful for small mercies. This war is finished, and perhaps we shall soon be arming ourselves to repel the eastern menace. I wouldn't call that a failure by any means. Would you?'

Hugh bows, a sense of palpable relief flooding his whole body and making all his muscles like fresh bread dough. 'Your Holiness is, as always, too kind.'

'Yes I am, and make sure you tell that to your magister.'

TAVERNA IL MAGNIFICO, TRASTAVERE, ROME. TWO HOURS LATER

The Florentine colony has only one real tavern for celebrating like this. The fact that good republicans have named it after Lorenzo de Medici shows a largeness of soul wholly consistent with the amount of wine they can consume when happy. They are on the corner of the *Via della Paglia*, a stone's throw from the basilica of Santa Maria, a church which was founded in the days of the church fathers. They have an excellent table near the fire, and the low ceiling is hung with pots and jugs matters little once you are seated. What a grand evening they are having.

Whatever Michelangelo orders in Trebiano, Jacopo Galli matches with earthen jugs of Greek wine Malmsey. Hugh sniffs his Malmsey cup in a state of near intoxicated bliss. It is redolent with the resins of maritime pines, and able to take him back to a hundred days as happy as this one before his capture by the Turks. They have feasted on boiled peacock. Then followed a Florentine specialty: jellies in the shape of little men and animals, which are made from almond milk, coloured with *zafferano* and scented with something that Hugh cannot divine, nor does he try, for part of the joy is in the mystery. He lets his eyes drift about the table with unadulterated wonder and delight. From Sangallo to Galli, Bembo to Donato. What an extraordinary mix one impromptu soiree can throw together. Galli, an octogenarian, remembers playing the *Pallioni* at the ball court with Piero de Medici – before the gout ruined his game – and also trading in Constantinople before it fell to the Turks. Opposite him is Girolamo Donato, the almost penniless ambassador of one of the world's wealthiest empires, who'd rather talk about cantatas than treaties, and who will probably make the best treaty that could have been made under the circumstances anyway. Next to him the old architect Sangallo has his hat off for once and is smoothing the few stray hairs over his otherwise bald head, listening with delight to the banter and repartee. And next to him is Buonarotti himself, surely the greatest painter as well as sculptor of his generation. He is still in thread worn woolens and still breaking off every now and then with his graveyard cough. No culture like Italy could create such contradictions and not see the joke. He relaxes his shoulders and leans back for a moment.

I am a rich man. Hugh repeats it to himself over and over. There is something so exhilarating for him to see friends assembled with wine in abundance. He feels right now a joy fit to bursting within him. Partially, no doubt, it is pure relief; he is off the hook with Julius, the Venetians, Cardinal d'Este and Vendramin even, but there is also something else which he cannot yet articulate fully.

His thoughts are broken as Sangallo toasts his shabby countryman for half finishing the Sistine Chapel ceiling. 'I thought that it would finish you off last winter. But now I see that this pope's ceiling will bring great glory to your name and to your beloved Florence. I salute you.' A moment later he salutes him again as *magnifico nostro carissimo* and kisses him tenderly on the cheek. Michelangelo cries a little and bashfully sends wine outside to his colour-grinder Michi, who is with Wilf, feasting on beef and watching the animals.

Hugh notices Jacopo Galli putting his fist to his mouth as if with hiccups. 'Are you all right, Signor Galli? Has the peacock given you indigestion?'

The old man recovers enough to say, 'No, no, don't worry about me, Hugh. If I get an attack of indigestion, I just have to think of those who are waiting to gain from my death, then I take courage out of sheer spite, and fortify myself with a celery stew.'

'You do very well, signor, for your age.'

'Well yes, quite, but in a dream, one is never eighty, Hugh. Every day is a gift; that is what I have learnt. And it is especially true at eighty. At my age I daren't even buy green figs, my boy. *Salute.*'

As Galli raises his goblet, Hugh receives a slight touch on the shoulder. 'Fra Hugh Erpingham? Do I have the privilege of addressing Fra Hugh Erpingham please?' He turns to see man of slender build in a black lawyer's robe and a scholar's black beret. His large nose and diminished chin gives him an unprepossessing air, but he seems friendly enough. Hugh does not refrain from acknowledging his identity and stands unsteadily to observe the usual formalities.

That done the secretary, or lawyer, or whatever he is, bows a second time and says, 'If it please you, signor, a lady wishes to speak to you in her carriage. She says it be to your advantage and only brief.'

'I see,' Hugh says, trying to sound sober and imagining Felice swooning for him in crinoline and damasks. 'I see, and...and who is this lady?'

'You can hardly expect a lady of my mistress' station to have her name spoken in a tavern. Please sir, come and do not delay.' More obsequious bowing.

Hugh looks back at the old man. Galli guffaws, his eyes twinkling with delight. 'That's the other thing, my friend. At my age you don't have to worry about avoiding temptation, it usually avoids you. Run along now, I'll keep your seat for you, and your reputation.'

Hugh excuses himself to the others and follows the little man to the door. He opens it and points onto the dark street where a carriage with fixed lamps is waiting. The man walks ahead in a straight line to the carriage, and Hugh attempts the same, finding it not so easy on the cobbles. He can see no insignia on the door and no one inside the doorway when he approaches. The little man holds the door wide open, and Hugh takes another step forward. To his horror the face of Prior Battista appears in the doorway. He is barely registering this new evil when his ear catches a tell-tale step behind him. The first cudgel blow fells him to his knees. Dazed and stupefied, he looks up at the prior.

'Welcome home, Hugh. As you advised, I brought more men this time, and as promised, this interview will be brief but only to your advantage, if you cooperate.'

A second blow to the head sends Hugh's face to the street. His cheek is ice cold and punctured with grit; his hair wet. His eyes stare stupefied at the horses' hooves before involuntary lids close, bringing darkness and oblivion.

GUEST OF THE PRIOR

Hugh awakes to find himself once more lying on a damp, stone floor. There is a smattering of straw about, some in his mouth. His face is wet with his own saliva, but other than a throbbing head, he finds himself unmolested. There is a strong odour of urine, partly his own, but he hasn't soiled his small clothes any other way yet, thank God. When he tries to stand however, Hugh feels the manacles on his right ankle. Fettered again. They chaff at the flesh of the anklebone. He tries with feverish, shaking fingers to move the shackle round a quarter turn so that the slightly wider portion near the bolt will ease the pressure but it makes little difference. *These are shackles for children surely. What is this place?* Hugh strains his eyes in the half light. A cellar of some sort, twenty feet square but double height with a small lancet window fifteen feet from the ground. No bucket, no table or stool and barely enough straw to keep a body off the cold flags. Hugh hugs himself, trying to rub some blood back into his limbs, that, and suppress the panic of demoniacal fear rising in his gut. Clank, clank. Fetters that bind and terrify. He holds still and strains his ears but cannot hear anything but the whistling wind. He tries to scale the wall to be near the light, but when he is only four feet off the ground the chain tightens, and he falls to the floor with a clatter that brings boots running. Hugh looks up as an oak door screeches open on rusty hinges. Two men enter, one with a sword, another with a flaming torch. Hugh's eyes grow wide with alarm as he sees white crosses on their surcoats. They are hospitalliers.

'The traitor is awake at last,' the first says. 'Get the prior.'

The second knight gives Hugh a boot to the face, then says, 'And you stay there while we fetch him.'

They close the door and leave Hugh to nurse his face and his worse fears. *Am I under the grand priory of Rome then? But the magister said that they had dealt with the prior, so how can he have a body of men still in the knights' livery? The Venice letter was in d'Amboise' hand and sealed with his seal. There is no doubt it was his writing so this doesn't make sense. Unless they have already taken the prior's side and were leading me into a trap. But I would have come if he had been ordered. My cheek bone, damn him. There is no need to treat me thus. I have kept troth. Have I not?* Hugh begins to see that since Assisi his loyalties have become, well, alloyed, nuanced, ambiguous even.

While he brings up reinforcements by way of counter arguments and one or two noble excuses, he also begins to hear other sounds above the beat of his heart. Footsteps. Light footsteps, not heavy like a soldier but shuffling like a septuagenarian – Prior Battista. Hugh braces himself. *I've done nothing wrong. Nothing wrong. Let him come.*

The door grinds open, screeching like the turn of a rack. Prior Battista steps into the cell, careful to sidestep some soiled straw. He is not wearing the surcoat of the knights, but an unadorned black woolen doublet with plain linen collar. His usually grey face shows pinkness in the cheek, and Hugh detects the odour of his sweat even when he is almost six feet away. *Is he afraid?* Hugh observes with silent disdain the prior arranging his face, clenching his fingers into fists, exhaling with irritation, and folding his arms in defense.

'So at last we are back where we started Hugh. No, don't speak. Don't say a word. Only answer me truly when I have finished what I have to say.' The prior licks his lips. His blue eyes have a fierce intensity, but they are shifting and unsteady in a way that tells Hugh all he needs to know. *Yes, he is afraid.*

'I am not angry with you. I bare you no ill will, no private malice, my boy. Rest assured. On the contrary, I admire you. I always admire men like you. First in the camp and forum and so forth; fight like Achilles; hunt like Diana. I admire that; I really do. Our order is built on that; Christendom relies on it. But it is not governed by it. Let us not fool ourselves on that count. Now, I, for example, am not a soldier's soldier like you. I know that. I'm no poet, no great courtier. My modest talents lie in the fields of governance and administration which, in their own quiet way, require a fortitude and tenacity not unworthy of – well, shall we say, not unworthy of many of the greatest men that have moved history onward. I have age and experience, Hugh, and with wisdom comes a foresight that cannot be expected of a man your age. So I say again, there is no private malice here, my boy, perhaps not even blame, but only an earnest desire to save you from yourself. Oh, don't look at me with such offence. Did you think I didn't know what would happen? Sending you after Vendramin, as the magister did? I told him, "Young men are too easily led astray. Young men are too easily tempted by ideals – like lambs before wolves. They do not understand the world." But the magister would not listen to me. He thought you would get results, and of course you have in a fashion. But d'Amboise did not know Vendramin personally, and I did. He is a persuasive fellow—cursed Venetians, a peculiar gift of theirs. He is one of those men whom weaker people follow for good or ill. I knew from the first look of you, Hugh, that you could not resist him. I saw again after your first meeting with him in Siena. It was not so much in your letter to Rhodes but in your face. I don't blame you. It was the magister's fault. But we cannot let that get in the way of what you and I know must happen. You must disclose what you are hiding from us. We must know the whereabouts of the gold.'

'We?' Hugh raises his eyes from the straw for a moment. 'Who is we? You don't mean the knights. You've been hand in glove with others; I know it. You turncoat, you Judas. I dare say they swarmed on you like flies the minute it was known that the navigator was coming to Rome on the Petronilla. I bet they promised you all sorts. Who was it—the pope, Petrucci, Cardinal d'Este, the White Cardinal? All of them? What villainy is this? And you have me chained and tell my brothers that I am the traitor.'

'Do not speak of what you cannot understand. Don't you dare forget your station, your oath.' The prior spreads his thin legs, planting two grey fists on his hips. 'How nice to have a mind so fine that no complex idea ever defiled it. Do you think there is only one way to serve the cause? Do you think that if you had all the gold right now loaded on one of our galleys, that Julius would allow you to embark for Rhodes? Don't be a simpleton, Hugh. My work here is to secure the knights' interests. I hold my position because I am trusted to know the situation in Italy and act accordingly. I do not flatter myself that I have some great reputation of my own to protect like you do, my young friend. What a curse it must be to have such a great name. What temptations you repulse at every hour. My actions are for the cause and not mere vainglory. Perhaps the great Hugh Erpingham cannot understand that.' The prior bends forward so that he can squint more satisfactorily at Hugh's face. 'Yes,' he says slowly. 'I know you. It is the bane of all you heroic types, the besetting sin: pride. You begin to think more of your opinion and reputation – your honour – than of twenty wise councilors. The serpent flatters and beguiles you until you cannot see the wood for the trees.'

'And you can?'

'Yes, indeed I can, and certainly more than you.' The prior straightens and folds his arms once more. 'The pope will not live long. All his supposed support for our crusade! Hah! What has he done but sow strife and penury within Christendom? He has the soul of a butcher, a merchant, a greedy moneygrubber, and not a prince.'

'Last year you said his intentions were honest.'

'Forget last year. Forget what I said. Forget what *he* says, only look unto his actions. The knights must look elsewhere for real succor, Hugh, not the dry paps of this pontiff. He is in poor health and will soon go to his reward. And we would do well to look to the future.'

'The White Cardinal?' Hugh says with a sigh of resignation.

'Like I say, you cannot be expected to understand how we do things here. This is Italy. But yes, the White Cardinal will be the next pope, and yes, you will tell me who your contact was in Assisi and where the gold is hidden. That way, when he arrives, I will be able to give him good news and also to plead successfully for your life to be spared.'

'I have no contact in Assisi, and I know nothing of the location of any gold. And even if I did, I wouldn't tell someone whose allegiance is more toward an ambitious prelate who thinks he can divine the future, than his own magister. No, I repeat, if I knew anything I would reserve it for a superior that I could trust. But, seeing I know nothing of help in any case, you will permit me to hold my peace.'

'I see, I see.' The prior moves towards a sideways stance. 'And that is your final answer. Hugh Erpingham, the great hero. Then I will tell you something, my boy. All nations and cultures like their heroes, they like the ideal, they like the comfort, they like the stories, but you perhaps will have noticed that the heroes they really like are all dead.' The prior sidesteps the fouled straw once again as he walks back to the open door. As he passes through, the prior casts words behind him. 'Think on that, my boy. A living dog is better than a dead lion. I can see that you do not know of whom you speak, or else you wouldn't have spoken as you did just now. But you will know soon enough – when he arrives.'

MADNESS, A WEEK LATER

'What day is it?' Hugh looks at the rat hanging near his head. The rat, however – mouth open with a vacant grimace – does not know the hour, and does not apologise for its ignorance. Hugh examines the wound on his ankle. The manacle is crusted with rust and blood. Toes blue. Skin grey and cold like marble. His mind is weary with sleepless delirium, and he is shrinking slowly into an inhuman stupor. He caught a rat yesterday evening. He felt it near his feet while half asleep. In that wandering state, he instinctively struck out with his bare feet and pinned it to the wall. Just as in the old days as a galley slave, all his nightmares have come true. He can hear his oar-companion Filcher's voice, his cynicism. *We are all rats; we eat, we shit and we die.* Being chained to him for weeks on end was like being chained to a cloven-footed devil. He voiced everything in your mind, and everything that would follow, too, if you had no restraint.

Hugh is not starving, but he killed the rat anyway. You never know when a rat will come in handy. It is best to leave them hanging for three days to let the skin loosen and tenderise the flesh and sinew – just like hanging game. He will eat its corpus in one go on Sunday when he hears the Eucharist bell at mass. Is Sunday tomorrow or the day after? He will be mad by then, or frozen to death. *Perhaps I am mad now.* He starts to sob at the thought. He sees people all the time. They come to him at night and speak to him. His mother, his sisters, even his brother Cecil came to him in the form of a beardless youth. And that is when he knew it was all wrong, for Cecil must now be much older than this phantom. *They cannot fool me. I am not so mad as they are – the prior and his people. Perhaps they are poisoning me – weakening me so that he will confess. I will not.* His father came to him last night. *God's oath.* No word of comfort he gave, only stood by the door with his arms folded and said that this was God's justice, that Hugh should be thus, for he had abandoned his family and not sought their honour. His mother was kinder, but said he should not eat rats for they are unclean. His sisters would have kissed him tenderly, only when they came near they drew back for he had soiled his hose. *I am abandoned truly. I am a leper. I am forsaken – a worm and no man.*

Succor comes from a strange quarter on Sunday evening: the grand prior appears with two soldiers in the dark. They pin Hugh against the wall while the prior interrogates him. They have found the letter in the lining of his doublet—the last communication he had from Vittoria. He kept it close to his person yet never replied, uncertain as he was as to what to answer. The prior, by some stroke of insane genius and want of other evidence, has decided that the letter is part of a secret code between conspirators. The smell of wine is suddenly strong in the cell. The three men seem even to Hugh to be overly confident, overly rough and overly stupid after some long bout at the table.

'Come on, Hugh,' the prior slurs. 'We both know that there is more going on Ischia than just parties and poetry. The duchess almost told you as much when we were both there that autumn. She and Vendramin were friends. The gold was stored for a time nearby in that cave. What am I now to make of this when I find you've been in correspondence with her, eh? When I find these carefully crafted letters, full of veiled religious references? What's a sane man to make of that, eh?'

Hugh can't resist a faint guffaw, for even in the state he is in, he cannot help appreciating the delicious irony of the prior struggling over words as he himself had, but for different reasons. 'We make of things what we want,' is his simple reply, for which he receives a fist in the belly.

'I expect you to cooperate with me, Hugh.' The prior slumps his shoulders against the opposite wall so roughly that wax from the light spills onto his hand. He curses, then resumes. 'I know that you will. I can get you food and wine within the hour if you help me.'

Hugh looks up from his doubled up posture and sees the old goat holding that precious paper before the flame of his candle. He cannot answer for the wind has gone from him. If it were not for these two other brutes, he knows he could not stand for a moment. His wretched mouth slavers at the mention of food. Food within his grasp even. *I won't betray my soul for food again. God let me die rather than do that. Vendramin said I would do the right thing. How can I? What slender threads hold me now?*

The prior continues with the letter. 'Let me see, Signorina Colonna – though doubtless that artful duchess – writes, "Sometimes our thoughts are bent on the Great Son." Now what is that, "the Great Son", but the gold? She's reassuring you perhaps, that she knows you're after it. "Upon the cross, by faith inspired, whence light, calm and serene, streams down in radiance bright, leading them glorious to the Almighty's throne." All right, but what is all this reference to light and the Almighty's throne?

Is this about the new location? Somewhere bright with learning or piety perhaps? Somewhere ecclesiastical or some university? "The Almighty's throne" – a bishop's seat maybe? A vice-chancellor of some university's chair – a cellar under it? Or even – or even – under the pope's throne – in the crypt of that stupid basilica Bramante is building? That would be just like that Vendramin, to hide it all in plain sight, just so that he could thumb his nose at us. Well? Or is this all some acrostic code?'

'You are an ass, Prior. That is all anyone can say. A stupid, drunken ass.'

Hugh doesn't see the fist that sucker-punches his head against the wall. But all of a sudden his head is swimming airless and detached almost from his body. He cannot focus on the prior's light – it shifts and blurs. His thoughts wander. It is a mercy that this has happened; that these words have been brought from across the divide of time and space to his attention just now, now when he is sinking. Vittoria's words he had committed to memory and mulled over often. Why had his memory not brought these words to him sooner? Why has it taken his torturer to do it? How does it go? Duh-duh, duh-duh, something, something; 'light, calm and serene, streams down in radiance bright, leading them glorious to th' Almighty's throne.'

> Now in the faithful soul, this favour done
> Will cause no pride to dwell, who has in fight
> Prevailed, putting the world and self to flight
> But all the honour gives to God alone.

He is aware of more blows and a shouting ferment of drunken brutes battering against his head and ribs. But they cannot get in now because he is losing consciousness anyway. *In fight prevailed. No pride to dwell in the faithful soul. Put the world and the self to flight.*

The iron taste of blood. Darkness.

ANOTHER WEEK LATER

'Good morning, Hugh.'

A pleasant voice calls Hugh out of a fitful slumber. He is huddled in his corner like a beaten dog. It is another chill, blue dawn and the frost is visible on the mullions and stonework inside his cell. At first he does not see that the door is open, but when he finally does, the figure of a man is standing in a grey riding cloak among the shadows of the cell's corner. *Is this another trick? Is it my father come to chide me again? I don't want him; I want my mother. No, no, I do want him. I want to say that I am sorry. I want to tell him that he was right. I had no business to leave Norfolk. I shall return to my father and say father, I have sinned against heaven and in your sight. Will that be good enough for him?*

'I said, good morning.' The shadow does not move, but the words cut through Hugh's rambling thoughts. There is something in the Toscana of that voice that suddenly reminds him of the syntax of Urbino. It is like when the painter Raphael speaks – always missing the middle of the word out. *Perhaps it is not a phantom after all.*

Hugh tries to shift his position, but his hip feels like lead. 'Who are you?' Is it the mysterious man he saw in Venice on the bridge, then at the *Arsenale* and then again more recently under the Medici palace wall in Rome? Hugh moves his head to examine the silhouette, but he can divine not one thing because of the large beret that flops to the right obscuring the total form.

'A friend, I hope. I have had business in the north, but have come as soon as I could. My boots, as you see, are fresh from the road.'

Hugh squints, and can see the mud on the black leather and on the fringes of the cloak. He has ridden.

'Why?'

'To see you. I was greatly desirous to converse with you.' No movement, but Hugh knows that he has heard this voice before.

'I am in agony here. I am in agony. I do not want to talk to anybody, only to make peace with my father. You are not my father. You are another phantom.' Hugh hunches his shoulders and retreats further into his cocoon of wool, where the smell of straw and urine greet him like familiar friends.

'No, my friend, I am quite real as you shall see.'

Hugh looks up again, as if for the first time realizing that he is not actually dreaming the whole thing. 'Are you the White Cardinal?'

'Some call me that. You looked surprised. Did you expect me to wear a white cloak perhaps?'

'Yes,' Hugh croaks, almost laughing at himself for his idiocy and coming to himself quicker and quicker. 'And horns.'

'Horns!' The shadow exhales with an almost imperceptible guffaw. 'I'm sure you already know, Hugh, that not even the devil is quite as black as he is painted.'

'Are you a real cardinal?'

'Oh yes, quite real. I have been a cardinal for many, many years. I was also the Chamberlain of Pope Alexander. Does that ring any bells?'

'Oh.' Hugh's half frozen and stultified mind grinds into gear. The chamberlain was the Borgia pope's closest confidant. He would have known about the shipment of gold. He was there on the night the pope and Cesar Borgia fell sick. *What was his name? I can't remember. Damn this cold.* While Hugh is trying to remember the name, and failing, a second thought crashes into his mind unannounced. He blurts out. 'You poisoned them. Both of them, didn't you?'

'Very good. Yes, I did. In my defense, they were monsters, both of them, and I had watched them – assisted them to – grow worse. Alexander...he had grown tired of me. When a man has sunk into a life of vice and lies, he will abide less and less the voice of one who speaks the truth. He was preparing to do away with me, as he had done others. He wanted my Palazzo Giraud most particularly. Bramante had done too good a job for me as architect, and I could see the pope's eyes more and more pleased with the place every time he visited. But I want you to know, especially you, Hugh, that I, like noble Brutus, did not rise against my master out of private malice or for base motives of self-preservation. I racked my conscience at every point, more than Marcus Aurelius even, and wrestled at every turn over what a virtuous man in my position of responsibility should do. I have risen from very humble beginnings, you know. I am thankful too. Cicero says that gratitude is not only the greatest of the virtues, but also the parent of all. To be as I am now is more than my parents could ever have hoped or dreamed. God in his wisdom and mercy willed it. I had no eye for Peter's seat except for two converging stars. First, I saw how easily a base man could fill it and then what carnage he could wreak. And second that a soothsayer once prophesied before many reliable witnesses that a man of mean birth and great wisdom called Adriano would one day wear the papal tiara.'

Hugh observes the cardinal caressing his own hands as his shadow peels from the wall and approaches the centre of the room in two slow steps. He crouches in a pool of sharp winter light, resting one hand clad in a calfskin riding glove on the bare stone to aid his balance. Hugh stares for a moment at the sharp nose, cheekbones and chin; the thin, over-stretched skin; the piercing blue eyes.

'Cardinal Adriano de Corneto.'

'Have you only just guessed? You surprise me, Hugh. When you happened upon me in Venice, I feared that perhaps you were already onto me, but obviously you are far behind the plot. Dear me Hugh, and to think I took such precautions to hide myself from you.'

But Hugh hardly hears, for he is suddenly breathless with astonishment. A disinterested, scholarly ecclesiastic! To think he had been imagining the White Cardinal to be one more monster worse than the last. But a cultured prelate, whose sympathies have been tempered by the richest learning – whose intentions were well-meaning? *Good God, what is the world coming to? Even the angels are carrying pitchforks these days.*

But hard upon this revelation comes yet another. A searing pang of self-knowledge and accusation come swift as a bolt: *who am I to talk, to accuse? God's oath! The road to Hell is paved with good intentions after all, aye and blood. The best of us have become the most devils, and being self-deceived are as Dante's condemned men, who all purposed great things and got their own way.*

'My God, why?' Hugh whispers, shrinking further within himself and, at this point, thinking more about the state of his own soul than anything else.

'I tell you God's truth, Hugh. I would not have begun to follow the course I have without that divine prompt – the prophecy Hugh, the prophecy. God wills it – that I should be pope, but as I said, I need a second self.'

'Oh, Cardinal,' Hugh says, his eyes shut and his mouth hanging open in a wince of pain. 'You quote Cicero to me. I seem to remember he also believed fidelity more venerable than you seem to have done.'

'Fidelity *and truth*, I think, was actually what he wrote. You cannot have one without the other or where would we all be? I said before *the devil is not as black as he is painted*, and perhaps even Rodrigo Borgia had some amiable qualities. But as time went on, I also saw what he became, and moreover, what he would become thereafter. I learned what he and Cesare ware plotting – to unite the sacred and secular powers. How could I know of this treachery towards Christ and his church, and do nothing? You see that don't you? With the arrival of the gold from the New World, he would have been unstoppable in his plans. What would you have done? I did what I could never have imagined myself ever doing: I invited them both together to my villa and served them a little more than just oysters.'

'But you were poisoned too? That is what someone told me.'

'I pretended to be ill. It is ridiculously easy when you know which of your servants is the Borgia's spy. You just make sure that he sees and hears only what you want him to. They congratulate themselves as being something so special, these schemers but really, a child could outwit them if he had the neck for it, or was bored enough.'

'But Cesare didn't die.'

'What can I say? It was my first poisoning. I am an accomplished churchman and scholar, but a *gentleman-amateur* with the Eternity powder. It is perhaps the least of my faults. And anyway, the action was an eventual success and I have kept my anonymity too – for one cannot be a successful poisoner and a famous one, you understand.'

'And Vendramin?'

'What of him?' The White Cardinal shrugs with nonchalance, but there is nothing casual in the tone of the reply

'Did you confide in him?'

'No, Hugh, I did not. But I did try afterwards to bring him to my cause, as it were.' The voice is distant, as if distracted. He changes his footing, and Hugh sees his head tilt upward in thought. When he speaks again, it is as a scholar teasing out a theorem in lyrical and reaching sentences. 'He is such an intriguing fellow, that man. Many of his generation were, you know. I suppose he is to my generation what I am to you. I truly believed that I could find in him what I ask of you today. But he would not parley. I suspected he did not trust me, which was very wrong of him. Things might have been different; he and I might have represented admirably that great tension between the Latin tradition of domination and the Hebraic tradition of protest. I, the former, he, the latter. The Aurelius in me would have been countered admirably by the Jeremiah in him, but now we shall never know. He disappeared, and soon everyone – every vile character in Italy – came forth from the woodwork in search of him.'

'Petrucci.'

'Yes, and Don Michelle – or Michelotto, whatever he was called, a murderous villain, and Cardinal d'Este, and Julius – all men of the basest character. They acted each according to their nature; the average mind of Petrucci, by experience; the dull mind of you knights, and Julius and d'Este, by necessity; and the base mind of Michelotto by brute instinct and animal cunning. What could I do? Cicero says the wise should be instructed not by necessity, experience or instinct, but by wisdom. I was a peaceable ecclesiastic, a scholar, a man of letters. I came to Rome as Plotinus came to Rome from his studies in Alexandria, 'in fear and trembling, not revealing the humble origins of my former life.' And there they all were, steeped in villainy and blood from their youth. They had led armies and waged great campaigns, but me? *Niente, niente*. Oh, the monotony and banality of evil, Hugh, these men and their base ambitions. Often, I wondered they did not tire of it. So,

I bided my time, and studied, and prayed – of course, I prayed a great deal. And while I prayed, then I remembered the house of my parents and the little loft where my brothers and I slept on pallets. Don't let me bore you, but do indulge me a little, Hugh.

In those years, and in our country there were ever so many spiders, so many you would not believe. They hatched in April, and they were so tiny on the walls, along the roof beams. No matter how many times we swept those beams there were always more. It was truly amazing. One year, when one brother had gone to Padua to study and another had gone to London to his guild, I was left alone and could not reach the ridge beam because I was not so tall as they. So, what do you think? Instead of clearing the highest beam I watched them. And soon I realized that to sweep everywhere was unnecessary because in time the flies became too few and the big spider in the corner – perhaps the parent, I don't know – but the biggest spider would eat up the others anyway. So, of late, I said to myself, I will learn from the spiders, I will not run around Italy revealing my intentions again, but wait until the spiders have eaten themselves and there is just one left. And then I will see what can be done with that last big spider. To fight on one front is better than to fight on two or three fronts, you will agree. And so here we are today.'

The Cardinal pauses for breath, perhaps expecting applause.

'Oh, good for you.' Hugh says, closing his eyes and grimacing. 'You let me and Vendrammin do your dirty work. Didn't want to dirty your own hands.'

'Is that really wrong? You know, Hugh, there was once a Burgundian prince called Conrad at the turn of the great millennium. A good and wise ruler who was beset by two enemies who came to attack him at the same moment. One was the Magyars and the other, the Saracens. But he had not the strength to meet either, so what do you think he did? I will tell you. He sent envoys to both asking for assistance against the other. Genius, pure genius. And then he sat back as they tore each other asunder, only entering the field finally himself to clear away the remnants of the two armies. But the strangest part is how foolishly historians remember him. They call him Konrad der Friedfertiger or Conrad Pacificus, the unwarlike, gutless. But Pacificus is a fine appellation for a ruler if he is as wise as that prince. I should not mind it myself. Would not you, too?'

'I...' Hugh's mind stumbles over the name Pacificus, for he has heard it recently and in it he senses something momentous that he cannot divine. 'What? Yes. But were we not talking about spiders? Were you not about to say that we knights are the final big spider on the beam, or something like?'

'The knights! Oh no, Hugh, not the knights, for they are history in any case. You, my friend, are that last spider. You are the only one who has seen Vendramin, and no other spider on the beam has been able to eat you up, and get from you that information. That is good. I knew that I chose wisely when I took the prior under my wing. You knights have such – what shall I call it – such an independence and sense of honour. And this I admire. Brings one so much in mind of the marshal vigor of Pompey and the Scipios. Truly, I believe that the reason we don't have such great men these days is because we are always looking for them. We have studied greatness as if it were literature, or philosophy, and have ensured that, in our own case at least, by merely studying, there shall be one less great man on earth. We have become fools. I truly believe that, don't you? Diogenes searched with a lantern for an honest man in every crypt and cave, but he never looked inside himself. I dare say he was not that honest. But Christ looked inside the thief on the cross and promised to elevate him to a seat in paradise. And that is, in effect what I am offering you, Hugh—not paradise by any means, but elevation, a seat of power and so forth. I am not looking for saints-absolute, Hugh. I know enough of this world to see that all men have a past. The knights seem to produce a certain sort.'

'Did you offer them a share in the gold for their defenses?'

'What?' The cardinal sniffs. 'What can I say?' More sniffs. 'The first man gets the oyster, the second, the shell. *Questa è la vita,* that's life.'

'And did our prior gain permission from the Magister to make such a deal?'

'Our negotiations have been delicate. But a man who robs Peter – so to speak – to pay Paul will always have Paul's support – only in this instant Paul should be aware that the intermediary alone has the power to apportion shares. I tell you all this because I know you can see past the pettiness of individual interests. What matters to men like you and me is the future of Christendom.'

'I am not sure d'Amboise will see it like that.'

The cardinal's voice suddenly flares up. 'Damn d'Amboise, what do I care? He's a bloody Frenchman for God's sake. Will he bring stability to Christendom? *Dio Mio*, his own brother at the head of a French army is more menace to us here than any Turkish fleet. The knights are an anachronism. How long will you hold out on your little island against an empire that size? You are a remedy worse than the disease. In fact, you make more problems than you solve. Why antagonize them? What is the point? Let them have their end of the Mediterranean, and we will have ours. Rhodes' fall is inevitable. I would rather have the knights in a more strategic position and not pour money into defending the indefensible. You cannot live in the past; that was Vendramin's mistake. He could not see time's great river moving forward with progress at the helm, but rather the broken pieces of paradise – some past utopia – floating by him. It is no way to live. I am sorry, my friend, but these are mere facts, indisputable. Venice is our best defence against the Turks. If Venice falls and is dismembered, the balance of naval power in the Mediterranean will inexorably tilt in the sultan's favour. Her defeat by Ferrara came too close. The loss of galleys was a blow to all Christendom, not just Venice. Doge Loredan would have sought terms while he still had the strength of Pitigliano as gonfalonier, so Pitigliano had to be taken care of, permanently, for everybody's sake. It was regrettable. But, as they say, an unjust peace is better than a just war.'

'So I have heard.' Hugh observes the cardinal's heaving and uneven sigh. *He is rankled, alright. And he seems to fit his new role as well as Rodrigo Borgia or Cesare ever did. Even sounds like them. Same depredations, same justifications, though this time Pro Fides*

The cardinal glances sideway, pursing his lip and then returns more apologetically. 'I am sorry. You make me say too much perhaps. But I feel I can talk with you as an equal, and that is as it should be. I have become diverted from my original intention to tell you how I came here. How I, a man of peace and learning, have outlasted the plotters and schemers and villains and all the mighty of Italy in pursuit of this treasure. They all thought that history would be on their side. Just a few more mercenaries, a few more ducats, a few more bribes. Fools. All of them, fools. History cannot supply the key to its own meaning. The human mind can barely cope with organizing its own affairs looking forward, much less bring the little god of Reason to arrange the past according to its will. I believe God has acted – through the words of this soothsayer and many providences small and great – to raise me to Peter's chair.'

'By killing a father and son who came to your table. The shadow of Cain falls even on the palace of Princes.'

'Oh Hugh, please!' The cardinal now attempts to speak with the ease of *noblesse oblige*. Under it though, Hugh detects a hardness and a man on guard. 'This is an uneven handed game you play. The scriptures say that Cain killed Abel because his own deeds were evil, whereas in my case, I was Abel killing Cain because of his evil deeds. There is all the difference in the world. I am sure you have killed with far less pretext. In fact, I know you have. I killed for Christendom, no less than you. I killed the Spaniard before he killed me; it was practically self-defense. As we say in Rome; *cosa fatta e fatta*, a dead man never makes war.'

Hugh shakes his head. Words, words. Then he whispers with deliberate pauses between the syllables. '*Et tu Brute*.'

'Me? Another Brutus?' He chuckles. 'I do not deny it. And I am not ashamed either. Why should I be?' The cardinal's head stirs slightly and then sways in a sort of bobbing motion that minds Hugh that he is being closely scrutinized. 'And I must have a Cassius in days like these, Hugh – a *second self*. I have been watching your progress through Italy very carefully. You impress me, impress me deeply: your noble sentiments, your learning, your piety – your valor. Of course, your valor. My informants are many, and I have paid much for every morsel of news of your movements and conversation, so that I may know you truly, and may bring you to my side.'

'Bembo? Is he an informant against me, too?'

'Yes, of course, but not in the way you mean it. He has repeated, quite innocently, the things that you have said and done to others, and they have repeated them to me for a small consideration. And that is how I know that we are very alike, that we value the same things: virtue, civility, learning, *les beaux arts.* The papacy has rested between whoremongers like Borgia and warmongers like Julius for too long, Hugh. Do not impugn Bembo; do not think it. He has been a good friend to you, and you have wrought wonderfully on him. I see that now. He is a changed man because of his association with you. And it is people like him, people with learning, with culture, with *sprezzatura*, who should be cardinals – and not these barbarian sons of the wealthy – these Medici, Orsini and Colonna. I have tried to advise Julius, but as the sage said, *advice to the aged is futile, for why burden a traveler with provisions when he is reaching his journey's end?* What good is it to change the cork when the wine has gone sour, Hugh? The vinegar of the Borgia, the della Rovere and their sort has set Europe's teeth on edge. We need new wine and new wineskins as Our Lord has rightly said. Julius has driven me away like a leper. I am only in Rome now in disguise. But I had to see you, for this concerns all our futures, and the future of Christendom.'

'Me? No, do not speak to me thus.' Hugh says, turning his head aside and hunching even more as if wounded.

'Are you affrighted, my son? You look stricken.' The cardinal stretches forth a reassuring hand. 'You remember me now, don't you? I was at that little soiree at the Casa d'Oro, and then again at the doge's palace talking with poor Pitigliano. They have entered him with the doges. Look at me, Hugh. Look at me. The church has become corrupt from the inside, and providence has offered us a way out. When I am pope, I will strengthen the Conciliar movement by populating the Curia with the best sort of men – not those rotund, chinless prelates who've been bred on peaches and the *realpolitik* – but real men of learning and sentiment: humanists like you, Bembo, Castiglione, Erasmus, Ariosto; men whose worth is always overlooked by the pompous princelings of the *Magna Curia*. Dante saw it, the church is the best hope Christendom has for unity, order, *sistemazione*. No more succession rivalries between the old families, but a guardian stock of Christian humanists dedicated to virtue, to learning and the arts.'

'Benedict and Calixtus XI said they would relinquish power but did not.'

'Hugh, Hugh!' The cardinal pleads, reaching out an open hand and almost touching him, 'Do you not think I know all this? Do you not think I do not know the corrupting nature of the power I seek? Can you not see that is why I need you, a second Cassius, a man to challenge me where I am weak – to keep me on a steady course. I will make you a cardinal and gonfalonier of the papal forces even, and together we will make such changes in Christendom that all history will remember us.'

Hugh does not realise his mouth is hanging open until he begins to jabber. 'What? Me?'

'Of course, you. No one will remember Julius, though he thinks he strides across the earth like a colossus. History will not remember him, but it will remember Michelangelo, and Ariosto, and Raphael if I have my way. Men forget their diseases and remember their remedies. They remember the day they first held their newborn sons. Such will be the dawning of our day, Hugh. And history will remember us, because you and I will carry out such reforms in education and the common-weal, schools, hospitals, universities; we will be patrons of such verse, commission such buildings, frescoes, and sculptures that all the world will marvel and ever after look back to us in wonder and gratitude. It will be hard to remake this cankered hulk into a great civilization – perhaps it would be easier to start over among the barbarian nations – but it is not impossible. I suppose you know that Michelangelo for many years saw that great lump of mouldy and deeply veined marble outside the municipal workshops. It seemed no one could do anything with it until he saw David within its form. That is what I am talking about; can you see that? We must dare to hope. We must have faith in the divine will, the divine power, Hugh. By God's grace we can be the change Christendom yearns for. We shall make peace throughout the west. We will harness the New Devotion north of the Alps with the New Learning here in the south.'

'And you do not think that the latter will swallow the former? That the clamorous pagan and epicurean elements of this new humanism will overspread and eat up the quiet piety of the saints?'

'Perhaps, I am not a fool Hugh. Perhaps it will if good men do nothing. And that is precisely why we have this moment to act. It will be a new golden age, I tell you.' He pauses then adds as an afterthought. 'If, if God allows. And verily I say that God wills it. What say you? Come, Hugh, imagine, just imagine, you will treat with kings and emperors. Do not be daunted by the task. I believe you are equal to it, indeed, have been set apart for it. Come man, think how large your world will be.'

'I think my world would be large enough, Your Grace, if I could only become smaller in it.' Hugh breaks the cardinal's implacable stare, and lowers his own to the floor where the rat's skull stares back at him through empty sockets. *Momento mori, Hugh, momento mori.*

There is some noise of disturbance far away along the corridor and up the stairs. It's a little early for shouting. *Perhaps someone has tripped up with the piss pots. Perhaps this offer is all piss and vinegar, too.* Hugh looks up once more. 'Would you offer me this if there were no gold?'

'Gold and Greek Fire, Hugh. Don't forget the Greek Fire – for lamentable as it is, the Greek Fire is essential, too.'

'But would you?'

Cardinal Adriano pauses. 'Of course, of course.' He repeats unnecessarily. 'But, but you understand how necessary they are: fire and gold, power and money. This whole world has gone mad with the abuse of them. It is time to put that right.'

'I do not know where they are. And I do not wish to know. If God truly wishes you to be a good pope, he will not need your money or anyone else's.'

'Hugh, I interrupt you and apologise. I do. I do.' The cardinal pivots on his haunches and straightens out his fingers toward Hugh, as if he were presenting a small box. His words become rapid, spiraling forth with a barely contained fever. 'I don't want you to say any more. I don't want you to commit yourself one way or the other. I have laid too much on you too fast. Forgive me, dear friend, but I have been rehearsing this conversation for so long. I have rushed ahead when you are tired, and cold, and hungry. That idiot prior has mistreated you. Let us remedy that first, eh? Give time for all this to sink in. I am tired from a long journey, too. Let us break bread, attend mass.'

'It is no use, Cardinal. My mind is already set. I have told you all I know.'

'But it is not the truth, not the whole truth anyway. Perhaps you have renounced the use of the Greek Fire. It is a weapon *sui generis*, diabolical. But that is why you are precisely the one who should wield it – because you renounced it – because you passed the test. You alone can be trusted. Can you not see that? You've been set apart, I say.'

'Trusted? I do not trust myself, Cardinal, and I doubt you even trust me enough to release my bonds. No, I think you have underestimated the power of power, to corrupt, to beguile. Tertullian was right: *nothing of God's may be purchased with gold.* If the meek really are to inherit the earth, I cannot think they will do it with Greek Fire and ducats. In any case, I have nothing to offer you.'

'You don't mean that, Hugh; you don't. This, this, this is Vendramin.' At the word *Vendramin* the cardinal's hands clench tight shut into trembling fists, and his face twists with rage. 'He has poisoned you. I knew it. Obdurate pride. He has poisoned you. I saw it in your eyes from the first. It's that villain.'

'Vendramin is dead.' Hugh bristles, and looks away. 'But you are right he did warn me not to entrust myself to you, nor will I for all the gold in Cathay.'

'So, you will abdicate responsibility to take your part in this world?'

'No, I did not say that, Your Grace, but I do say that I will not take *your* part in it. I answer you as Bishop Antonino answered those who would have made him a cardinal, "*I could not do it without peril to my own soul.*" And really, that is the politest way I could put it. Maybe you should take his example, too.'

The cardinal stands, his brow hardened, his face set like flint, voice brittle. 'And so, you will force me to be a barbarian and have you tortured as if I were a Thracian peasant like Maximinus. You force me to do this, even after all I have just shared with you? You would make me play the tyrant?'

'Play? You are already a tyrant without knowing it.' Hugh speaks slowly and with a pathetic resignation. He doubts he has the strength to reach the cardinal's throat, and even so, what would he do then? He is chained to a wall. The cardinal won't have a key. And even if Hugh should escape, then what? Fall into the hands of the next covetous villain, the next maniac prelate? *Let him do his worst,* Hugh thinks. *I'll hold up against him out of spite; force him to see what a monster he really is under all that Cicero and Bologna silk. I am ready to die. God knows where I am if he wants me. A man can't run forever.*

Suddenly though, as the words complete their circuit around his mind, Hugh hears the steps of someone running down the long corridor toward his cell. As the footsteps grow louder, a heaving broad-chinned man appears in the doorway.

'You must fly, Your Grace. We are discovered.'

'Fly? What?' the cardinal says imperiously. He looks down at the man's bleeding hand. 'Good God, what has happened to you? Discovered, you say. Is it the pope? Is he here?'

'No, it is the prior of Rhodes,' the man gasps, holding his hand and glancing back down the corridor. 'His men are killing without quarter.'

'The prior? Our prior?' the cardinal says, aghast. 'I don't believe you.'

'No, Prior Battista is slain. It is the Grand Prior from Rhodes, de Blanchfort and his men. Quickly please.'

'De Blanchfort! Here?'

'Your Grace, we must fly now while there is time. There is a way out from the cellars – the others are waiting, but we must go now.'

The cardinal casts a baleful eye about the cell and then at Hugh. Hugh almost feels sorry for him. *Fortuna is such a bitch. Machiavelli says she favours young men. It will be hard for a man who has been shown such condescension from the king of England to find himself on the wrong end of de Blanchfort's sword. Perhaps Plato's guardian stock under the patronage of Cardinal Adriano will not preside over a golden age after all. Probably for the best.*

'Damnation.' The cardinal slams his right palm hard against the door. 'How can this be? And now of all times?' He paces left and then right across the cell, shaking his head and fists. 'Very well, it is as it is. Your mind is made up, Erpingham?'

'It is.'

'Very well, I give up.' He turns to the injured soldier. 'Kill him and follow me.'

The cardinal storms out leaving the broad-chinned man staring at Hugh from the doorway. Something strange shines in his eyes. He looks stunned. Is it the wound, the order, or something else? Hugh braces the muscles of his chest and stomach. As he has done to many, so will it be now to him. It is just. And in his mind rises the possibility of some small merit in dying for keeping secret the location of the gold and Greek Fire. The man comes within blade's reach. He holds forth his cross hilt with a trembling hand. His eyes are wide, trembling and strange. Hugh feels his stomach churn, his strength melt like snow before a fire.

The blade comes level. He closes his eyes.

But then he hears the man say, 'I know you. You are the knight. He just said your name. You are the one.' Hugh glances up, unbelieving. The man's is face is lined with anxiety and wide-eyed with fear, shudders. 'Do you not remember me, uh, Gabriel—the navigator? You rescued me from the assassin.'

'What!' Hugh ejaculates, almost bursting into tears as he begins to see in the well fleshed visage the emaciated wretch he rescued from Bembo. 'Gabriel, good God. But how? Why?'

'Vendramin took me that day in Rome. He interrogated me, but let me go. The cardinal found me pretty soon after. I told him everything in exchange for work, and food.' Gabriel looks askance at the blade in his hand as if it were an unclean thing. 'You know what it is like for people like us, people who have worked the oars. I swore I would never go hungry again. I am sorry; I did not know it would come to this.'

'What will you do now?' Hugh's heart misses a beat as he observes the navigator's fist clenching the crosshilt with tremulous vigor. 'For God's sake man, surely you will not murder a man who saved your life?'

'I am foresworn.' Gabriel breathes heavily and repositions his grip.

'Not to murder chained men, I warrant?'

Gabriel's eyes break from Hugh's as he glances from the straw to the wall and back again, still breathing heavily. But when his eyes finally surface, Hugh understands.

The blade tip drops to the floor. 'A life for a life, signor. You and I have suffered enough for two lifetimes.' Some beginnings of a bitter smile overspread his unshaven face. He nods slowly and looks up toward the high lancet window. 'God forgive me. Do you think men like you and me can know peace in this life?'

'What?' Hugh squints up at him, the comment has caught him broadside. *Hell of a time to have this sort of conversation.* Someone is battering a door above them with a sound like constant thunder. Hugh swallows hard. 'I don't know. But Vendramin did, for I was there when he died.'

'You killed him?' Gabriel says, his hand tightening visibly on the sword.

'No, he died of an ague to the lungs, but peacefully. It's hard to explain.'

'No, it's not. He was a strange man. There was something about him. You and I know evil men, I think. He wasn't evil, of that I am sure. I am glad you didn't kill him.'

'So am I.'

'I thought you would, you know.'

'So did I.'

'Life is strange, no?'

'Hmm.' Hugh, looks toward the door. 'So, are you going to go with the cardinal?'

'No.' Gabriel follows Hugh's eyes toward the open doorway and then upwards to streams of lime plaster descending from the masonry above them. 'No, I think somehow the cardinal will not take kindly to me when he finds out you are still alive. Do you think the knights will give me work?'

'If I put in a good word, they might. Perhaps you should hide that sword and sit here with me. Forgive the mess.'

DE BLANCHFORT, THE OTHER PRIOR

A minute later Hugh hears an almighty crash of masonry and splintered timbers. Dust billows into the cell like smoke, only narrowly preceding the stamping boots and arrival of the knights of Rhodes. When Prior de Blanchfort enters, he pushes past the first three knights in his eagerness to see Hugh. Hugh glances up and is surprised to find himself staring at the white-haired man from the bridge in Venice, and from the *Arsenale*, and more recently from the Medici Villa in Rome. But now he is wearing his eye patch again, and brandishing the same carrack sword he had once lent to Hugh.

Another breathless soldier rushes in behind the prior a moment later. 'The enemy has fled via a back door, should we pursue?'

'No, leave the snakes. I know where Cardinal Adriano lives if I need him. Besides, I've got what I came for.' De Blanchfort bends down and lets out a long sigh. 'So you are alive, are you Erpingham? Good.'

'You!' Hugh says with alarm, trying desperately to understand what it all means. 'I didn't recognize you. I mean, I saw you numerous times but, well –'

'Well what? Because I grew my hair like a frigging dervish and lost the eye patch. It's called a disguise, you idiot. You're not as sharp as you were. These Italians drink like fish; maybe your brain is addled.' He braces up, taking a deep breath before speaking. 'Yes, I came to Venice to see what the hell you were up to. All those letters of conspiracy. You, Prior Battista, it's a bloody mess. Either way, the magister knew we'd be left with our collective arses in buckets if we didn't nip it in the bud. So I came to Venice, had you followed, went to see how our new galley was coming on at the *Arsenale* – which by the way you nearly fired when you showed up there that day. *Mon Dieu*, can't you keep out of a fight for twenty-four hours? Anyway, when we understood that it was the prior who was up to his neck in – how would the magister put it? – disadvantage alliances, and you were up to your neck in shit, I decided enough was enough.'

'I see,' Hugh said, still wondering whether he should consider himself saved or fear the sword before him now, crimson with fresh blood. There is something familiar, almost comforting in the curt, coarse Gascon French of the prior. But what does it mean?

De Blanchfort follows Hugh's eye toward the blade, which rotates, before the prior says, 'I told you to look after this.'

'I did, but Battista – '

'Yes, I know. I found it upstairs, but never mind him. It's the last thing that traitor saw, bloody Italians. As I said, enough is enough. But who's this fellow? He looks rather too well dressed to be a prisoner.'

'He is the navigator whom we ransomed from Barbarossa. He saved my life and wants to work with us.'

'Does he now? Hmm.' The prior raises a skeptical eyebrow. 'We'll see about that. But it is you I've come to see, Erpingham, tearing up and down this country making trouble for us.' The Grand Prior nods to his men. 'All right, you lot, take the navigator out of here. I need to speak with Erpingham alone. And find a key for his bonds.' The men file out with Gabriel, and soon Hugh can only hear the labored breathing of the prior.

'Let's have it then. Have you found Vendramin?'

'Yes, sir.'

'And? Come on, spit it out.'

'Dead, sir.'

'You killed him?'

'No sir, he died of an ague to the lungs. But at peace, all the same.'

'I see.' The prior's face relaxes slightly at the jowls, which sag from his winced cheeks. 'The gold?'

'Given to the poor, he said. The Greek fire—he took that secret with him to the grave. He had not told anyone, and I have no reason to doubt him. He became a Franciscan and worked at their leper colony in – '

'In Assisi, *naturellement.* Now I see why you went there. We lost you after Perugia and like idiots kept following your baggage wagon. So you went to Assisi, did you? Well, well. And Marcantonio became a friar there of all places. Hah, it would be just like him, the ass. We used to joke about things like that. But with him you always knew he might do the unexpected at any moment. He once told d'Aubusson in a council meeting that the knights would do greater good to give up their sword and canon, and turn the fortress into a friary. He actually said that. *Merd*, they all thought he was joking. But I wasn't so sure. He was a great soul, but a troubled man, you know.' De Blanchfort fingers the edge of his goatee, then lets his thumbs rub at the thick stubble on his neck. 'Hmm, so you went to Assisi. I thought you might have. I said as much to one of the men when we realized we'd lost you. Sort of place a man goes to find a confessor, I said. The city of the pauper saint. But I was wrong, I suppose.'

'No, far from it, Prior. I remembered what you told me back in Rhodes at the harbor. I confessed to a friar in Assisi whom I found, or at least, who found me.'

'Vendramin?'

'Yes, but don't ask me to explain it, for I scarce understand it myself. I fell into his hands twice, and he may not have spared me but for your sword which he recognized.'

'Is that right? Hmm. He was always a great soul. I am glad you met him.' De Blanchfort bends to clean the colhonna's blade in the straw. 'I suppose I ought to give it back to you then.'

'I am honoured, but no. Not for the moment. I have many things to think about first.'

'Hmm. I see. We can talk about that anon.' The prior straightens up. Footsteps and the jangling of keys echo in the corridor. 'So there is no gold and no Greek fire, according to our mutual friend. And what would you say to a search being made of the friary?'

'I would say it would be a mistake.'

'I agree,' de Blanchfort says, with resignation. 'Besides, Vendramin would be too clever for that. You'll never get one over on a Venetian. They drink in guile from their mother's milk, I swear it.'

A soldier enters with a set of rusty keys. Hugh recognizes him as the captain he spoke to on the bridge in Venice – the one he backed away from. 'We'll have you out of here in a moment, Fra Hugh.'

'Where is here?'

The soldier unlocks Hugh's fetters one by one. 'The old knight's priory on the edge of the Roman Forum. No one comes here much—low lying, miasmic, malarial. The old prior had quite a collection of prisoners down here. Him and his stupid cardinal, I should say.'

'Hmm, cardinal,' says de Blanchfort, turning on his heels for the door. 'Whom the gods wish to destroy, they first tempt with the papal tiara. His final judgement will not be sleeping, that is for sure. Come.'

EPILOGUE

FOUR WEEKS LATER. A SPRING DAY ON THE ISLAND OF ISCHIA

The sun reaches Hugh's eyes and heart like a golden spear, probing and warming him. He stands in a high terraced garden along with other wedding guests, looking east across the ocean while the newlyweds process along the line. He talks while she distributes sea thrift from her bridal bouquet. This is the garden where once she escaped and hid from her old tutor, *la Bafana*—the same garden where now she walks with her husband like the first couple in Eden.

Most guests stand in the shade for the cool of morning has passed, but Hugh embraces the sunlight, his heart feeling something like a calf let out of winter stalls. *The air here!* A quartet of musicians on their *viole da arco* suffuse it with tunes seemingly composed to match the very birds, which add their own chorus on this proto-resurrection morn. There are many whom Hugh now knows and who know him, for this is one of the most significant weddings of the year. As he stares at the upper terrace and along the one on which he stands, it looks like a group portrait of the magnati of the *Magna Curia* and the *Dolce Sol*, with more than a few northerners thrown in for texture. Swords and cannon for once have given way to lace and brocade.

Everyone ate a hearty wedding breakfast before the ceremony—slices of melon and *berlingozzo*, followed by a boiled capon, prime sausages and veal, thrushes, roasted pigeons, pheasants and trout. To the shrill accompaniment of fifes, the duchess summoned trolleys on which were edible buildings of various sorts—bases of parmesan cheese, columns made of tripe and capitals of roasted chicken. So here at least, on the enchanted island, no irascible old grandees start or continue family feuds. It is a breath between storms perhaps, but in the pause even the dullest heart can hear the music.

The pope is not present, but has sent Johannes Burchard – who for once looks as if he has finally found something pleasant to do in his otherwise exhausting and relentless work with successive popes. His colleague Paris di Grassis is not here, but the banker Chigi is and so is Bramante – who never misess an opportunity to acquire new patrons. Pietro Bembo, Castiglione and Raphael form a clique under an olive tree on the upper terrace. Directly to their left the Duchess Elizabetta Montefeltro of Urbino is talking with her lady-in-waiting, the Lady Emilia Pia. Behind them, shaded by the creepers of a high wall, the Dominican Inquisitor Fra Giovanni Rafenelli—always on duty—strains to hear their conversation. Further along, on stone seats sit other *magnati* whom Hugh has come to know on his progress through the Italies: Duchess Constanza D'Avalos, Madonna Felice Orsini with her husband Gian Giordano Orsini. Also, the Duke and Duchess of Ferrara, and the Marchesa of Mantua. *They look well,* he thinks, *and well pleased too.* The war is ended. Their fiefs and dukedoms remain intact. No sign of the Marchese of Mantua. He's probably still in prison under the doge's palace – but he'll be all right, Hugh thinks. *And no sign, thank God, of certain cardinals that I would rather not see.* Lucretia looks like a goddess, so does Felice in her own way. Hugh will never understand what women are; perhaps they are a mystery best left to truer poets, or a burden best left to Atlas, as de Blanchfort and Bembo say. *But even I know they hint at things very great in this cosmos of ours.*

And the bride? Hugh glances again as the couple approaches: Ferdinando Francesco d'Avalos, Marchese of Pesaro, bedecked in the light blue silk of Naples, garlanded in honours and glory from the war against Venice, rejoices over his bride. Vittoria, the playful and giddy girl of his former visit, is radiant. Her eyes shine with the whole energy and beauty of the lover and beloved. Her face powder is streaked with the tears from her vows at mass. The bridegroom teared up, too, at one point; even Hugh felt it. *There's a thought*, Hugh muses, revolving his empty glass gently between scarred fingers. *The man who charged Trevisan's bulwarks blubbed like a babe before the face of that mystery*. Its power and meaning are hidden from so many and for so often, but marriage surely is richly poetic and suggestive too. We see a man, a woman, but also a world within a new story of two lives. And reflected within that grain of sand, perhaps we see the unseeable; the whole meaning of this world in the hourglass of time.

Hugh lifts his glass to the servant with a copper pitcher full of Malmsey. He knows it is going to his head and scattering his thoughts, but better Greek wine than Greek Fire. He spies De Blanchfort approaching from one side even as the newlyweds approach from the other. The weight has gone. He can take great gulping breaths. Spring has come at last.

The bridal couple eventually stop on the gravel in front of him. The marchese, pink of cheek, yet proud and strong, bows with a military speed, but Vittoria rushes forward to take Hugh's hand. Her eyes and hands raise him from where he too is bowing. 'And what shall be done for the man who saved the life of my fiancée that he might return to me and make me the happiest woman in all Italy?'

'There is nothing, I mean, that is,' Hugh stammers, 'than that you be happy together. Very happy.' He can feel a huge lump in his throat. *Idiot man.* He looks down for a moment and then up at his former comrade in arms. 'And perhaps see to it that she refrains from excessive sentiment in her verse, no straining for effect. It is unbecoming.' The marchese's face creases into a broad grin.

'That I will, Fra Hugh, and anything else that I may do to honour you.' He bows again.

'Anything, my lord?' Vittoria repeats, with a peevish smile.

'Indeed,' the marchese replies, trying to keep as straight a face as he can.

'You are in earnest my husband?'

'Truly, my love, I am earnest as Herod,' he says with the beginnings of a snort of laughter. 'Let him ask up to half my kingdom, the life of his enemies. Let him ask it.'

'Well,' Hugh says, recovering slightly from the wine, and catching the new mood of jollity. He demurs with a tilt of his head, but then glances conspiratorially at the prior, the marchese, and finally at Vittoria before saying. 'Then perhaps I could also ask for the exile of split infinitives?'

The marchese claps his hands with a great guffaw and takes Hugh by the arm. Looking into his eyes but speaking to the prior, he says, 'You have a good man here. Do not lose him.'

Prior de Blanchfort says, 'I do not plan to, Your Grace.'

And with one further hand squeeze from Vittoria, the couple move on, leaving Hugh and de Blanchfort alone before the shimmering, azure sea.

'Well.' De Blanchfort gives his characteristic, equine snort. 'What now? You said you needed time to think. I am not such a fool as to force you.'

Hugh glances briefly to his left to observe de Blanchfort again. Their eyes do not meet, they rarely do. The Grand Prior is chewing on his inner lip and listening to the call of the great sea. His heavy-lidded eyes squint and search the horizon for something. *An Ottoman fleet perhaps? Maybe, maybe not.* Hugh follows the line of his gaze. Perhaps he is looking toward the Isles of Procida where Vendramin disappeared, where he was reborn, where he changed his armour for a habit, his sword for a staff, where the soldier shed his surcoat and the sinner became the saint. Hugh would wager he's thinking about Vendramin. *On a day like this we are all searching for the same thing – sons seeking fathers, father seeking sons. Pere et Fils.*

'Let me know,' the prior grunts, then sniffs and walks down the steps in front of them, so that he can stand on the edge of the terrace. Hugh closes his eyes for a moment and drinks in great, deep breaths. Augustine said you should not only seek as if you will find, but also find as one who will go on seeking. He knew there was more. Wise men always know there is more. Today the whole world seems so pregnant with symbols and mystical meanings that he only wishes for sharper wits to perceive them. His reflections are cut short by the gruff voice of the prior. 'And another thing, Erpingham. Something that might help you decide right—dispatches I recovered from the priory in Rome show that your brother Cecil has joined the order and is sailing to Rhodes this spring.'

As the words sink in, Hugh feels memories calling like far away thunder. His brother. Is he really that old? Little Cecil, a knight? This is more than unexpected. *Am I my brother's keeper?* The seas of his imagination froth and swirl. But under the choppy waters of unwanted circumstance, Hugh feels the deep undertow of providence, and with it a knowledge beyond thought that this is all part of some larger plan. For the first time in three years, he knows he can finally write home to his mother. And to his father, even.

He digs his left hand into the bottom of his scrip. Crumpled by coins and compressed by water, it is still there – the letter he tried to write on his voyage to Italy nearly two years ago. He doesn't need to read it. He knows what it says. He remembers with a shudder the man he was then. He kept it always with him, intending to post it, but never did because he always hoped that he could write a better one – be part of a better story. Perhaps if he had posted it they would have kept Cecil at home. It's too late now; he's coming. And I will be there to meet him. If it please God, I will save him where I could not save myself. 'Perhaps now I can.' Hugh mutters the words absently and unintentionally. He suddenly feels someone at his shoulder. He turns to see Bembo, grinning like an idiot, flushed with the wine.

'Well, Hugh,' he says raising a glass toward the receding bridal party, now fifty yards away. 'They will make a handsome couple.'

'They do already.' Hugh squints at a wine stain on Bembo's sleeve. 'Looks like you've been enjoying yourself, *caro*.'

'Raphael knocked into me; the little prick can't hold his drink. What have you been up to – looking out to sea as if you're about to take ship?'

Hugh points to the horizon. 'Those are the Islands of Procida. Do you see that cluster of buildings on the craggy headland? It is the Franciscan friary.'

'Ah, I see. Maybe you are thinking that you could disappear like Vendramin, and be reborn?'

'I don't have the balls to be a Franciscan.'

'What then, return to Rhodes? I suppose that is what your prior is hanging around for.'

'Rhodes, Rhodes.' Hugh sucks the air. 'The White Cardinal said its fall is inevitable. Perhaps it is. Perhaps that is what attracted me to Rhodes in the first place – to be like Hector fighting with his back against the walls of Troy.'

'Ooh, that is picturesque, Hugh, really very good. Is that your own?'

'No, it was what Castiglione said to me the first time we met. He said that no one ever claimed their cities were founded by Achilles. It struck me at the time. We are a strange breed, we knights, as I see it—émigré princes, refuges and exiles fleeing from the collapse of chivalry. It is a penetrating observation. I thought so then as I do now. A man only has one life.'

The two men fall silent, and remain gazing across the sea towards Procida for almost a whole minute.

It is Bembo who breaks the silence. 'I suppose you remember that it was Hector who said of his son Astyanax, "Zeus, all you immortals! Grant this boy, my son, may be first in glory among the Trojans. One day let them say, 'He is a better man than his father." That is a worthy epitaph Hugh and a noble sentiment, you know, to want something greater for the children and the cities that we love. You told me that

Cardinal Adriano tempted you with the reigns of Christendom. Would it really have been such a bad thing?'

'Undoubtedly.

'Hmm, suppose. And a man may ascend the most exalted of thrones, yet still be sitting on his arse for all that.' Bembo is looking for a smile but finds none. 'You know that Ariosto – oh, I wish he were here with us – once told me that there is a town north of Savona – what is the name? Forgotten – anyway, he said that the church roof of the town – or was it the town hall? I can't remember – is the very divide of the watercourse. One side of the roof drains into a small river that reaches the Gulf of Genoa after only a few miles. But the other side of the same roof drains into the mighty Po basin that transverses the entire country hundreds of miles toward Venice. Ariosto—he is such a poet—said that the beating of a bird's wing or the faintest breath of wind might change which side a water drop landed on. So much of our lives, of history even, rests on such slight circumstance: a chance meeting, an illness, an advancement, a friendship, an enemy, an incarceration.'

'Yes,' Hugh says. *The father I did not have, and the one I did.* 'I did well to find Vendramin when I needed him most. He was right; a man is most free when he finally says, I am what I do. I am not my memories; I am not my past; I am what I choose to do today and tomorrow. But what about you? What will you do now?'

Bembo sighs. 'Go back to Urbino and write. It's gratifying to be wanted somewhere, and I do like it there. Think the air suits me. After that? I don't know.' Bembo elbows Hugh lightly in the ribs. 'Perhaps I will finally purge myself from the lusts of the flesh, and win my spurs as a knight of Rhodes. Upstage you.'

'Hah, the penitence of Fra Pietro Bembo, now that does sound like an epic worthy of the annals.'

'I've only one thing to say about that.' They are surprised from behind by the familiar Norfolk-baritone of Wilf. Hugh turns to see him with ruddy cheeks and beads of perspiration on his forehead.

Hugh smiles warmly. 'Dear Wilf, what could you possibly have to say about it.'

'Namely, don't expect me to do for you both if he does come to Rhodes. I've enough work looking after you, master.'

'Well, Hugh,' Bembo says in mock disgust. 'Your servant bespeaks himself very freely.'

'Bembo, my friend, I think he has the right to after all this.'

'For sure I do,' Wilf says to Bembo. 'Why, I was there the night he was born, so I was. I saw him 'fore ever his own father saw him. I was the one what took the news to his lordship. I was the one who held him first and all – little runt that he was.'

Bembo laughs loudly so that other guests turn. Wilf's been drinking, but Hugh doesn't care, for he suddenly understands him as if for the first time. Sons seeking fathers and fathers, sons. If the trappings of chivalry and courtly love collapsed then so much the worse for them. Fealty and troth still abide.

'What?' Bembo says. 'They let you hold a babe? God's oath, next you will tell us you were called upon to name him at the font.'

No. Hugh smiles inwardly and raises his gaze one last time toward the far distant island of Procida and the cluster of Franciscan buildings.

Only God can give a man his name.

Historical Note

I feel that I owe it to the reader to briefly add a further historical apology, and also a summary of later developments that might add texture to the general picture painted in this work of fiction.

The predictions made by the beleaguered ambassador of Venice, Girolamo Donato, came true to the letter. Venice did indeed wriggle free from the treaty she had signed under duress. There were more intrigues and more reverses, even to the point where Julius allied himself with Venice against France – a cynical twist in affairs that he ironically called *The Holy League*. But Julius, like his French nemesis Cardinal George D'Amboise would be dead by 1513, leaving the European stage for others to settle. *Omnia Vanitas. Momento Mori.*

I chose Cardinal Adriano as my ultimate villain for various reasons, not least because he is most likely to be the villain of the present age and the future. That is because he represents that most subtle and dangerous element in all of us: the good in us that would harness evil for noble purposes. We are trained to expect a James bond-type villain, that is, a parody, or cartoon villain. We want another Michelotto, another Cardinal Ippolito d'Este, another Hitler or Stalin, because it keeps the problem of evil at one remove from ourselves. It is a dangerous moral delusion. The truth is that when western civilisation implodes, it will be because of the apparently benevolent intentions of men, women and economic systems more like the enlightened Adriano than the brutal Michelotto.

The tragedy of Cardinal Adriano – a noble prelate of formidable learning and humane sympathies – is that he was almost exactly the real-life villain as I have described in this book. It was he who conspired with Cardinal Alfonso Petrucci (see Book I) to assassinate Leo X – the pope elected immediately after Julius, and who had the unenviable position of presiding over the Catholic Church during the Reformation. Adriano only narrowly got away with his life, which was more than young Petrucci. But why did he do it? A century later, our own Francis Bacon gave us an answer worthy of Macbeth.

> '... he was animated to expect the papacy, by a fatal mockery, the prediction of a soothsayer, which was; "that one should succeed Pope Leo, whose name should be Adrian, an aged man of mean birth, and of great wisdom." By which character and figure, he took himself to be describ'd; though it were fulfilled of Adrian the Fleming, son to a Dutch brewer, cardinal of Tortosa, and preceptor unto Charles the fifth; the same that, not changing his christian-name, was afterwards called Adrian the sixth..."1

Oh, the vile *equivocation of the fiend!* It is said that Adriano was murdered by a servant when on his way to the conclave that elected Pope Adrian VI. But Leo (whom Hugh met in Venice at the Contarini palace as Giulliano de Medici) survived the plot. Amongst his favourites he raised Baldasarre Castiglione to ecclesiastical preferment (after the death of his wife). Castiglione, the amiable ambassador-turned-papal nuncio and bishop, died in 1529 in Toledo after a distinguished career that took him as far as England.

Pietro Bembo also became a cardinal, and later even a knight of Rhodes. Poor Botticelli died in 1510 of the complaints enumerated in Book I and he was indeed laid to rest at the foot of Simona Vespucci's tomb. Both Felice and Vittoria outlived their husbands and achieved much amidst difficult times. Felice, who suffered great anxieties at the hands of her children and step children, was also instrumental in negotiating with Michelangelo to finish enough of Julius' tomb that we might at least enjoy one quarter of it today. She endured great financial reverses at the 1527 sack of Rome and died in 1536. Vittoria also had many dealings with Michelangelo, not least through the *Spirituali* movement of Christian renewal within the Catholic Church that was supressed by Cardinal Caraffa and the Inquisition. Her correspondence with Michelangelo remains. She died in the convent of San Silvestro in 1547. In this novel I have moved the date of her wedding forward a few months to the spring because it aided the chronology of the work and the wider symbolic importance of their union.

Of those books and cultural tropes referred to in Books I and II, few remain visible today. Like the tips of an iceberg, or the fragments of a ruined building, we see just a fraction of the content and meaning which underlies them. Of course, we have many of the great artworks referred to, but what is meant by them is still unintelligible and irrelevant to most of us. Bembo's work, together with Castiglione's The Courtier and Cortese's The Cardinal quickly became obsolete, and they are rarely, if ever, mentioned today.

Machiavelli's *The Prince* is the exception, for as we might expect, any source that lends the fig leaf of legitimacy to wickedness is bound never to be out of fashion. He eventually wrote it while in an enforced exile from Florence hoping to ingratiate himself with its Medici ruler – something that did not happen. He is as much a tragic figure as Cardinal Adriano, though perhaps more a symptom than a source of the troubles that undid him and countless others. Machiavelli's other books, 'The commentaries on decades of Livy' and his plays seemed to be suffused with his own failure and bitterness – the private failure of great man who never became important, and even the public failure of a sophisticated and over-civilised nation which never achieved the unity and discipline necessary to defeat foreign invaders.

Both he and noble Francesco Guicciardini started young in civic service. Both were Florentine ambassadors and both were fascinated by governing men and achieving power. Both were eventually thwarted, retiring to country estates where they studied and wrote historical works, and reflected on history's mysterious laws. The tragedy of Italy's inability to be united (and therefore be properly governed) haunted them both too. Guicciardini's father Piero had been an able statesman, but Francesco, for all his wisdom, eventually experienced the same betrayal as Seneca did from Augustus. As the ablest politician of the day, he had helped Cosimo I d'Medici mount the throne only to be cast aside by his protege. In his disappointment, he sought solace in religion, becoming a priest and cultivating an ancient piety. He died aged 58 as a man of contradictions: a priest who hated politician-popes yet who served two, and a Florentine who hated tyranny yet irrevocably led Florence under the yoke of tyrants.

Ariosto, who made so many hearts soar with lofty sentiments and virtue, had popularity in later centuries and among those you would not always expect. The famous Whig politician Charles James Fox said, 'For God's sake learn Italian as quick as you can so that you can read Ariosto as soon as you can.' And even though the chivalric conscience continues to have an ever-anachronistic power in popular culture – from Disney to Marvel – its sixteenth-century champion is rarely spoken of these days. He and Titian, are perhaps the two men in these books whose company I would gladly trade for all others.

Titian, that sun among small stars, was eventually made a knight and pensioned for life by the Holy Roman Emperor. In fact, it is said that Charles V once even picked up a brush Titian had dropped, such was his respect. The Venetian painter lived to a very great age and in 1575. While a plague raged in Venice, and in one of his last works, he painted himself into a *Pieta*, prostrate and half-naked before Christ, pleading for his son's life to be spared. But both he and his beloved Orazio succumbed soon afterwards.

In many ways, Italy herself forms the most tragic of all the book's characters; her comprehensive history, the terrible memory of greatness, and the ignominy of a people unable to be governed by rules, a people who could not achieve national unity, centralised government, modern industries and free institutions until the late modern era. Or perhaps even, the pathos we feel, I certainly do, is that part of it is that very same world weariness felt in late antiquity by Augustine, a knowledge that even the best efforts of humane civilization are somehow not enough, that the intractable mystery of human nature cannot be internally diagnosed, let alone treated. For this reason, and because I am sure that this trilogy's readers have a deep love of Italy already, I wish to conclude this historical note with some observations on her and her story. To seek to know another person or culture is, by one definition, to love them or it. But it is also, as philosopher Paul Ricoeur says, *a means of understanding ourselves.*

1492 seems to be a watershed moment in Italian and world history. It was the year that the Genoese sailor Columbus discovered America and thus diverted world commerce into new channels. It was the year of the Borgia papacy, which set the clock irrevocably ticking toward the reformation a quarter century later. It was the year Spain became a nation after conquest of Granada, thus directing her unspent energies westwards to foreign fields. Their discovery of the New World's gold (and syphilis) made their domination of Europe a tragedy all of its own. Back in Italy, 1492 was also the year that Lorenzo de Medici died: that man who gave political mass to the delicately balanced alliances that kept Italy safe from foreign invasion. In the same year, Ludovico Sforza invited Charles VIII of France to invade Naples. The French came two years later, 'the first of our disastrous years' says Guicciardini.

Piero de Medici, Lorenzo's successor, gave Charles the keys to the Apennine passes that he held. The Florentines, furious though they were, were made to pay up 120 000 florins in the days of Savonarola, whose end-time prophecies appeared to be coming true. As the French moved south, the Borgia pope shut himself up in Castel Sant'Angelo. Julius (the pope from these novels) and Asciano Sforza were cardinals at his side back then and it must have been a formative episode in their own lives. This French invasion and the humiliations that would attend it, set the stage for the tragedy which is modern Italian history.

The pivot of all this was arguably the Battle of Fornovo. It only lasted fifteen minutes, and yet it has cast an oversized shadow throughout Italian history. Francesco Gonzaga, who discusses it with Hugh in this book, always wanted to portray the battle as the victorious beginning of Italian unity. In his vainglorious cavalry charge, he shouted, '*Italia, alla morte*' before his horse was shot from under him. He built the gargantuan *Chiesa della Vittoria* (The Church of Victory) in Mantua to mark the occasion and had a gold medal struck with 'Ob restitutam Italiae libertatem,' *for the reestablishment of Italian liberty*. I recently saw a fine painting in the Louvre showing him after the battle kneeling before the goddess Victory.

History has been less honeyed in its praise. Gonzaga planned the battle as a complicated display of his military genius, and for which he needed to lead a cavalry charge in person. Even by the protocols of his own day, he should have led from an advantageous position where he could have better coordinated the mayhem that ensued. But, as I say, his horse was shot under him and he never got to capture Charles, who was fighting bravely at the head of a small band of troops. Eventually, 4000 lay dead in the field, two thirds Italian and Charles escaped, though only narrowly.

In his book *The Italians*, that keen observer of his own countrymen, Luigi Barzini, wrote, 'if they had won, they would have discovered the pride of being a united people, the self-confidence of defending their common liberty and independence.' But Gonzaga's *Stradiote* went for the baggage train whilst the greater prize, the king of France, escaped.

But worse was to come of it, for it showed Europe how rich and how easy were the pickings south of the Alps. Austrians, Burgundians, Germans, French and Flemish, Spanish, Swiss, and Hungarians all brought their armies over the alps to plunder Italy. The local princes and republics, who were unable to form military alliances among themselves to defend their country, always joined this or that coalition of foreigners. In their internecine strife, and out of sheer spite of their local rivals, Italian rulers sent their subjects in droves to fight and die in innumerable and incomprehensible little side wars.

In 1527, after 33 years of bloody trouble, a new imperial army marched on Rome and for nine months the city was abandoned to the lust, rapacity and cruelty of thirty thousand men without an authoritative commander to check them. Nothing was sacred, no one exempt from the humiliation. Even Julius II was dragged from his tomb and relieved of a weighty ring. The Catholics behaved as viciously as the protestants, the Italians soldiers as viciously as the foreigners, the Roman populace as viciously as the conquerors. Vittoria Colonna and Felice both survived it, the latter by an outrageous payment using (a complicit) Isabella Gonzaga as an intermediary. The sack of Rome, itself a distant consequence of the Battle of Fornovo, was a catastrophe from which the Italians never recovered, a trauma that left its indelible mark on the national character. Not one of them doubted that it had come about from their own faults. It is a national humiliation without parallel in European history, says Barzini, even the fall of Paris in 1940 does not come close.

The Italians became a demoralised and resentful people, even as the Chinese became under British exploitation and degradation. Both were over-civilised cultures that could not unite to defend itself. The boxer rebellion and the rise of communism in China and Italy, 'all have many roots, some of them distant, half – forgotten defeats and the desire for revenge.'

In 1530, the same emperor who had sanctioned the sacking of Rome, Charles V, was crowned with the ancient iron crown of Lombardy in Bologna. It was same one used to crown that exceptional queen Theodalinda a thousand years before and may even have been Constantine's, containing iron from a nail from calvary. As the pope placed it with all pomp on Charles's head, so ended the cultural ascendancy of Italy. The church was left its moral and spiritual rights but the power was now with Spain or whoever was bold enough to supplant her.

Barzini remarks with sorrow, 'the loss was irreparable.... the ceremony closed a miraculous age of unprecedented intellectual splendour and immense suffering for Italy, and inaugurated a new era, a period of more than three centuries of subjection to foreign rulers, during which time it can be said that Italy had no history of her own... What happened to Italy is what usually happens to old ladies who were once famous beauties. Just as they relinquish only reluctantly the gesture, curls, witticisms and fashions of their sunset years, so Italy still clings to the manners and ideals of the two centuries which followed the coronation of Charles V.'

Barzini called this terrible and interminable sunset of Italian culture, 'The perennial baroque.' Beneath the surface of Italy's perfect *trompe-l'oeil* he observed 'a new kind of bravura'. Especially in the arts, the painters like Veronese, Tintoretto, Caravaggio and Guido Reni developed a technical excellence on the canvas while Borromini, Bernini and Juvara sent marble sculpture, *chiesi, palazzi and piazzi,* flying skyward. And yet something in the ever-increasing spectacle spoke of a generation keeping themselves alive only as if *with the knives of the priests of Baal.* They lived off the gold of an exhausted cultural capital and beat it finer and finer in an attempt to make it last forever.

Before Italy's unification, the 19th century poet Heinrich Heine also sensed that the tragedy of Italy as something too deep for paint, or stone or even words. 'To poor enslaved Italy', he wrote in his *Reisebilde*, 'words are not allowed. She can only describe the anguish of her heart through music. All her hatred against foreign oppression, her enthusiasm for liberty, all the anguish at her own impotence, her longing for her past greatness, pathetic hopes, watching, waiting for help, all this has transposed into her melodies.'

During this epoch of emulation, Barzini suggests that 'everything was done not for itself alone but for the effect it would produce. For two centuries or more an immense number of men had dedicated their incredible talents to the national belief that show is, *faute de mieux*, a good substitute for reality; they filled the world with masterpieces in order to find compensation for the insecurity, emptiness, disarray, impotence and despair of their national life, to forget their humiliation and shame, to forget their collective guilt. It was a frenzied search for consolation and revenge against the crude and overbearing foreign devils. Proud Italians felt the shame of not being ruled by laws...'

'Italy, who had given birth to apostle and martyrs in earlier centuries, ' the philosopher Benedetto Croce writes, 'and would beget more in the Risorgimento, did not produce any in the Baroque age, because such men cannot exist when there is a lazy tranquility and resignation of spirit.' There may not have been many visibly great souls, but there were certainly many who suffered because there were none, and found a lack of purpose and emptiness in their lives unbearable. Many of them immigrated. Even if Italy had no history of her own, individual Italians tried to become historical characters in other lands.

Even when Italy's eventual unification (*Risorgimento)* came, it was no popular and rising tide, but rather liberal and progressive minorities of the aristocracy leading an enlightened bourgeoisie. The rest watched with skepticism and indifference. The kingdom struggled on for 60 years with a high point being the defeat of the dispirited Austrians and Hungarians. But the brittle state of affairs in the aftermath of WWI was only covered temporarily by the fascist state, which propped up the state like wooden beams on a crumbling edifice. Mussolini was one more symptom masquerading as a cure. When the crowd cried 'Duce, you are all of us,' they spoke a deep and tragic truth.

'The moment of truth cam in 1945 when the Italians finally understood that what they had believed was the final solution to its age-old problems had itself turned out to be yet one more baroque creation, one that cost the lives of millions. After the war, the tourists came back, most to take a holiday from their national virtues. But how many of them understood the tragedy that they beheld with such gasps and acclaim. One of Ignazio Silone's characters describes a certain "intimate sadness which comes to chosen souls simply from their consciousness of man's fate. This sort of sadness prevailed among intelligent Italians, but most of them, to evade suicide or madness, have taken to every known means of escape; they feign exaggerated gaiety, awkwardness, a passion for women, for food, for their country, and, above all, for fine sounding words; they become, as chance may have it, policeman, monks, terrorists, war heroes. I think that there has never been a race of men so fundamentally desolate and desperate as these gay Italians."

Perhaps Orson Welles spoke with great perception when he observed that Italy is full of actors, '50 millions of them, in fact, and they are almost all good; there are only a few bad ones and they are on the stage and in the films.'

These people, who so 'instinctively neutralized all the men who tried to force moral greatness on (them),' continues Barzini, 'not only defeated their rulers but also managed to invent splendid and melodramatic ways of making each humble or ignoble hour as bearable and satisfying as possible. This is the reason why their manners, their food, houses, cities, love-life are so delightful. This is also why their art, or most of it, is principally designed to give the public oblivion and bliss. They have naturally been accused of being frivolous and never going beneath the brilliant surface of things. The reproach is justified, of course. But they are not frivolous because they cannot be anything else. Many great artists left private documents showing that they were deeply tormented by the tragedy of their life. Italian literature is filled with anguished cries.'

Even before 1492, those poets with the keenest gaze, felt it. Dante, spurned and exiled in his day, railed bitterly: "Ah, slave Italy, the abode of sorrow, ship without a pilot in a tempest, not the ruler of domains but a brothel!" And Petrarch, a priest who travelled widely as an independent observer of the Europe of his day, saw Italy as covered with sores that no words could cure – and that is a metaphor coming from a man who lived through the plague years that carried away half of Italy. He believed that her truest repentance could only be proved by deeds.

Virtue against fury shall advance the fight,
And it i' th' combat soon shall put to flight;
For the old Roman, valour is not dead,
Nor in th' Italians' breasts extinguished.

’

If these observations are only partially true, then we begin to see an Italy that was understood little by later travellers. Byron's garden of the world was, in fact, more nearly a graveyard overgrown with beautiful-though-wild flowers. So complete was Barzini's perenial baroque, so beguiling the artifice, that few understood the pain behind the crumbling façade. The Italy of Shelly, Henry James, Browning and Milton was part mirage. Some, like the Enlightenment historians McCauley and Gibbon, were deceived because they went with an historiographic imperative. (Fake tourist sites already proliferated for the Grand Tourist: Cicero's villa at Formia, Virgil's tomb at Naples, Nero's tomb on the Cassian way in Rome.) Others, like the Romantics, were deceived because of an aesthetic imperative – to satisfy a yet unfulfilled desire for life and beauty, a mystical joy, a *Sehnsucht* missing in the colourless north. Goethe wanted Italy's moonlight brighter than daylight as an elixir to save him from *sturn und drang* of Nordic romanticism. Perhaps only Stendal, Heine and John Addington Symonds took time to understand her, to see the grieving widow behind the lace veil and pretty face. Perhaps each nation, like each family – as Tolstoy says, *is unhappy in its own way*. We British face our own past, present and future with similar feelings of pathos, fear and hope. But we must affirm and keep on affirming that *to know is to love*, and that no one who desires truth need fear reality.

On that note, we must finish with one man who, supreme among these cultural influencers of his day, that has hitherto gone unmentioned in this end-note. Erasmus of Rotterdam (once referred to as Europe's first free floating brain) completed his Greek New Testament, and as he expected, the effects were seismic when they permeated Europe as a source for indigenous translation. The unintended consequences of the spiritual renewal resulting partly from his scholarship, was a great schism that sundered Western European Christianity. The bandwidth for necessary renewal that Erasmus had hoped for, was not achievable within the structural confines of the papacy at that moment when it was needed. Thus, came the Reformation. It was something that grieved him greatly. Erasmus laid an egg that Luther *et al* hatched. The deterioration of relations between the Catholic Church and the reformed churches can be seen in the correspondence between him and Luther. The tone, the paradoxes and the recriminations are all there in miniature. Erasmus attempted to defend a scholarly neutrality but eventually, denounced by Luther as a 'viper,' 'liar,' and 'the very mouth and organ of Satan,' and much saddened by the schism, he died in July 1536. Even as he was laid to rest at Basel, King Henry VIII began to despoil the monasteries of Britain – which is where Book III of this trilogy begins.

Henry Vyner-Brooks
Latterhead, Loweswater, August 2022

www.ingramcontent.com/pod-product-compliance
Lightning Source LLC
Chambersburg PA
CBHW030813310726
48980CB00006B/479/J
* 9 7 8 0 9 5 6 9 4 2 7 7 7 *